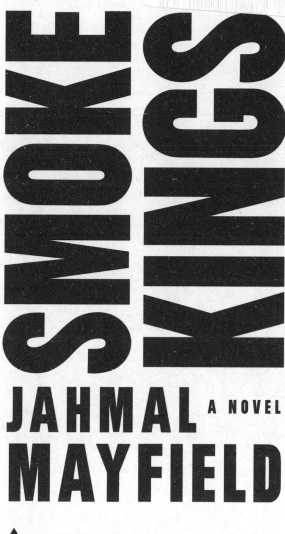

SMOKE KINGS

JAHMAL MAYFIELD

A NOVEL

🏠 MELVILLE HOUSE
BROOKLYN · LONDON

First published in 2024 by Melville House
Copyright © 2023 by Jahmal Mayfield

All rights reserved
First Melville House Printing: December 2023

Melville House Publishing
46 John Street
Brooklyn, NY 11201
and
Melville House UK
Suite 2000
16/18 Woodford Road
London E7 0HA

mhpbooks.com
@melvillehouse

ISBN: 978-1-68589-111-4
ISBN: 978-1-68589-112-1 (eBook)

Library of Congress Control Number: 2023945048

Designed by Patrice Sheridan

Printed in the United States of America
1   3   5   7   9   10   8   6   4   2
A catalog record for this book is available from the Library of Congress

SMOKE KINGS

For Andrew, 5/27/18.
The brightest lights cannot be dimmed.

And they are lucky that what black people are looking for is equality and not revenge.

—KIMBERLY JONES

SMOKE KINGS

February 20, 2017

2:37 a.m.

The victim's advocate *meets them on the sidewalk in front of the hospital. Despite the woman's warm eyes and gentle smile, Joshua will forever associate her with stinging pain and loss. Doesn't help that when she showed up on his doorstep earlier with the cop, she'd tried to soothe Joshua by telling him "Grief is love with no place to go." Some bullshit off the internet.*

"This is my cousin, Nate," he tells her.

"Pleasure to meet you, Nate. Wish it was under better cir—"

"Can we get this moving?"

"Yes, of course, Nate," she says. "Detective Mullen is waiting for us."

Us.

As if they're in this together. Even with her promised follow-up, Joshua knows this is a lie. He's the one who failed to protect all that is near and dear. This woman can't nudge him through what's to come.

"You said someone's sitting with your mother?" she asks as they move through the building.

"My girlfriend, Alani," Joshua says. "And two friends, Rachel and Isiah."

"Good. I'm glad your mother isn't alone."

There's a layer of something ethereal gauzing everything. One minute they're walking, and the next they're on an elevator and Joshua's not even sure how they got here. His heart is racing. Thoughts spiraling. Stomach queasy with nausea.

A ping sounds with a lit-up G. Ground level. The doors flash open.

The victim's advocate steps off. Then Nate. Joshua lingers in the open elevator.

Nate turns to him. "You sure you can do this?"

Joshua nods a lie and steps out.

Halfway down a hallway that's long but not long enough, the cop meets up with them. He's close to the end of his "twenty," looks ready to put his Glock 19 in a gun safe for good. Without speaking, he leads them to an unmarked door, a gray box on the wall next to it. This is one of the older areas in the hospital, down in the bowels of the building, with ready access to the loading docks. For the hearses, Joshua realizes.

The cop hesitates, his hand hovering over the gray box. "Again, I'll encourage you to wait until after the funeral home has picked up—"

"We're not waiting," Nate says. "We want to see him."

Nate's impatience counters the grief that thickens the air like humidity. He's steady as always, shatterproof. Joshua's thankful his cousin is here. His own brain is stuck in a loop of that earlier conversation with the victim's advocate. She'd explained how she helped families. Particularly those whose loved one was murdered.

A burning, tingling rash prickles Joshua's neck and chest, and he scratches at it.

Hives, on top of everything else.

"You really don't need to be here," the cop says. "We have preliminary ID from—"

"That's fine," Nate interrupts again. "But we'd still like to see him."

"We don't typically allow—"

"Nothing typical about this situation, Detective Mullen."

The cop glances at the victim's advocate, and when she looks away, he sighs, flips open the cover of the gray box. Snatches the phone housed inside. Mutters a few words and then a buzzer sounds and the unmarked door clicks. The cop holds it open for Joshua and Nate to enter. "Down to the end of the corridor," he says. "Last door on the right."

Joshua's dazed but manages to shuffle his feet.

Beside him, Nate skulks, keeps his head forward, not looking in any of the rooms they pass.

Joshua can't help looking.

Stainless steel tables, drains in the floors, scales. Lots and lots of sinks.

The last room at the end of the corridor on the right, though, is different. Could be a lounge with its carpet and soft lighting. Which leaves Joshua with a fleeting hope he'll discover this is all a terrible mistake.

Nate's first into the room. His legs buckle as he takes in the carefully positioned gurney. He cries out, curses, punches a wall.

Joshua steps in behind his cousin, holds his breath like he's underwater.

The cop and the victim's advocate stand back, but when Nate kicks over a chair, the cop's shooting hand drops to his waist, and he takes a step in Nate's direction.

Joshua is instantly in the cop's path, blocking his way.

The cop squints his eyes.

Joshua angles his head.

"We'll give you a moment," the victim's advocate says, and she gently takes the cop by the arm and pulls him back. The door snicks shut behind them.

Joshua lets out that held breath. Now that the woman and the cop are gone, he's left to deal with the wreckage in this cold, unwelcoming room.

He plops in a chair by the gurney, loosens the knot of his tie.

Bruises are often secrets on darker skin. But his little brother's face is mottled with blotchy purple discolorations. A gash in his chin, a busted lip, right eye swollen like a chocolate Easter egg.

It's inexplicable that anyone would do this to Darius. He was all about his computer designs, his sneakers, and this new girl he'd been seeing. Wouldn't stop talking about some artificial intelligence class he hoped to take in September.

Rutgers University won't be happening now.

Instead, there'll be an autopsy. The medical examiner will cut Darius up. Joshua can't bear the thought. He desperately wishes he could rewind time all the way back to strolling the boardwalk down in Seaside Heights, dragging a tiny, wide-eyed Darius along to attract girls like a three-week-old Labrador. Nate letting Darius beat him at air hockey, tenderly wiping powdered sugar off Darius's face from the funnel cake.

Rachel and Isiah are devastated. Darius was like their little brother, too.

Who would do this?

The door opens and the cop sticks his head in. Everything about him breeds distrust. He's been coy and guarded from the start. *Fixin' to chalk this up as just another dead black boy?*

"Fuck that," Joshua says out loud.

And Nate, almost as if he's reading Joshua's mind, nods and says, "Not this time."

Part I

1

Two years later . . .

Searching the swamp for bear scat wasn't originally part of the deal. Neither was listening closely for grunting feral hogs. It didn't help Rachel's mood, either, that the crotch of her waders was cut too low, and where the boots and legs seamed there was a sharp edge that bit into her calves, and the waterproof nylon trapped heat and perspiration against her skin. Once this was finished, her sweaty clothes would have to be peeled from her like an orange rind. Calamine lotion for mosquito bites.

"Tried to tell you all," Isiah called out. "There's nothing here."

For all his gifts, he didn't seem to pick up on Rachel's state of mind.

She ignored him and trudged forward through muck the color of pea soup. Keeping an eye out for the silk of a banana spider. Webbing that could stretch across the path, glowing a golden yellow as it reflected the sunlight.

"Rache?"

"Let's head back," she snapped.

"Wait. You're upset with *me*?"

There was so much Rachel could've said in response but, again, she chose to focus on her movement through the swamp. With each step she took; especially mindful of snakes.

She hated snakes.

She also didn't like Isiah's recent hesitance to the crew's plan.

"I never wanted it to be like this," he said.

Rachel stopped, turned to him, an angry scarlet blush to her café au lait complexion. "Yeah? What did you want it to be like? I'd really like to know, Isiah. 'Cause your bitching is getting old."

"My bitching?" he said, the wound clear in his voice.

Plus, that hangdog look in his eyes.

Rachel sighed. "I'm sorry. I shouldn't have said that. I'm just . . . never mind. We've all got to stick together."

She wasn't sure the apology was landing smoothly, but Isiah held up his arm. "Lead the way."

They walked on in silence. Finding nothing on the path worth reporting back to Nate.

The boathouse where they'd set up operations was a heap along the bank of a stream carpeted with duckweed. Bleached gray from years of abandonment and mucky swamp air. Ratty, once-white sheets still hung in the windows as curtains. A rusty barbecue grill, small table, and two mismatched chairs took up what passed for a porch. One of the chairs a straight-back cane model, the other plastic, and the blaze orange of a hunter's vest.

Rachel eyed the dumpy lean-to and before taking its steps up to the front door she paused. "I know you're not feeling this, babe. But . . . we need you."

"Don't worry, Rache, I'll be a good little soldier," Isiah said, and tried to smile. It didn't reach his eyes.

"Thank you," she told him, and as a mea culpa added, "And I can't wait to marry you."

Isiah nodded and climbed the makeshift cinder block steps to the boathouse like a man condemned to the gallows.

Rachel had no such reticence. The sweltering heat and

uncomfortable waders aside, this was what she was here for. The real action. She pulled a pair of clear latex gloves from her waders and snapped them on. It was jarring seeing her right-hand ring finger bare. She'd left her engagement diamond boxed back in Jersey so it wouldn't get damaged out here in the swamps of Alabama.

Inside the boathouse, Scott York was as he'd been when they'd left, propped up on an orange chair that matched the one from the porch. His arms were secured behind his back with cable zip ties.

Nate glanced over as Rachel and Isiah rejoined the "party." Rachel gave him a nod.

All clear.

Nate, not skipping a beat, focused back on their captive. "Do you believe me to be a serious man, Mr. York?"

Scott York's voice was an embarrassing croak. "Ye . . . yes."

Rachel eyed the stain down the front of York's pants, the damp pool beneath his feet. A strong ammonia odor in the air. Scratches and bruises on his face. He trembled like a washing machine in spin cycle.

Nate placed a hand on York's shoulder and the captive flinched. "You're familiar with the Tyler-Goodwin Bridge?"

"I don't think so," York said, eyes starting to tear up.

"No," Nate said, shaking his head. "None of that, Mr. York. Chest out, head raised. Have some pride."

"What is . . . what is this about? What are you going to do with me?"

"I asked you about the Tyler-Goodwin Bridge."

"I . . . I never heard of it."

"Quite possible," Nate said, nodding. "They tore it down when you were a toddler."

York swallowed, said, "Okay."

"You've heard stories about '57, though?"

"The . . . the year?"

"Yessir," Nate said. "There's one story in particular I'm keen to discuss with you."

Rachel couldn't help but admire Nate's calm, the precision of his language, as if he were negotiating a business transaction.

"Mr. York . . ."

"Okay," he said again.

Nate paused to take a sip of a Muchacho, the can slick with beer sweat, then set the can back on the floor by York's feet. He belched, wiped his lips with his hand, then got back to it. "One of your fore-bears and three other whites forced a black man to jump off the bridge."

Up until then, Joshua had been standing in the corner, silently holding a crooked tree limb at port arms across his chest. He'd used the tree limb to poke York forward through the muddy sloughs of the swamp. He murmured now at the mention of those white men from the past forcing Johnnie Williams to leap to his death. Very little had changed in the more than sixty years since. But Rachel figured Joshua was more concerned with the last two years. The injustice in Darius's murder was the reason they'd *all* committed to do this work.

His death couldn't be in vain.

They wouldn't allow it to be.

Nate frowned at the captive. "An innocent black man losing his life at the hands of someone in your family doesn't even elicit a reaction, Mr. York?"

"Which . . . which forebear?"

"Your grandfather."

"Pawpaw? Impossible." York shook his head, and his posture straightened. Energized, it seemed, by the task of defending his family's honor. Or, less benevolently considered, holding on to the lie of his past to keep from getting the comeuppance he deserved in his present.

That's how Rachel saw it.

"You doubt what I've told you?" Nate said.

"Somehow you've got your wires crossed."

"My wires crossed?"

"I mean no disrespect."

"Hmm."

There was menace in Nate's utterance of that one exclamation. Scott York seemed to realize it, too. Rachel noticed him looking more closely at the four of them, most likely to gather whatever he could make out through the openings of their coal-black balaclavas.

She pictured it as York must've, from his bigoted perspective.

Nate. Six-five, the brown of cinnamon. Slim and sinewy. Eyes as intense as an out-of-control blaze.

Joshua. Black as licorice, stocky. Wielding that tree limb as a weapon.

Isiah. Smooth, tawny skin, sharp cheekbones, and small, nearly lidless eyes behind wire-rimmed glasses.

And Rachel herself. Pale-green irises, skin so light that few connected her with a black-and-white heritage. She was confused for Puerto Rican, Italian, but almost never black. Even by black people.

She wondered whether Scott York was perceptive enough to realize what he'd gotten into.

The answer came quickly. Of the four of them, York chose Isiah to address. A Korean ally? Would someone like York even know the difference between a Korean, a Chinese, and a Japanese man?

"You're okay with what they're doing here?" he asked Isiah.

Rachel was pleased that her fiancé didn't respond.

"Cracker judge dismissed the charges," Nate interjected, getting back to the bridge. "Claimed no cause of death had been established."

York shook his head. "Pawpaw wouldn't have been involved in any of that."

"'Merely forcing a person to jump from a bridge does not naturally and probably lead to the death of such person.' Those were the cracker judge's exact words."

"Listen. I feel your pain. I do. The man on the bridge was kin to you?"

"No."

York frowned. "Why are you taking it so personal then?"

"Each week, by five p.m. Friday at the latest," Nate instructed, ignoring the question, "you will deposit three hundred eleven dollars and fifty-four cents into an account we will provide to you."

"What?"

"The exact amount I quoted you," Nate said.

"Every week . . . for how long?"

"In perpetuity."

"Jesus. What's the money even for?"

"We like to think of it as a community-building fund," Nate said. "But you can consider it reparations."

"Reparations? You mean like to make up for slavery? I had nothing to do with that. And I know you're trying to pin something on my pawpaw, too, but . . ."

Nate's eyes clouded over, and he reached out his hand to Rachel. "Rope."

She glanced at Isiah before unfurling a snake of chunky lariat from a compartment in her waders. One end tied off in a familiar loop. A hangman's knot. Noose. She tossed it to Nate.

York lurched back in his seat. "The hell . . ."

"Your bloodline is tainted," Nate said. "And it'll remain an endless cycle if you aren't held accountable. Your daughters are already following in your grandfather's footsteps. Following in *your* footsteps. Ava liked a post making fun of Mexicans and the wall. Maddy wrote in a post that AOC might be tolerable if she was *any other color.* Clever, I'll give your Maddy that."

"How do . . . how do you know these things?"

"Signaling System vulnerabilities are easily exploited, Mr. York. We've been listening in on you and your family's cell phone calls, reading your texts."

"Why are you doing this to me?"

Nate edged close to York again, touched the man's face. A gentle gesture with no good intent. The captive tried to shirk away from him but couldn't.

"Your company was awarded a 4.8 million-dollar grant to repair the sewage system in a place called Uniontown. You were supposed to build a spray field but have yet to do so even though you took the money. Can you explain why that is, Mr. York?"

"I don't even know what a spray field is," York whined. "My company is in recycling. We haven't received any grants."

"Every time it rains," Nate continued, flexing the noose now, "the lagoon spills over, flooding fields, cow pastures, contaminating the water supply. I suppose you don't care because the affected are mostly black farmers and residents. Well, a little boy got very sick and nearly died. It's a miracle he lived. Others probably won't be as lucky."

"Listen to me," York said, revving his voice. "I'm in recycling."

"You should've made this easy for yourself, Mr. York. All you had to do was agree to deposit the money each week."

"You've got this wrong."

"Hold him, please," Nate said, turning to the others.

Joshua gently set the crooked tree limb on the floor. Rachel rubbed her gloved hands on her thighs and shot Isiah a look. He frowned but pulled a digital camera from his waders, trained it on York. And they all moved at once, a sublime synchronicity that came with practice, lots and lots of practice. Six of these so far.

York shook his head. "Don't do this. Please. You've got this all wrong. I'm in recycling."

He squeaked his chair backward, and it almost toppled. They

grabbed hold of him, dragged him and the chair back to the room's center. Nate eased the noose over York's head and down around his neck. "Come on . . . please," York begged. "You don't have to do this."

Rachel could sense Isiah's hard gaze trained on her but wouldn't look in his direction.

Nate said, "The pull at the end of your drop will lever your jaw and head upward. Wrenching your vertebrae apart."

"You've got this all wrong."

York sobbed, closed his eyes, the rope cutting into his windpipe as he was forced to his feet.

2

It was an old-school trick, keeping a jar of Vicks VapoRub handy, spreading it around the rims of the nostrils. Supposedly it masked the rancid odors of death, though its true effectiveness was dubious. Either way, Mason Farmer, formerly with the Birmingham Police Department, used it now as several techs from Homicide pulled a body from Shades Creek, a tributary of the Cahaba, which itself was an offshoot of the Alabama River. The techs looked exhausted, disinterested even. Holiday weekends were awful. The exhilaration from the Fourth had faded and left behind a melancholy that came with seeing the worst the world had to offer.

"Jesus."

The victim was a white male, slim in the hips, leached gray by the water, flayed in a clean line that started just above his ribs and ended just below where his penis would've been—had whoever done this to him not shorn it off and tossed it to God knows where.

"Dollars to donuts, we're dealing with asphyxiation. Looks like rope of some kind."

Teddy Terry, an old partner of Mason's still with the BPD.

Mason nodded in acknowledgment. Even though the victim's flesh was bloated and discolored, he could clearly see the necklace of an abrasion around the span of his throat. He hadn't been in the water long. "Sick, someone would do this."

"Hate," Teddy Terry replied. "This looks personal."

"I'm thinking more than one doer."

"It's possible. He got worked over pretty well. One holding him down, while a second and third . . ."

"Yeah."

One of the techs, a pocket-size Asian woman, peeled off her gloves and stumbled toward a clump of bushes. Vomiting at a volume that made it seem as though she were exaggerating with each retch. But it was genuine.

Teddy Terry's nose wrinkled in displeasure. "There goes the chow mein."

"I see you skipped the fine city of Birmingham's sensitivity training," Mason said, smiling.

"Tell me you weren't thinking the same, Farmer?"

"I'm not police anymore, Teddy. I don't get to banter."

"What a shame. The private money must be good if you're willing to stifle man's inherent need for rejoinders and repartee."

Feeling as though an entreaty for some on-the-side work was imminent, Mason clapped his old colleague on the shoulder. "Thanks for following this through for me, Teddy. I'll get out of your hair now."

"Sorry it wasn't a better outcome. Your firm will still see some money?"

"We were contracted to track him down. I'd say he's been tracked."

They shook and Mason started the climb up the slope of grass. He was about halfway up when Teddy called his name. Mason sighed and turned back. "Yeah, Teddy?"

"Bella doing all right?"

Mason hadn't expected that. He would've preferred Teddy try to hit him up for a recommendation to the firm than ask about his wife. "Same steady battle ax," he said, forcing himself to smile, to keep his voice even.

"Good to hear it."

Mason could tell his old partner hadn't believed him, and by the time he reached his car a brush fire of rage was sweeping through his gut. Fuck Teddy for dredging up a fresh wound. He banged the wheel and accidentally bleated the horn. Then pulled out his cell phone and shakily dialed the house. The landline rang and rang and eventually dumped him into voicemail. No point calling Bella's cell phone; she didn't even bother keeping it charged anymore. But now his head was swimming and he needed to talk with someone to get his mind off his wife. There weren't many options. Nicole, his daughter, was out of the question in his current mood. Despite everything, she'd surely ask him how her mother was doing. And what would he say?

Same.

A fucking recluse not participating in her own life, just because some homeboys hanging around UAB's campus had tailed her from yoga in Five Points South one night and forced her off the road. She'd had the presence of mind to lock all her doors and call 911, kept her cool as they banged on her windows and jumped up and down like a shrewdness of apes. It hadn't lasted long, the homeboys gone by the time a patrol car showed up, four minutes and thirty-six seconds after Bella's call to emergency services. Four minutes and thirty-six seconds that left Mason with a wife who wouldn't step out of the house now to pick up *The Huntsville Times* from the curb. And to think he'd sold the old house and moved ninety minutes north to buy her a sense of comfort. Had to take on private work after retiring from the BPD to stay ahead of her prescription costs—an arm and a leg even with his pension's medical insurance.

"Same, my ass," he said aloud. Bella had gone most of the weekend without showering. He sighed, started his car, and pulled onto the highway. A few minutes into his drive, thoughts of his wife had receded, and his focus was fixed solidly on his next stop. He wouldn't need Vicks for this job, thankfully. White-collar crime was tidier.

The landing page of Oxmoor Management Corporation's website explained they were an investment management firm focused on alternative ventures, with approximately $6.6 billion in regulatory assets under management as of January 31, 2019. Mason had done a deep dive into their business over the past few weeks and could do a decent impression of an asshole with seventy thousand in student loan debt. Risk parity, managed future accounts, commodity pools. *Now hand over my MBA.*

Oxmoor's headquarters were on Richard Arrington Jr. Boulevard, named after Birmingham's first black mayor, which was fine with Mason. He didn't understand, though, how some of the same people who championed the dedication of an entire street to the man could then turn around and fervently demand a simple statue of Jefferson Davis should come down, that it didn't deserve its place in history. Hypocrites.

The building loomed up ahead, at the corner. Mason found a spot on the street side, got out, and took care of the parking fee. Turned and let out a long, slow exhale.

Inside the building, he walked directly to the security desk. The woman on sentinel had shoulder-length black hair, eyes dark as shadows, skin like a milk chocolate candy bar. Not black, though. "*¿Cómo estás?*" Mason said to her.

She frowned, then regathered herself, said, "What can I help you with, sir?"

Mason told her his name, his purpose, and thankfully—because she'd been alerted beforehand to expect him—she saved him a wait by ushering him up to the third floor and into the conference room herself.

"Mr. Miller will be with you momentarily, Mr. Farmer."

"Wonderful. Appreciate you taking the time to see me up here. *Gracias.*"

She swallowed. "Anything else I can do for you?"

"What's your name? I'd like to mention you to Mr. Miller."

"Parineeti Chopra," she told him, and then she was gone.

Mason settled into a leather chair, pulled out his phone just to check. No missed calls.

The door opened as he was easing the phone back into his pocket. He sat up, and then stood altogether to greet Sean Miller, shake his hand. Mason himself was a hair under six-one, and Miller had that hair and probably another inch. And speaking of hair, his was beginning to thin. He also had some paunch. Meanwhile, Mason had all his hair, dark like an Irish stout with a frothy bit of gray at the temples, and a stomach as flat as a two-by-four. He wondered whether Miller's wife—presuming he had one—flinched when the man reached for her in bed at night.

"Sit, Mr. Farmer. I'm anxious to hear what your firm has discovered."

Mason's firm, Tsaro International, ran the gamut from surveillance to missing persons, from bug sweeps and cheating spouses to unsolved crimes and litigation support. And, of course, corporate investigations. Most of the investigators were former supervisory federal agents. Though Mason didn't have that background, he modestly felt as though he was among the firm's best.

"On average," he started, "fraud schemes last about eighteen months before being detected."

Miller inhaled. "Sounds as though you're telling me this thing happened. And it's gone on for a while."

"Can you have her brought in? I'd like to ask her a few questions."

"Should I stay?"

Mason shook his head. "I'll debrief you afterward."

The "her" in question was a black woman named Tamara Blake, a seven-year employee in the payroll department. She dazedly took a seat at the conference table. As soon as she sat, Mason stood up, took off his jacket, and draped it over the back of his chair. He placed his butt on the corner of the table and fixed his gaze on Ms. Blake. Didn't say anything, just stared at her. He had to give it to her, she held on for a heck of a lot longer than most.

"What's this about?" she finally asked, voice cracking. "Who are you?"

"No one told you?"

"Nothing," she said. "Just that someone needed to speak with me in the conference room."

"I work for a firm that investigates, among other things, corporate fraud."

"Fraud?"

"It's sophisticated stuff," Mason offered. "You wouldn't believe the tools we have at our disposal. Continuous monitoring, anomaly detection, pattern recognition. Just in data mining alone there's decision trees, machine learning, cluster analysis."

One of the young women from his firm, Ash, had shared the various means with him during their talks, and it sounded impressive, though he couldn't have spoken on any of it beyond the basics, meaning the names of the tools only.

"What does any of that have to do with me?"

"You have a little boy and a girl, correct, Ms. Blake? Jade and Jamarcus. Neither of their fathers in the picture."

"Excuse me?"

"I don't envy you."

"What is this?"

"The cost of ceramic crowns, braces . . ." He shook his head. "And that's times two in your case. Talk about a money pit."

"What did you say your name is?"

"I didn't."

"I'd like it, please."

"Farmer. Mason Farmer." He grinned. "You know, like James Bond."

"What is it you believe I've done, Mr. Farmer?"

"Created ghost employees," he replied without hesitation.

Tamara Blake didn't say anything.

"Amy Pizzolatto. Christine King. John Cruz. Flynn Coyle."

"Those names s'posed to mean something to me?"

"Yeah, they *s'posed* to," Mason said. "All of them separated from the company during the time you've been working in payroll. But magically, they remained on the rolls for months after their actual termination dates. That'd buy Jamarcus a lot of *Black Panther* action figures. What's Jade into?"

Mason couldn't make out her reply. He asked her to repeat herself.

"Was it Peter Jacoby started this?" she said.

"It's not appropriate for me to—"

"Because I filed a complaint on him that never went anywhere. He promised to make me pay for it, just the same."

Mason frowned. "Complaint?"

"Apparently, I remind him of Misty Stone."

"Who?"

"Exactly. I googled her. Don't make that same mistake."

"I'm afraid we've veered off course here," Mason said.

"You were off course before I even walked in."

Mason shook his head. "I don't think so, Ms. Blake."

"I don't understand it. You white men got the world, and it still isn't enough."

"This doesn't have anything to do with race."

"Or common sense," she said. "This scheme you're claiming I cooked up would be bound to fail. The payroll system would eventually issue inflated W-2s, and that wouldn't take nothing to detect."

"That's true."

"But I'm *supposed* to be that dumb?" she said.

"Most criminals—"

"I've had enough of this," she said, cutting Mason off. "Oxmoor has a great health plan and I have a CareCredit card with a zero balance, so I've never worried about ceramic crowns and braces for my kids. And I know I've never pocketed any money from some so-called ghost employees, so if I get fired over this you can best believe I'll have my brother—he's an attorney, by the way—either represent me himself or hook me up with someone from his firm. I'll even add you to the lawsuit."

Mason laughed at the notion. "On what grounds?"

"Racial profiling."

"That's ridiculous. Not that I must tell you, but my daughter has a biracial child."

"*Your* daughter?" Tamara Blake chuckled in disbelief. "Well, I feel sorry for her."

Mason thought of Bella and his own reaction when he'd learned of Nicole's pregnancy, and, sadly, he couldn't think of one damn rejoinder to the Blake woman.

Teddy would be appalled.

3

One of the oldest cemeteries in New Jersey. Joshua eyed his brother's headstone. Under different circumstances the black granite would've been impressive. He grunted. About fifty yards away a group of mourners gathered around a fresh grave site. Some were standing, some sitting on tan folding chairs set at the edge of the unwelcome hole covered in green felt cloth. A minister was speaking in a booming, rhythmic voice, but his words were lost to the distance. Joshua could only pick up snatches. "Pain and suffering," and "no more grief and sorrow." The ideas were incongruous, that you could move from suffering to feeling no grief. But perhaps the preacher was speaking to the numbness Joshua still felt, two years after his brother was taken from him.

DARIUS ADAMS
OCT 12, 1999 – FEB 19, 2017
SON AND BROTHER

The words carved in the stone floated toward him, mocking in their finality.

Darius had been so young he hadn't gotten the chance to stalk his dreams.

Son, brother. Would've been so much more if he'd lived longer.

"RIP, Bred."

Joshua snapped his head around, startled. And for a brief, bewildering moment, he couldn't make sense of the tall man standing beside him. Six-five, with a baritone to rival the minister's voice. His cousin Nate. He'd come up with the nickname Bred—a blending of black and red, as in the old Jordans—because Darius was such a sneakerhead. Vain to the point of ridicule about his kickz.

"We should head out now," Joshua said, rising from his mental fog. He draped a pair of burgundy shoelaces over the headstone like a shawl. Next to a grimy gray pair and some dirty ones he remembered as being yellow. He and Nate came here after every job, so that meant the elements had taken six other pairs.

"Stay cool," Nate told him.

Joshua said, "What's up?"

"Alani." Nate nodded off in the distance. "Looks like she has a bouquet."

Joshua turned, squinting. His ex's hair was trimmed and dyed platinum blonde. She was a few pounds heavier than when he'd last seen her, but the added weight only accentuated her already ridiculous curves. Beautiful as ever, with rich mocha skin and hopeful eyes. Even from a distance, Joshua could see the desire burning in them.

"Let's go out the other side," he said.

Nate frowned. "You're not even going to say hello to her?"

"No."

"Woman's still laying flowers on Darius's—"

Joshua didn't care to hear any of that. He took off walking. Once he'd reached the gravel skirting the parking lot, he heard the crunch of Nate's footfalls behind him. He didn't stop moving until he'd slid safely inside his cousin's Explorer. Nate eased inside and sat back against the driver's seat, keys on his lap. "Help me understand, Joshua. Why won't you talk to her?"

"Nothing to say."

Nate sighed. "Listen, you've been through a lot. I know by now you would've expected to be a finance manager with some company."

"Bullshit accounting degree," Joshua muttered.

"Point I was making . . . nothing about your life has taken the trajectory it should have. Alani's dependable and ambitious and . . . she was good *to you* and *for you*. Don't you think it would help to have that in your life now?"

"Sure," Joshua said. "And you can go back to working for the senator. Rachel and Isiah, too. We'll all just pretend the last few years never happened and go back to our old lives."

"I didn't mean to upset you."

"Doesn't matter where the fuck I thought I would be," Joshua said. "I'm here now. We all are. So, we press forward. All right?"

"It's not healthy for you to—"

"Don't, Nate. Don't. I can't deal with your moralizing right now. You up and go to Hawaii for reasons you won't explain while we're in the thick of this shit and no one calls you on it. Show me the same courtesy right now. I don't want to talk about Alani."

Nate nodded. "Fair enough."

"But we should speak on you and Isiah."

Nate's features tightened in a frown. "What's to speak on? He's a lying piece of shit."

You've got this all wrong. You've got this all wrong. I'm in recycling. Even now, Joshua could practically hear Scott York's voice, how insistent he'd been that they were making a mistake. Eventually, Nate had turned to Isiah and asked him what their captive was talking about. Isiah did all the vetting for their work and explained that York's company exploited eminent domain. Stole land from the Creek Indians to build a recycling plant. That essentially, he was no different from his grandfather. York had been right. He had nothing to do with the black farmers in Uniontown. "Those Creek Indians are every bit as impacted as the black people with the crappy sewage system," Isiah had argued. Nate hadn't bought it. No one suffered like black people.

"Fucking Indians," Nate snarled now. "*Indians.*"

"Isiah's been saying all along that we should expand the scope of our work. Everything doesn't have to be about black folks."

"I don't give a shit about anyone else, Joshua."

"Won't say I feel too differently. But you can't see this from Isiah's perspective?"

"No."

"When he wanted to look into that situation with the Korean grocer who—"

"No," Nate said, cutting him off. "We're not disrespecting the importance of what we do—getting a semblance of justice for Bred and all the others like him—by entangling ourselves with I.T.'s quest for absolution. He's about as Korean as I am. His parents made sure of that. And he reaped the benefits for a long time without any complaints."

"That's not exactly fair, Nate."

"You want to know what's not fair? Let a few Chinese girls get pushed around, asked if they 'sucky, sucky' on the DC Metro. It wouldn't take a week for Congress to pass a bill addressing hate crimes directed at Asian-Americans. Meanwhile, the civil rights movement for us will still have to be waged in the streets."

"This won't work with you and Isiah at each other's throats, Nate. And where will that leave all the families we've been helping? That we've tried to make whole with the reparations."

"I wouldn't worry about that, Joshua. I.T. can be dealt with."

"That's the last thing I wanted to hear."

"Nevertheless," Nate said, and again fell silent.

This time Joshua didn't push him. Didn't say a word until they were pulling up in front of his mother's house.

Nate cut the engine. "I'll be in to say hello to Aunt Dot after I make this quick call."

"We're bound to fuck up if you and Isiah keep playing against each other," Joshua reiterated. "One major lapse and we're risking federal time."

Nate hopped from the vehicle, pulled out his cell phone, moved to the boundary of the small front lawn with the phone pressed to his ear. Avoiding the uncomfortable.

Must be a family trait, Joshua decided. And he hopped out, too. Before his mind could flash on Alani.

The house was stuffy inside, air conditioner on the blink again. His mother wasn't in her usual spot on the sofa.

"Shit," he said, rushing to find her.

There was only the living room, kitchen, her bedroom, Darius's old room, and Joshua's spot in the basement. He checked all the rooms except his brother's and flipped on the lights in the bathroom.

Stumbled back on his heels as his mother's screams pierced his ears.

Dorothy Adams weighed over 440 pounds. Her body was littered with mole-like growths caused by chafing. Her salt-and-pepper hair shorn close because she couldn't make it to Set 'N Style anymore. Most concerning, though, were her shins. They were covered in rusty, dark skin that was shiny like a flat-screen television. Chronic venous insufficiency, the doctors called it. The veins in her legs weren't strong enough to move blood back to her heart. It left her in persistent pain and discomfort. She didn't let the pain shape her features or her mood, though, and that strength of spirit made Joshua love and admire her even more.

His gaze landed on the bucket of fried chicken balanced on the tabletop of his mother's lap. Crumbs were spread across her bosom. He took the bucket and sat it on the sink.

"Go on and say it, Shoe."

Josh-*shoe*-uh. And thus, Shoe.

Like Nate, she was fond of using nicknames. She was the only person on the planet who called him Shoe, an irony when you considered Darius's affection for his sneakers. She'd been saying it even more since her younger son's death. Joshua wondered whether that was intentional.

"Don't just stand there gaping at me," she said. "Help your mama up."

Her walker had tipped over and lay just out of reach. Joshua bent and righted it, set it directly in front of where his mother sat on the commode. "Didn't learn from your fall, I see."

"Shirley's at choir practice," she replied, patting her housedress. "Got the TracFone you gave me in this pocket. I figured the Mighty Voices of Worship wouldn't have a problem getting me up, if it came to that."

"Doctor said you need to lose fifty pounds before he'll even consider the surgery, Ma."

"Might as well have said five hundred." She waved a meaty hand. "Lose weight to get a surgery to lose weight. Makes no sense."

"You don't have to do this alone."

"No?"

"If you'd stop fighting me, sneaking food," he said, "I could help you."

"Oh, I've had enough of your help, Shoe."

"What's that supposed to mean?"

"Hummus? What black folks you know eating that stuff?"

"More should be," he shot back. "And it wasn't just any old

hummus. Blended with roasted red peppers. A sweet, smoky flavor with just the right amount of zip."

"Yeah, it made me zip all right," his mother replied, patting the armrests of the commode.

Despite himself, Joshua smiled. "Listen, Nate's outside. He should be in any moment."

"Nate?" His mother smoothed her housedress. "Get me to the living room then, Shoe. Can't have my nephew seeing me like this."

"You never want Nate to see you as anything but the perfect aunty. Maybe I should tell him about your fall. About you sneaking food."

"Don't play with me, Shoe. Let's go!"

"Okay, okay." He trapped the walker in place with his foot, took hold of her left arm. While she rocked, building up the momentum that would bring her to her feet, he considered all she meant. How good she'd been to him and everyone around her. She'd never lain a hand on him in anger; though, Lord knows, he'd deserved his share of beatings. And then there was Joshua and Darius's father, Jesse, who'd run off on the family and had only come back as the cancer was whittling him down to the bone. Despite that, their mother had taken care of the bastard to the end. Put on more than a hundred pounds in the year after his death. Who but someone good through and through would even mourn someone bad?

"Upsy-daisy," his mother exclaimed, and with his help she was on her feet.

He assisted her to the couch in the living room, supported her as she plopped down heavily against the sea of pillows. She spent most of her time on the couch and pressure sores were always a concern. The pillows helped.

"Thanks, Shoe," she said, out of breath.

"It's nothing, Ma."

"You're so good to me."

"Have to be. You're all I've got," he said, swallowing.

"That's sad. A young man your age needs . . . a different kind of companionship."

Knowing Alani's name would come up any moment, Joshua said, "You're my girl, Ma. I'm good."

"Girl? This old sow ain't been a gilt in many a year, Shoe."

"Wish you wouldn't talk about yourself like this, Ma."

"You know Alani really wants—"

"I'll check on Nate," Joshua said. "He's chopping it up on the phone with somebody."

Nate looked up as Joshua stepped outside, held up a finger. Joshua nodded and sat on the stoop. Scrolling through his cell phone, he stopped on a story he'd learned about while they were down south. Cedric Browne. He'd been ripped away from his family back in May. So far, none of the officers who'd killed him had been charged. In the three years since Philando Castile's fatal traffic stop in Minnesota—shot dead with a child in the backseat—very little had changed. Joseph Curtis Mann. Korryn Gaines. Alfred Olango. Chad Robertson. Too many names to track.

He pocketed his phone, unable to stomach another Twitter hashtag, another candlelight vigil, another graffiti memorial.

"All right," Nate said, joining him.

"That was a spirited conversation. Who were you talking to?"

"No one," Nate said, and then, likely realizing how ridiculous that sounded, he added, "It's not important."

"Had to have been a twenty-minute call."

"Leave it be, Joshua."

"Just making sure everything's okay. You were yelling."

"I said leave it be."

"All right, cousin, no problem," Joshua said. "You got it."

He hovered by the front door as Nate stepped inside, his cousin immediately switching on the charm. Nate leaned down and kissed Joshua's mother. He was her only nephew, her deceased sister Janice's son. "Staying out of trouble, Aunt Dot?"

"Ain't no fun in that," she replied.

"I heard that."

"Shoe hasn't said much 'bout your trip to 'Bama. Everything went okay with your PAT?"

"PAC, Ma," Joshua called from the doorway, a childlike squeal in his voice that only came out with his mother. "Political action committee."

"We held a fundraiser for Talladega College," Nate told her. "State's oldest private black college. Met with a young woman running for State Senate in District Twenty-Three. Keisha Rawlings-Baker. She's an adoptee. A physician. The first black female major general in Army medicine."

"Sounds like my kind of woman. Are you giving her money?"

"She didn't leave the same impression with the others as she did with me."

"Rachel didn't like her?"

"Not particularly."

"Isiah? He's the rational one."

"I.T. took the most issue with her," Nate said.

"My goodness. Isiah loves everybody. What did this Keisha woman do? You'd think Isiah would relate to her being adopted."

Nate smiled, a tight smile, said, "She's a little too in your face about being a strong, proud black woman."

"Humph." Dorothy sucked her teeth. "Gotta be. Plenty of people wanna make you feel ashamed of your skin when you black. And that goes double for a black woman."

"I'm with you there, Aunt Dot. But I.T. feels she doesn't speak to the concerns of all her constituents, just the black ones."

"Black folks need champions," she said.

And Joshua looked up, feeling the heat of Nate's gaze.

"That's what we are, Aunt Dot," Nate said, looking straight at him, a lopsided smile on his face. "Champions for black folks."

February 19, 2017

4:51 p.m.

Sofia, Sofia, Sofia *Angelini. Italian bellezza with wild brunette hair and eyes the color of cola. Blessed with a God-given tan; for a while his boys thought she was Puerto Rican. Darius's chest still swells with pride at how Chuckie couldn't stop staring at her that one time they met. And how Bizz had lifted the collar of his shirt to wipe drool from his lips. Jalen, smooth as always, gave her a head nod, said, "Que lo que." That's how Dominicans greet each other, not to mention Sofia isn't a Latina of any kind, but she'd nodded, replied, "Nada. What you all 'bout to get into?"*

Only four years in the United States and she sounds like she grew up in Newark.

Cool as hell.

Why he loves her.

Took him two hours to get here. Caught the number 59 bus at Watchung Ave., then a train from Elizabeth. Cost him twenty-seven beans round trip, people stepping all over his brand-new kickz, but still worth it. Nothing beats spending time with Sofia.

They're walking a long stretch of road now. Residential area. A slew of stately houses with manicured lawns, solar panels on the roofs. Gleaming SUVs or luxury sedans in the driveways. Even though New Jersey's a blue state, there's nothing but Republicans in town. White folks who attend council meetings to complain about different ordinances and infrastructure projects.

Spring is still a little over a month away, so he's coated up. An all-black, hooded goose down with a scarlet R above the heart, for Rutgers University. Matched with distressed blue jeans and a pair of all-white Adidas. Sofia's wearing a green and white hoodie, ripped jeans, bulky sunglasses. No jacket. So hot she's unbothered by the chill in the air.

"Pretentious," he says, snatching the glasses from her face.

"Darius! Those are Bulgari, you better not fucking break 'em." She lunges to get them back, and he steps into the street to avoid her, a car swerving and honking its horn. "Watch out, fool. Gonna get yourself killed."

"Walking while black," he says, smiling.

"This town is like the city in that manga you forced me to read. A utopia. Nobody here is tripping 'cause you're black."

Darius doesn't bother correcting her. Sofia's innocence is too lovely to ruin. "Well, I hope you would've got in touch with my cousin Nate to tell him a Saab turned me into a pancake."

"Not Joshua?"

"He would lose his shit if he knew I was out here with you."

"I'm sorry, your brother sounds racist as hell."

"It's not even that," Darius says.

"What then?"

"It's complicated."

"Bet he'd come around if he knew how fine I am," Sofia says, wagging her ass.

Darius swallows. "They have condoms at this store we're going to?"

"Not happening, chief."

Sofia lives down one of a million cul-de-sacs branching from one of the roads off this main stretch. Today isn't the first time Darius has been to her house. By his count, it's the fifth in the last two months. And her parents *don't have a problem with his going up and hanging in her bedroom, even with the door closed. He doesn't think they're overcompensating, either. Like they're going out of their way to show they're open-minded. Sofia always said her parents trusted her to make good choices, and they didn't see color. He'd originally doubted that second part. But Mrs. Angelini was neither rude nor syrupy sweet. Mr. Angelini didn't open his gun cabinet or dust off a baseball glove and ask Darius whether he wanted to play catch. Sofia's parents are bland, normal. Fine with their daughter dating whoever she wants.*

"Not happening, huh," Darius says, coming out of his thoughts to respond to Sofia's jab about the condoms. "That's cool. I'll bide my time until the fall, find myself a lil' something-something when I get to campus."

Sofia's cheeks turn a fiery red and her eyes harden.

"Hey," Darius says, "I was kidding. I wouldn't—"

She turns and marches away from him. And march is the right word, too. Her head up, shoulders pushed back, an exaggerated lift in her legs with each step.

Darius trills his lips, touches the necklace in his pocket. Heart-shaped. Sterling silver chain. Amethyst and tanzanite stones—purple is Sofia's favorite color. He had to hustle hard to save up for it. They'd seen The LEGO Batman Movie *last week for Valentine's, shared appetizers at Chili's afterward, exchanged homemade cards. But the chain will be the first major gift either of them has given the other.*

He wants to be first.

This entire walk he's been trying to find the perfect time for the surprise.

4

Mason flipped open a pack of Winston Ultra Lights 100s with one hand, raised it to his lips, and clenched the filter of one of the cigarettes between his teeth, then withdrew it in one fluid motion. There was a bit of a tremble in his hands as he thumbed his lighter and held it to the tip, but he got the damn thing to flare. Though he expected to be rusty, he didn't choke or cough on the smoke. Inhale fast and deep, exhale quick and smooth. Like riding a bike.

He glanced up at the antique clock hanging above the door of his den. Bella had found it at a rummage sale, up in Jackson, just across the line from Tennessee. Talked the seller down to fifty bucks, later discovered it was a Seth Thomas. She could've fetched over two thousand for the clock, easily, but wasn't of the mind to part with it. It represented her guile, her strength of spirit, her wisdom. Age might eventually rob her of those qualities and the clock could serve as a reminder of what she'd once possessed. At least that was the theory she'd shared with Mason.

He squinted and tried to blow out rings of smoke. It didn't work. So, he *was* rusty after all. He picked up the nearby wastebasket and used it as he flicked off gray ash. Then he went ahead and ground out the cigarette on the edge of his desk and tossed it. Outside, he heard

the squawk of a horn. Might be Nails, a few minutes earlier than
Mason was expecting. He stood and moved to go check.

Bella must've heard the horn as well because she was flitting down
the hallway like a skittish cat. They crashed right into each other. In
days past, Mason would've instinctively reached for his wife to make
sure she didn't fall. But despite everything, this was a graceful woman,
a dancer at one time. She brushed aside the bump like lint off her
sleeve. Frowned and leaned forward, sniffing.

"Thought you'd quit," she said.

"Cold turkey. That's exactly right."

"What is it I smell then?"

"Relapse."

"Prefer black lungs, do you?"

"*Black* lungs? Gosh no," Mason said. "Then you'd have nothing to
do with me."

She didn't take the bait. "Sorry to hear of the relapse. You had
some time in. Two years?"

"Twenty-seven months, to be exact," Mason told her. "I don't feel
badly, though. Dr. Miele sold me a bill of goods."

Please, he thought, please ask me what I mean.

"In what way?" Bella said, which was close enough.

"He told me smoking damages the nerve endings in the nose and
mouth, dulling taste and smell. Within forty-eight hours of me quit-
ting, the nerve endings would begin to regenerate, and I'd get back
those senses. He said I'd have more energy, would have an easier time
fighting off colds."

"What part of that isn't true?" Bella asked.

"I didn't finish." Mason gave her a smile that wasn't a smile. "He
also assured me my sex life would improve."

Unfortunately, before she could react, before Mason could get the
payoff of that riposte, that *rejoinder*, the doorbell rang. Bella flinched

and grabbed his sleeve. He peeled off her hand, one finger at a time. "My apologies," he said. "I forgot to mention Nails would be stopping by."

"Nails? Why does that name sound familiar?" Her voice was strained and an octave higher than normal.

"One of the baseball kids," Mason said. "Well, I shouldn't say kid, I guess. I believe he'd be about forty-two by this point."

"I didn't realize you'd stayed in contact."

He hadn't. Nails had called him today, out of the blue. Probably twenty years or more removed from their last interaction. He sounded as though he needed someone, badly. The want in his voice had sold Mason on a meetup. He understood want.

"I'm sure he'd love to see you," he told Bella. "Your sugar cookies were a hit with the boys."

She shook her head. "Think I'll lie down. I have a bit of a headache."

"I hope it wasn't the smoke."

"Enjoy your visit with Nails," she said, heading for the bedroom. Mason watched her the entire way and a moment longer after she'd disappeared up the stairs to the second level. He sighed and went to answer the bell.

The lanky kid he'd coached in Little League, down in Sylacauga, could probably still fit into the jeans he'd worn back then. He still resembled the old Mets and Phillies centerfielder, Lenny "Nails" Dykstra—hence the nickname—and looked as though he could still turn a 3–2 double play from first. That was just his build, though. Because a closer inspection of his face revealed bloodshot eyes and a web of wrinkles. Plus, he was jittery. Mason had plenty of practice cataloging the curses of anxiety.

"Coach."

"Been a long time since anyone's called me coach," Mason replied.

"Same for me with Nails. It's kind of nice. Takes me back to a good time in my life."

"Would you like to come in, Nails?"

He nodded and stepped inside. Mason headed toward the kitchen, then changed his mind and veered toward the den instead. Something with the acoustics, sound rose from in there; you could hear enough of the murmur of voices upstairs in the main bedroom to keep you awake. Bella had complained about Mason playing his old 45s in the den and he'd removed his vintage Victrola with no complaint. It was down in the basement now, dusty and unused. Another sacrifice he'd made.

"Get you a drink or anything before we get too settled, Nails?"

"I'm fine, Coach."

They both dropped down into chairs. Mason cleared his throat. "I don't bother with Facebook. You married? Kids?"

"Yes, and yes," Nails said.

Mason got the hint. "I was surprised to hear from you. What's on your mind?"

"Heard you'd retired from the Birmingham police."

"That's right."

"But you're still . . . still in the field? You work for a security firm?"

Mason imagined his face must've colored with disappointment. This wasn't a personal call. "Whatever you're dealing with," he said, "you should contact my firm and explain your need. You can request me if you'd like."

"Is there any way we can bypass that step?"

"I don't think I understand," Mason said.

"I've been through something, Coach. I was told to never talk to the police. Not to change my cell phone. That's why I called you using a colleague's phone."

Mason frowned. "Not to change your cell phone. Why is that?"

"They're in it. They can see my texts. Listen in on my calls. I've been a nervous wreck. I'm thinking that's part of the point for them."

"Hold on," Mason said, raising a hand. "I'm sorry but I'm not tracking any of this. Who are *they?* I need you to start over from the beginning and tell me what's happened."

The kid once called Nails disappeared and a weary, middle-aged man took his place. He was on the verge of tears, an articulate guy having trouble finding the right words in this instance. His recollection of everything that had happened to him was strong, but the telling of it was disjointed, to say the least. When he'd finally finished, he sat back in his seat, let out a breath that seemed unending.

The swamps of Alabama, a gang of four kidnappers, a noose, and some crazy talk of reparations.

"That's some story," Mason told him, after taking a moment to process it all.

"Thought they were gonna kill me."

"That bit with the noose is . . . troubling."

Scott York nodded. "They threatened my daughters, Coach. Why would anyone do that? Maddy and Ava have nothing to do with any of this."

5

Isiah woke to find Rachel sitting on the end of his bed, staring off into space. Shivering in her panties and bra, even with a sheet draped over her shoulders like a shawl. As was often the case, his breath caught in his chest, just from looking at her. Seafoam-green eyes, wild and wavy chestnut hair, a small mole on her left cheek. Her father, Marko Vucinich, was Italian and Serbian, and spoiled her rotten whenever he flew from overseas to visit her in New Jersey. The reason, Isiah believed, Rachel pouted and crossed her arms over her breasts whenever she didn't get her way. Perhaps that inflexibility could be attributed to her mother as well. Miss Pratt had never wanted marriage and taught her daughter how to use a switchblade. Interesting woman, Miss Pratt, liked to describe herself as a French quadroon.

"Hey." Isiah yawned and sat up on his elbow. "Get any rest?"

Rachel shook her head, pulled the sheet tighter around her body so she was cloaked in it. It'd been this way for the past few days, since they'd gotten back from that nasty business in the swamp, Rachel avoiding her apartment and hanging out here at Isiah's, unable to sleep. Melatonin hadn't worked. Neither had valerian root. She'd blamed her skin flare-up on the lavender he'd sprayed on her pillow. Glycine was a thought, but Isiah had read online that on rare occasions it could cause soft stools and abdominal pain.

"Hungry at all?"

Another headshake.

"You should try to—" He pulled up suddenly as a strobe of Firecracker Popsicle lights painted the bedroom. Police lights. Rachel hardly blinked as he bolted toward the window and parted the curtains. "Derby," he said, relaxing, turning back. Next-door neighbor. Either the marijuana plants he grew, or he'd put his hands on Inez again.

Rachel was still staring at nothing.

"You should eat," Isiah told her, because that's what he needed himself. "I'm going to grab a bowl of Frosted Flakes. You sure you don't want anything?"

Rachel fixed those green eyes on him, said, "You shouldn't have done it."

"Done what?"

"Tricked us like that."

"Don't you mean tricked Nate?"

"It could've ruined everything."

"What's the big deal?" Isiah said. "Those Indians have intermarried with African Americans. And they're dealing with all the same prejudices. Isn't that what matters?"

"That's not a good enough justification for you lying to all of us."

"Nate," he said. "You mean Nate."

"Why must you antagonize him? It's getting out of hand."

"*He's* out of hand, Rache. You're not going to talk about him making you carry that noose?"

"Nate didn't make me do anything. That cracker had it coming to him."

"Cracker?" Isiah laughed. "Nate's really got you drinking the Kool-Aid. I hope you don't think that lil' drop you got from your mother really makes you black."

She was up and out of the room in a blink. The sheet she'd had around her shoulders now lay on the floor by the doorway like a puddle that had to be stepped across. Isiah sighed, grabbed his laptop from the dresser, and headed out to find her.

In the living room, on the chaise, long legs folded under her.

"Look, Rache. I know how that sounded. I admire you for embracing your culture. I'm trying to do the same with my—"

"I need a moment," she said, raising her hand. "A fucking moment's peace to think."

"This is my place, Rache."

A frown etched together her eyebrows. "Pardon me?"

"Nothing," Isiah said, backing out of the room. "Take as long as you need."

On the way to the kitchen, he muttered, "Shit," angry at himself for giving in so easily, for not holding Rachel's feet to the fire. Perhaps he would've benefited if his adoptive parents had taken a different approach with him. If his mother had taught him how to use a switchblade rather than grin and walk away when the kids at school wondered whether he ate dog, whether she and his father had responded when he started calling them *Umma* and *Appa*, whether they'd have encouraged instead of mocked him when he worked to teach himself Hangul, the Korean alphabet.

"To what purpose, Isiah?" his mother had asked.

"It's my heritage, Umma."

"You don't appreciate all your father and I have done for you?"

"Of course I do."

"Then . . . ?"

A pointless argument. His mother was implacable.

Much like Rachel.

Isiah shuddered away the memory and gathered a bowl, poured in cereal and milk, then settled on one of the high bar chairs in the kitchen. He flipped open his laptop and typed a search term in Google. Normally, his fingers blurred over the keys, but mainly when he was working. This was work, too, he supposed, of a different sort. After a while, he was consumed with it, so much so he didn't hear Rachel enter the room.

"The lil' drop I got from my mother means I must cover my hair when it rains. Means people ask me all the time whether I speak Spanish. Means white people look at me as a curiosity, and black people look at me with distrust. I would hope the man I intend on marrying would understand and not contribute to the hurt I've dealt with, still deal with."

Isiah didn't want to go there with her, not now. He cleared his throat, slightly turned the laptop so she could see the screen. "Found a photographer I think you'll approve of. Offers bridal portraits, digital files, online proofing, same-day edits, which is fantastic."

"Did you hear what I said?"

"And listen to some of the comments I found on The Knot. 'They had us fill out a detailed form going over our must-have pictures and moments we wanted captured during the wedding.' That's thorough, right?"

Rachel fumbled with her engagement ring, twisted it on her slim finger.

"Here's another," Isiah tried. "'They focus on storytelling, so their photos and videos really capture emotion and detail.'"

Twist, twist.

Isiah cleared his throat again. "'From our initial consultation meeting through our engagement photo session and our wedding day itself we were treated with the upmost professionalism.' Should be *utmost*, but no need to quibble."

Rachel turned to leave.

"Okay, okay," Isiah called.

She turned back.

"What is it you need from me?" he asked.

"An apology."

"I'm sorry."

"You owe one to Joshua and Nate as well."

"I'll speak with Joshua. Nate's getting nothing from me."

"You're going to ruin this. What we're doing is important."

"At one time, I thought so."

"What does that mean, Isiah?"

"What happened to Darius is inconceivable to me," he told her. "That kid was going to be something. Could sit and talk to me for hours about frame rates and position tracking and all sorts of geek shit. I don't think I'll ever finish building the OCR system we were working on together. I'd probably be a blubbering mess if I even tried."

"Sounds like all the more motivation to continue. Darius was killed and left to die in the street like an animal . . . and no one pays for it. You're okay with that?"

"You know I'm not. But we dreamed up this crazy-ass reparations scheme to right as many wrongs as we could, Rach. And for a while it made sense. Maybe it still does for you, but it doesn't for me. And now we're just out here lynching white people."

"No one was lynched."

"Nate came close to doing it."

"Would you blame him if he did?"

"Hell yeah," Isiah said.

Rachel sighed. "When I was five, I asked my mother for a little brother. She told me all I had to do was close my eyes when I got into bed at night and say a prayer. Feels like I'd kept on praying for a little brother until Darius came along."

"What am I supposed to say to that?"

"I don't want you to *say* anything," Rachel said. "It's about *doing*."

"A great many people have been aggrieved, Rache. Not just black folks. And I'm all for getting those people some justice. I don't feel as though the rest of you feel the same way."

"I look at some of the pictures of Trayvon, and he looked so young.

Darius was so young. Boys with a lot of living left. Then there's Eric Garner and Philando Castile and . . . Jesus, babe. White people can be so horrible."

"All white people?"

"I mean—"

"Your father," Isiah said. "Is he evil?"

"What?" Rachel frowned. "Of course not."

"My parents have their issues," Isiah went on. "But are they *evil?*"

"Babe . . ."

"Ms. Rupert, wrote that beautiful recommendation letter you've told me about, helped get you into college. Is she evil cause she's white?"

"I scored twenty-two fifty on my SATs," Rachel said. "That's what got me into college."

"I said *helped*. And you didn't answer my question."

"She's not evil," Rachel whispered.

"There are bad white people. Bad black people. Bad Asians. Et cetera. But we're doing Darius a disservice making this just about terrible white people. Don't you see that?"

For a moment, he thought he had her, that he'd won the argument, possibly even swayed her thinking.

Then she said "No," and slipped from the room.

6

There was a settler's cabin on Mason's land, and beyond that a stream. The water flowed steadily, creating a melody with the night owls, cicadas, and the occasional sigh of a breeze. When he and Bella first moved here, when he still thought it made a difference, Bella would meet him out here after dinner, after she'd wiped down all the surfaces in the kitchen, cleaned all her cooking pots by hand, loaded the dishwasher with everything else. Mason would be standing by the stream, looking at nothing and everything, and his wife would appear at his side, in one of her flowing sundresses, carefully removing her shoes, dropping them to the soft ground, then dipping her toes in the wet, foamy water. They might settle into a conversation—that trip they'd taken to Trinidad—and share smiles over the naughtiness at Pigeon Point Beach. Or they might not speak at all, either there by the water's edge or in the grass as they fumbled out of their clothes.

Mason grumbled away those thoughts and let his latest cigarette fall to the ground. He smothered it with the toe of his shoe and turned to head back inside. So much had changed for them, but they still ate takeout dinner together every evening. Bella insisted. Tonight, it'd been a tomato pie Mason picked up from Carlile's in Scottsboro. Of course, it had been colder than a witch's tit by the time he made it home, but a warming in the oven hadn't robbed it of any of its flavor.

Fresh tomatoes, bacon, and basil. Salt, pepper, green onions, mayonnaise, and cheese as a saucy garnish. Then Bella surprised him with banana pudding for dessert. A bit heavy on the custard and skimpy with the coins of banana, but he appreciated her effort. He'd told her as much and wrapped an arm around her waist as she rinsed out their drinking glasses at the sink. When the schoolgirl laugh hadn't come or a mischievous gaze into his eyes, he'd stepped outside with his pack of cigarettes.

Hopefully his wife would be down for the night as he trundled back into the house now.

She wasn't.

Mason startled as he turned on the lights in the kitchen. Bella was sitting on one of the tall bar chairs, by the butcher's block table in the center of the room. She didn't bother with makeup anymore, which prevented her tears from smudging her cheeks black with mascara now.

"What's wrong?" Mason asked. He slammed his pack of cancer sticks on the butcher's block, so she'd have to see. Her gaze, though, it remained focused on the wall beyond him. "Bella?"

It took him waving his hand across her field of vision like a hypnotist's watch to get her to look his way. When she smiled at him, he again remembered the woman who would frolic with him in the grass out back. He swallowed to keep from crying himself.

"I was reading today about MacKenzie Bezos," Bella announced.

"Who?"

"She's divorcing the man who started Amazon."

"He's a fool," Mason said. "His ex-wife stands to clean up."

Bella nodded. "She's getting thirty-eight billion dollars' worth of Amazon stock in the settlement."

Mason whistled. "Talk about happily ever after."

"They loved each other at some point," Bella whispered.

"It's just the way it changes, like the shoreline and the sea, Bella."

"You've given it some thought," she replied.

"I'm afraid Leonard Cohen gets the credit for that one."

Bella smiled.

"What?" Mason said, frowning.

"Thinking of how you were always listening to your records. They put you in such a state of peace. Why did you stop?"

He shrugged. "Maybe peace doesn't suit me."

"Perhaps you're confusing yourself with me."

"I could easily dust off the ol' Victrola, I guess."

"I love you, Mason. I hope you know that."

"You'd better," he said. "Even though I don't have the Amazon guy's money."

"How did it go with Nails?"

"I'm working on something for him," Mason said.

"You just got a gleam in your eye."

"The work keeps me going. Otherwise, I might rust up."

"You've got a lot left to give, Mason."

There was something familiar and beautiful about the light, playful way they were talking to each other. Mason plucked the pack of Winstons from the butcher's block, made a turn to move away. If he did so now, before the conversation shifted, he could hold on to its memory, use it to get a good night's sleep for a change.

"You hate me because of Nicole," Bella called to him. He was nearly out of the kitchen. He sighed and turned back.

"You two were inseparable," Bella added. "So much for the bond between mothers and their daughters."

"Nicole loved us both, Bella. Loves us both."

She nodded. "I haven't made it easy. But our daughter has a kind soul . . . like her father."

"No one's ever accused me of that."

"And yet it's true."

He didn't want to have this conversation with Bella, but it was unavoidable now. "We don't have any pictures of Zion anywhere in the house. You realize that?"

Bella was silent.

"I'm a kind soul?" Mason said. "Well, I've got a question for you. What do you see, what do you feel, when you look at our grandson?"

Tears once again ran a silver streak down Bella's pale cheeks.

"The gorillas that followed you from UAB? Pulled out their dicks and smashed them up against the car windows? That what you see with Zion, Bella?"

She didn't respond.

"Well, guess what?" Mason finished. "I do, too." And, with that, he turned and walked off. This time his wife let him go.

February 19, 2017

4:54 p.m.

Sofia stomps past *a dry cleaner, a health food store, and an Exxon gas station. The A-Z Mart looms ahead.*

"Sofia, hold up a sec," Darius says, coming up behind her. "You know I was joking."

Now she's feeling the chill, he can tell. She doesn't usually walk with her shoulders hunched in like this. She looks like she wants to rub her hands together and blow on them.

"Slow down a minute," he says. "I'll give you my coat to wear."

She doesn't slow.

There are bundles of firewood selling for $7.99 stacked up against the convenience store's brick facade. A standalone cooler advertising seven-pound bags of Sea Isle ice for $2.99. A Redbox vending machine. A silver Acura with 20 percent tint idles in a parking spot out front, bass-heavy music rattling its windows. Hospital-bright lights inside the store.

Sofia stops by the door to tap dirt from her shoes. She squints against the sun, low and about ready to set. It's fiercer here without the cover of trees. "Here," Darius says, moving to ease the sunglasses back on her face. She turns her head and goes inside. Darius lets out a long sigh, pockets the sunglasses, and heads into the store himself.

The aisles aren't crowded, and the shelves aren't stocked with dusty, out-of-date products. There aren't any loose cigarettes or White Owls for sale. You could eat off the floors if that were a thing. Nice lemony smell to the place. Darius feels lost a moment without the Raid bug spray and stale Newport smoke he's used to circulating at Raja's Grab & Go around his way. He recovers and nods at the older guy manning the register. Dude has short, mixed brown and gray hair, a glower carved into his weathered face. There are four shoppers in the store. Two white boys a few years older than Darius, and two girls with them, quite a bit younger. One of the white boys looks Sofia over as he moves by her, sort of smirks. He's wearing gray sweatpants and a Nike shirt with sleeves to his wrists, the black Air Jordan Retro Space Jams. No coat. None of them are coated up. These white people don't feel the winter.

Space Jam bumps into Darius as they cross paths in an aisle.

"My bad," Darius says to him.

"Yeah," is Space Jam's reply.

Darius settles beside Sofia as she plucks a Snickers from the shelf. "You know him?"

"I'm not standing for you interrogating me, Darius."

"Interrogating you? I'm asking because he was staring at you like a meal." He looks up to see Space Jam hanging by the door while his friends pay up. "Still is."

"Another horndog," she says, shrugging.

Darius says, "I hope you aren't going to stay mad at me," his fingers reaching for the necklace in his pocket.

"Didn't you say you wanted Rice Krispies Treats? You're smothering me. Why don't you go handle that?"

"Yeah," he says, letting the chain fall from his grasp, "I'm on it."

"Later," Space Jam yells as he exits the store.

No telling whom he's directing the comment at. The cashier has his back turned. He's stacking cartons of cigarettes on the counter behind the register.

Darius eyes Sofia. She's concentrating hard on the candy shelf. Like she's working out a model for exponential growth and decay in AP Calculus. "Hey, Sofia . . ."

But he decides not to even press her about Space Jam. Leaves her and moves down the aisle that's one over, pastries and cookies. The front door opens as he contemplates buying Devil Dogs. He looks up expecting Space Jam's return. Even worse, a patrol officer strolls in. Darius drops the cakes and grabs a Rice Krispies Treats from the shelf and a Mountain Dew from the cooler. He's too anxious now to look for marshmallows to take home to his mother as a surprise.

It takes a moment to locate Sofia. She's up near the checkout counter. Haloed by the sunlight streaming through the glass doors. The cop's hovering on her left, chatting up the cashier. Darius approaches from Sofia's right, whispers, "Let's get out of here."

"I'm getting a hot dog," she replies, not even looking at him. "It'll be a few minutes. He just put it on the grill."

Grill is a bit of a stretch. Darius eyes the rolling bar set up behind the counter glass. It will take forever and a day for a hot dog to cook on that thing. "We need to go, Sofia."

"We'll go after my hot dog's done, Darius."

Raising her voice catches the cashier's attention.

The cop's as well.

He steps over, asks Sofia, "There a problem, ma'am?"

7

Forecasts were calling for it to reach the midnineties, and even though it was still early, the sky was already burning bright with a fireball sun. Despite the temperature outside, Nate walked into an armory that was as cool as the other side of the pillow. He typically was greeted by a wall of heat in the lobby that squeezed the air from his lungs. It was pleasant, then, to find it so comfortable today. The pleasure of that surprise lasted only the time it took him to take the elevator up to the third floor, and the suite of offices for the PAC he ran with Joshua, Rachel, and I.T. All three of them were in the reception area already and their voices hushed as he walked in.

Nate glanced at his watch. "Guess I'm late for a meeting I didn't know we were having."

"We need to talk about Alabama," I.T. said, standing, his feet widespread, arms crossed over his chest.

Nate took him in, barely suppressing a chuckle. "Something bothering you, I.T.?"

"Alabama," he said.

"You want to have this talk here? Is that a good idea?"

"I've swept the suite for bugs already. We're clear."

Their PAC had grown in the twenty-three months since its formation, now boasting over a hundred thousand contributors. After Nate,

I.T., and Rachel's time working together in Senator Riehle's office, they'd wanted to create something of their own, to impact change on a more personal level. Enter the *Actions Speak Louder* PAC. A grass-roots organization building power at the local, state, and federal levels. Electoral work and issue advocacy—fighting for democracy issues and economic priorities. They'd raised over $3 million in donations for progressive candidates, many of them black and brown and opposed by the corporate political machine as well as the "forgotten" majority who were feeling left behind and neglected by a changing America. They had enemies like the idiots down south in Charlottesville, marching through the streets with tiki torches, chanting, "You will not replace us."

Not to mention their other "work."

Still reeling from Darius's murder, they'd convinced Joshua to leave the comfort of his job with Johnson & Johnson and come aboard as the PAC's treasurer and custodian of records. Isiah would serve as assistant treasurer, Nate and Rachel as consultants. None of them collected more than $50K annually in salary, so it was a big step down from what they would've made in the open market. It meant Joshua living in his mother's basement, Isiah next door to a weed dealer. Rachel had the benefit of her father's financial support, if needed, and Nate's home was the one possession of any value in his late mother's estate, a well-kept colonial that nonetheless led to more than a few sleepless nights considering the exorbitant property taxes.

But running the PAC gave them great cover to do what mattered most. Avenging Darius's death.

Even for Isiah, Nate hoped that was still the case.

"Say your piece," he said, eyeing I.T.

"Scott York."

"What about him?"

"You went overboard with the noose."

"Rachel agreed to hold it for me, pull it out at the appropriate moment. You've been giving her shit for that?"

I.T. didn't respond.

Nate said, "Didn't think so."

"You're deflecting."

"Right. Has York deposited the money in the account? I'd like to send it on to Ms. Williams. It won't bring her father back but—"

"She's not the only one who should be getting that money."

"If you're thinking about those Indians," Nate said, pointing a finger at I.T.'s chest. "Please know they aren't getting a *red* cent."

"You're an asshole, Nate."

"Call me whatever names you want. But be thankful I'm giving you a pass for that stunt."

"Giving me a pass? You're my father now?"

"Certainly not . . ." Nate smiled. "*Min-su.*"

Min-su. I.T.'s birth name.

His white adoptive parents decided to keep it as his middle name, then proceeded to erase every aspect of his culture. It'd been one of the things that had drawn Nate to him when they'd met working for the state senator from Livingston. That erasure had inspired in I.T. a passion that was palpable. Seemed like a million years ago. That passion had long since evaporated.

"You're out of control, Nate."

"Yeah?"

"You pushed this one too far," I.T. said. "We agreed there wouldn't be any violence."

"There hasn't been."

"I guess we're looking at it differently then."

"If we're going to talk Alabama," Nate said. "Let's start with the cops who killed Cedric Browne. Walked away free even though they took a man's life. Same as the muhfucka who murdered Bred."

Joshua let out a long breath.

"Or let's talk about the black folks in the Belt having their water contaminated," Nate continued. "Shit, we can even talk about your Indians. But I will tell you one thing. I'm not about to stand here feeling sorry because I made some white boy piss his pants. Cool?"

"Cool," I.T. said.

"Good." Nate rubbed his hands together. "Let's move on then. We can't have these distractions. That's how you lose momentum. So, I was thinking for our next one we might—"

"Doesn't matter what you're thinking," I.T. said. "I have the next one figured out."

Nate narrowed his eyes. "You know that's not how this works."

"This time it will," I.T. said.

"What makes you think I'm going to stand here and listen to this shit from you, I.T.?"

"That was really cute, Nate," he said, "throwing in that bit about Signaling System vulnerabilities with York. How we were able to get into his text messages. For a second, you even had me fooled. I was beginning to think you knew what the hell you were talking about."

"Fuck you say?" Nate said, edging close.

"Course, you don't know jack about the actual process," I.T. went on. "How to run Linux and SS7 SDK, fooling the network into thinking the hacking device is actually an MSC/VLR node."

"Get to whatever it is you have to say, I.T."

"I set up the bank accounts, route the money to the victims in a way that doesn't get traced to us. I'd say I'm pretty important."

Now Nate crossed his arms.

"Regardless of what you seem to think," I.T. continued. "Black people don't have a monopoly on being discriminated against. And knowing what we know of Darius, I think you can agree he wouldn't want us making this so . . . limited. He'd want us to help all sorts of victims. Especially since we claim to be doing this to honor him."

Nate turned to Joshua. "This is what I was trying to tell you."

"It's been headed in this direction for some time, cousin," Joshua replied. "We can't be so quick to dismiss how Isiah feels."

"Rachel?" Nate said, facing her.

"All of us, or none of us," she whispered.

Their motto from the start.

Isiah said, "If I'm going to do this, I need to be comfortable with it. Don't you think?"

"Just tell us who the fuck you have in mind," Nate said, his voice pinched.

8

Pulling away from the house, Mason glanced in his rearview mirror as the woman from Instacart set grocery bags on the plastic Adirondack chair Bella insisted they keep on the porch. Normally, that sight would've upset him, a reminder of all that was lost, but this morning he felt something close to serenity. Bella had at least tried last evening. He could still smell her shampoo; maybe soon he'd be able to say the same about her lotion.

Smiling at the thought, he pulled out his cell phone, dialed a familiar number. After three rings a woman picked up. "What do you have for me, Ash?" Mason asked.

"Hello to you, too, *Mase.*"

Mason smiled, merged into traffic on I-565W, headed for Birmingham. "Okay, I'll start over. How are you, *Ashley?*"

"Blessed and highly favored, Mason."

"Speaking of favors . . . I wanted to see how you were doing with the one I asked of you."

"The four kidnappers in the swamp?"

"Yes. You said to give you a few days."

"Hubris."

"Oh, no. This isn't sounding good."

"In Russia, if there's a divorce, women get 10 percent of the marital assets. In Dubai, they get nothing. Which leads successful American men to do some real deep thinking when the nuptials start to fall apart. The wealthiest ones will have an adviser, some shady genius who suggests they set up a trust in the Cook Islands. Cook courts typically don't recognize US court orders, including divorce judgments. To sue a Cook trust, you must fly out to the island, in the middle of the South Pacific. We're talking six thousand miles southwest of Florida."

"And this relates to my situation how?"

"The Channel Islands, Liechtenstein, the Caribbean," Ash said. "Panama."

"I'm not following."

"What's the next level up from genius?"

"Is there a level up?" Mason asked.

"I wouldn't have thought, but apparently so. Not only does your bank account have a nominee . . . I won't bore you with the details, but that's basically a hired proxy for official documents—a dead end in this case, by the way—but your guys also created a fake identity. And they've added additional layers of protection by having the money jump around like a pinball. All those places I just mentioned. The bank account you gave me is a landing spot, but the money doesn't stay there for very long. I was able to follow it for a bit, but then the labyrinthine nature of the additional accounts left me lost."

"Jesus."

"Who are these people, Mason?"

"Good question."

"I like a good challenge, so I'll keep working it. I make you no promises, though."

"Appreciate it, Ash."

And just to rankle her a bit, Mason disconnected the call without a proper goodbye. He'd hear about it the next time he spoke with her, but that was fine. Ashley Kellerman was one of his favorite people at Tsaro, and he was certain she felt the same way about him. It was an unlikely pairing on the surface, he being well over fifty and squeamish about tattoos and piercings, Ashley in her midtwenties, both her arms "sleeved" with tattoos, diamond studs along the curve of her right ear, a brass lotus through her septum.

Indigo-blue eyes, though. A perpetual ballet-slipper blush to her cheeks, blunt blonde haircut. She reminded him of Nicole.

It'd been almost a month since he'd last spoken with his daughter. A conversation that started out fine and quickly deteriorated. Nicole would say that was because Elijah had called her and she'd put Mason on hold for four minutes, but that had nothing to do with the shifting tide of the exchange. Mason couldn't recall now what had been the catalyst, but that's how it often went with Nicole; she was a storm when it came to her father. It was even worse with Bella. And yet they all loved one another. Dysfunction was their fertilizer.

Rather than dwell on any of that, Mason popped in a CD of Emmylou Harris's *Heartaches & Highways*, immediately swept up in the pity and sadness of "Love Hurts." It made him want to call Bella. Call Nicole. Remind his daughter he was born on March 4, 1968, exactly one month before Martin Luther King Jr. was assassinated, that he was named after the Mason Temple, where King delivered his "I've Been to the Mountaintop" speech. Of course, Nicole would shoot back that Benjamin Waterhouse was also born on March 4, and in addition to cofounding Harvard Medical School, he'd been the first doctor to test the smallpox vaccine in the United States—on his own family. Also, HMS didn't admit its first black students until sixty-eight years after its founding. What was up with that?

It was never a fair fight when Mason challenged the two loves of his life. Bella won, always, because she forever left him *amazed at the way she pulled him out of time*, to paraphrase Paul McCartney. Nicole always won because she was, quite simply, smarter than her father on his best day, a natural debater. And she knew her father better than he knew himself.

Emmylou was still with Mason, almost two hours later, as he took the exit toward Sylacauga East. She was with him on US-280, then his left onto Overton Road, the red dirt girl by that point of the CD wondering whether he'd suffered at the end and would there be no one to remember. She was with him as he pulled up to Reichert Recycling on Urban Center Drive.

Once inside, Mason was given a yellow safety helmet and orange vest, ushered to the plant. "He's up in that lookout," the young man who'd guided Mason here said, pointing at an oversize birdhouse-looking thing near the top of the structure at the other end of the plant floor. Mason thanked him for his help and started walking in that direction, awestruck by the sheer size and scale of the building and machinery. He'd learned on the walk over it was called a material recovery facility, or MRF for short, seventy thousand square feet. He'd also learned more than he ever wanted to know about the single-stream recycling process, which he saw firsthand now.

Trucks unloading a blended mix of paper, plastics, glass, metal, and cardboard onto conveyor belts. Workers presorting, screening, and picking out their assigned commodity. Large bales of recyclables that would be sold to manufacturers and turned into brand-new products.

Efficient.

And apparently very profitable. On the walk over, the guy had said the state-of-the-art machinery cost the company more than $15 million.

Mason's knees creaked as he climbed the structure that would take him up to the birdhouse. The rails of the stairs were bright yellow, while the structure itself was a dark green. Mason wondered why those two colors.

Scott York met him as he reached the top of the stairs. They stood near what appeared to be a command center for the operation, workers all around them manning the conveyors. "Saw you on your way over, Coach."

"Why don't we ease up on the past?" Mason said. "I'm nobody's coach."

"That's fine by me."

Despite his own declaration, Mason said, "You know I was just twenty-seven when I coached you all? Fifteen years older than you but it felt like a million. I was already married five years to my Bella by that point."

"Miss Bella . . ." Scott York stopped, a berry blush painting his cheeks.

"Say whatever's on your mind."

"I was thinking out of turn," Scott said. "Don't mind me."

"Tell it," Mason insisted.

Scott sighed. "I can't say any of us liked Miss Bella's sweets, especially those awful sugar cookies. But we were always happy when she came around. She was . . . easy on the eyes."

"Still is," Mason told him. "And her cooking has significantly improved." He glanced around, not wanting to dwell on talk of his wife. "Some arrangement you all have here."

"We're eliminating waste, decreasing the need to eradicate the Earth's natural resources."

"You make it sound like a calling, Scott."

"I suppose it is, of a sort."

"Something has been niggling at me," Mason said, getting this started. Otherwise, they'd be here all morning, talking about green energy and all that other progressive bullshit.

"What's that?"

"No luck so far with the bank account, by the way, but I have a tech person looking into it." Mason cleared phlegm from his throat. "The four of 'em took you, did all the psychological-thriller shit to you, then gave you this oddly specific amount you had to deposit in an account each week, called it reparations?"

"That's the sum of it."

"Reparations," Mason said again. "Once more, that's an oddly specific word. Did they say what these reparations were for?"

"I'm imagining slavery."

Mason kept quiet, just eyed Scott for several beats. His former first baseman was having trouble meeting his coach's eyes. Eventually Scott's head dropped, and he said, "You ever hear anything bad about my pawpaw, Coach?"

Mason frowned. "Bad like what?"

And Scott told him everything he'd learned about that fateful night on the Tyler-Goodwin Bridge. When he finished, Mason let out a breath.

"A lot of terrible stuff happened back then," he said.

"I know it."

"We learned from it. You wouldn't see any of that nowadays."

Scott nodded. "I'd like to think so." He looked around the plant. Most of the workers were a shade of brown. "I'm not here often," he said, "but we send a clear message from corporate that diversity is valued and expected."

"Just not among the administration."

"Pardon?"

"In the main office," Mason said. "I couldn't help but notice the leadership portraits you have displayed. All white men."

"That's just because—"

"I'm not judging you for it. I understand, believe me. I'm just wondering if one of your workers here might've noticed as well. It's the kind of thing that might make these people upset enough to do something."

"None of them are involved."

"You sound certain. What aren't you telling me?"

"Can you find the people who did this to me or not?"

"I can find 'em," Mason said. "But it's going to take serious resources."

"You mean money?"

Mason nodded.

"Not a problem," Scott told him.

"What are you looking to do when I find them?"

"Probably best you just pass that info on to me. I have people that'll take it from there."

"Sounds ominous," Mason said, but he still held out his hand to shake.

9

They'd moved from the armory to Isiah's place, and the more the other three talked, the more Rachel realized she had nothing to contribute to the conversation. She ignored her unease, though, and took another glug of her Heineken. It was not at all uncommon for her to feel as she did now, lost in a way she couldn't articulate. Detached, as if she were hovering overhead, watching her own life unfold and unable to offer any input. To make matters worse, her feet hurt in her flip-flops. The straps were cutting into the interstice between her toes. She quietly let the sandals slip off her feet. There was one beer left in the refrigerator, she remembered, and she stood to go retrieve it for herself.

She didn't make it back to the table with Isiah, Nate, and Joshua to continue with the planning for their upcoming job. Instead, she found herself in the living room, curled up on the couch with the television remote and flipping aimlessly through channels. She stopped on one in the ESPN family. Two fighters on the screen, one black and one white. Of course. The white one was short, hyper, heavily muscled, with a broad face and scarring in his eyebrows. The black one was thinner, calmer, the outline of his ribs like the gills of a cartoon shark. They met in the center of the ring, touched gloves, and then returned to their respective corners.

"The sweet science."

She turned to discover Joshua standing in the doorway.

"Sorry I bailed," she told him.

"Is that what you're calling it? I just thought you needed to take a minute."

"I'm about nine over, if that's the case."

"Ten minutes then."

"The details are overwhelming for me," she offered. "I just needed to . . . I don't know."

"Get some distance in case of flying shrapnel?"

She smiled. "I made sure to check the cutlery before you guys walked in. The butter knives are dull. Don't think they'd do much damage."

"That skillet on the back burner's got some heft to it."

"Shit," Rachel said. "Told you I wasn't one for details."

Joshua smiled, moved into the room, went to settle in a chair, changed course when Rachel patted a spot beside her. "Don't worry. They're behaving. Right now, at least."

"I think Nate respects Isiah for standing up to him and picking this latest target."

"Yeah? Well, you know my cousin better than me."

"Mmm."

"Are you doing okay in here?"

"I am," Rachel said. "What's happening with the boys then?"

"Isiah's doing background. Appears our *target* works in a building with an attached parking garage. Your brilliant fiancé is attempting to find out what kind of security cameras they have installed. If it's a Pelco, there's a backdoor password reset flaw he can exploit."

"I take it Nate isn't helping with that."

"No, Nate's leaving the technical stuff to the pro," Joshua said. "He's trying to put together a fundraiser to benefit A&T and Fayetteville State."

Rachel nodded. "That would be nice."

"Gives us cover, while we're down there."

They looked at each other, just briefly. Then Rachel cleared her throat and nodded at the screen. "I ever tell you my mother sent me for boxing lessons?"

"Miss Pratt was no joke." Joshua shook his head and laughed. "When was this?"

"Eighth grade," Rachel said. "Year before we moved to Jersey."

"You were living in Connecticut back then, right?"

"Massholes, but close enough."

"And what made Miss Pratt want to turn her daughter into Laila Ali?"

"Todd Simmons. He was a year younger but had a five o'clock shadow. He'd follow me around and ask creepy white-boy questions. Was I more silk or wool down there? Shit like that."

"Sounds awful."

"It was, but I dealt with it gracefully for the most part. Didn't mention it to my mother until Todd pinned me against a wall one day and tried to stick his tongue in my mouth. Said he wanted to see if I tasted like caramel."

"I hope you blasted him in the balls."

"I did indeed," she said, and looked off at that distant memory. She'd gotten detention for the incident. Todd had told someone in the principal's office she'd attacked him. The school hadn't bothered investigating to see whether there was any provocation.

"Really, are you okay?" Joshua asked, pulling her back to the present.

"I don't think I ever told you this, but on my first day working for the senator, Nate came up to me and introduced himself. He said, 'I heard we had a new mulatto on board. Welcome.'"

Joshua whistled. He was the only one of the three of them who hadn't worked in that office. "My cousin can be . . .'"

"Right," Rachel said. "I'd heard worse coming from those white boys in New England, but it was stunning hearing something like that from Nate. I didn't initially know how to react."

"Same treatment you gave Todd Simmons when he tried to kiss you."

"I was close. But then Nate told me to never let anyone else define me. Being called a mulatto, for instance, shouldn't cause me shame. And if I needed a reminder, to think of it as—and he smiled as he said it—*making ugly labels always tough to observe.* I didn't get it at first, but when I did . . ." She shook her head, chest rising from an exhaled breath. "I didn't realize how much I needed to hear something like that."

"Sounds like something my cousin would say."

"Isiah doesn't understand our fixation on race," Rachel said, turning to look directly into Joshua's eyes. "But I don't want you to think he's not angry about what happened to your brother. Isiah was just talking the other day about how he and Darius could geek out together."

"Either catch Darius at Foot Locker or on his computer," Joshua said, speaking softly.

"Talk about brilliant . . ."

Seventeen. And oh so very brilliant.

Rachel reached for her Heineken. Took considerate care polishing away the sweat on the bottle with the hem of her shirt. A bitter tang, a biting burn as the beer slid down her throat. A clunk when she set the bottle back down on Isiah's coffee table.

"I'm sorry," she said, unable to even look at Joshua.

But she felt his gaze.

"For?" he asked.

"Isiah thinks he's sticking it to Nate, insisting we go after this guy. I don't think he's given any thought to how it must make you feel."

"Because the guy's black?"

"Yeah."

"*Hate* killed Darius," Joshua said, laying his hand on Rachel's knee. "I can't be upset with Isiah. I understand where he's coming from. This guy did some vile shit to that poor girl, and he shouldn't be allowed to get away with it."

Rachel faced him. "Isiah's dealt with a lot of racism himself. He's still trying to find his way."

"Aren't we all?" Joshua said, and stood. "Anyway, you needed some time to yourself. I just wanted to check on you. Make sure you were okay. I see that you are."

He was almost out of the room when Rachel called him. He turned back.

"I know we can't bring back Darius. We can't bring back any of them. Still, there's good in what we're doing?"

"Weren't for this, I would've slaughtered the motherfucker who took Darius from me," Joshua said, a sad smile on his face. "And of course, I would've been the first person the police would've looked at. What we're doing . . . it's saved me from myself."

He stepped out of the room then.

Rachel turned and looked at the television screen.

The black boxer was having points deducted for hitting below the navel.

February 19, 2017

5:02 p.m.

"Ma'am? I asked *if there's a problem," the cop says.*

Ma'am? Sofia's seventeen, same as Darius.

"I'm fine," she tells him.

"Sure?"

"Are you hard of hearing?"

The cop ignores that, looks over her head, at Darius. "You live in the area?"

"Visiting with my girlfriend, Officer."

"Girlfriend," the cop says, and he glances at Sofia. She cocks her head as if to say What of it? The guy behind the counter grunts.

"And where'd you two happen to meet?" the cop asks her.

"Why does that matter?"

"I put a CAD drawing up on the 'Gram," Darius cuts in. "And Sofia commented on it."

"CAD drawing?"

"Computer-aided design," Darius explains.

"You some kind of techie?"

"I dabble," Darius says.

Placed fourth in the Google Science Fair. One of the top high school students in the region. With a small assist from his and his brother's friend Isiah, he'd created a wireless virtual reality system. Rutgers had since offered a full-ride academic scholarship. But he wasn't about to tell the cop any of that. It likely wouldn't matter. "Pink Nikes for Breast Cancer Awareness Month."

"What now?" the cop says.

"That drawing I'd put up on the 'Gram," Darius says. "My aunt died from breast cancer, and I did it to commemorate her."

The cop smiles. "The wonders of social media. Bringing people together who might not otherwise have ever met."

"Don't act like you think that's a good thing," Sofia says.

Darius groans, closes his eyes for a moment. Don't do this, he thinks in the quiet of his mind. He and Sofia have an almost telepathic connection. He hopes she can intuit his thoughts now.

"World's sure enough turned into a rainbow," the cop goes on, and smiles. "What's that commercial? Taste the rainbow? Guess you two didn't realize they were talking about Skittles."

Sofia squints, trying to read something on the cop's chest. Oh Jesus, she's searching for a badge number. After a quick glance to make sure the cop isn't watching, Darius buries the Mountain Dew and Rice Krispies Treats in an endcap of single-serving chips. He moves closer to Sofia, gently taking hold of her arm. "We should go," he says through gritted teeth.

"Go? My hot dog's not ready yet."

"Please, Sofia."

She looks at his face, sees something, and in a whisper says, "All right, we'll go."

"You okay with him grabbing your arm, ma'am?" the cop asks.

"Mind your business," Sofia snaps at him.

10

Mason crossed the Madison County line as rain and thunder began to whirl across north Alabama. He'd been listening to Emmylou again, her cover of an old Buck Owens B side, and had completely missed the signs of a coming storm—dark, roiling clouds the color of wilted orchids, sudden gusts that shook his car, a steep drop in the temperature. Had he been paying any attention he would've sped up to get home sooner instead of driving all leisurely, because his wipers were beat to shit and doing a feckless job of gaining him any visibility. Now, intent on getting back to Bella safely, he set aside his pride and pulled over on the shoulder of the road, clicked on his hazards. He'd wait it out. Luckily it was July, and he didn't need to be as concerned about a tornado siren.

Rain hammering the roof of the car, he thought about the crumpled pack of Winston Ultra Lights 100s stuffed under the bric-a-brac in his glove box. He reached for the storage handle twice before going ahead and flipping open the door, rooting breathlessly through the mess until he had the pack in his shaky hands.

Orchestral piano chords filled the car interior, startling him.

In the commotion, he dropped the pack of Winstons in the dark foot well on the passenger side. That's where he tossed fast-food containers and other garbage. It was worse than his glove box. Unless the pack had settled on top of the landfill, it would take some doing to recover.

Another string of piano chords. Mephisto's Dance. The ringtone Nicole had programmed.

Mason leaned to the side to fish for the phone from his pants pocket, and once he had it, he reached overhead to turn on the dome light, squinting to read the caller ID on the phone screen. A 205 area code, but a number with which he wasn't familiar. He had no idea who would be calling him so late and was surprised to hear Glen Saunders's voice on the other end. Tsaro's chief legal counsel. Years ago, they and their wives had gotten together at Mason's house for dinner. Although it had only happened just once, Mason considered the lawyer a friend.

"Catch you at a bad time?"

"Not at all." Mason turned down the volume on Emmylou. "What's going on, Glen?"

"Tamara Blake."

It took Mason a moment to place the name. "The black girl at Oxmoor?"

Saunders sighed in his ear, said, a little put out, Mason thought, "She's thirty-one. And I really wish you hadn't led with her race."

"What's going on here, Glen?"

"Do you remember speaking with an Indian woman as well when you were there?"

"Indian? I don't recall anyone in headdress and feathers, so I'd have to say no."

"Jesus, Mason."

"Is there a problem here, Glen?"

"Were you joking just now? Please tell me you were joking."

"Of course I was," Mason said, mainly because he could tell that's what Glen Saunders needed to hear. "What's going on? The Blake woman making a stink about getting shitcanned?"

"Making a stink, yes. But she wasn't terminated."

Outside the car, a flash of lightning split the sky, then a roll of thunder, rain hammering the road. "Take the mashed potatoes out of your mouth and tell me what's going on here, Glen."

"Oxmoor has informed us they will not require our services for any future matters. Ms. Blake and Ms. Chopra have—"

"Who?" Mason interrupted. "What was that second name?"

"Chopra. The woman from security. Claims you made a point of speaking to her in piss-poor Spanish."

"Sí," Mason replied. "And what of it?"

"She's originally from Jamshedpur."

"Is that supposed to mean something to me?"

"You know what? Forget I called. I wanted to give you a heads-up that Deighton would likely be bringing you in to talk, but . . . yeah . . . just . . . I didn't call, okay?"

Thaddeus Deighton, whose grandfather had been a founder, was one of the firm's partners. Mason had seen him in the halls around their headquarters, but he was certain Deighton wouldn't know his name if he spotted him four letters. "Calling me in to talk about what, Glen?"

But the other man had disconnected the call. Mason tried the number twice, got dumped into voicemail both times. Frustrated, he decided sitting idle on the side of the road wasn't for him and pulled back out onto the highway to continue home. It was slow going with the storm raging, but he was pulling up to the house a while later.

Bella was asleep and buried under the covers. She stirred, though, and gave him a brief smile as he kissed her forehead. He settled downstairs, behind his desk in the den. And, although it was probably a terrible idea, he dialed his daughter's number. She picked up right away.

"What's happened?" she said.

"Nothing," Mason assured her. "I just wanted to talk to you. How are you doing?"

"I'm fine. You're sure nothing's wrong?"

"Certain. And Zion? Elijah? They're doing okay as well?" When his daughter didn't respond, he called her name. "Nicole?"

"I'm here."

"Thought I'd lost you for a moment."

"Would that bother you?" she asked.

"I think you're reading a little more into the statement than I intended."

"Right. How's Mom doing? Taking her medicine?"

"Costs as much as the mortgage, so she better be. You should call her sometime."

"These phone doohickeys are remarkable," Nicole replied. "Did you realize you can dial in *and* out on them?"

"Your mother made a lot of sacrifices to ensure you were on the right track, kiddo. Gave up ballet, put her own—"

"You two still sleep in separate rooms?"

Mason's mouth went dry. He wasn't sure how to answer. He knew, though, his silence would be an answer, and managed, "Your mother's been through a lot. I'm patient with her."

"Doesn't she realize you aren't black and therefore not inherently inclined to rape and pillage pure white women?"

"Pillage?" Mason said, trying to keep it light. "Isn't that a Viking thing?"

"Talking to you makes me sad," Nicole told him.

"I don't always come away feeling warm and fuzzy inside," Mason said. "But I love you. And so, I keep trying."

"You're missing out on Zion. I know I'm biased, but he's . . . amazing."

Mason swallowed. "What has he done now?"

"One of the women at Little Rascals told me he used the word ambiguous the other day. In the correct context."

"That's impressive."

"Elijah's a big reader," she said. "He reads to Zion every night."

"Very nice."

"Yeah, sure."

They were quiet for a time.

Mason, ending the lull, asked her, "Things going all right for you at work?"

"I'm writing a grant. We want to start offering prevocational training. Especially for the tech field."

"Tell me again how you refer to the kids you work with."

"They're on the spectrum," Nicole said.

"That's right. That's right."

"How's work going for you, Dad?"

"I told you about the missing-person case I was working on the last time we spoke. James Frazier?"

"Married father of three from Bessemer? Just up and disappeared one day?"

"That's right. I passed along some info to Teddy and—"

"Mr. Terry? Y'all still keep in touch?"

"When the situation warrants it," Mason said. "Anyway, I passed along some information and the BPD was able to find Mr. Frazier."

"Alive?"

"Floating in the Cahaba," Mason said. "Whoever did it strangled him and . . . cut some pieces off him."

"My God, that's horrible. I'm sorry, Dad."

"Sure."

And then he told her more. Especially regarding the situation at Oxmoor. Glen's call.

Nicole scolded him over his actions with Tamara Blake, educated him regarding the Chopra woman.

This call had already lasted far longer than usual, and he craved more time with his daughter. So, he let out a breath and went into the situation with Nails, Scott York, not getting into names or too much of the specifics but laying it out enough for Nicole to get a sense of it. "Didn't even know you'd coached baseball, Dad," she said once he'd finished.

"Before your time."

"Before my time . . . makes you sound old."

"I'm well over the fifty-yard line," he said. "Not much field left to play."

"Football field is a hundred yards, Dad."

"Think I might've mixed my metaphors."

Nicole laughed. It was such a sweet sound. Mason could sit for hours on end and listen to his daughter's laughter on replay.

"I was talking with our executive director the other day," she said, "and we got into a conversation about ignorance. People don't understand autism, which is fine, I suppose, though more and more will be affected by it. But anyway, my issue is those that are affected and choose to remain ignorant. There's so much information available. They should take the time to read up on it. Step outside their comfort zones and learn about someone different than themselves."

"Why do I feel as though you're directing that comment to me?"

"I'm going to email you the link to a website. Check it out."

"You know I don't like fooling around on the computer, Nicole."

"It'll help you with your case, if that motivates you."

"Which one?"

"Kidnapping, reparations," Nicole said. "All of those details about the Tyler-Goodwin Bridge. That's not a history many people know about."

"All true. But what does this website have to do with any of this?"

"You'll see. But listen, Dad, I have to go. Elijah's working on an important presentation for work, and he's asked that I give him some feedback."

"Okay, sure, you go ahead. Tell Elijah . . . tell him I said good luck with his work stuff."

Nicole disconnected the call without responding. Mason closed his eyes and tapped a fist against his forehead. Wishing her boyfriend good luck on his "work stuff" was probably the wrong thing to say. He didn't want to go another month without speaking to his daughter, and he didn't want it to be strained between them whenever they did speak again. There was so much to consider, and he wished they could just have a natural relationship, that everything he said and did didn't have to be so . . . ponderous. He missed being able to talk to Nicole, for hours at a time, without worrying his next word would either move her to a stony silence or make her decide to end the conversation altogether.

He'd change so much if he could. But what was that old saying? Three things that never come back: the spent arrow, the spoken word, and lost opportunity. Mason had said things to his daughter, particularly in the beginning, when her stomach was swollen with Zion, that he would've loved to have erased from his record. That was impossible, of course, and the fact that she was still speaking to him was a triumph.

"Be happy with what you have," he said aloud, as if hearing the words would make the sentiment true in his heart.

It didn't.

He wasn't happy with what he had. Far from it. He looked up at the ceiling, Bella asleep above him. He wasn't happy, and he wanted more. Sighing, he powered up his desktop computer. It clicked and whirred and eventually came on. He logged into his email and smiled.

Elijah's presentation may have been hot shit, but Nicole had made sure to email the website link she'd promised before she settled down for the night with her baby daddy.

Mason clicked on the blue link.

And less than five minutes into exploring the website, he sat bolt upright in his chair. "Whole-lee shit."

11

Despite spending several days in North Carolina, they hadn't set aside time for leisure. Rafting the French Broad River or sunbathing at Elk River Falls. Catching a glimpse of the wild ponies on the beaches in Corolla or walking the gardens at the Biltmore Estate. Instead, their focus had been on watching the target Isiah had forced on them, for a sense of Devon Robinson's movements, the rhythm of his days. Turned out he was a kindred soul, all work and no play. A security guard, ironically, in an office tower in Durham.

By the end of the third day, they knew he'd claimed a space for his car on the third level and always pulled out the keys to his Sentra as soon as he stepped from the building into the parking garage. They knew he walked the 142 steps to his car with little consideration for his surroundings, not at all attentive to possible trouble lurking in dark corners.

An easy mark.

He emerged from the door on the third level now, moving gingerly. Drained after another long day of work. His dark blue security uniform shirt was already untucked. His Sentra parked in a blind spot for the cameras, next to a support column. Breaking from the habit of the three days they'd watched, though, Robinson didn't chirp the locks when he was within earshot of his car. He pulled up on his heels, let out a breath, then grinned and picked up his pace for the last remaining steps.

Rachel had her back to him, bent near the bumper of his Sentra, her ass on full display while she stuffed a scattering of papers from the ground into a file folder. As the sounds of Robinson's steps drew closer, she eased a hand into her pocket.

"Looks like you could use a hand," he called. Rachel gasped, acting startled, and Devon Robinson chuckled. "My bad. Didn't mean to scare you, baby girl. Don't worry, I don't bite."

Rachel wheeled around and pressed a stun gun to his chest, squeezed the trigger. Two electrodes on the business end that could penetrate for skin contact even through a thick layer of clothing. If Robinson had the wherewithal to attempt wrestling the stun gun from her hands, there were shock plates on the side that would put him down.

He didn't have the wherewithal.

It was akin to touching an electric fence, a power surge that hijacked his nervous system. After two seconds of contact, his muscles seized up. Rachel helped him to the ground.

Then Nate and Joshua moved in.

Joshua took Robinson's keys, fired up the Sentra. Nate secured Robinson's hands behind his back with zip ties, nodded at Rachel to take ahold of the man's feet. "Where the fuck is I.T.?"

"He's coming," Rachel said.

Twenty more precious seconds and I.T. rolled up in an Econoline van.

They hustled Devon Robinson into the back cargo space, Rachel holding his head on her lap. He was still dazed. Moaning and disoriented. The plan was to follow Joshua to a nearby shopping center where he'd dump Robinson's car and then join them in the van.

Joshua couldn't have been doing more than the speed limit, but his taillights were like laser sights up ahead. "What the fuck, I.T.," Nate yelled. *"Yujihada!"*

"I'm trying to keep up, Nate. You want me getting pulled over for speeding?"

Nate decided not to push. Not now. He went silent as they finally pulled into the mall. Didn't say a word as Joshua stormed inside the van, sat back, and closed his eyes. Stayed silent until they were pulling up to a ramshackle house, the only one on a hidden little spit of dirt road. They'd scouted it carefully and knew they could work here without fear of being interrupted. Robinson had regained much of his consciousness now, so all of them coalesced to get him on his feet and moving toward the rear of the abandoned house. He was beastly strong in his fright, amped up on adrenaline. "Stunner," Nate said, fluttering his fingers at Rachel. She hesitated, then handed it to him.

He pressed it to Robinson's chest. Another two-second zap.

Devon Robinson's knees scrubbed the ground, and they had to hold him up by his armpits to drag him inside. They got him into the dank, unfinished basement, shoved him onto a chair beneath a dangling light bulb. Other than its beam, powered by a generator they'd picked up at Lowe's, the basement was dark. They duct-taped Robinson to the chair in three places—ankles, thighs, waist. After a while, he started rocking the chair.

"Don't bother," Nate told him. "You aren't getting loose."

"Fuck this," Robinson barked. "You better let me up, nigga."

"Nigga?" Nate shook his head. "Now see, that's a word I never use. And spare me 'It's with an *a* and not *er*.' Don't want to hear that you're thumbing your nose at the white man. Taking what he used to hurt us, flipping it into a term of endearment. I don't find it endearing."

"Fuck you talking about, nigga?"

"You sure love the word. What I'd call self-hate. Must be all that milk in your coffee."

"Whaddya mean?" Robinson said, his forehead lined in confusion. "Milk in my coffee?"

"Means your great-great-great-grandmother Peg couldn't fight off Massa John from getting up under her osnaburg shift. Means Peg probably baked a few Oreos in her oven."

"I ain't got no white in me, nigga."

Nate laughed. "You serious? Line you up next to Vin Diesel and you'd make him look like Wesley Snipes."

"Fuck you."

Nate nodded, then pressed the stun gun to Robinson's chest and squeezed the trigger, muttering "High-yellow buffoon" as the man involuntarily jerked in the chair.

"Hey . . ." I.T. called.

Robinson grunted, said, "Who . . . who the fuck are you?"

"Call us the Smoke Kings," Nate said, glancing over at I.T., smiling though it couldn't be seen through his balaclava.

"Smoke Kings?" Robinson said. "Hell does that mean?"

"Means you should read W. E. B. Du Bois."

"I ain't reading shit, nigga. Let me go."

Nate sighed again, said, "Brew's Pub across the line in Greenville."

"Aww, shit," was Devon Robinson's reply.

"Good, you understand now," Nate said. "You come by your fondness for ugly words quite honestly. What did your father call that boy he hit outside the pub?"

"Shit."

"Punched him in the face so hard, he broke the boy's facial bones. When the kid hit the concrete curb, his brain stem detached from his brain. Your father left him there to die. And what did he call the boy? Witnesses heard what your father said, so don't lie to me."

"Come on, man."

"Oh, now I'm a man. Not a nigga?"

"Please."

"What did your father call that boy he hit, Mr. Robinson?"

"I was little, man."

"You've heard the stories. What did he call him?"

"Jesus, man. That's old news."

"What. Did. He. Call. Him?"

"You know the word," Robinson said. "Boy was gay."

"You've got your father's blood, Mr. Robinson. Tainted blood."

"Tainted? He run off on my mama. I ain't see him but a handful of times my whole—"

"Tainted," Nate said, shooting volts into him.

"Hey . . ." I.T. once more.

In the glow of the light bulb, Nate looked at Joshua, then Rachel, couldn't make out anything on either of their faces. After that business with the noose, I.T. had insisted they all agree on a safe word. *Lotte.* Hotel in Seoul. Didn't appear as though Joshua or Rachel were close to uttering it. Nate took that as permission to continue. He turned back to Robinson. The man's eyes were glassy, unfocused. But he was doing his best to look directly at Nate.

"Confession time," Nate said. "What do you feel guilty about? We're here to give you an opportunity your daddy never took. Chance to confess your sins and ask for forgiveness."

"I don't need a fucking priest."

Nate placed the stun gun to Robinson's chest again.

"Shit, man . . . I, uh . . . used to steal Cheerwine Krispy Kreme donuts from the Harris Teeter."

"Bet you wet the bed, too," Nate said. "But we're looking for something more recent."

"I can't think of anything. I swear it."

"You better," Nate said, squeezing the stun gun's trigger. Devon Robinson squealed.

"Cheated . . . Texas Hold'em," he said, his voice pinched. "Cheated my potnas outta nice pot one time. Close to fifteen hundred."

Nate said, "Which potnas? Juke Irving and 'em?"

"Shit," Robinson said. "That's what this is about. Juke sent you?"

"So, you know him."

"Did some work with him from time to time."

"What kind of work, Mr. Robinson?"

"You know about Juke, then you know."

Nate nodded. "Juke has a little sister, doesn't he? Debra? Denise?"

"I told him I ain't touch Dana, I swear. The girl's retarded. How you gonna believe her?"

"Retarded? You're just a dictionary of ugly words."

"She's got something wrong with her. She don't look you in the eye."

"She's autistic," Nate said.

"Whatever, man."

"You got enough of Juke questioning you about what happened and told him Dana asked for it. What did she ask for, Mr. Robinson? You weren't clear in your texts."

"I was drunk when I sent them. Tell Juke I didn't mean—"

"Answer the question," Nate said. "What did Dana ask for?"

"She offered to suck my dick, okay?"

"And you let her put her mouth on your little creamsicle and that was it?"

"Pretty much," Robinson said.

Nate pressed the stun gun to Robinson's chest again. Robinson winced. "She looks normal, you understand," he said. "No isn't a word I want to hear when I get . . . you know, titillated. I'm sure you understand that."

"You raped Dana Irving?"

"Why you gotta say it like that, man? I didn't mean her any harm. I actually like the girl. She looks normal, like I said."

"You raped her," Nate said again.

"I ain't copping to that."

Nate moved the stun gun down to Robinson's ball sac. "I can make it so you only get hard during a thunderstorm, *nigga*."

"Come on," Robinson gasped. "Yeah, I guess you could say I raped her."

"Say it yourself," Nate said. "And say her name, too."

"Come on—"

Another two-second zap.

Spit forming at the corners of his mouth, Robinson managed, "I raped Dana Irving."

"You get it?" Nate asked I.T.

"We got it," Rachel answered for him. Some bite in her voice.

Nate shook that aside and turned back to Robinson. "North Carolina has no statute of limitations for rape. We have your confession recorded. Each week, by five p.m. Friday at the latest, you will deposit three hundred eleven dollars and fifty-four cents into an account we will provide to you."

"Three hundred a week," Robinson said, looking up, his voice rising. "I don't have—"

"Not my concern how you get it," Nate cut in. "But you will get it. The exact amount I quoted you."

Robinson sagged. "Why that amount?"

"Reparations," Nate said. "There was an article in the *New York Times* back in May that I used to figure the calculations, if you're interested."

"This is bullshit. How you gonna have me paying reparations, man?"

"It's a debt owed."

"I'm black, man."

"Debatable," Nate told him.

"Fuck you, nigga."

"There you go again with the . . ." Nate bit his lip, forced the stun gun up against Robinson's testicles, savagely clicked the trigger. Like someone angry with a remote that wasn't responding.

"Lotte!" I.T. called.

Nate kept squeezing the trigger.

"Lotte! Lotte!"

Nate stepped back, breathing heavy, wiped his mouth. Robinson's head lolled a moment and then he began to jerk. The chair juddered with his wild movements.

"Shit," Joshua said, taking a tentative step forward.

"He's fine." Nate waved his hand. "Probably an act."

One of the chair legs came off the ground, echoed like a firecracker as the chair clacked back on all fours. Robinson continued to jerk.

Rachel pushed her way forward. "Fuck," she said. "Get him on the floor. He's having a seizure. We need to turn him on his side."

Nate was exasperated. "I didn't mean—"

"Never mind that," Rachel snapped. "Help us get him on the ground."

It took all four of them to rip away the duct tape and get Devon Robinson in position. Rachel eased him to his side. "Need something soft and flat to put under his head."

Joshua emptied the small tools and such they'd packed in a cloth rucksack and handed it to Rachel. Then he let out a long breath, ran a hand over his scalp, and disappeared in the darkness of the basement, away from the dangling light bulb. Rachel folded the rucksack and pillowed it beneath Robinson's head.

"Is he going to be all right?" Nate said.

Rachel didn't respond, but I.T. snapped, "You don't get to ask her that."

"I can help," Nate said. "Just tell me what to do."

Rachel loosened the buttons of Robinson's work shirt.

Finally, mercifully, he stopped jerking and coughed. Nate let out a relieved breath. I.T. glared at him.

"Relax," Nate told him. "It's going to be okay."

I.T. tossed the digital camera at Nate and didn't bother sticking around to see whether he caught it. Rachel stood and gave Nate a look, then stalked out herself.

On the ground, Robinson coughed again.

Nate stifled the desire to kick him.

12

"These are terms you should know, Dad: unconscious bias, microaggressions. And what year did they come up with Title VII?"

"I don't think it's that serious, Nicole. I'll beg for forgiveness and then this'll be the end of another sad chapter in the life of Mason Andrew Farmer."

"Andrew . . . yuck," she said. "You're talking two of the most unabashed racists to ever sit in the White House. Jackson and Johnson; must be something in Tennessee's water. Johnson gave amnesty to the Confederates and voided forty acres and a mule."

"I hardly ever use my middle name, if that helps."

"Funny."

"By the way, I checked that website you sent me."

"And?"

"Blew my mind," Mason said.

"Will it help with your case?"

"A good chance. I should get off now, kiddo. They'll be here any minute."

"Good luck, Dad."

"Don't need it," Mason told her. "But thanks anyway. And Nicole . . ."

"Yes?"

"It's good to hear your voice."

"Twice in one week. That must be a new record."

After she'd disconnected the call, Mason sat there, the smallest conference room in Tsaro's office building, wondering how it could've come to this. How speaking to his daughter twice in a week was deserving of commendation. The notion made his stomach turn. There were so many things that had to change. He wouldn't survive much longer if they didn't.

The door opened and he quickly shoved the phone back into his right pants pocket. Thaddeus Deighton strolled into the room. Tall, like most men with power, in his midthirties, soft in the middle, already starting to gray, hard eyes the color of pistachios. Mason stood and extended his hand. Deighton moved past him without acknowledging it. Glen Saunders walked in next, and a woman trailing him whom Mason didn't know. She was on the older side, anywhere between seventy and eighty, brownish hair shot through with blonde highlights, fine-boned. Mason had splurged on a Valentine's Day gift for Bella two years ago and knew the woman's bag was a Birkin. The one he'd bought for Bella was over four thousand dollars and his wife used it to store scarves she no longer wore.

Mason came out of that memory and found he was the only one still standing.

Glen set a portfolio case on the table, flipped it open, and pulled out a sheaf of papers. "If you'll have a seat, we can get started, Mr. Farmer."

Mason frowned. "Mr. Farmer?"

"Please," Glen said. "Have a seat."

Deighton had chosen the head of the table at the other end, the woman in the closest chair to his right, Glen the same on his left, the three of them forming a square missing one side.

Mason took the head on his end. The woman watched him with curiosity, Deighton with disdain. He didn't like either approach.

Glen tapped the stack of papers on the table. "We're here today because—"

"I know why we're here," Mason snapped. "You gave me a heads-
up, remember?"

The corporate attorney colored. "I remember apprising you of
the situation and attempting to get a feel for where you stood on
the events."

"There weren't any *events*," Mason said. "I conducted an investigation which concluded that Ms. Blake, key personnel in the payroll
department, was defrauding her employer through nefarious activi-
ties carried out during her duties."

The words sounded unnatural, overblown, and Mason immediately regretted uttering them. It didn't help that Deighton looked un-
impressed. Or that the woman was unreadable, busy rubbing the top
of her Birkin as if there were a Maltese sticking out of it.

Glen said, "Ms. Blake suggested an alternative narrative to
the one you presented, and her employer was more compelled by
her version."

"Foolish," Mason said.

"I understand Ms. Blake raised her concerns with you. That she
made it clear she hadn't done what you were accusing her of."

"Prisons are full of the innocent," Mason said. "To hear them tell
it, at least."

"Mmm."

"If the woman's looking for an apology from me, even though she's
guilty as sin, I'll hold my nose and give it to her. I don't want to hurt
the firm. I'm a team player."

"I see."

"Will that get us out of this mess?"

"Ms. Chopra is another matter," Glen said, shuffling through the
papers. "She shared with Oxmoor HR that she had a troubling interaction with you as well."

"Troubling because I didn't have a clear sense of her ethnic orientation?"

Was orientation the right word?

"Oxmoor was a valued account for us. And we've established other accounts, larger accounts even, based off their network of connections and strong recommendations. I hope you can appreciate how troubled we are by losing their trust, Mr. Farmer."

"Ease up with the Mr. Farmer bit, Glen. You know me. I'm a simple man. Just Mason."

"Very well."

"This is all very official. Is it possible I could at least know who I'm meeting with?"

Mason let his gaze fall on the woman.

"Gretna Sandiford," she announced. "My late husband was one of the founders."

"Mrs. Sandiford," Mason said, nodding. It pleased him that she returned the gesture.

Even though he knew who he was, he looked at Deighton.

"Thaddeus Deighton," Deighton said. "I believe we've met in passing."

"Good to see you again, Mr. Deighton."

No response.

Mason thought of his daughter's advice from earlier. "Look, I'm aware I may have some unconscious biases. I'm working on that. And I'm sorry all of you had to get dragged here for something so small."

"Our governance bylaws state that a minimum of two partners—or their proxies—must be present for matters of this sort," Glen explained.

"Understood," Mason said. "But again, I feel terrible about this. I've been reading through Title VII, familiarizing myself with the protected classes. Evaluating what I've said or done to make sure I wasn't showing any microaggressions."

"Sounds as though you've taken this seriously."

Mason nodded. "Without question. And anything the firm can offer in terms of training and education . . . I'm all for it."

Glen pursed his lips, crinkled his brow. Gretna stopped rubbing her Birkin. A tiny smile played at the corners of Deighton's mouth.

Mason realized what was happening.

He rose to his feet. "No, no, no."

"Please sit down, Mr. Farmer."

"Don't you dare Mr. Farmer me, Glen. Tamara Blake keeps her job, even though she's crooked as the letter S, and I'm tossed out on my ass because I didn't know the Chopra woman took a plane and didn't tunnel under a wall to get here?"

"See, that's why we're—"

"You don't understand. This . . ." Mason wavered, tried to regain his composure. He'd begun to tremble, which he hated, but a bit of humility could swing this. "My wife," he said, speaking softly. "She takes medicine. That's . . . that's crucial to her well-being. It's over a thousand bucks a month."

Tranylcypromine.

For major depressive disorder, especially when there was also an accompanying anxiety component. Bella's doctor insisted she take the brand, *Parnate*, rather than a generic.

"This is difficult for you," the lawyer said.

"Difficult for me?" Mason sniffed a laugh. "That time we went for dinner, I couldn't help noticing your wife looking at you in a manner I couldn't pinpoint. It comes to me now, Glen. Disinterest. Damn right this is difficult for me. You don't have anything more creative to offer?"

"'Fraid not," the lawyer said, crossing his arms over his chest.

"I'm working something," Mason said. "It could be big and I'm willing to share the glory. A crew of vigilantes. I believe they're personally looking to correct what they consider to be some sins of the past. I know of one person they've kidnapped. They put a fucking noose around his neck."

"Mason . . ."

"And there are plenty of sins for them to correct, sadly."

"This is all fine and well, but—"

"There's a website, Glen. I'm going to be meeting with the woman who runs it. I read of one case where some Klansmen took an old black man and slit his throat, cut out his heart and intestines, and threw his corpse in a nearby creek."

Gretna Sandiford turned a pale white and stumbled to her feet, scuttled past Mason and out the door, the Birkin clutched to her chest. Deighton leaned over and whispered in Glen's right ear.

Mason dropped back down in his seat.

He still had some time. They had to call in a different partner now that Gretna had left, right? The governance bylaws said so, didn't they?

February 19, 2017

5:07 p.m.

Once they're outside the A-Z Mart, Darius lets out a breath, says, "Damn. What the hell was that?"

"I know, right," Sofia replies. "Fucking asshole."

Darius frowns. "I meant with you."

"Me?" She stops walking, turns to him with her hands on her hips.

Darius steals a look at the store. He can see the cop and the cashier, both looking back at him. "We can talk about it later."

"No. We'll talk about it now, Darius."

"Sofia. Shit, come on. This can wait."

"That cop's a flaming asshole, but you're finding fault with me. Hell no, this can't wait."

"You're right about him." Darius looks again and sees the cop has moved closer to the store's entrance and is still looking out at him. "All the more reason to keep it moving. I didn't like that you were antagonizing him."

"Antagonizing him? I was sticking up for you, Darius. For us."

"Well, if that's the way you do it . . . don't."

"Wow, this is great. I can't believe you're siding with Twelve, over me."

"Twelve?" Darius laughs. He's never heard her use that slang before. "Don't get sucked in by everything you read online."

"What are you talking about?"

"You've been spending a little too much time on Urban Dictionary," he says.

"Whatever," Sofia says, her eyes watering. "Have fun with your bitches at Rutgers."

"That's what has you so worked up? Sarah Lawrence is only an hour away by car. We agreed we'd take turns visiting each—"

"I'm so fucking over this," she says, turning and heading down the street, back in the direction of home.

"Sofia . . ."

She doesn't look back.

Darius feels the skin tighten at the back of his neck, his scalp. He loves Sofia but the shit she pulls is too much. Having sex with him those three times at the beginning, reeling him in, then going chaste ever since. Claims she wants to be certain he's in it for her and not only what she gives him. And he doesn't pressure her because she gives him plenty. But still, isn't that the point of a relationship? Link up with someone who's happy to gift you the special parts of themselves? Find someone you feel the need to do the same for? He's given Sofia every ounce of himself, every inch. She knows things he hasn't shared with his mother or Joshua. Things he hasn't told his boys or his cousin Nate.

Whatever.

He certainly isn't going to stand here sweating the girl.

Doesn't want the cop busting him for loitering or some other made-up shit.

Jalen has recording equipment in his grandmother's garage. Darius could ignore the weed smoke and lay down a track, pretending he's Drake for a hot minute. Or he could get into some Call of Duty on Bizz's Xbox. Drop by Chuckie's to finish watching One of Us on Netflix. They'd left off on the episode where Juliet was selling tabs of LSD to raise money for *her daughter's operation. He and Chuckie got into a heated discussion about that. A moral dilemma, for sure, but wrong was wrong. That's what Darius had argued.*

Anyway, if none of his boys are around, he can . . .

"Damn," *he mutters, pulling Sofia's necklace from his pocket, and rushing to see whether he can catch up with her.*

13

When Rachel woke in the early dawn, with Isiah snoring beside her, she didn't know where she was. She rolled out of bed and felt her way across the dark room to the window, parted the curtains, the tension leaving her shoulders as she took in the dirty stucco of the house next door. Derby's place. She wasn't in a motel room in the bayou, or a Tar Heel Airbnb. She was back in Jersey, at Isiah's. He stirred but didn't awaken as she eased back under the covers. Sleep came so easily for him. "Hey," she said, shaking his shoulder. "Babe, wake up."

He didn't.

Not at first.

But after a while his eyes opened, and he tried to sit up. "Shhh," Rachel said, forcing him flat, straddling him.

Despite the fog that must've been in his head, his hands found her hips and together they fell into a practiced rhythm. Rachel tightened her thighs and scraped her fingernails across his chest. Leaned forward with all her weight as he bucked and moaned.

That was enough for her in the moment, *his* pleasure. Hearing him wail as if he were kneeling at a prayer wall in Israel. She lowered her hands, guided him from inside her just as he erupted. Wet wipes were on the table on her side of the bed. She pulled two and cleaned him up.

"That was—"

"I know," she said. "I know."

"Did you . . . ?"

 She shook her head. "Not this time."

"I could . . . I could get you to finish."

"No, babe. I'm fine. This was everything I needed."

"You're sure?"

"Go back to sleep. I'm going to go for a run."

"I love you, Rache."

"What do you love about me?" she asked, smiling; this was one of their rituals.

"That your eyes are like emeralds when the sun catches them the right way. How you ball your fists and scowl during the action scenes in movies. The coy way you cover your mouth when you laugh. How you . . ."

He drifted back to sleep, whispering the many things he loved about her.

Rachel smiled, touched his eyelids, kissed his lips.

She rooted through her designated drawer and found a sports bra, tights, ankle socks. Slid into them and secured her hair with the Buff headband Isiah had bought for her when she first started running. Slipped her feet into her ASICS.

Gave Isiah another kiss before leaving.

July was not only the hottest month in Jersey but also the wettest, and she smelled the sweet, sharp tang of ozone in the air. The flowers were throwing their scent as well.

Rain was coming.

She picked up her pace, the effort mentholating her lungs and firing up her calves. A new sheen of sweat started to pop from her pores. It'd taken her months to get to the point she was at now, capable of running all out for five or six minutes without slowing to a walk. Her soles slapped the asphalt as she turned a corner and made for the long stretch of road that connected this town to the next. Jersey was like that, congested, towns sitting on top of each other.

About halfway up the road, she stopped to give herself a moment's breather. She was thinking of Isiah, snuggled under his covers, when a dark Ford Explorer with tinted windows pulled up beside her. An aftermarket muffler system, known on the street as a "cherry bomb," produced an obnoxiously sharp cracking sound.

It looked like an unmarked police vehicle.

Rachel's stomach sank and she became conscious of her heart knocking in her chest.

The passenger-side window skidded down.

"Get in," the driver called.

"I've been doing everything I can to put you out of my mind and like a bad penny, here you are."

"Bad penny? You really are an old soul. Sounds like something my—"

Rachel took off running. Once she paused, to catch her breath, the dark Ford Explorer again pulled up beside her.

"We need to talk."

"You could've come to the house," Rachel said.

"You're never at your place anymore. I wanted to catch you away from I.T."

"I wonder why that is."

"Because he's unreasonable."

"We almost killed this man, Nate."

"I fucked up," he admitted. "It won't happen again."

"You keep saying."

"Please, Rachel. Five minutes, and then you can finish your run."

"You sure you want to spend five minutes talking to my high-yellow ass? Shouldn't you save your energy for a *real* black woman?"

"*That's* what you're upset about," Nate said, frowning.

"I'll be timing you," Rachel told him, indicating her watch, a Garmin Forerunner, also a gift from Isiah.

Nate pushed open the door for her.

She looked around, then moved inside.

"You've stuck with the running," Nate said.

"Five minutes doesn't leave you much time for small talk."

"You're really this upset?"

"Four minutes and twelve seconds."

He sighed again. "Just wanted to let you know I appreciate how well you handled yourself with this last one. You kept it from going completely sideways."

"We were in the car for eight hours coming back. You mentioned that a time or twenty."

"Well, I'm telling you again, Rachel."

"Three minutes and forty-eight seconds," she said.

"How often do you think about your mother?"

"What?" The sudden shift short-circuited her attitude.

"Once a week? Once a month? Hardly ever?"

"Every day," she answered.

Nate nodded. "Same."

"What does—"

"It was just the two of us, so my mother was more of a friend than a parent. She mentioned it to me right away when she first found the lump in her breast. Said it was bruised and shaped oddly. Hurt like a bitch."

Rachel wasn't sure how to respond, so she kept quiet, just watched him. Scraggly lines at the corners of his squinted eyes.

"She convinced herself it was just a cyst, that her oil glands were clogged or something. I begged her to get it checked out, but she was adamant sunflower lecithin and warm compresses would set it right. Before long, though, it was the size of a walnut. The skin started to dimple, and her nipple inverted. I'd read up on some stuff and knew that wasn't a good sign."

"Why are you telling me this?" Rachel said.

"You and I are one and the same."

"We aren't."

"Miss Pratt also died of breast cancer."

Rachel bit her lip. Shook her head. "I've given you everything I have to give, Nate. I've been nothing but devoted to our cause. Now I'm wondering if I've been a fool this entire time. If you think I'm just another Rachel Dolezal play-acting like she's black."

"It fits," Nate said. "Rachel and Rachel."

"Oh my God. I hadn't even thought of that."

"I'm joking, Rachel. You know I don't think of you like that."

"The stuff you said to Robinson."

"He's a joke," Nate said.

"But I'm not?"

"No."

Rachel looked at him, hard. Sighed. "Isiah is convinced you're a live wire. Unpredictable and selfish. He's got a lot of grievances. None of us really said anything, but he's particularly pissed off about you running to Hawaii without—"

"We went into this one on the wrong foot," Nate interrupted. "I'll accept that I had a bad attitude about it. Is I.T. willing to admit he shouldn't have forced this one on us?"

"You should have seen the look on your face when you were using that stun gun on Robinson."

"Robinson's a buffoon," Nate said. "But you're right, I should've shown some restraint. I accept that. Again, when is I.T. going to acknowledge that he's contributed to the problems we've been having? Lying about York, making us take on Robinson."

"I wish you'd stop antagonizing each other."

"That's all on him," Nate insisted.

"We're *Smoke Kings*," Rachel mimicked, reminding Nate of what he'd said back with Devon Robinson, and how he'd looked at Isiah as he said it. From one of W. E. B. Du Bois's poems. *I am the Smoke King / I am black!* An expression of black pride. "You know you said that just to agitate Isiah."

"I.T.'s an honorary Smoke King."

"You were upset at Isiah. And you went overboard with the stun gun because you know even a hint of violence makes him uneasy."

"I wasn't sure he has the stomach for this anymore. I needed to see how he'd react. Not a clear verdict, I'd say."

"Maybe we need to stop then."

"No, no, no."

"You ever considered that our *work* may have run its course?"

"Not for me." Nate smiled. "And most certainly not for you."

"I think you're reading me wrong. I'm not sure my heart is in it anymore."

"That what you're telling yourself?"

"You don't know what I'm feeling, Nate."

"I know what I saw. This is some rough shit we're doing, and it's bound to fuck with your head from time to time. But when it's time to go . . . you go."

"Isiah did all the prep."

"Sure."

"He drove the van."

"He was behind the wheel. It's a stretch to call what he was doing driving."

"Don't be an asshole, Nate."

"Regardless, we obviously need him. I.T. won't completely fall off if you help him keep his eyes on the prize."

"It would be a mistake to push this, Nate. We agreed at the outset if even one of us lost heart, we'd simply stop."

"Let's you and I make sure that doesn't happen."

"You and I?" Rachel laughed that thought aside. "You really don't realize how uncomfortable I am just sitting here alone with you?"

"Why?"

"You're not seriously asking me that, are you? After everything we've been through."

"What I'm asking is for you to put your personal feelings aside," Nate said, "in service to a greater purpose."

"You're the only one on that greater-purpose shit. Joshua doesn't even say it anymore."

"Desiree Walton posted on Facebook that she isn't being evicted after all. She's able to pay her mortgage thanks to a large gift from an anonymous benefactor. She was thanking whoever sent her the money."

"That's nice."

"Rhonda Perkins posted the scholarship check her daughter received. Tina's going to William Carey."

Rachel didn't say anything.

"We did all of that," Nate said. "It can't make up for what was done to their grandfathers but . . . We're putting this money to good use, Rachel. Reparations indeed."

"Damn it, Nate. You're a manipulative motherfucker."

"That's fine. Can I count on you to handle I.T.?"

"No. Isiah's not someone to be *handled*."

"Work with me here, Rachel. You and me, come on, we've got this."

"You need to chill with the 'you and me' shit, Nate."

"Oh?" Nate smirked. "I remember a time when you and I were quite . . . compatible."

This was why being around Nate made Rachel so uneasy. The intense history between them. The hint of a threat in much of what he said. She'd told Isiah a lot, but she hadn't told him *everything*. And Nate could fill in the blanks in a way that would destroy what she'd so carefully built with Isiah.

"Rachel?"

"Just stop antagonizing Isiah," she said. "No more fucking talk of Smoke Kings."

She pushed open her door then, slammed it closed behind her. Didn't dare look back.

But she knew, with certainty, Nate was smiling that devilish smile of his as she took off running again.

In a rush to get back to Isiah's place before the sky turned dark gray and opened up in a violent downpour.

14

Mason was too damn old to be back in his mother's basement, yet here he was. And, as Mildred Farmer would've said were she still alive, "three sheets to the wind" on top of it. Snot-slinging drunk. Good thing it wasn't actually his parents' basement, rather a poorly kept secret spot he'd discovered when he was still on with the police. Below a pet supply store, the homey bar was just as you would expect. The walls were wood paneling and there were pinball machines, a pool table, and a dartboard. You could sit at the bar or on either of the mismatched couches—one colorful with orange-and-blue flowers, the other drab, the color of oatmeal. Cold beer was kept in a locked fridge and came paired with a choice of pizza rolls, taquitos, cheese balls, or, that old fan favorite, good ol' PB&J. The walls were lined with pictures of people's mothers.

"Another?"

Mason looked up from his spot on the plain couch. "I should call it quits," he told Shihadeh, who was part of the staff but also part of the *vibe*. She'd been the one to convince him to try the Treehorn, a hard cider from over in Georgia.

"Alrighty," she said.

"I said *should*."

She smiled. "B-r-b."

It took Mason a full minute to grasp what she'd meant. *Be right back.* Jesus, if he wasn't a fucking tyrannosaurus, then he didn't know who would qualify. It was difficult for him to imagine anyone wanting to take on his old bag of bones at this point, wisdom and seasoning and all that happy-go-lucky bullshit aside. He was used goods and knew it. An employer with even an ounce of discernment would easily recognize the stink of mildew on him.

Shihadeh returned, and as he reached for the can she snuck it through his guard, rolled it across his cheek. Cold and sweating, it made him lurch back. "I'm a bad influence," she told him. "Just wanted to wake you up a bit. This is your last one."

"Shihadeh . . . that's . . . ?"

"Made up," she replied, again smiling, a dazzling smile, a smile that had gotten him where he was now. "If I told you my real name, I'd have to kill you right after."

"Can't say I'd mind meeting my maker with one of your secrets on my lips."

"Aren't you sweet," she said.

"Sit with me a moment."

"You don't need me, sweetie. I heard somebody blowing up your phone. And I'm too old to be fighting over somebody else's plus-one."

"She means nothing to me," Mason said, grinning.

"Wrong answer, Mr. Mason. But I'll blame it on the alcohol."

Once she stepped away, he trapped the can of beer between his thighs and pulled out his cell phone, squinted at the screen. He'd been sitting in here long enough to miss five calls from his daughter. Miss being a generous way to put it—he'd flat out ignored Nicole's calls. Couldn't face her after the humiliation back at Tsaro. Not that avoidance was an effective measure. She'd finally given up calling and sent him a text, making it clear she'd figured out why Mason wasn't picking up his phone.

Their loss.

Reading it again now made his eyes water.

He dropped the phone on the coffee table they had set up in front of the couches, in the process knocking over one of the empty Treehorn cans he'd lined up. The six remaining cans didn't mind. He went ahead and guzzled the latest. Looked around.

A young white woman in cutoff jean shorts, a fitted white halter top, obviously not wearing a bra, had one eye shut and was threatening to throw a dart at the board. The group of women with her, similarly dressed, laughed and made goofy faces to distract her.

Shihadeh was over by the bar, smiling and leaning into some metrosexual asshole wearing a striped button-down shirt, khaki pants, and boat shoes. Type of asshole who wore contacts and got his hair cut at a salon.

The only black guy in the place reached up and pulled his hair loose, slipped the rubber band that held the mess together onto his wrist. Dreadlocks, Nicole had explained, that first time after introducing Elijah to her parents.

"So, he never washes his hair," Mason had said. "Wonderful."

She was a fucking saint to put up with Mason. He didn't deserve her. And as though kismet, his cell phone rang out at that very moment. He grabbed it and swiped to answer the call without hesitating. "I told 'em what you taught me. They didn't bite. Their loss, right?"

"Mason Farmer?"

"Huh . . . what?"

"I'm looking for Mason Farmer."

"Who's this?"

Whoever she was, she had a rich alto voice that was mournful and pounced on the syllables of her every word. Sounded like Gillian Welch. A voice that would be a blessing to wake up to each morning. Much better than the silence he awakened to now.

"We've been emailing back and forth," the woman continued. "I

promised to meet with you when I had the opportunity. You thought
I might have info that could help with your investigations."

Mason sat up. "The woman from the website."

"Yes," she said. "Elizabeth Brantley. Is this a bad time?"

"No, no. Can I call you back in a minute, though?"

"Shh . . . sure."

"A minute," Mason said, and disconnected the call.

He tried to catch Shihadeh's eye on the way out, but she was deep
in conversation with the khaki pants–wearing asshole, laughing and
tossing her hair and reaching to touch him every few seconds. His
hand, his arm, a playful shove of his shoulder.

Mason bit down on an emotion and continued attacking the
stairs. He had to pause several times during the climb. It took far
longer than a minute.

"Elizabeth?"

"Yes."

She sounded hesitant now.

"I apologize," Mason told her. "My work takes me to more than a
few dark corners. They tend to be loud spaces as well."

Could she tell he was drunk?

"I understand," she said.

"You were mentioning you had an opening in your schedule for
us to meet?"

Nothing from her end.

Mason switched the phone to his other ear. "Elizabeth?"

"Sorry, yes. I'm here."

"When can you meet?"

"I was going to say early this evening if you were able. I know you
have to drive down from Huntsville."

"I'm actually in Birmingham now."

"Oh."

"Name the place and I'm there."

Sometime later, after a quick detour to Cowboy's for a black coffee and Ivory LeShore's cheesecake to sober up and settle his stomach, Mason was parking on the side of a road. It was peaceful along here, murmuring maples and elms, the sun just beginning to slip toward the horizon, the air clean and green and not at all touched by the fetor of Bradford pear trees, which were everywhere nowadays. Mason leaned against his car, working through a Winston, waiting.

Elizabeth Brantley was late arriving, almost twenty minutes after he'd gotten here, and when she pulled up in one of those pointless hybrids he'd heard about, a Toyota Prius, Mason was prepared to give her a little attitude. Not too much, just enough to let her know his time carried some value and he thought her clown car was a joke.

Then she stepped out.

Mason's mouth gaped enough for the cigarette to fall out. He crushed it with the toe of his shoe and kicked it under his car and tried to brush the smoke from his clothes.

She stood at attention on the other side of the road, and he moved toward her, putting some thought into each step so he didn't stumble.

She smiled as he approached. "Mason?"

He nodded.

"Thanks for humoring me," she said, looking around. "I know this meetup location is umm . . . unconventional."

Another nod as the lyrics of an old Charlie Rich song came to mind. *Like a breath of spring, warm like the summer rain.*

"And I apologize for being late," she went on. "I stopped by the Irondale Cafe for their toasted coconut cream pie. Sadly, it's an obsession."

"No problem," Mason told her, transfixed by her voice.

"You must not be a dark corner," she said, smiling. And seeing he didn't get it, added, "You're not at all loud. I'm wondering if you make a sound."

"Give me some time," he managed.

Either it was a good line, or she was simply a charitable soul, because another smile lit her face. A striking face. Skin white as milk, violet-colored eyes, long, black hair dark like a raven's wing. Healthy. Some would say overweight, but no, healthy. The yellow sundress she wore would've been flowing on a lot of women, but it hugged Elizabeth Brantley. Mason put her at about five feet ten inches, and so he did a double take when he looked down at her bare feet.

"Old habits die hard," she said, noticing his gaze. "Grew up on a farm in Crossville."

"You'll burn your soles."

"You're concerned? No need to worry. My feet have evolved over time, Mason."

It frightened him how much he liked the way she said his name. He cleared his throat, focused on the landscape around them instead of her face. "So, this is . . ."

"The road Elizabeth Lawrence was walking down when a group of white schoolchildren threw rocks at her."

"Nineteen thirty-six, you said?"

"'Thirty-three."

"She was a teacher?"

Elizabeth nodded. "Probably why she reprimanded the children. She wouldn't have given a thought to them being white, saw it as a teachable moment."

"And she was lynched," Mason said, frowning.

"A mob of the schoolchildren's parents. They burned down her house as well. Forced her son, Alexander, to flee to Boston."

"That's a grim story," Mason said.

She nodded. "I'd spent most of my life going by Lizzie until I learned of it."

"Your website's very informative," Mason said, allowing himself to look at her again. "I can't imagine the time you put into the research."

"Other groups have done the same. You're aware of Bryan Stevenson and the Equal Justice Initiative?"

"Yes," Mason said. "Haven't delved into their stuff yet. But it's on my list."

Jesus, why did he say that?

Could it have been the music in Elizabeth Brantley's voice when she mentioned it?

"It was nice to hear from you," she said. "We've documented 4,743 lynching deaths between 1882 and 1968, and it's not talked about enough."

"You said the last known lynching in America happened here in Alabama?" Mason asked.

She nodded. "Michael Donald. In Mobile."

"Do you usually track anything on the families?" he asked, keeping his voice level.

"The families?"

"Of the victims. Descendants and so forth because I know most of this is ancient history."

"Ancient history?"

"I'm not being flippant," Mason said. "I just mean . . . some of this goes back to 1882, like you said."

"That's right."

Mason's plan, after his own preliminary search had come up blank, had been to use Tsaro's reach to see whether he could track down any surviving family of the man whom Scott York's grandfather allegedly forced to jump off the Tyler-Goodwin, but of course that was off the table now. He felt bad about pulling Elizabeth Brantley's strings like this, she appeared to be so earnest, so genuine, but he needed her resources and connections. Scott York, good old Nails, was willing to pay and pay a lot for any information about the four who'd taken him and brought about the worst day of his life, out in the swamps. In Mason's mind, it made sense the doomed man from the bridge would've had some people left for which his death was still a festering wound. They might've been angry enough to enact some revenge.

Mason could appreciate that.

"The case I originally asked you about," he said. "Tyler-Goodwin Bridge. I'm curious if you know what came of the surviving family."

"I've spoken with his daughter and grandson," Elizabeth said. "They're nice people. Scarred and still very much hurt, as you would imagine."

"Grandson?" Mason couldn't tamp down the eagerness in his voice this time. Could he be one of the four who'd taken Scott York? "Tell me about him."

15

She took a long, hot shower, dried off, and slipped into fleece pajama bottoms and one of Isiah's T-shirts. Even though her hair remained damp and turbaned with a towel, she felt a million times better now that the stickiness of her morning run had been rinsed off her skin. Reenergized, no longer light-headed, or tired, and the pain pills she'd swallowed earlier had quieted the throbbing headache behind her eyes.

She opened the bathroom door and stepped back out into the apartment. Isiah was in the bedroom, sprawled on his stomach across the made bed. He rolled over and sat up as Rachel moved into the room. Their eyes met for the briefest of moments but neither of them said a word.

Rachel searched the table on her side of the bed, then moved to Isiah's side and did the same thing. Hands on hips, she surveyed the rest of the room, let her gaze fall on the dresser, the rocking chair in the corner, the expanse of the carpet. She was just about to lift the hem of the comforter, look under the bed, when Isiah raised an arm. The remote; he had it. When Rachel reached for it, he snapped his hand back like a child touching a hot oven.

"We need to talk, Rache."

"No. I'm showered and feeling relaxed."

"And before that you were ready to rip my head off."

He was right, of course. She'd returned from her run and spent most of the morning avoiding him, which clearly had confused Isiah, especially considering how she'd behaved before the run, fucking him back to sleep after waking him up in the first place. And when he'd worked up the courage to confront her on it, what had she chosen as a reason for her coldness? The fact that he had eaten a Belgian waffle in the bedroom. The kitchen had been a wreck—congealed pancake batter spilled on the counter, the syrup left out along with a pat of butter that had softened to the consistency of cake frosting, and Isiah splayed across the bed, oblivious, crumbs all over the comforter, the sheets gummy with Aunt Jemima as well. Rachel the one left to clean up. However, none of that had been the reason for her blowing up on him, and she knew it.

"I overreacted," she admitted.

"That an apology?"

"Closest you'll get."

"What's going on with you?"

"You and Nate are wearing on me," she said. "I thought pissing contests were for boys."

"He's sloppy, Rache. We're lucky you were able to attend to Robinson."

"It was an accident. Could've happened when I used that stun gun on him."

"But it didn't," Isiah said. "Nate's arrogant and self-righteous. Thinks what matters to him should matter to everyone. He's becoming more impulsive and it's making him dumb."

"You feel the same way about me?"

"What? No, of course not."

"Because what matters to Nate, it matters to me as well. Matters to Joshua. You seem to be the only one of us who doesn't give a shit."

"That's not fair, Rache."

"We targeted our own kind, and that still isn't enough for you."

"There you go with that tribal bullshit," Isiah said. "I feel sorry for you, Rache."

"Don't."

"Robinson's darker than you, and Nate picked at him, said he wasn't black. That didn't bother you?"

"Nothing I haven't heard before. You yourself made a comment about my lil' drop of black. That lil' drop is more powerful than a million drops of something else."

"Listen to you," Isiah said. "I think you actually hate the white part of yourself."

"You make me want to cry, Isiah."

"That's not my intention."

"I don't know what your intentions are anymore."

He tossed her the remote. She snatched it out of the air. Hopped up on the bed next to Isiah with her legs folded underneath her and turned on the television. On the screen, Representative John Lewis, a civil rights leader who'd marched with Martin Luther King Jr. in the sixties, was speaking to his colleagues in Congress. *I know racism when I see it. I know racism when I feel it.*

Isiah sighed and took back the remote from Rachel and pressed the volume down arrow, so low he could've simply used mute. Rachel watched him, expectant. He reached for her hands. "I don't want to fight. I know I don't see this the way you do. The way any of you do. But I hope you know I'm trying to understand. Trying to believe in the vision. That the reparations can somehow repay these people's families for the harm done to them."

"It's . . . something at least. I don't think anything can truly make up for what was done."

"Right," Isiah said. "I'm trying to believe."

"You really got involved in the planning details for this last one."

"I love the technical challenges, for sure. And Nate . . ."

"Yes?"

"He could sell water to a whale. But once you've bought in, you realize you may have been duped. You've got junk bonds and a time-share in Friedenswald."

"Where?"

"Exactly."

Nauseous, nauseated, what was the proper term? Rachel couldn't remember. Whatever the case, she felt uneasiness in her stomach, the contents as if they were ready to empty. Lying didn't come naturally to her. Lying to Isiah was even worse. She squeezed his hands, ready to end her deception. "I need to tell you something about Nate."

"No," he said. "I shouldn't have said that. It isn't true. Nate's always been up-front."

There was her out, and she cowardly took it. "I was looking through your spreadsheet."

"Yeah?"

"Mississippi, 1964," she said.

"The three civil-rights workers stopped on Highway Nineteen, for speeding inside city limits."

"Right."

The deputy who arrested them instructed the jailers to play dumb if anyone should call asking after the three men. Then he met up with his fellow Klansmen, to work out the details of an evening release and execution. After the three civil-rights workers paid the speeding fine, the deputy caught up with them before they crossed over into Lauderdale County, a relatively safe community for Negroes. He ordered the three men out of their car and into his cruiser. Drove them to a deserted area, two cars loaded with Klansmen bringing up the rear. The deputy turned the three men over to the white hoods and they were beaten to death, buried at a dam site.

"Makes me sick those Klansmen were never held accountable for what they did," Rachel said. "We can do something about that. Staying idle doesn't sit well with me. I feel as though I'm letting Darius down. All of 'em down."

Isiah sighed. "What if the Klansmen's descendants are all clean?"

"That," Rachel said, looking deep into his eyes, "would be a first."

February 19, 2017

6:14 p.m.

It's the dark *side of the day now, fourteen minutes after six. The sky above him is a black tarp etched with sparkly white constellations he doesn't know the names of. Years ago, he'd learned the Big Dipper is part of Ursa Major, and about Orion the Hunter. But all that is a jumble in his head in this moment; he can't recall much of it. That depresses him. Mrs. Pederson would be aghast. She was the first teacher to call him "bright," to believe in his potential. She'd be so disappointed to learn that little of what she'd taught him had stuck. He blinks to keep from tearing up. And the surge of emotion has nothing to do with Sofia ignoring his calls, either.*

Yeah, right.

Like his cousin Nate says, worst lies you tell are the ones you tell yourself.

He dials Sofia's number again. Straight to voicemail.

"Sofi here. If you're part of the problem, hang up. If you're part of the solution, drop a line and I'll get back to you."

Her voice makes him ache with longing, but leaving another message would be undignified. Demeaning. He's already left four. He refuses to leave another. Not gonna do it.

"I've walked around for thirty minutes in the cold trying to find your house," he says after the tone. "I should know the name of your street.

That's my bad. I'm asking you to cut me some slack here, though, Sofia. I don't hear from you in the next five minutes . . . I'll find my way to the train station and that'll be . . . Hey, call me back. Please."

He pockets the phone and turns a slow circuit there on the sidewalk. Eyes the Victorian he's standing in front of. A bicycle leans against the porch. A camping tent is set up in the middle of the front yard. Porsche Cayenne in the driveway. Lights burning inside the house. Venetian blinds in the windows, so there's no curtains to part. No one is peeping out at him from any of the neighboring houses—at least no one that he notices. These folks are too busy with their own charmed lives to be worried about him. Eating their dinners now. Chicken cutlets seasoned with a sprinkle of Mrs. Dash. Whole grain rice, steamed broccoli, a nice bottle of red wine. Welch's white grape juice or filtered water for the kiddies.

He touches a button on his watch and the face lights up so he can check the time. Sofia's had her five minutes. He blinks again and starts walking. You can hear the trains arriving and departing in the distance. There's a new one headed north at the same time every hour. If he hurries, he can make the 6:44.

Might have to cut through a few yards.

Not a big deal.

These folks are busy eating their dinners.

16

Mason flicked his left blinker, waited for a familiar MAX Transit bus to pass so he could make the turn. The bus was blue, white, and yellow and had 17 Eastwood lit on the destination sign. Searching his memory, Mason was fairly sure its last stop would be at Central Station on the north end of Morris Avenue. There used to be a nightspot named Zen over there. Kid got stabbed to death on the dance floor back in '09, Mayor Langford calling for the city to revoke the club's licenses. Same as they'd done after the fatal shooting at Banana Joe's a year earlier.

Two thousand nine.

Mason struggled to make sense of all that being ten years in the rearview. Time moved at warp speed. This meant with each passing day he had less and less of it left. He wondered whether Bella thought about this stuff, what a valuable commodity time was and that it shouldn't be wasted. Probably not. She was busy trying to motivate herself to put one foot in front of the other for trips to the bathroom to wash and to the kitchen to eat.

Mason shook his head and made a turn.

Elizabeth Brantley was well ahead of him, eating up the road in her clown car, rounding a bend without touching the brakes. Mason punched the gas to catch up even though he knew exactly how to get to where they were headed. Marks Village, a public housing community here in Gate City. At one time there'd been nineteen entry and exit points in those projects, but the housing authority had since put in sixty concrete traffic barriers, creating roadblocks they hoped would cut down on crime in the area. An artist had primed the barriers, painted over them in white, added colorful geometric shapes. Mason had never been able to see the point of that.

All the buildings in Marks were redbrick, faded, two levels, looked for all intents and purposes like a military barracks. One of the constant criticisms Mason heard when he was still with BPD was that he didn't live in the area he policed—which was pure insanity. Who would willingly choose to live like this if there were other options? Then again, he couldn't relate in any way with these people's mindsets. Many of them were without jobs, and yet everyone in Marks appeared to have more than one car. Correctly arranging their priorities wasn't exactly a strong suit for these folks.

Elizabeth Brantley parked her clown car along the curb in front of one of the buildings, and Mason pulled up behind her, close enough to kiss her rear bumper. By the time he got out of the car, she was already waiting for him on the sidewalk, still barefoot, the prettiest sight for miles. And that included the painted traffic barriers.

"I'll handle most of the talking," she said as he reached her. "Jean trusts me but she's suspicious of pretty much every other white person she encounters."

"And her son will be here?"

"Yes. But he won't have much to say about what happened to his grandfather. What he knows is from stories he's heard and been told. Jean, though, she's done her level best to make sure her father isn't forgotten, that people are aware of what those horrible men did to him."

"And you say she only has one son? Does he have any close cousins? Friends?"

Elizabeth frowned. "I would guess . . I mean, I don't really know. Why's that important?"

Realizing he was pushing too hard, Mason shook his head and smiled to put her at ease. "It likely isn't important, just spit-balling. I appreciate you setting this up, Elizabeth. And on such short notice, too."

Elizabeth Brantley was earnest and quickly back on track.

"Jean can use all of the allies she can get," she replied, reaching for Mason's arm and giving it a squeeze.

His voice cracked, but he managed, "Ready when you are."

A group of black men sat in metal folding chairs on the lawn in front of a makeshift table they'd constructed with milk crates and a sheet of plywood. All of them took occasional sips from red Solo cups, and two large bottles swaddled in brown paper bags lay in the grass. They were playing checkers. Then, on second glance, Mason realized it was chess. He'd tried to learn the game himself years ago but had given up. He remembered every player got eight pawns to start, the knights were the pieces that looked like horses, bishops had pointy heads and could move diagonally, rooks could move up and down the board and left to right as much as they wanted. It was a lot to square away, so he doubted these guys were all playing it correctly.

"How y'all doing?" Elizabeth said, giving the men a tiny wave. They regarded her, letting their gazes rove over her, head to toe, but none responded. Undeterred, she told them to enjoy what was left of the day before moving on.

That last declaration made Mason look up at the sky. He squinted as the sun continued to slip toward the horizon. Despite Elizabeth's ease of comfort, he knew they couldn't spend a lot more time here. It would be foolhardy to think Marks Village would be kind to him and Elizabeth after dark. Nonetheless, he followed her down the sidewalk to the correct apartment.

"Remember," she told him, "I'll do most of the talking until she's comfortable with you."

"Sure."

The doorbell's plastic housing was cracked, wires left exposed. The main door was open, though, a television blaring from inside. Sounded like *Family Feud.* Mason used to watch with Bella when they still did that sort of thing. She'd initially felt as though Steve Harvey was funny. Mason found the man to be loudmouthed, fool-acting, not at all on par with Richard Dawson. So, it hadn't really been a loss when Bella couldn't stomach watching anymore.

"Jean?" Elizabeth called out. She banged the screen door with the side of her fist. Seeing her knock that way, Mason had to run his tongue over his teeth, lick his lips, let out a few breaths. It's how he and practically every cop knocked.

The sound of the television faded.

A black woman appeared. "This door ain't exactly industrial-strength, Elizabeth."

"Sorry."

"This is your friend?"

Elizabeth turned to Mason. "That's right. Mason Farmer, this is Jean Williams."

"Pleased to meet you, Miss Williams."

"Just assumed I'm not married, huh?"

"I—"

"You were the police in Birmingham? I don't recall ever seeing you?"

"I was around," Mason said.

"What does that mean? Around?"

"Broke up my share of fights and drug deals at Lewis Park. Wanted it to stay family-friendly, you know?" When Jean Williams didn't respond he went on. "Helped hand out food at Holy Rosary. Donated books for the reading program at Ann Seton."

"Any excessive-force complaints against you?"

Mason smiled. "That's an interesting question."

"I'll take that as a yes then."

Jean Williams was an inch over five feet, neither skinny nor fat, with a mixed gray-and-black Afro, dark skin almost the same color as her eyes, a wide gap between her top two front teeth. She had a smoker's rasp, wrinkles etched into her face. All of which added up to one intimidating woman, despite her slight stature.

"Mason contacted me to learn about lynching and other hate crimes of the past," Elizabeth said, no doubt an attempt to ease the tension.

"What's his interest?"

"Ask him."

The old black woman trained her dark eyes on Mason. "What are you up to?"

"Up to? You make my interest sound degenerate."

"I don't know about that," Jean Williams replied, "but I'm noticing you ain't much for answering simple questions. More like a smarmy politician than ex-police."

"Would it be all right for us to continue this inside, *Ms.* Williams?"

She studied Mason for a moment, then unlatched the screen door and pushed it out. Elizabeth thanked her and stepped inside. Mason moved inside as well. It was a small, cramped apartment. He couldn't imagine more than one person using the space.

"Your son is home, Ms. Williams?"

"Resting," she said.

"Think you could wake him?"

"Terrell ain't got nothing to tell you."

"You never know when—"

"We can sit in the kitchen," she said. "Only got the one couch in the living room."

The two rooms were divided by a half-wall, the top surface of which Jean Williams had turned into a religious display. A King James Bible lay open and under the tangerine illumination of a small lamp. There was a framed picture of a ridiculous black Jesus and several fans from a Baptist church, spread like a deck of cards. Just enough chairs waited for them in the kitchen, and to Mason's surprise they were from the same set. The table where they sat down was topped with glass, a few chips here and there but no smudges whatsoever, which was also surprising.

"It's white folks more likely to keep a dirty house," Jean Williams said, watching Mason as he checked out his reflection.

He looked up. "House? Not much here for you to keep up."

"What did you say?"

Elizabeth tried to intervene. "Mason didn't mean—"

"Why'd you bring this man here? Should've known when you said he used to be police."

"Please give this a chance, Jean. Mason's curious about what happened to your father. He'd like to see someone held responsible. He's retired from the police but works for a private firm now and still has lots of connections."

"What those connections gonna do for me?" the old black woman asked.

Mason said, "What was it . . . '99, you convinced the district attorney to reopen your father's case? Even got her to put it before a grand jury in Montgomery County. They agreed with the new medical examiner's determination your father was forced to jump and the jump was the cause of his death. But they didn't indict anyone for it, even though there was a great deal known about who was involved."

"Surprise, surprise." Jean Williams sat back in her chair, crossed her arms over her chest. "You looking to track down the men done it? I hate to tell you, they all dead and gone by now."

"But they have people who aren't," Mason said. "Children and grandchildren just like you and your son."

"So?"

"Sounds like an opportunity for some get-back," Mason said. Out of the corner of his eye, he could feel Elizabeth staring at him, probably frowning.

"Get-back? These children and grandchildren most likely wicked in their own way," Jean Williams acknowledged, "but they ain't have nothing to do with my father."

"Agreed," Mason said, nodding. "I'm wondering if your son feels differently, though."

"What the hell does that mean?"

"Where is he? I'd really like to have a word with him."

"Told you, he's resting."

"That's a nice flat-screen you got in there, Ms. Williams. You hit the lottery?"

"What now?"

"Seems out of place. Sixty-inch, Samsung. That'll run you about eight bills."

"Not that it's any of your business, but I got some money for unclaimed property."

"Unclaimed property?"

"They sent me a letter with a check. Might be some more coming, they said."

"That's not how it usually works."

"I'm lying?"

"Can I see the letter?"

"You most certainly cannot."

Before he realized what he was doing, Mason was up on his feet, and darting out of the kitchen and down Jean Williams's narrow hallway. She yelled for him to stop. Elizabeth rushed up behind him, calling his name, trying to get a grip on his shoulder.

It would be dark soon.

This needed to end. Now.

Mason tried a door, peered inside. Likely Jean's room, judging by the perfume bottles arranged on the dresser, the dress lying across the bed.

Next room was the bathroom.

"Mason, stop this," Elizabeth pleaded.

Next room was the son's, Terrell.

Mason didn't move beyond the doorway.

Terrell Williams craned his neck, frowned. "Who's there?"

His eyes were the color of dirty dishwater.

Blind, Mason realized.

Jean Williams brushed past Mason and into the room. She placed a hand on her son's shoulder, eased him back against his pillows. "Just some crazy white folks," she told Terrell. "Don't worry, they's leaving now."

17

Nate answered his door in baggy Monmouth University basketball shorts and a dingy tee with holes at both armpits. On the other side of the threshold, his cousin Joshua couldn't keep the surprise from his face, no doubt stunned by the bags beneath Nate's eyes, the several days' growth of beard, the need of a haircut. Looking in the mirror earlier, Nate had been dumbfounded himself. So much had transpired in the few days since they'd taken Devon Robinson.

The weather was marigold and cerulean, which was a stark contrast to what had been a rainy, gray afternoon. Nate moved to the kitchen, plopped down heavily at his small glass-topped table, and tried massaging away the band of tension that had wrapped itself around his head. There was an open pizza box on the counter, two waxy slices left from the pie. And next to that, a lineup of Modelo cans and an uncorked bottle of Château Latour.

Nate heard the clunk of the bottle as Joshua picked it up, heard his cousin turning it appraisingly in his hands, then heard a low whistle. "What happened to Two Buck Chuck?"

"Don't you know," Nate said, forcing a smile, "I'm a man of bearing and sophistication."

Joshua set down the bottle, a frown etched in his face. "Really, what's going on here, cousin? Rachel told me about you rolling up on her earlier while she was on her run. She's concerned about you."

"She should focus that concern on I.T."

"I think you're spiraling. I'm wrong?"

Nate's nostrils flared. "I.T.'s playing some kind of power game. It's bullshit."

"He checked the Mississippi descendants Rachel wanted to take on. The only one who's an issue is already doing ten at Parchman."

"Convenient. So once again it'll be I.T. picking who we target."

"Is that so bad? I mean, Isiah does all the vetting anyway."

"Some bullshit," Nate muttered.

"I think we're seeing now that you and I would've been too . . . emotional. It's good Isiah is on this."

"Fuck that."

They fell silent.

After a while, Joshua cleared his throat, said, "I been thinking about what we talked about the other day. Your time in Hawaii."

"Is there a question in there, Joshua?"

"Where were you really?"

"Looking for rainbow-colored fish and protected tide pools at Hulopoe Bay's marine sanctuary. Hikes along the cliffs up to Puu Pehe. Watching the sun set at Kaumalapau Harbor."

"Sounds like something you read off a brochure."

"Initially," Nate admitted. "That travel marketing gets you every time."

"You've always done your own thing. Did you find Darius's killer and do something to him?"

"You know he's in the wind," Nate said.

"I don't believe you went to Hawaii. It came about so sudden, and you were so vague in explaining it."

The doorbell rang before Nate could respond. A welcome diversion. He didn't want to get into the time he was off the board.

Supposedly in Hawaii, as Joshua saw it. There was too much to explain about his time away. Too much that couldn't be explained.

Another ring of the doorbell.

"Want me to let them in?" Joshua asked.

"Yeah."

"Go easy on Isiah, Nate."

"Power play," he said. "I don't like it."

After Joshua stepped out of the room, Nate rose to his feet and trudged over to pick up the bottle of red. He raised it to his lips, took a swill. Then he swept the empty Modelo cans into his blue recycling bin, tossed the wine bottle in on top. Ran warm water from the sink over his face and dried it with a dish towel.

"I'm here."

Nate turned and looked at I.T., then beyond him at Rachel and Joshua standing back in the doorway. He moved and sat down heavily in one of the kitchen's dining chairs, folded his hands, and placed them on the table.

"This is how it's going to be?" I.T. said. "I could've stayed home."

"Just giving you the full attention you deserve," Nate said.

"Now you're being patronizing."

At that, Nate stood and left the kitchen. He had a second bedroom he used as an office and for storage. Boxes were stacked on the floor along one wall. And he'd bought a plastic shelving unit from Home Depot, and its four shelves held more boxes. He lifted one from the middle shelf of the unit, calling up a tornado of dust. It was from his mother's attic, which was left as he'd found it a little more than five years ago right after she died.

He set it on his desk, removed the lid. Reached inside and pulled out several dusty books. *The Autobiography of Malcolm X. Invisible Man*, by Ralph Ellison. Maya Angelou's *I Know Why the Caged Bird Sings*. He reached inside the box again and pulled out a stack of worn magazines and yellowed newspapers held together with twine.

Amsterdam News, and the *Chicago Defender, JET*. He stopped at one specific *JET*. He'd placed it in a Ziploc bag when he first found it among his mother's things.

Nate carefully slipped the magazine from the Ziploc, opened it to a page he'd marked with a Post-it. He studied the page a while, aware of the heat coming off his skin like a food-warming lamp. I.T. had come up beside him in the room. Rachel and Joshua lingered by the doorway. "Since we were considering Mississippi," Nate said, and handed the magazine over to I.T., who appeared hesitant. "Go on, take it."

I.T. licked his lips, reached for the ancient *JET*. A breath escaped him as he took in the image on the page.

"We've all heard the story by now," Nate said. "How Emmett Till's mother, Mamie, insisted they photograph her son in the coffin, run it so people could see what was hauled out of the Tallahatchie River. Bloated, missing an eye, nothing recognizable of the handsome, fourteen-year-old boy he once was."

Nate smiled sadly, seeing I.T. couldn't close the magazine, couldn't set it aside, couldn't turn the page. Couldn't look away. He did, however, sniff and wipe his eyes with the back of his hand.

"Gentleman named David Jackson took the picture," Nate said. "I looked him up, but unfortunately, he's passed. No mainstream publications ran the photo. They barely covered the story. That responsibility was left to black media."

"This is . . ." I.T. couldn't come up with the words to express what he was feeling either, it seemed. "I'd heard about the photo but . . ."

"Yeah," Nate said, nodding. "Seeing it for yourself is something else."

"I can't believe . . ." And again, I.T.'s voice trailed off.

"What we're doing means something, I.T. I'm not saying black folks are the only oppressed. I'm not saying we have a monopoly on pain and suffering. What I'm saying is, right now, at this moment in time, is it possible, is it okay, for us to get a little healing? Emmett Till was in 1955 and here Trayvon was just seven years ago. Darius, two years. FBI reported 1,943 hate crimes against black folks last year. So, I ask again. Can we please get a little healing? Please?"

"Yes," I.T. said, gently closing the magazine, handing it back. "I get it, Nate."

"Do you?"

Nate watched as I.T. looked at Joshua, who had his head down. As he looked at Rachel. Her eyes shiny with tears. But her jaw firm, her posture taut. Then I.T.'s focus was back on Nate. He reached out a hand and they clasped. Speaking softly, he said, "I have something, Nate."

"Yeah?"

"Give me your word," I.T. said. "We keep this nice and clean, so no one gets hurt."

"Of course. We're not savages, I.T. What do you have?"

"Mingo Jack" he was called, a onetime slave who'd worked a string of odd jobs once slavery was abolished. He was known for being a dedicated worker, keeping his nose clean. In March of 1886, though, a white woman, Angelina Herbert, was raped and beaten. She couldn't identify the man who had attacked her, but recalled his asking her, "Do you know Mingo Jack?" That was enough to get him arrested. And a mob of people chiseled holes in the wall of the jail where Mingo Jack was being held, and they fired their guns through those holes, hoping to kill him. When that didn't work, they stormed the jail, beat and hung him. The trial was a farce, all the defendants easily acquitted. Mingo Jack left behind a wife and five children. Years later, another black man would confess to the crime, though many believed his testimony to have been coerced. Justice was difficult to wrangle, a thorny and nebulous idea that never worked out well for black people.

A wife and five children.

That was the sticking point for Nate and the three others.

They could've been those children. Not literally, being that it was so long ago, but still, it resonated with them.

"Eatontown," Nate said once I.T. finished going over the details.

"Right here in our own backyard."

"How come I've never heard this story?"

"Same thing I wondered when I stumbled upon it."

"And there's a memorial in Wampum Park?"

I.T. nodded. "Part of Eatontown PD's night patrol. The original was torn down, and they don't want that to happen again."

"Torn down by who?" Nate asked.

"One of the descendants. An asshole goes by the name Chipper."

18

"I just want to know why," Elizabeth said.

Mason didn't have a good answer. He'd chased her all the way from Jean Williams's apartment in Gate City, flashing his high beams the entire way, finally getting her to pull over on the side of a road on the outskirts of the projects. Her Prius was parked haphazardly, under a canopy of longleaf pine. Mason's car was angled so the two of them were yellowed like jaundice by its headlights. He would've preferred the pitch dark because somewhere along the line Elizabeth had bunched together her long, black hair, exposing what he considered a particularly lovely neck. The sight of it further threw off his equilibrium. He licked his lips and tried to call up some spit.

"It took some doing to earn Jean's trust," Elizabeth went on, "and it meant something to me that I'd gotten it. Now I'm just the latest white person to disappoint her, to exploit her pain."

"This is all on me. Let her know you were blindsided as well."

"You've done enough, Mason. I don't need you to tell me how to clean this up. It's over. I wouldn't think of bothering Jean ever again."

"I'm sorry."

"Why the hell did you barge into her son's room like that?"

"I was fired today," Mason heard himself say.

"Fired?" Elizabeth frowned. "What for?"

"The truth would further disappoint you, I'm afraid."

"I'll just go then."

"Wait," Mason said, raising a hand to stop her from passing. "Hear me out."

"Please let me pass. I don't like being manhandled."

Mason dropped his hands to his sides. "Forgive me. My head is spinning. I'm not thinking clearly."

Elizabeth studied him a moment, then said, "Answer me: why did you barge into Terrell's room?"

"Thought he might be guilty."

"That's right. What was that foolishness you were talking about get-back? What's going on here, Mason?"

He grunted, wrung his hands, grimaced.

"Mason . . ."

"I haven't been honest with you," he said.

"Really? You're kidding?"

"I'm sorry."

"I'm sorry you keep saying that. I asked what's going on. And if you can't—"

"I didn't contact you out of concern for the families of the blacks who'd been lynched and such. I contacted you thinking one of them might've been involved in a kidnapping."

"A kidnapping? What are you talking about, Mason?"

"I manipulated you," he said. "It was clear from the first email you were passionate. So, I figured you would be thrilled if someone wanted to investigate the sins of the past. Someone who could possibly get some justice for the victims' families. And you were. So, I ran with it."

Elizabeth hugged herself, her pale white cheeks reddening as if she'd been slapped. And in a way, she had, Mason supposed. He found it deeply hurtful he'd been the one to inflict the blow.

"Keep going," she whispered. "This is still not making sense."

And so, he told her all about Scott York, his old first baseman from Little League. Told her about Scott's connection, through his grandfather, to the Tyler-Goodwin Bridge. Told her about what had happened to York in the swamp. Jean Williams's unclaimed property windfall was more likely from the reparations the kidnappers collected. "Robin from the hood," he joked.

Elizabeth didn't appreciate his attempt at humor. "They slipped a noose around his neck?"

"Yes."

"Pretty brazen for them to do it in broad daylight."

"These are vigilantes on steroids," Mason said. "Smart, spiteful. That's a dangerous combination. How long before they kill someone?"

"Kill?"

He nodded. "In my experience there's always an escalation in these situations. They'll kill someone if they aren't stopped."

"You believe they've done this to others?"

"Bet on it. From what Scott told me, they are a well-oiled machine. That kind of precision doesn't come from drawing up blueprints on some basement whiteboard . . . it comes from doing. I need your help, Elizabeth."

"What do you plan on doing if you find them?"

"Cross that bridge when we come to it," Mason said.

Elizabeth shook her head. "That's not good enough for me."

"What's your concern?"

"You," she said. "That was ugly back at Jean's. The way you spoke to her. How you looked at her. That you felt entitled to move through her apartment without permission."

"Not my proudest moment," Mason admitted. "But what does that have to do with catching these guys? And girl . . . or, er, woman?"

"I have a framed reproduction of an article on my office wall," Elizabeth told him. "It's from 1930, in the *Raleigh News and Observer*, reporting about a lynching. There's a passage about whole families

coming to this particular one, even young children. Men joking about
the bleeding body, and girls giggling as flies fed on the blood that
dripped from the Negro's nose."

Mason swallowed. "I wouldn't have been among that number."

"No?"

"I'll admit I have my prejudices . . ."

"Why were you fired?"

"What?"

"I'm pretty sure you heard me, Mason."

He let out a breath and didn't hold anything back in telling her
the rest of it. Tamara Blake, the Indian woman from actual India,
everything Nicole had imparted for his edification. Unconscious
biases, microaggressions.

"You mentioned in an email that your son-in-law is black. And
you have a grandson."

"Yes," Mason replied, a strain of emotion evident in his voice. "But
it hasn't been joyous, not in the way I presented it to you. My daughter's relationship with Elijah upset me quite a bit in the beginning.
Still does if I'm being completely honest."

With more than a touch of sadness, he thought then of Bella.
He'd implied to Elizabeth his wife was gone. Death, divorce—he
hadn't said, and she hadn't pried. But if she were to ask now, he'd tell
her the truth. He wouldn't lie to Elizabeth again.

"This is a lot to digest," she said.

Mason nodded. "Yes, it is. I understand if you're having trouble
squaring it all. I'm trying to be as honest as possible."

"I appreciate that. I think. I still feel foolish, though. How could
I have been so gullible?"

"My performance was pretty convincing," Mason said. "I took full
advantage of your goodness. And trust me, I'm ashamed of that. But
that's my weight to carry. Please don't let my failings shape how you
think of yourself."

"That's easier said than done," Elizabeth told him. "I *took you* to Jean."

"And I'm terribly sorry about that. I know you valued your relationship with her."

"I did. But it's over. She'll never trust me again."

"I hope . . ." Mason cleared phlegm from his throat. "I hope the same can't be said about you and me."

She didn't respond.

"For what it's worth," he went on, "I genuinely believe the lynchings and the rest was terrible. A stain on our country. And I wouldn't have stood by to watch. But what these four vigilantes are doing isn't right either. I don't know how progress can be achieved if both sides keep hurting each other."

With a frown etched on her brow, Elizabeth turned to face him. "Did you say both sides?"

"Yes, I did. Is there something wrong with that, Miss Elizabeth?"

"I don't drive well when it's fully dark," she announced. "I'm going to go now."

Mason tamped down the urge to reach forward and grab her wrist, instead asked, "So will you help me? I want to put a stop to what they're doing . . . before they kill someone."

"You take care of yourself, Mason."

He was still standing there on the side of the road as Elizabeth pulled away from under the grove of tall, skinny, longleaf pines. Still standing there as her Prius disappeared from sight. Still standing there as nightfall covered him like a thick wool blanket.

Sadly, heading home just didn't hold very much appeal for him.

February 19, 2017

6:36 p.m.

It's where everyone *sleds when powdery, white snow blankets the ground. A sloping hill beyond the tennis courts, full-length basketball court, and baseball field. He can't believe how good these white kids have it, as he climbs toward the middle school building at the top. He'd have bargained with the devil for something similar when he was this age. Thurgood Marshall Middle School was a sea of cracked blacktop. Painted, though, with crooked white lines for kickball during lunch and gym. Had to go to the Y if you wanted to play tennis or b-ball. He has no idea where they would've played baseball.*

There are woods off to the right, and it looks spooky in the gloom. He doesn't have to broach it, though. He'll cut down the side of the school and come out on Wicker Place, shaving a few minutes off his walk to the train station. He's got eight minutes before he'll hear the 6:44 pulling away.

Sofia still hasn't called back, so he resorted to texting her. At least he can tell whether she reads them. So far, she's read all six, but hasn't responded.

Whatever.

He reaches the school building, turns sideways because of the narrow alley. That makes him feel claustrophobic but he's able to manage. Still, he's grateful as he makes it through, comes to the buttery glare of the streetlamps in front of the school. Wicker Place is a straight shot to the train station. Half a mile.

He'll make the train if he rushes.

A car parked on the street rumbles to life as he touches the sidewalk. It rolls forward, headlights off, a few paces behind him as he begins to jog. He hadn't bothered trying to see who was behind the wheel of the car. Wouldn't have mattered if he'd tried. Dark tint on the windows.

Dark tint.

He frowns, stops jogging, turns back to look. The headlights flash on.

He shields his eyes as the car approaches. Just as he'd suspected. A silver Acura.

He stands there, challenging the driver. The car stops rolling, and all four doors open. White boys scurry from inside like ants smoked out of a dirt hill. Darius owns his spot on the sidewalk as Space Jam moves toward him.

"Hey, bro," Space Jam says, "you got a thing for trespassing?"

"Are you following me around?"

"Word is out you've been running through people's yards. Climbing fences, crushing their rosebushes."

Darius wasn't running. Didn't climb any fences. And rosebushes? In February? This is foolishness. He turns and starts walking again. No point missing his train for this.

"Bro?" Space Jam trails behind him like toilet paper stuck on a shoe.

Darius wheels to face him. "What, man? What do you want?"

"This is my town," Space Jam says. "Seems you're not putting any respect on its name."

"You listen to too much Hot 97. I'm leaving your town now if you'll stop harassing me."

Darius doesn't expect the group of boys to charge at him. For them to grab him and drag him to the dark alley on the other side of the school building.

But they do.

At least it's not as narrow as the side he'd come down. He has room to maneuver and fight back. A losing battle, though. They're pummeling him. A blizzard of punches and kicks to every inch of his real estate. Stomach. Legs. His face. He feels his lip split like a grape.

Best he can do is cover up and let them punch themselves out.

White boys don't feel the winter chill and, to his dismay, don't tire, either. They keep pummeling him for what feels like an eternity.

Finally, they stop.

Two of them hold Darius's arms as Space Jam rifles through his pockets. "Hell is this?" *he says after a while, holding up Sofia's necklace.*

The two goons let Darius go, and he reaches for the necklace.

Space Jam hides it behind his back. "You stole from that girl?"

"What? No. I was gonna give her that."

Space Jam also has Darius's wallet, plus the chisel-tip Sharpie that he keeps in his pocket, and a folded sheet of graph paper for when inspiration strikes. The paper is flimsy from use and smudged with rough drafts of designs. Stuff he'll bring to life with CorelCAD later.

"Took her artwork, too," *Space Jam says.* "You some kind of kleptomaniac?"

"That's mine, man."

"You're a menace, bro. I'm glad we stopped you."

"I'm not looking for any trouble," *Darius tells him.*

"All-white Adidas," *Space Jam says, chuckling, shaking his head.* "You do have a type."

"What does—"

"Think they'll fit me?" *Space Jam asks.*

"Come on, man."

"Take 'em off."

"I'm not walking around in the cold without my shoes, man."

Again, they're on him.

He curls his toes, but they're still able to remove his Adidas.

Space Jam tosses the Sharpie to one of his friends, who's now holding a pilfered sneaker. "Hold on to that for sticky fingers here." Then he turns back to Darius. "Let's talk about that jacket now. I'm really feeling it, bro."

"Take a picture," Darius says. "'Bout as close as your dumb ass will ever get to Rutgers."

More pummeling. More covering up.

"You've taken on a lot of trouble for yourself," Space Jam says, breathing heavy. "All for a stuck-up puttana*. Worth it, bro?"*

"Sofia's worth everything," Darius tells him, spitting blood and an incisor. "Beat me all you want, and she still wouldn't let that little pink worm you got anywhere near her sweet fica.*"*

Space Jam grins and then punches Darius in the stomach. "I'm not gonna stand for some black turd, Migos-looking motherfucker talking shit to me in my own hood," he says.

Definitely listens to too much Hot 97.

Space Jam and his friends are relaxed, as if they expect Darius to continue engaging. When he takes off running it catches them by surprise.

Darius hustles past the school, hesitates a moment, then melts into the woods.

He blurs through trees, hard and unforgiving branches lashing out at him. He's coated with dirt, cold sweat, and blood. The carpet of soft ground offers little comfort to his damaged feet. In the end, he knows, his body and its limits will not matter much. This is mental calisthenics more than anything else. Either he'll get away, or they'll catch him and . . .

Something hard plucks him in the back, between the shoulder blades, as he scampers into a clearing. His feet tangle, and he's tumbling before he can process how to break the fall. His chin bounces off the ground like a ball, rattling his teeth and jarring his brain. He groans and rolls over on his back. It would be nice to look up at the stars and collect himself. But there's nothing nice about what's happening to him.

Space Jam peers down at him. "That wasn't graceful. Thought you brothers were superior athletes."

"Why are you doing this?" Darius whispers.

"Put your sneakers back on."

"I haven't done anything to you."

Space Jam drops an Adidas toward Darius's chest. He raises his arms, but it careens off him and plops in the dirt. "Can't catch, either. Shit, bro. Please tell me you can rap."

"None of this happened," Darius says. "You don't have to worry about me telling on you."

"Put on the sneaker, bro."

"I mean it. Not a word."

"Don't make me tell you again."

Darius fumbles for the sneaker. Grimacing, he sits up, takes a breath, then tries to slip it on his foot. He's concussed, he thinks, because it's not fitting. Round peg in a square hole.

"Shit, bro," Space Jam says. "This is ridiculous. Just give it to me."

He snatches the sneaker from Darius and asks his friend for the Sharpie. Uncaps the marker and slashes writing on the sneaker. Then drops it by Darius and focuses his cell phone flashlight on it. "Might've wasted my time. Can you even read?"

Darius's eyes water. He wants to see what was written on the sneaker. Wants to read it so this can be over. But the writing is far too faint.

"It says, 'Da left,'" Space Jam tells him, sounding exasperated. He turns and focuses the cell phone light on the other sneaker, a few feet away. "Didn't mark that one but—"

"It's obviously Da right," Darius says, joining in on the joke. Hoping that will buy him some goodwill among them.

"Put 'em on," Space Jam says. "The police are nosy around here. We need to get moving."

"Moving?" Darius tears up again. "Come on, man. I just want to go home."

"Exactly," Space Jam says. "We'll take you to the train station."

"I can manage on my own."

"I insist . . ." Space Jam's voice trails off a beat. "I'm realizing we don't even know your name, bro."

"If this is all about Sofia, I give you my word I won't see her again."

"That goes without saying, all the shit you stole from her."

"I didn't—"

"The fucking sneakers," Space Jam barks. "Put 'em on, stop dicking around."

It takes some doing for Darius to slide his feet in them, and even more for him to then stand up. Space Jam is right up on him, the others standing well back. Twenty feet at least. Like they don't want to be a part of this. He wonders whether they'll even give chase once he runs for a second time.

"You're mumbling, bro. Your jaw broke?"

Darius's jaw does feel creaky and loose. His tongue stings from where he bit it. He's producing saliva like a Saint Bernard.

"I'm talking to you, bro."

Space Jam leans in close.

Darius spits in his face and turns to run at the same time.

He was wrong. All the boys give chase.

He hears the slapping rhythm of the boys' feet, and deep animal breaths on his trail. He doesn't dare look back—that would slow him down. He runs like his life depends on it.

And it does.

He's a few feet from the tree line and an exit from the woods when they catch up to him. Pepper him with a cascade of blows. A bunch to the face, his stomach. Someone punches him hard in the chest. He feels an immediate tightness, a rolling wave of nausea, and sinks to his knees. The pain is overwhelming.

"Shit, Austin, you jabbed him," someone says, and Darius makes out from their conversation it wasn't a punch that brought him down. He's been stabbed.

The boys scatter like roaches with the lights on and it's Darius, alone. He feels blood soaking into his shirt, which pains him—it'll ruin his Rutgers jacket.

He lays on his side, as tired as he's ever been.

He wants to raise his arms, sit himself up, but can't get any body parts to obey his brain.

It's getting harder to breathe.

He feels his heart racing and gasps for a spoonful of air. His lungs are filling, but with gallons of water, it seems, instead of oxygen. This sets him into a panic. Is he drowning?

Tears leak from his eyes.

No way he's making that 6:44 train.

Or the one after.

Or the one . . .

19

Duane "Chipper" Kelly's face was weathered from a lifetime outdoors and covered by a gray-and-brown beard, the tip of which reached to his chest. His head was shaved clean and, paired with his eyes, which were blue like a stove flame, gave off a hint of the menace that lived inside him. Not to mention, he was of a size that made men either bullies or gunshot victims. Looked as though he could've opened a fire hydrant with his bare hands, no wrench necessary.

Seeing him up close like this made Rachel wonder whether they'd made a mistake. Whether it was too late to gracefully bow out. Even the stun gun in her purse offered her little confidence.

Up on the stage surrounded by blue and red balloons, two women in G-strings and nipple tassels were cycling between wrestling with each other and tossing money in the air. The DJ's black T-shirt read *Hustlin' Made Me Rich*, and he was busy cutting up some of that white-boy music. Def Leppard or AC/DC or something, Rachel wasn't sure.

She'd bet herself it would take less than five minutes before Chipper worked up the nerve to approach her—he'd been staring at her more than at the dancers. A glance at her watch now as he made his way over showed four minutes and fifty-six seconds since the bet, right to the wire.

"Bucket list, I hope," he said, standing over her.

She looked up. "Excuse me?"

"You ain't one of them LGB-whatever, are you? I'm hoping you just wanted to see what all the fuss was about gentlemen's clubs."

"Are you a gentleman?"

"I'm asking if I can join you before I sit down, aren't I?" he said.

Rachel patted the spot next to her on the velvet bench seat.

"Anybody ever tell you that you look like Taylor Swift?"

"Never." There was some truth to it, though. At least today. Baby-blue contacts over her light-green eyes, a bloodred lipstick marketed as Cherry on Top, a blonde wig styled in a short bob with flat bangs. Dressed to impress, too. Heels, tight black jeans, an even tighter silk top. "I imagine you think that's a compliment?"

"Meant it as one."

"What are you drinking?"

"Michelob Ultra."

"I would've taken you for a Guinness man."

"Eight-fifty a bottle," Chipper said, blowing out his lips, "no thanks."

All the bartenders here at Lace were women, and busty. They all wore a variation of the same getup as well: tight spandex boy shorts and snug white top with the strip club's name spread across it from nipple to nipple in vivid purple lettering. Rachel waved over Tonique, a Bahamian woman with bronzed skin, exquisite cheekbones, and breasts like mammee apples. She had a belly piercing, a tattoo on her right forearm that appeared to be longitude and latitude numbers, and a smile that didn't make it to her eyes.

"Another chocolate martini, *bey?*"

Rachel shook her head. "Michelob Ultra for this gentleman, please."

Tonique stared at Chipper a moment, then said, "You got it. Be back in a sec."

Soon as she stepped away, Chipper, one eye cocked, said, "You're buying *me* a drink?"

Rachel placed a slender hand on his knee. "Play your cards right. In about thirty minutes, you'll be earning your keep."

He gulped. And seventeen minutes later was following Rachel out the back exit. She'd told him there were conditions: her place, she'd drive, and if he left so much as an air bubble in one of the Magnum condoms she kept stocked in a drawer of her bedside table, she would call the whole thing off. He looked a bit sheepish at that last part but nodded anyway.

"Didn't catch your name," he said as they stepped outside.

"Didn't throw it."

"You're clever."

"Bet you're not used to that, are you, Chipper?"

He pulled up short. "How do you know—"

Rachel couldn't help it, gazing past his shoulder, and that gave it away. He wheeled around as Nate socked him hard and fast in the jaw, making him stumble forward, Joshua leaping in as well and kicking Chipper's legs out from under him. But Nate's punch hadn't landed flush, and the big man quickly found his feet, surprised Joshua with a kick to the groin that would've made a horse proud. A burst of air shot out of Joshua, and he dropped to his knees.

Rachel stuck her hand in her purse.

Nate moved on Chipper, feinted left, then came in with a looping right that would've decapitated the big man if he hadn't ducked and rolled. He peppered Nate's ribs with several short jabs. Terse punches were more powerful when they landed.

Nate took them, though, and returned his own fire. A hard elbow to Chipper's midsection, then another to the back of his head when he doubled over. A lesser man would've fallen. Chipper wrapped his arms around Nate and ran him into the brick wall of the building.

Rachel whispered, "Shit," and moved up behind the big guy. He was busy rubbing his hands together, chuckling, admiring his handiwork, and didn't hear her approach. She zapped him with the stun gun, three full seconds, likely felt as long as a generation with that many volts shooting through him. All it did was stagger him enough for Nate and Joshua to recover. Still, that was good. They both rained blows on the big man, getting him halfway to the ground.

Rachel moved in and zapped him again. Another three-second blast. That got him, finally, to fall.

Joshua kicked his ribs. Nate punched Chipper in the mouth, then the throat. The big man coughed, spit up blood, went still.

"Fuck," Nate said, breathing heavily. "Let's get him secured."

Isiah pulled up in the Econoline right as they finished wrapping Chipper's ankles together with a ribbon of duct tape long as Highway 61. They'd gotten his hands zip-tied behind his back as well. Knotted a bandanna over his eyes.

Isiah dropped down from the driver's seat, opened the rear doors.

The back of the van was set up like a dog kennel, with an actual cage. They lifted Chipper like a roll of plush carpet, dropped him inside, shut the cage door. Nate jiggled it to make sure it was locked tight.

Then he turned to the others. "Piece of cake. Let's roll."

Twenty minutes into their drive, Chipper stirred. He sat up suddenly, tested the strength of his binds, swiveled his head, searching for an angle where he could see through the blindfold.

"Chipper Kelly," Nate said. "Proprietor of the best little motorcycle repair shop in Monmouth County. '*No job too small for us to tackle. Pipes, jetting, tune-ups, we do it all*'!"

Chipper stopped moving, tracked the direction of the voice. "What's your name, friend?"

"Mingo Jack," Nate replied.

"Mango? You don't sound like a Chink to me."

"You should be careful what you say, Chipper. I could be Asian."

Chipper laughed. "Nah, I'm pretty sure you're a burrhead."

"What's that supposed to mean?"

"Happy to be nappy."

Nate gritted his teeth, kicked the cage. "You understand what's happening here?"

"Sure enough, Sambo. You've gone and signed your death warrant."

"Be smart about this and—"

Snore sounds filled the cab. Chipper let his head loll to the side. After a few seconds of that act, he sat up again, said, "In all seriousness, I'm paying the price now for burning the candle at both ends this week. Wake me when we get to wherever you're taking me."

"I'm not your—"

More snore sounds.

Rachel looked at Nate, and even through the balaclava she could feel the anger rising off him. If it were just the two of them, she might've placed a hand on his shoulder, taken one of his hands in hers even. But it wasn't just the two of them. She caught the reflection of Isiah's eyes in the rearview mirror. His hands were shaking on the steering wheel.

No one spoke the rest of the way.

Salem held the distinction of being New Jersey's least populous county. Fewer than seventy thousand people across its more than 370 square miles. Isiah had discovered a four-bedroom Cape Cod on the abandoned property list, its inclusion never appealed by the owner. The property was still mired in legal remedy close to four years later.

Rachel let out a breath as they turned off a five-mile stretch of quiet road. There was no cutout, not even a crude dirt path, so Isiah had to drive through thick undergrowth, trampling all sorts of vegetation in the process, the van rocking and the engine straining.

"So much for my beauty rest," Chipper called, yawning loudly.

Isiah pulled up to a closed cattle gate, jumped out, and pushed it wide enough to drive through, then hopped out a second time to swing it closed behind them. The house was just up ahead, partially obscured in a forest of sun-scorched fauna. As they drew aside it, Nate opened the rear door of the Econoline. "Stunner," he said to Rachel, waggling his fingers.

She handed him the stun gun.

"Remove the blindfold and cut loose this duct tape," Chipper called. "I'll save you trouble by walking myself."

My God, Rachel thought, *he's as relaxed as a stroll.*

"You hear me, Mango Blackjack?"

Nate snatched open the cage, grabbed ahold of Chipper's feet, strained to pull the big man out. Chipper didn't make it easy. He let his body go slack and chuckled as if that was the funniest thing in the world. Nate shot some volts into him, and the laughter faded like a shout in the wind.

Joshua and Isiah helped him drag the big man out of the cage. They dropped Chipper in the tall grass. He groaned.

"Armpits," Nate said. "Let's lift him and drag him inside. Carefully. Watch he doesn't head-butt you once he gets his bearings."

Inside, they placed him in a chair they'd set up in the unfurnished living room. There was a folding table in the room as well, tools and building materials scattered across the surface. Just props. Nate picked out a twelve-inch spike. They were used to secure railroad ties or landscape timbers, had a galvanized shank at one end. He handed Rachel the stun gun. "Stand close by."

She nodded.

Nate moved to Chipper and yanked off the blindfold, wrenching the big man's neck. Chipper spat blood. He nodded at Nate tapping the spike against his palm. "That 'sposed to spook me, *Spook?*"

"Rachel."

She zapped Chipper. He groaned and slid down in his chair. Recovered fast, though, and scooted himself upright again.

"You serve?" he asked Nate, his voice pinched.

Nate shook his head.

"Didn't think so. You ain't got the discipline."

"You're up in the strip club before dinnertime and I'm undisciplined. That right?"

A cell phone rang out.

Chipper smiled, nodded at the pocket in the front of his shirt. "Someone want to pull this out and answer it? I won't bite."

Nate trapped the spike under his arm, moved to Chipper, carefully, and slipped the cell phone from the big man's pocket. Stepped back and glanced at the screen. Smiling himself then, he passed the phone to Joshua. He looked at it and also smiled.

"Speaking of the strip club," Nate said, seeing the confusion on Chipper's face. "*Chanel*. Gotta hand it to you, Chip. I've seen pictures of your lady. She's thick. Fine as hell . . . for a white bitch. Shame she gave Lace up and you never did."

Some of the color drained from Chipper's face. Still, he held on to the bravado. "Yeah, I share a little too much on Facebook. Kudos to you all for doing some research. You're still probably the dumbest niggers I've ever met, though. You gonna snatch someone, you make sure you liberate them of their technology. Guess they didn't teach you bluegums about GPS at Malcolm X High or wherever the fuck you got your schooling."

The cell phone rang out once more. "Chanel again," Joshua said, glancing at the screen. He turned to Isiah, called out the number for him to remember, then ground the phone into pieces under his boot.

"Hey," Chipper said, practically coming up off his seat. "That's an iPhone XR, asshole."

"Stay focused," Nate said, waving his hand in front of Chipper's field of vision. "You haven't asked why we've taken you. What we want."

"Don't give a shit. You niggers are known to be impulsive. Probably got the idea from a Kanye West song or some shit. You people don't have much to show for yourselves besides Barry Obama . . . and Oprah."

"Why don't you cool it with the act," Isiah called out. "You're scared shitless."

"Well, if it ain't the damn UN of kidnapping," Chipper said, looking over at Isiah. "Is it true your eyes are like that 'cause you have to squint to see your dick?"

"You're a coward."

"How you figure, Ching Chong?"

"We know you vandalized the monument for Mingo Jack."

"I didn't," Chipper said, but Rachel made note of the changed register in his voice.

Isiah was getting to him.

"I poisoned the DNS cache on a forum I found in your computer history," he said. "Redirecting requests to an intermediate proxy allowed me to track IP addresses, even anonymous cowards like you. You were boastful in taking credit for tearing down the original monument. Threatened to do it again when they constructed a new one."

"You're some kind of computer wizard?"

Isiah shrugged.

Chipper said, "But it's wrong to stereotype?"

Nate cleared his throat. "You're a shithead, Chipper. From a long line of shitheads."

"Fuck off, jigaboo."

"Rachel."

She moved forward to zap Chipper once more.

Later, playing it repeatedly in her mind, she would ruminate on how quickly it all happened. Chipper bounding to his feet, using his shoulder to knock her back on her ass. By the time she dusted off the hurt and her pride, Nate had already charged at Chipper and put an end to that confrontation. Rachel stood and moved to see what the other three were staring at. They'd formed a loose circle.

Chipper lay beached on the dusty hardwood, turned halfway onto his right side with his arms awkwardly twisted behind his back.

His eyes were open but flickering like a dying candle. His teeth were smeared red, which briefly confused Rachel. Then she noticed his chest. About a third of the twelve-inch spike jutted from it, pointed down at an odd angle that made it impossible for the sharpened end to have avoided piercing Chipper's heart. Dark red blood pooled the front of his shirt and was already beginning to clot, Chipper's last few breaths spraying it from his mouth as well.

One breath.

Two breaths.

A long pause that would last forever.

Done.

Joshua stared at the dead man with a look of disbelief.

Nate dabbed at his hands and face with the tail of his shirt. He was painted with Chipper's blood. He looked over at Isiah. "Didn't hear you call Lotte," he said.

Cold as an ice cap.

Rachel felt the opposite, overheated, a dark veil coming down over her. Before she realized what was happening, the floor was rushing up at her.

Part II

20

Samuel was pleased that the new guy wouldn't have stood out in a crowded mall food court or on the checkout line at the local Walgreens. He had pale-blue eyes, sandy-brown hair cut close, a clean-shaven face, and wore a simple white T-shirt and black jeans. However, on the negative side of the ledger, there was evidence suggesting he might be a dumbshit. Not long off a federal bid, he'd plead no contest to robbery charges after taking down not one but two 7-Elevens in one night, at gunpoint. The two convenience stores were less than three miles apart and the New Jersey State Police were waiting for him as he strolled out of the second. He claimed to have been drowsy off alprazolam at the time, as if that made it any better.

"Alprazolam," Samuel said. "That's Xanax, correct?"

"Yes, sir." Nodding like he was still on something.

"Ronald Owen Atkins. You have an extremely fortunate name."

"Sir?"

"ROA," Samuel said, raising an eyebrow. "You know? 'Race Over All.'"

"Oh, yes, sir. My parents were nothing if not forward-thinking."

"We have that in common then."

"Sir?"

"My middle name's Wayne. Samuel Wayne Pringle, SWP. 'Supreme—'"

"'White Power.'"

"You were under the impression I needed your help, Ronald Owen Atkins?"

"I'm sorry, sir."

"And why don't you stop slouching like you take it in the ass and paint your toenails?"

The new guy shot up in his seat like a shovel that had been stepped on. Quick compliance, Samuel noted. Obedient as an elevator. That was good. The Righteous Boys were an exclusive group. It took character to pass muster and join their ranks.

"You have any more questions for me, sir?"

Ronald Owen Atkins had shared the details that sparked his evolution in thinking, the politicians he hated the most, as well as those who had his deepest admiration, examples of situations where he believed violence was rightly justified, and what he considered to be the greatest threat to America. He'd admitted to never reading Mussolini's "The Doctrine of Fascism" but committed to correcting that by the weekend. He knew all about David Lane and could recite the Fourteen Words—*We must secure the existence of our people and a future for white children*—without glancing up and to the left. He appeared to be in decent shape and would likely do well with their weekend sparring matches and the group push-ups. He understood the Righteous Boys were the right kind of progressive and, though complimentary of the past, had grown beyond old Third Reich slogans such as "blood and soil."

"We welcome you with open arms, Ronald Owen Atkins," Samuel said, giving a conciliatory nod. "Committed patriot, you're now an enlightened member of the Righteous Boys, tasked along with us, your brothers-in-arms, with reclaiming an America that's true and pure."

"Thank you, sir. I'm chuffed."

Samuel frowned. "I ever hear you say you're chuffed again and we're going to have ourselves a fundamental problem. And I happen to be Samuel. Your father is sir."

"My old man doesn't get that respect," Ronald replied. "He's allowing my sister to date a boy with a Puerto Rican mama. His dad's pure as the driven snow, but still."

"Thought you said your family was forward-thinking, Ronald Owen Atkins?"

"My name was probably accidental," he confessed, a red flush creeping into his cheeks.

Through gritted teeth, Samuel said, "We have mahi-mahi tonight, with spinach and mango salsa. Go grab yourself a plate before it's all gone."

"Thank you, sir."

Alone again, Samuel returned to cataloging his arsenal. He moved everything around like chess pieces on the long oak table positioned in the center of his office. There was .38-caliber ammunition and .223 rounds, the latter used in the bolt-action hunting rifles he favored. There were two snub-nose .357 Magnum revolvers, plus an AR-15, which still left a bad taste in his mouth after he'd learned one of the brothers thought the AR stood for assault rifle. That'd meant an extra sixty push-ups for the imbecile, Samuel recognizing the urgency in keeping the brothers' minds and bodies sharp and in synch.

Speaking of which . . .

He moved over to his desk and picked up the landline, punched in a familiar ten digits. "Send me a girl," he said, and hung up without waiting for a response. By this point, his yearning was well-known. The girl had to be thin enough he could see the lines of her ribs and the points of her hips. She had to have perky nipples that did most of the work in filling an A-cup. Her skin needed to be starved for sun, and her eyes needed to be the color of a robin's egg, and her hair needed to be blonde and cut short like a boy's. She had to be able to engage in a meaningful conversation, had to bruise easily, and had to be the type to never flinch. Ever. If she had a raspy voice, he considered that a bonus.

This one happened to sound like she smoked Pall Malls with her breakfast eggs. She arrived within twenty minutes, gave a short knock to Samuel's office door, and stepped inside the room, bringing with her a haze of black coffee and white flowers. Yves Saint Laurent's *Black Opium*. Samuel knew it and, lucky for the girl, found it agreeable. Her look was agreeable as well. A layered blonde pixie cut, eyes the color of a painted ocean. She wore a black, one-shoulder cutout dress that showed off the fine bones of her chest and absolutely no cleavage. Her lips were painted in a midnight red like a merlot.

"You're . . . *sizeable*," she said. "Six-six? Seven?"

"You have a lovely accent. Botevgrad?"

"Close," she said, her eyes crinkling. "Vratsa. How did you know?"

"What's your name?"

"I'll give you three guesses."

"They didn't tell you I'm staid and not into games?"

"I was told a lot about you."

"That can't be true," Samuel said. "You're smiling."

And she continued smiling as she stepped around him, not even remarking as she passed the table of guns he still had laid out. She settled by the shelves of books stocked in his library, a prodigious collection numbering more than five hundred at last count. Ran her slim fingers over the spines, halting on one, saying, "Oh . . . *The Brothers Karamazov*. You read a lot of Dostoyevsky?"

"Just that, and never all the way through." Samuel moved beside her, gently took the novel from her hand, and pressed it back in its fitted spot on the shelf. "It's an inside joke with myself, because of my father."

"Difficult relationship?"

"Why don't we go sit?"

"Don't be like that," she said, and pouted. "I'd like to know everything I can about you. Is your father also big and handsome? I'd love to meet him. I'm captivated by mature men."

"Too late, I'm afraid. He passed going on eight years back."

"I'm sorry. What of?"

"Suspicious circumstances," Samuel said, smiling.

She didn't reciprocate with a smile of her own. In fact, she colored and raised a hand to her throat, calling attention to the locket hugged against it. It was at the end of a pitifully short chain, which practically turned it into a choker. When Samuel lifted it for a closer look, the woman made a tiny sound and had to stand on her tiptoes, her face shading toward the red of her lipstick as she held in her breath. The girl in the locket was this woman's spitting image, Samuel noticed, though much younger. Perhaps age thirteen or fourteen. There was a story there and he needed to hear it before anything else could happen.

"Who is this?" he asked.

"Sister," the woman gasped, still on her toes, still red in the face.

"Is she dead?"

A tiny nod.

"What happened to her?"

"I'd . . . I'd . . . rather not talk about it."

Radder not tawk.

Samuel smiled at how terribly she'd butchered the words. It wasn't her accent, but rather that her tongue was struggling for space in the small O of her mouth. He'd expertly bunched the locket and a portion of the chain together in his fist, which left it cutting into the woman's neck and spiteful to her circulation. Even though her eyes were beginning to water, she managed to hold Samuel's gaze. "You asked about my father," he said, speaking softly, too softly, "and I told you what I could. But turnabout isn't fair play with you, I see."

"Please," the woman gasped.

"He was a womanizing piece of shit, my father. A heavy-handed and quick-tempered motherfucker, especially coming off a drink. But in fairness, he did the best he could do for me and my brother. Taught me and Chipper to be self-sufficient and not take anyone's shit. And now, looking back, I truly appreciate those lessons."

The woman's eyes were starting to cross. "Please . . . please . . ."

Samuel closed the locket even tighter around her throat.

21

Hands shaking, Joshua managed to pull off his balaclava and use it to mop his head and face. He tried stuffing it in his back pocket, gave up after a few attempts, and left it hanging out like a janitor's white rag. After the initial adrenaline rush, his heart was beginning to slow. Now all he felt was tired, as worn down as he'd ever been. Still, he knew idleness wasn't an option. They had to move. He forced his legs to carry him over to one of the windows, looked out on a side yard choked with Johnson grass and bull thistle. There was nothing else as far as he could see. Isiah had picked the perfect spot. It was secluded out here, safe.

He turned from the window.

Rachel was still on the ground, though now sitting up at least, Isiah crouched beside her, rubbing circles in her back. Nate sat in the chair Chipper had leaped from, flexing his hands, glaring at the dead man on the floor. This had all started because of what had happened to Darius, and now, watching the rest of them frozen in place, Joshua realized he would have to be the catalyst for action.

"We need to get moving," he said.

They all looked in his direction. In all their talks, their planning, they'd never discussed this scenario. It hadn't occurred to them this outcome was a possibility. And they were all showing the effects of it, in their own way. Isiah's skin had a green tinge; Rachel's gaze was a thousand yards off into nowhere; Nate had stopped flexing his hands and was sitting back in the chair.

"What do we need in order to bury him, so he's never found?" Joshua asked.

"Mesh covering," Nate said, coming alive. "Couple of thirty-pound bags of fast-acting lime."

Isiah stood up. "We're going to just pour lime on this man and let it eat up his bones? That's what we're doing, Nate? And you always talk about us not being savages."

"Rachel's got you watching too many Netflix thrillers, I.T. All the lime does is slow decomposition and cut down on the odor. Oh, and we'll need shovels as well. The digging will have to be a team effort."

"This is insane," Isiah said. "You killed him, Nate."

"I'm aware. He called the play, though. I was just defending myself."

"Is that what you'll tell yourself so you can sleep at night?"

Nate got up from the chair and stepped over to Isiah, face-to-face. "See, I'm not a bitch, I.T. I don't have to tell myself anything. He called the play."

"No, you're a psycho," Isiah replied. "I can't believe I ever fell for your bullshit. This has never been about the spirits of your ancestors or that other so-called woke shit you're always talking about. You've been itching to kill one of these *crackers*."

"Well, mission accomplished," Nate said, smiling. "And thank you for your help in getting it done."

Isiah's eyes watered. "I trusted you, Nate. We all did."

Joshua was preparing to step over, put a hand on Isiah's shoulder, but Rachel rose out of her torpor, literally, making it to her feet and pulling her fiancé close. It was a tender display and hauled up thoughts of Alani for Joshua. If he was honest with himself, though he'd hoped it wouldn't come to this—blood on their hands—he'd known the chance existed. Nate had become increasingly volatile.

And they'd all seen it and allowed him to seduce them into continuing. Joshua hadn't liked who he was becoming, either, who he'd become, and had thought it best to leave Alani out of it, out of his life
period. So, he'd broken it off with her. Other than the shit with his
little brother, the breakup with Alani was the most difficult thing
he'd dealt with in a long time—ironic they should happen back-to-
back. His mother talked often about seasons of trouble. Maybe this
was his. Could he come out of it . . . ? He'd almost thought to himself
unscathed, but the dead man answered that question. There was no
getting out of this clean.

"I'll go to the store for the stuff," he announced.

They all turned to him again. He felt terrible, seeing the raw emotion on Isiah's face, his friend's eyes glistening, a tremble in his entire
body Isiah couldn't will away. Rachel, too, she looked pained, though
quite a bit more composed. Nate was Nate.

"Give Joshua the keys, I.T.," he said.

Isiah hesitated a moment, then reached down into his side pocket,
yanking at the key chain. He couldn't get it to dislodge. Nate shook
his head. Rachel gently took ahold of Isiah's wrist and pulled his hand
out of the pocket and reached in herself. She tossed the keys to Joshua.
He snatched them out of the air.

"Two different stores," Nate said. "Break up the order. Pay cash."

Joshua nodded, turned to leave. Turned back just as quickly.
"This is going to be it for me," he said. "But I want you all to know
I really appreciate what you've tried to do for me. Toughest time in
my life, the shit with Darius, and you all were there for me. I'll never
forget that. And, Isiah, I feel as though we *have* settled a few restless
spirits. So, no regrets. All right?"

22

Chanel Anderson thought of herself as a raw talent, an obscure gem, one of those dwarf planets she'd heard about, yet to be discovered. A curvy size ten, with blue eyes that "popped." A head of unruly hair, but it was blonde, and naturally blonde at that, which meant something. She also had a decent enough singing voice, and a rather good personality, so acting wasn't a stretch for her. In fact, some years back now, a producer had come into Lace with a group of Chinese investors, and he'd told Chanel, straight out, he was going to commission— that's the word he'd used—the writer of his latest script to revise the screenplay by adding a character with lines of dialogue especially for her. That was some months before she'd taken up with Chipper, and so, yes, she'd slept with the guy. It wasn't all bad, even though no part in a movie ever materialized and the producer eventually blocked her number. After all, he'd been the one who'd told Chanel her eyes popped, and she used that all the time now to describe herself.

A raw talent, an obscure gem, a dwarf planet with blue eyes that fucking popped, which made it even more pathetic, and deeply angering, that Chanel had to march her ass down to Lace, her past employer, several fucking times a week to pull Chipper out from under some bitch with dimples in her thighs, stretch marks like a clew of earthworms, and regular old eyes.

It was demeaning.

And today Chipper had the audacity to ignore her calls on top of it. Usually he'd pick up, stripper music blaring in the background, and do his best to convince Chanel he was working on someone's bike. All this talk of burned-out clutches and slipped chains to try to throw her off his scent. He'd flash that crooked grin of his as she'd pull him from Lace by the ear and they'd barely make it outside before Chanel would be hypnotized by that smile and slipping off her panties. It was like old times, fucking in the backseat of some old beater at the edge of Lace's parking lot. Sad, really, seeing as she no longer worked the pole here.

Damn you to hell, Chipper.

She was wasting her best years of potential stardom on his ginormous ass. Put a hold on moving from Jersey to California. And he had the fucking audacity to ignore her calls? She was going to kill him.

Lace's familiar smells assaulted her as she stepped inside. Johnson's baby powder, Dollar Tree perfume, beer-soaked ones and fives, Tennessee whiskey and trace amounts of Red Bull. DJ Blaze One was mashing up Maxo Kream's "Meet Again" with some Saweetie. One of the main reasons Chanel had given up the pole— Chipper couldn't tolerate his woman dancing to jungle music. That high morality didn't stop him from coming here, though, early most days, four o'clock, as soon as the place opened.

Chanel expected to find him in his usual spot, the leftmost corner, partially hidden in the shadows, but close enough to the stage so he could slip a bill in the featured girl's breakaway thong without having to work up too much of a sweat. Not seeing him there made her pull up short for a moment. He'd better not be in one of the private rooms getting a lap dance. They'd talked about that after he'd slipped up with that bitch Trinity. To move beyond that drama, Chanel had set some clear boundaries. Had to explain them to Chipper several times, and in a few different ways, because he was shrewd enough to take a person's words and twist them to suit his own purposes.

Lucky for him, he wasn't in one of the private rooms. She'd checked them all, twice.

He wasn't in the head, either.

Chanel pulled aside one of the new recruits, a drink girl, Raevyn, such a silly name. "Hey. Have you seen Chipper?"

The girl was struggling to balance a tray of Stella Artois, teetering in her high heels, makeup caked on to cover a flare of acne. "He was in that Jamaican girl's section," she said.

"Jamaican girl?"

"The one with the numbers tatted on her arm."

"You mean Tonique?"

"Yeah."

"She's Bahamian."

Raevyn shrugged. "Not much difference to me."

"You said Chipper *was* in her section," Chanel said, eager to move on.

"Yeah. Been a minute since I seen him, though."

"Chipper's hard to miss, big as he is."

"Riiight?"

"All right, Raevyn. Thanks."

"No problem, Cherry."

Chanel didn't bother correcting her. Wasn't like they'd ever be more than passing acquaintances. Tonique was the only friend she had here now. And she aimed to keep it that way. After what happened to Briar, Chanel was shy about growing close to the dancers and other talent.

Briar, sweet Briar.

Hustling Chanel to the side on her first night at the club and imploring Chanel to never sit on the velvet couches. "Dried-up jizz and other nasty shit that'll turn your bits into a petri dish," Briar had whispered. Chanel, ripe green at that point, asked what "bits" were, and Briar had laughed until she'd turned lobster red.

Chanel still wrestled with dark thoughts at night, remembering how numb Briar's five-year-old daughter was at the memorial. The journalists parked outside the club, hungry for a steamy tidbit about the dead stripper.

Chanel shook aside those thoughts and scanned the area.

Tonique was over by the bar. Chanel leaned in close and raised her voice so she could be heard above the pulsing music. "What da wybe is?"

Tonique turned, something instantly off with her eyes. "Een nothin'," she replied with no feeling.

Sensing Tonique's discomfort, and remembering she'd been the one to spill the *sip sip* about Trinity, Chanel didn't want to ask the question at hand. Instead, after swallowing, she said, "How's Amerie doing?"

Tonique's daughter.

"Growing like a weed," she said.

No smile, Chanel noticed. Normally, just the mention of her daughter lit Tonique's face like strobe lights.

"Second grade?"

"'Bout to go into third."

"Is she still having trouble sleeping at night?"

"Giving my sister fits," Tonique said. "Renessa's been pressuring me to quit. Find a nine-to-five."

"Mmm."

"You miss it?"

"The money," Chanel said. "Otherwise . . ."

They fell silent. DJ Blaze One had the walls thumping with the bass of Billie Eilish's "Bad Guy," cutting it up, not letting it get beyond the first stanza. Two, three, no, four times, Chanel opened her mouth to say what needed to be said, but each time she faltered.

A deep frown creased Tonique's forehead. "Chipper was getting cozy with some chick looked like that singer girl, she's got the video where she's dressed up like a cyborg in a white bodysuit."

"You mean Taylor Swift?"

Tonique shrugged. "If you say so. I'm not into her music."

"This girl with Chipper one of the new dancers?"

"Patron. She bought him a drink."

"Michelob Ultra," Chanel whispered, because she couldn't think of anything else to say.

"Yeah. He didn't even register that you and I were friends."

"Did he and this woman . . ."

"I saw them head out through the back together," Tonique said. "I'm really sorry."

"His truck is in the lot."

"Wait him out then."

Chanel shook her head. "I don't think I will. I appreciate you letting me know about Taylor Swift."

"You gonna be all right?"

Chanel smiled. "What did you tell me when you were going through all the shit with Duncan?"

"That whole situation's a blur to me, I'm sorry."

"Men are only good for two things," Chanel said. "Fixin' shit . . ."

"And breaking shit." Tonique nodded. "Now I remember."

"I'll see you around, bey."

Tonique gave a tiny smile as Chanel stepped away.

Once outside, she fumbled her phone from her pocket, shakily punched in Chipper's number. And for probably the fifth or sixth time it went straight to voicemail. She left a brief message that was clear and unambiguous enough that Chipper would understand it and not think he'd be able to twist her words. "You are so dead."

23

Isiah stared out into the distance, the air thick with the smell of roiled earth and rotted vegetation. He was exhausted from shoveling, eyes grainy and bloodshot. The four of them going about the work silently. So, this was it? The end. Other than his upcoming marriage, he couldn't think of anything that made him happier. They'd begun this with a noble enough purpose, but that had finished a long time past, if he was being honest. Nate had corrupted them all. Isiah was surprised to find he felt something near hatred toward his friend.

"This is deep enough."

"Oh, yes, most grand exalted ruler," Isiah said, saluting and letting his shovel fall to the ground like toppled blocks. Rachel was beside him and kicked his foot. Joshua pulled the balaclava from his back pocket and wiped his face and head again; he'd been doing that relentlessly this entire time. Nate stared across at Isiah from the other side of the dug grave. The separation was good. Isiah was wired so tight he might be crazy enough to try to wrap his dirt-caked fingers around Nate's throat.

"We're in this together," Nate said to all of them, but Isiah felt the need to respond.

"Wasn't me that jabbed a stake in his heart like he was Dracula."

"It was you that found the perfect place for his eternal rest, though."

Isiah swallowed because there was inarguable truth to that. They were burying Chipper right beside the abandoned two-story Cape Cod Isiah had found online less than a week ago. He remembered rushing in on Rachel, who'd been showering at the time, and telling her, "I found a place." His heart had been kicking in his chest, and not just because his future wife was naked and dripping water.

"Let's lift him and lower him in," Nate said.

Again, silently, they all moved to Chipper, laid out on a drab green army blanket. They each crouched and grabbed a handful of a corner. Without anything having to be said, they lifted at the same time. Of course, Isiah felt his grip beginning to slip. The dead weight of Chipper's corpse *pluffed* the dirt before he could call out to warn the others. "Shit. Sorry."

"I'd say something," Nate remarked, chuckling and shaking his head, "but what is there to say at this point? You're nothing if not consistent, I.T."

"Fuck you."

"Why don't you let Rachel hold *both* corners, and you can give her . . . encouragement?"

"Double fuck you."

Nate snickered. "Jesus. Just lift."

They tried it again, Chipper's arm falling over the side as they got him raised, just a man lazing on a hammock. Isiah gasped. He didn't like to gasp but found he did it often.

"What now?" Nate said. "You need us to lower him so you can stop to wee-wee?"

"No," Isiah said, speaking softly. "So we can remove the Apple Watch we missed."

Nate frowned and took a closer look, his shoulders going slack as he saw that unfortunately Isiah was right.

They'd fucked this up in so many ways. Gotten so frazzled fighting off Chipper at the strip club they'd forgotten his truck in the lot. And now the watch.

No chance it wouldn't come back to haunt them.

24

If not for the Toyota Prius parked in the small lot, he might've thought he had the wrong place. A dentist's office, maybe. Or an insurance agency. A photographer's studio, though with everyone having first-rate cameras on their cell phones these days, he couldn't imagine the talent and grit it must take to make a go of that. Nevertheless, the sign on the front lawn, which was bordered with boxwoods, azaleas, and hydrangeas, listed the sole occupant of this ranch as *December's Promise*.

Elizabeth Brantley's nonprofit.

Mason shut off his engine and sat there awhile, working up his nerve. It didn't dawn on him for several minutes that his presence, the only car besides the Prius in the lot, probably had alerted Elizabeth and brought her to look out of one of the windows. Surprise was no longer in his favor. He'd given her enough time to have locked all the doors and called the police.

"Well done, Mason."

He sighed and stepped out of the car, letting the door slam closed. What did it matter? As quiet as it was here, he couldn't have made a noisier entrance if he'd come with a college marching band, the brass, woodwind, and percussion sections working seamlessly through an arrangement of Stravinsky's *The Rite of Spring*.

Walking across the lot, he played over what he would say to

Elizabeth. Another apology was in order and then he'd confess that he hadn't slept well since they last spoke on the side of the road under an umbrella of longleaf pines. He would once again admit that he'd badly bungled the visit with Jean Williams, he'd betrayed Elizabeth in the process, and, honestly, he didn't deserve the "seven times seventy" forgiveness talked about in the Bible. If Elizabeth never wanted to see his face again, that would be understandable. More than understandable. But if she could find it somewhere in her heart to forgive him and start over, he'd be extremely grateful.

"Who are you talking to?"

Mason jumped. How had he missed her, crouching on the side of the building, rolling up what looked to be a blue tarp?

"Elizabeth," he said as she stood to her full height. Barefoot, as usual.

"What are you doing here, Mason?"

"'Bout to do some painting?" he asked.

She frowned. "What now?"

He nodded at the tube of plastic she'd rolled up on the ground. "That's a drop cloth, isn't it?"

"Banner for a fundraiser next month. I had it displayed out front. Someone tore it down."

"I'm sorry."

"The human capacity for evil doesn't even surprise me any longer, Mason," she said, focusing her gaze on his face. "I see it *everywhere* I look."

"You do all this alone?" he said, changing the subject. "I noticed it's just your car in the lot."

"Amazing. Look at those deductive powers on full display."

"You have a right to still be upset with me."

"Appreciate you giving me the permission."

Mason squinted, and not from the sun. "Probably everything I say will be wrong, won't it?"

"From the relatively small sample size of which I have to judge you," Elizabeth said, "probably so."

"Ouch."

"Why are you here, Mason?"

"Didn't like how we left things. Thought I'd give it another try with you."

"I'm not—"

"Damn," Mason said. "Hold that thought."

He didn't run so much as walk briskly back to his car. He clicked the locks as he neared it. White Styrofoam container sitting on the passenger seat where he'd stupidly left it. He leaned across and pulled it out.

"Toasted coconut cream pie," he told Elizabeth as he rejoined her. "From the place over in Irondale you mentioned."

There was something in her violet eyes, but she said, "Bribery won't work."

"Consider it more of a peace offering," he told her. "Couple things I wanted to ask you. To say to you. Thought you might be more willing to hear me out if I brought your favorite pie."

"Gimme," she said finally, waggling her fingers.

Mason did. And followed her inside to her office setup. Sat down across from her as she settled behind her desk. "You have until I finish this slice," she said, cutting into the pie with a plastic fork, shoveling the piece in her mouth.

"December's Promise," Mason said. "The name has something to do with Rosa Parks?"

Elizabeth Brantley stopped chewing, looked at him. But she didn't speak.

"What was it . . . December first, 1954, when she—"

"Fifty-five," Elizabeth corrected.

Mason nodded. "One of the seminal moments in the civil rights movement, and right here in Alabama. I thought it might be what you meant."

"Lucky guess."

Mason smiled. He'd made up some ground with her.

Honesty would have to be at the forefront moving forward. He sure hoped she would allow them to move forward.

"What is your deal?" she asked.

"I'm married," he blurted.

"O . . . kay."

"Her name's Bella."

"Beautiful name. Does it suit her?"

"Very much so," Mason said.

"That's nice."

"I haven't told her I was fired."

"Why not?"

"We're . . ." He searched for the right word. "Broken."

Elizabeth smiled. A sad smile, he thought. It didn't reach her violet eyes.

"What about you?" Mason asked her. "Are you married?"

She looked around at her office. "I most certainly am. To this."

"I can't tell you how much I admire your passion and commitment."

"I don't need you patronizing me, Mason."

"I wouldn't think of doing that, Miss Elizabeth."

Her throat rippled from a swallow, and he knew for certain then that he was getting some traction. And that mattered. He wanted ever so badly to crack through her surface.

"My wife," he began, and took a moment to clear his throat, gather his thoughts, "she hasn't left the house in . . . she was assaulted by a group of boys, black boys, and it did something to her. To us."

Elizabeth frowned, said, "Is that why you're—"

"No," Mason said. "Well, maybe a part of it. Honestly, I don't know how to think any differently about things than I do. I wasn't raised to look at anyone as if I was better than them. And for the most part, I haven't. I know I'm not supposed to mention I've had black friends, but I have. Not recently. And not my closest friends when I did, but . . . friends. Natural. Nothing I ever put too much thought into."

"Okay."

"But I witnessed some things when I was with BPD. Anyone wants to argue the blacks are their own worst enemy at times won't get any pushback from me."

"It's a shame you feel that way."

"I'm being as truthful as possible here, Elizabeth."

"I know you are."

Mason didn't respond to that.

"Legacy matters," Elizabeth said after some time. "You've read about the lynchings on my website. That's just one ugly part of it, Mason. Slavery, wage inequity, inferior educational opportunities, inadequate health care, mass incarceration. And on and on. Most of it systemic and purposefully carried out by white people."

"I'd like to be able to look at this stuff the way you do, the way my daughter does."

"But . . ."

"I've seen too much, Elizabeth. And that's shaped me, I'm afraid. But I don't like the idea of having hate in my heart. Toward anyone. I've witnessed firsthand what that does. It's poison. It destroys things that should matter."

"Are you talking about your marriage, Mason?"

He thought for a second. "I guess I am."

It hadn't crossed his mind until this moment that his marriage was completely and utterly destroyed. Destroyed meant something was damaged beyond repair. Did that hold true for him and Bella? Sure felt like it. After what had seemed like a breakthrough just a week or so ago, she hadn't allowed him to touch her these past days, walking around in a stupor, not giving any indication she heard him when he ventured to speak to her.

And his desire to say much of anything to his wife, to fight to regain what they once had—in all honesty, it really hadn't been there. Destroyed.

"I noticed something sad in you," Elizabeth said, pulling him back from his thoughts. "I wondered where it came from. You said a few things that made me think you might be a widower, but I didn't want to pry."

"You could've asked me."

"I suppose so."

"Will you help me, Elizabeth?"

"With what?" she said, touching her neck.

"I need to find the four I told you about."

"Right down to business, huh?"

"We both could benefit."

"How so?"

"I'm a mess. Always have been, I suppose. My daughter, Nicole, she'd tell you. My . . . Bella would say the same if she was being honest. But there's one thing I'm good at."

"I won't even venture a guess."

"I'm a dog on a bone when it comes to getting at the truth of something."

"Okay."

"You've shed light on a dark part of our country's history, but"—and Mason raised a hand—"what good has your research done for Jean Williams and others like her?"

"Interesting strategy," Elizabeth said. "Diminishing my life's work to get me to help you. Call me convinced."

"The four maniacs I told you about are going about it the wrong way, but they've hit on something. Somebody does need to be held to account for all the bad stuff that's happened. I believe in law and order."

"Sounds good, but I'm afraid Jean was right," Elizabeth said. "My zealousness has made me foolish. The men responsible for killing her father are dead and gone."

"Maybe in her case. But that's not true across the board, I bet. You help me catch these four and I'll make sure your work has some real lasting impact. Together we'll make sure the bad deeds of the past don't go unpunished. At the very least, we can call some real attention to what was done, maybe get some courts to take a closer look."

"I don't know that it's a good idea for me to get involved with you, Mason." She colored. "I mean, we think so differently. It would be an uneasy *business* arrangement."

"Get a sense you don't like things easy, Miss Elizabeth."

She sighed and sat there for a moment. Then, finally, she said, "How would I even help you?"

"I want to talk to some of the descendants. You have names and other records that would help greatly."

"That didn't work out so well with Jean, Mason."

"The white descendants," he said. "Surely you trust me with them."

25

The cottage was in Montague and exactly what one would expect from a pricey Airbnb. Whitewashed walls, dark hardwood floors, decor sourced from Cuban flea markets. A sprawling view of the rolling pickle-green hills off in the distance. Joshua crouched by the front door. Lifted a galvanized steel bucket bursting with pink hydrangeas. A key lay exposed like a revealed lie. He hesitated a moment, then picked up the key and placed the bucket back in place.

Once inside the cottage, he moved down the entry hall to the den, where a wall of windows flanked a stacked stone fireplace. A woman lay fast asleep on a leather sectional.

Joshua shook her shoulder, and she came awake in stages.

Sadie Webb's caramel skin, bold cheekbones, and lively hazel eyes defined her. She carried herself with the bearing of a woman who ruled over a kingdom. Language, posture, clothes. The central air-conditioning was blowing hard, and she wore a cream wool sweater paired with black pants. A pair of the Louboutin heels she preferred sat upright on the floor. She had expensive tastes and never went hungry.

"Mr. Adams," she said, sitting up and stretching.

"Mrs. Webb."

She blinked her eyes, likely an effort to get her vision in order. "What time is it?"

"I know," Joshua said. "I'm late."

He'd debated not coming.

"I cooked," Sadie said.

"Really?" Joshua said, surprise clear in his voice.

"It's scary that I can't seem to lie to you." Sadie smiled. "I ordered well, how's that?"

"That's fine. But I'm not starving."

"For food, you mean?"

Joshua forced a smile of his own. "You have something else in mind?"

"Do I ever."

They'd met at a DNC fundraising event last summer, headlined by Donna Brazile. In the year since, they'd hooked up five times that he could remember. Sadie probably had a better recollection since she had to coordinate their time together with her husband's time away.

"Don't let me forget to tell you about this couple I want you to meet," she said.

"What couple?"

She smiled. "Can't that wait until after?"

"What couple?"

"Geez. Somebody's irritable."

"Sadie . . ."

"Okay," she said, raising a hand. "Power couple making waves in DC. Husband's an architect with some big-shit firm in San Francisco. Commutes between there and PG County. When Abu Dhabi identified Al Maryah Island as its new financial center, they hired his firm to create a comprehensive design plan for the development. He led the project."

This was more Nate's purview, and Joshua suddenly wondered

why he was here. Why he'd picked *this* married woman to get involved with. They didn't fit.

Did he have any morals at all left?

"And the wife?" he asked.

"Was a model," Sadie said. "Born in London, Brent. English father, Jamaican mother. Went to Malorees Junior School and Hampstead School. King's College in Cambridge. I'm telling you all this, but she'll tell you as well. She makes a point of bringing it up in *every* conversation. Also, she's quite proud that she grew up on a council estate and made it out."

"Council estate?"

"You'd call it the projects," Sadie said, her nose wrinkling by instinct.

Joshua nodded. "Great. Can't wait to meet them both."

"I deliver donors, Mr. Adams. You know Sadie has your back."

"You almost sounded down to earth for a moment there," Joshua said.

Sadie frowned and stood from the couch. She moved close to him and reached for his hands. He let her take them. "You're a good brother," she said. "I know we don't have an existential relationship, but if you were ever in trouble, I hope you know you could come to me."

He couldn't.

That's part of the reason he'd been able to justify this . . . whatever it was.

"I know it," he said.

"I don't know what's going on with you. You're tense. What's happening?"

"What isn't?"

"That's not really an answer, Joshua."

"You been following the Cedric Browne news?"

"Who?"

"Black man in Alabama. Cops killed him."

"I don't worry myself with that nonsense," Sadie said, waving off the notion.

"What is politics if not activism?"

"Power," Sadie said. "I thought you knew that."

He'd parroted one of Nate's lines and got back what he deserved. A response that made him feel even worse about himself and everything he'd done in the past few years. All the talk of making sure Darius didn't die in vain, that his memory lived on, and here Joshua was in bed with a woman who represented almost nothing he claimed to hold dear.

He was a fraud.

A fraud with blood on his hands.

"I bet he did something," Sadie said.

Joshua, lost in his thoughts, frowned. "I'm sorry. What?"

"The man in Alabama. I'm not one for believing the police are just going around targeting black men for no reason."

"And women," Joshua said.

"What?"

"Sandra Bland."

"Didn't she kill herself?"

"That's just—" He didn't even know how to respond.

"Enough of this," Sadie said, pulling at his hand. "Come blow my back out."

"Down to earth," Joshua whispered, and he let her lead him to the bedroom.

He wasn't feeling inclined toward sex, not deep in his bones at least. But there was the hope that going through the motions could quiet his gusty mind.

In the bedroom, Sadie tore off her clothes and he did the same and tossed them to the floor.

Soon as they'd finished, Sadie rose from the bed and started plucking her clothes from where she'd tossed them. "I have a thing I need to get to," she said. "Stay if you like; it's rented through the weekend. Don't forget to put the key back. I'll be in touch to introduce you to the Carmichaels."

"Carmichaels?" Joshua said, barely a whisper.

"Couple I was telling you about."

"Right."

Sadie kissed his forehead and was gone.

Tears fell from Joshua's eyes when he heard her Land Rover crunch over the gravel outside.

He sat with them.

26

Though it wasn't anything new, it surprised Nate to answer his door to a young girl with unruly, rust-colored hair and lively brown eyes. Darius's girlfriend was wearing a short lavender sundress and her usual white sneakers. Deeply tanned, so Nate couldn't tell whether there was any redness splotching her nose and cheeks. She hadn't been sheepish, as it were, in sharing her newfound fondness for Smirnoff Grape vodka. It kept her nightmares about Darius at bay.

The first time she'd come, Nate had asked her a lot of questions. The second time, the roles reversed. Each time since had been them getting to know each other. Feeling each other out. He'd wanted to know what made Darius love her. She'd wanted to know whether Nate had any limits.

They moved this silent conversation to the kitchen. Nate pulled two tall glasses from the cabinet over the sink, filled both with ice cubes and tap water. They settled in chairs, on opposite sides of the dining table. Sofia tinkled the ice in her glass. Took long swallows of the cold water, drumming her fingers on the table between gulps. Nate nursed his drink.

"Well?" he said.

It took her a moment. "I have news. Austin's living in Pennsylvania."

Nate frowned. "Who told you that?"

"It's kind of convoluted."

"You really should be in college, Sofia."

She blinked and Nate felt something inside of him shift.

"You ready for the address?"

"Keep it."

"What?" Sofia's voice notched up an octave. "But you said—"

"Doesn't matter what I said."

"You're not gonna do anything?"

"Like what?"

She shrugged. "Make Austin pay for what he did."

"An acquittal's an acquittal," Nate said, not even believing his own ears. "His attorneys argued self-defense and won, Sofia."

Her eyes brimmed with tears. "You're gonna let them get away with it?"

"They won."

"Darius wouldn't have attacked those boys. Austin was starting shit with him in the store."

"You had your say in court."

"Bullshit verdict," she muttered.

"I know it," Nate replied, his voice raspy.

"But you won't do anything?"

"Nothing I can do."

"It doesn't make you mad they got off?"

"You have no idea how mad it makes me," he admitted.

Sofia wiped her eyes with the back of her hand. Straightened her posture. "Then I don't understand. Why won't you track them down—at least Austin—and make him pay?"

"If I did, would it bring Darius back?"

"Course not."

"No point then," Nate told her.

"I can't believe it. You're a pussy."

"Think it's time for you to go, Sofia."

"Punk-ass bitch."

Nate stood and moved around to her side of the table, tried to take her arm. Sofia shrugged him aside. Rose from her chair on her own. Defiant, though, rooted in place, glaring at him.

"It's all right for you to buy some sneakers other than white," Nate told her. "And, please, get yourself in school. What's your community college down in Monmouth County? Brookdale? You could enroll there if you aren't up for four years just yet."

"You think I give a shit about an associate degree. You know why I came to you? 'Cause Darius thought you cared about him."

"I—"

"Fuck you!"

Nate didn't walk with her as she stormed from the kitchen. Didn't move, even after he heard his front door slam. She had no idea what she was talking about. No idea the cost that came with seeking revenge. She hadn't struggled to look at herself in the medicine cabinet mirror these past few days. Pupils the size of dimes because she hadn't been sleeping and her nose had been running and her eyes had been watering and she'd gone a bit overboard with the Benadryl.

She knew nothing.

Nothing about revenge.

Nothing about death.

Nothing about the toll of either.

Nate took her glass and set it down with care on the landfill of dishes in his sink. He'd load them in the dishwasher later. Now he wanted a hot shower and an Ambien nap. Craving sleep was surprising because Chipper tended to start talking shit to Nate as soon as Nate closed his eyes.

He was in the bathroom, testing the water with his fingers, when he heard the chime of his doorbell. He hoped Sofia had gotten her arms around her emotions and was ready to talk about the future. Her future. Nate wasn't certain he had one.

He turned off the water, dried his hands on the towel hanging by the door, and went to answer his bell. He'd be gracious if Sofia apologized for calling him a pussy. Darius had loved her, and Nate was doing his best to give her some approximation of love. He hoped to continue getting a close-up look at the heart medallion and silver chain around her neck for a long time to come. It looked so much more at home there than in the plastic evidence bag the police had given his aunt Dot and Joshua.

Remarkably, he was smiling as he opened the front door.

But the smile died a quick death.

Not Sofia.

A man in slacks, a collared shirt, Windsor-knotted tie.

Tailored jacket with extra material around the waist.

Likely to hide the bulge of the police-issued gun in its holster.

27

"**Would you like** some breakfast, Karina?"

She shook her head and blew blood from her left nostril. Samuel handed back her ripped black dress and she used it as a handkerchief. Did the same for the other nostril and sat there on the side of the cot in his office, clutching the dress. Tears streaked down her cheeks. The undersides of her eyes were smeared black. Reddish-brown marks tracked up both of her skinny arms and across her stomach. Cigarette burns. She hadn't given up her name easily.

"You're sure? We're serving chocolate chip pancakes."

Again, she shook her head.

"Use your words, Karina."

"No," she said. "I am not hungry."

"You sound irritated."

"Will you let me go?"

"Of course," Samuel told her. "Eventually."

Sooner than later. He was tiring of her. It'd taken longer than he would've liked for her to set aside her fear after he'd choked her with the locket. However, to her credit, once she'd done so, she'd been a revelation. Durable as fuck, intelligent, good with her mouth. Not that it lasted. Like riding a roller coaster, dealing with this woman. As the early evening had stretched to late night and, now to a new day altogether, Karina had grown morose. Samuel suspected she wasn't enjoying herself. He certainly wasn't anymore. "I can't leave us on this downturn," he said, stroking her face. "That would be bad mojo. I say we liven up things a bit before you leave. How does that sound, Karina?"

Her eyes teared up, and her jaw trembled. "Please . . ."

"That's the spirit," Samuel said, smiling.

He slipped into his pants and moved to his desk. Picked up the landline and dialed a number he'd just recently committed to memory. "Come up to my office," he said, and hung up. His calls were always brief and one-sided.

Karina started working at lifting the dress to ease over her head, wincing with the movement.

"Not yet," Samuel said, taking the dress from her, dropping it on the end of the cot.

"Someone is coming. No?" she asked.

"Not enough time for you to fix your makeup. But perhaps you can find your smile?"

A soft knock sounded at the door.

Karina began to immediately sob again.

Samuel yelled out that the door was unlocked.

It opened a hair and Ronald peered into the room. "You wanted me, sir?"

"Come in and close the door," Samuel said. "Lock it behind you."

"What's . . . what's going on, sir?" Ronald asked, his gaze darting between the naked woman and Samuel.

"Ronald Owen Atkins, Karina," Samuel said. "Karina, Ronald Owen Atkins."

Ronald nodded and gave her a small wave. Karina's crying only intensified.

"Take off your pants, Ronald Owen Atkins," Samuel said.

"Sir?"

"Posthaste." Samuel waved his hand. "Karina's already warmed up for you."

Ronald swallowed.

"Is there a problem?" Samuel asked him.

"I'm not sure she wants this, sir."

"Don't let the tears fool you. There's nothing Karina wants more. Isn't that right, honey?"

Ronald said, "I'd rather not—"

The short flourish of a trumpet stole his thought. Royal Fanfare. A ringtone. Samuel grabbed his cell phone from the table where he'd spread his guns yesterday. They were stored and locked away now. He hadn't wanted to test the battered woman from Bulgaria with that temptation.

He disengaged the lock, stepped out into the hallway, leaving the door to his office open wide. "Chanel?" he said into the phone. He had her number programmed, but she never called him. He never called her either. She was his brother's fat whore and of no concern to Samuel.

"Something has happened to Chipper," she said, getting right to it.

"What something?"

"He left Lace with a woman. I think it was a setup of some kind. His truck's still in the lot."

Samuel didn't say anything, processing what he was being told.

"Chipper never stays gone overnight," Chanel added. "He knows better. I'd never let him back in."

"Tell me about this woman he left with."

"Taylor Swift."

"Chipper left with Taylor Swift?"

"Sorry," Chanel said. "A look-alike."

"Leaving with this woman doesn't really mean anything. She could've been having car trouble and learned that Chipper's a mechanic."

"He works on bikes."

"Something to consider is all, Chanel."

"Chipper doesn't know it," she said, "but I downloaded the Find People app and shared the location when I gave him that Apple Watch."

"He's aware," Samuel said.

"What?"

"He told me he didn't have anything to hide from you," Samuel said. "That he's off the wayward path."

"You're being for real?"

"Yes, ma'am."

A beat of silence, then, "Now I think I'm even more worried."

"Where is the app saying he is?"

"Salem County."

Samuel frowned, said, "There's nothing out there."

"Exactly."

"Text me the info. I'll check this out."

They disconnected and he went back inside his office. Karina was still sitting on the cot, once again holding the black dress. And Ronald stood at the foot of the bed, holding his pants. He'd taken the time to fold them into a neat rectangle. Despite seeing that, Samuel couldn't muster the energy to be angry. He told Karina she was free to go, and she hopped up and breezed past him, wiggling into the dress as she moved, not even wincing. Adrenaline, probably.

Ronald's face reddened as Samuel turned to face him. "I couldn't—"

"Never mind that. We've got a full calendar of events with the brothers today. Then we're taking a little trip."

"Where to?"

"Just get dressed. Where we're going doesn't matter for you."

Salem fucking County.

Over one hundred miles, and close to two hours' traveling time.

What the fuck would Chipper be doing way out there?

Samuel didn't like the possibilities.

28

Isiah stepped out of his bedroom and shuffled in stocking feet toward the kitchen for a glass of orange juice. Since they'd buried Chipper, he'd been moving around his place without thinking too much. That wasn't to suggest his mind was free and clear—impossible after all that had happened. But a sense of calm had settled over him and he knew what had to be done. In the twelve-step programs, it was the fifth step: admitting to God, to ourselves, and to another human being the exact nature of our wrongs.

"Look who's finally among the land of the living."

Rachel called him from the other room. He didn't respond. Instead, he moved past her and into the kitchen, where he grabbed a tumbler glass from one of the cabinets, poured it full of juice, took a sleeve of Ritz crackers from the box on the counter, and settled down at the table. Not the best breakfast, but he'd make do.

"I've been researching honeymoon locations," Rachel said from the doorway.

"I thought we'd agreed on St. Lucia."

"That was all me," she reminded him. "You argued for something different."

"And you said what mattered was that we were together."

She came in and sat across from him. "Australia. Place called the

Whitsundays. It's comprised of seventy-four islands, only eight of which are inhabited. 'Exhilarating sunsets over turquoise waters and romantic nights under swaying palm trees' is how the site I looked at describes it. It could be just the two of us on a beach, Isiah. Isn't that amazing?"

"Do you know anything about Australia's coat of arms?" he asked.

Rachel frowned. "What?"

"It has a kangaroo and an emu on it. It's thought neither animal can move backward, but that's not true. They just seldom do."

"Interesting," Rachel said in an uninterested voice.

"Advance Australia is sort of the country's unofficial motto. Advance. As in move forward rather than backward."

"Are you okay, Isiah?"

"Better than ever," he said, smiling.

"I don't think that's true."

He looked at her, really looked at her, and the entire pretense slipped away. His shoulders sagged and he let out a long breath, sat back in his chair and closed his eyes. "I can't stop thinking about Chanel."

"His . . . girlfriend?"

Neither of them could say Chipper's name any longer, all personal pronouns on the few occasions they'd referenced him. Nothing personal about it, despite the description.

"She must be going out of her mind," Isiah said. "How would you feel if I went missing?"

"Terrible. But you need to stop thinking about that."

"I'm not sure I can."

"You're obsessing over her, and it isn't healthy. Don't think I didn't notice her resemblance to your sister."

Isiah didn't say anything. Julie was thinner, her hair longer, eyes not as vivid and blue as Chanel's were in her Facebook profile. But, yeah, there was some resemblance. Still, he doubted Chanel grew up as the prized birth daughter in a white family who adopted a stray from Daejeon. Doubted she had a little beige brother she coddled and loved, protected and defended. He doubted that brother had grown apart from her, breaking her heart, that he'd eventually resented her like he did the rest of the family.

"Babe?"

Isiah reached across and picked up the tumbler glass, took a sip, set it down hard. Juice splashed. "I have to do something."

A frown from his wife-to-be. "Do something? Like what?"

"I could send her an anonymous message, letting her know he won't be coming home." Isiah felt as though he might cry. "She can at least have closure."

"Not a good idea. Nate would go apeshit if he heard you talking this way."

"Fuck Nate."

"You're just bursting with unhealthy emotions."

"Hating that motherfucker is unhealthy?"

"Since when do you use these words, Isiah?"

"Since that motherfucker dragged us into this shit, made us accessories to murder."

"Accomplices," Rachel said.

"Huh?"

"We were there . . . and involved. Every step of the way."

Isiah grunted and took another sip of the juice. "Fucking Nate," he muttered.

"It's not on him, Isiah. We knew what we were doing. From the beginning, we knew. And we kept going. Because we were angry about Darius and didn't know what else to do with our rage. Nate came up with a plan. A good one, despite how it's turned out."

Isiah frowned. "You're an evangelist for the motherfucker now?"

"Please stop talking this way. It doesn't suit you."

"Oh, what, I'm not bad-boy enough to talk how I'm actually feeling?"

"It's not about being bad, Isiah. Don't lose yourself in all this."

"Too late for that, wifey."

"What are you going to do?"

"I told you."

"Contact this Chanel woman?"

Isiah nodded.

"I'm asking you not to," Rachel said.

"This will have to be one of the few times I defy your orders," Isiah replied, smiling.

"I'll have to tell Nate what you're planning."

His smile disappeared. "The fuck you say, Rache?"

"It's not a good idea, babe. You're not thinking clearly."

Isiah studied her, really studied her. "I'm wondering why you're always defending him."

"What are you talking about?" Rachel said, her voice quavering.

"It's like you're a cheerleader for the motherfucker," Isiah said.

Rachel pushed back her seat, a loud screeching sound on the linoleum, and stood to her feet. "Think I'll go take a run. Please don't do anything rash."

"You were going to tell me something about Nate the other day and I stopped you."

"It was nothing," Rachel said.

"You fucked him, didn't you?"

"What?"

"Nate," Isiah said. "You fucked him."

"Why would you ask me that?"

"Why haven't you answered?"

"You know what, Isiah? Fuck *you*."

He flinched a minute later as the front door slammed.

Yeah, Isiah, he thought, fuck you.

29

Mason touched his brakes and cursed. The road was flooded by the storm. Quite frustrating, because after the long drive from Elizabeth's office he was at the verge of I-65 North, three-quarters of the way home to Huntsville. He'd have to find another way now. He completed a K-turn to backtrack, weaving to avoid a minefield of potholes brimming with rainwater. His knuckles were red from gripping the steering wheel, the muscles churning in his jaw. "What a holy fuck of a day," he exclaimed, and in the next instance, he hit one of the ruts square-on, and his car briefly veered out of control, then sagged at the front end. A carload of teenagers just missed rear-ending him. The driver leaned on her horn as she blew past. Several of her passengers hung out the windows and gave Mason the finger.

Truly a holy fuck of a day.

Once he got his heartbeat to slow, he flashed his hazards and stepped out into the hard, slanting rain to check for damage. His front right tire was a scarf on the rim, completely flat. He stared at it dumbly and blinked water from his eyes. Changing a tire in these blustery conditions was the last thing he wanted to do. Right next to going home. Sighing, he moved back inside his car, pulled out his cell phone. It took a couple of tries with his fingers wet, but eventually he was able to punch in a number.

"Aren't you tired of talking on the phone today?" Elizabeth asked.

"I've got a slight problem."

"That's an understatement."

"Blew a flat," Mason said, trudging ahead despite her attitude. "Storm is raging. And in my infinite wisdom, I gave up Triple A a year ago."

Bella had warned him not to.

"Sorry to hear that," Elizabeth replied. "But what do you want from me?"

"Honestly, I don't know. I'm sorry I disturbed you. I'll let you get back to whatever you were doing. Take care, Miss Elizabeth."

"Crap," she said softly. "Where are you?"

Mason told her and then the phone went silent. She'd disconnected. He assumed that meant she was coming for him. It might be a poor assumption, but it was all he had in the moment. He started the car and risked driving it the ten feet that put him on the grass and out of the roadway.

With nothing to do but wait, he closed his eyes and his thoughts drifted back to the hours he'd just spent in Elizabeth's office, her sitting shoulder to shoulder with him as he started working through calls to the descendants. Something about Elizabeth's closeness energized him, even though she was clearly troubled by what he was doing and didn't attempt to hide it.

"Just one documented lynching in North Dakota," she said. "They wrote the story as a poem in the local paper. It's shocking to read. Callous. That's what I mean when I talk about legacy. This is serious stuff, Mason. None of us should ever forget what was done to black people in this country. Is still done."

Mason, unsure of what to say, kept quiet. The wrong response.

"Nothing?"

"Elizabeth, I—"

"Forget it." She'd turned her laptop screen so he could see the

Facebook page of the grandson of one of the men involved in that long-ago offense. "Stephen Thomas."

Thomas was a double amputee with a sleeve of tattoos on his right arm and a long, scraggly red beard that hung down the front of his olive drab T-shirt. His eyes were hidden behind gas station sunglasses but were likely pale blue, possibly green. One of the more prominent posts on his page was of a Bible verse, Malachi 2:3. *Behold, I will corrupt your seed, and spread dung upon your faces, even the dung of your solemn feasts, and one shall take you away with it.*

"I sort of lost interest after 'God is great, God is good. Let us thank Him for our food,'" Mason had said. "But I can appreciate Mr. Thomas's zeal."

Elizabeth looked at him.

"How did you manage all of this?" he asked. "Compiling the details of all those lynching deaths."

"Murders."

"Right. Lynching *murders*. Plus, phone numbers for many of the descendants . . . black and white." He nodded at her computer screen. "Their social media, in some cases. I can't even imagine the work that went into this."

"Grant funding," Elizabeth said. "It allowed me to bring in interns from UAB at a prevailing wage. They should get the credit."

"I'm sure you didn't sit around on your hands," Mason said. "That's not who you are."

"Why don't you go ahead and call Mr. Thomas?"

"I just—"

"It's getting late, Mason. And it's looking like a storm."

Outside, the sky had been colored in a strange, purplish haze. Definitely a storm brewing, she was right about that. He'd squinted at the spreadsheet Elizabeth had printed for him, used a finger to line up the row for Stephen Thomas, reciting the phone number aloud as he reached for his cell phone.

It rang several times on the other end and then a rough voice came on the line directing the caller to leave a message. Mason cleared his throat. "Mr. Thomas, my name is Mason Farmer. I'm an investigator. I'd like to talk to you about something your grandfather was involved with. In Grand Forks."

He left his number for a call back.

"All is right with the world now," Elizabeth snarled.

"I hope you know I'm trying to do the right thing here."

"Makes two of us," she replied. "But I'm not feeling very simpatico with you, Mason."

"I'm sorry to hear that."

"Sure. Who's next?"

"I hope you realize—"

"Next," she snapped.

Mason sighed and glanced at the spreadsheet again. Next up was a man in Maryland. And after that, a guy in New Jersey whose family had been involved in the killing of a man named Mingo Jack. The list also included people in Virginia, Rhode Island, Ohio. Lots of phone calls to make. Hopefully one of them would lead to the kidnappers. Why should those fuckers roam free while he scrounged to rebound from being fired? Unjustly.

A horn blared, breaking his reminiscence. He glanced in his rearview mirror and saw the Prius coming to a rough stop behind him. So roughly he flinched. Elizabeth flashed her lights. Mason sighed and got out. Rain soaked him as he made the walk to her car.

30

There were only three chairs in the conference room. Two of a style found in any office, and the one they'd offered to Nate—outfitted with a cuff bar and bolted in place. The walls were painted Tar Heel blue, the solid concrete flooring underfoot glazed with a moss-green epoxy. A light in the overhead fixture guttered in the way of a dying candle flame. No doubt the cops had been intentional about not having it replaced. They hunted for an advantage wherever they could establish one. Mind games, threats, physical force. Nothing was beyond the pale. The fidgety light, after all, might rub off on one of the dirt bags. Unnerve them, cause them to make a critical mistake. That's what the cops thrived on. You fucking it up for your own self. Made their job a lot easier.

"Blue and green," Nate said, looking around. "Cool colors. Meant to soothe, calm."

"Is it working, Mr. Evers?"

"Not really."

The cop smiled but Nate wasn't about to fall for that. Detective Barnes had the build of an NFL wide receiver—long-limbed, impressive hands, and just enough bulk to cause a solid door to shudder and split apart from the jamb if he rammed it with one of his wide shoulders. Expressive, too. One moment he'd nod thoughtfully, and a look of dismay would flit across his face. The next minute there'd be a smile, full and not the least bit bashful even though one of his incisors was chipped and all his teeth were mottled with the yellowish stains of a heavy smoker. He was down to earth, which meant he couldn't be trusted.

"All right we move this along, Detective?"

"You have somewhere to be?" Smiling.

Nate didn't respond. The less he said, the better. Barnes took the hint, cleared his throat, opened the manila folder in front of him. Nate subtly stretched to look but couldn't make out anything on the pages inside the folder. For all he knew, they could be blank.

"We found him with a .380 Bersa on his person. You familiar with it, Mr. Evers?"

"I don't know anything about guns," Nate told him.

Barnes nodded. "Seven-shot magazine, adjustable sights. He'd acid-burned the serial, made a suppressor with a Maglite."

Nate felt the pulse lurch in his throat as Barnes leaned forward. He suspected that'd been the cop's intention all along—pull out a reaction and then pounce. Nate nodded to mute what he was really feeling, not trusting his voice.

"You don't tool up and go to those lengths unless you're looking to cause someone serious harm," Barnes said.

Nate swallowed, nodded again.

"You hear about people being radicalized," Barnes went on, "and it sounds so sinister and evil. Media paints it that way." He shook his head, pursed his lips, leaned back in his chair—all part of his performance art. "I don't think it's always that black-and-white myself. I'm sure your outfit didn't realize you were grooming a domestic terrorist."

There it was.

"Travis Nelson worked for us less than three months, Detective," Nate said. "Mostly grassroots marketing. Handing out flyers, making a few phone calls. We paid him by the hour, and he never spent any significant time in our office at the armory."

"He mentioned your group in most of his Facebook posts."

"PAC," Nate corrected. "And I'm not big on social media, so I can't speak to any of that."

"Anything he said or did that you found concerning when he was with you?"

"Again, I didn't have much interaction with him."

"Okay."

Barnes sounded dispirited. Nate almost felt sorry for the man. Almost. In the end, though, this was a cop, and cops were charged with protecting the public and bringing criminals to justice. Even being in proximity with a cop puts the average citizen on edge. Nate wasn't the average citizen; he had a lot to lose the longer this went on.

"I'm sorry," he told Detective Barnes, making his voice as earnest as possible. "I really didn't know Travis well. He answered a job post we put up on Indeed, did what we asked of him for those three months, and I haven't heard from him since. It's shocking to hear from you what he was plotting."

Barnes sat back in his chair, sighed, his shoulders sagging. "These extremists are emboldened, coming out from under their rocks, causing all kinds of . . . trouble. I appreciate you answering my questions, Mr. Evers. I knew it was a long shot but . . . nothing beats a fail but a try."

Reduced to well-worn bromides. Nate *did* feel sorry for him.

"Am I free to go?" he asked.

"Of course, of course." Barnes stood and offered a hand.

Firm handshake.

Nate was surprised to find himself so composed, so calm. Maybe the cool colors worked. Ironic he would've been in such a funk these past few days and all it took to snap him out of it was a sit-down with a police detective. Outside, he slipped into the Explorer and, before even processing what he was doing, dialed a number on his cell phone he knew he shouldn't be calling.

A woman picked up on the third ring.

Offered no hello.

Nate said, "Hey."

After another beat of silence, she said, "What do you want?"

"I'm outside the police station. A detective showed up on my doorstep this morning."

"What?" Her voice rose and Nate pictured her sitting up.

"Former employee was plotting some kind of attack," he said. "Cops wanted to know what I could tell them about him. Which wasn't much."

"All right," she said, relaxing. "I'm glad it didn't turn into something . . . bigger."

"You and me both," Nate said.

Silence from her end of the line.

Nate rubbed a hand over his scalp. "Are you alone?"

"You don't get to ask me that."

"Ever think about us getting—"

"No," she said, cutting him off. "Don't even go there."

"You don't even know what I was going to ask."

"We both know that's not true, Nate."

"I love you," he told her.

"Okay."

"You won't say it back?"

"No."

"Because of *him?*"

"I better go now. Take care of yourself."

"Hey . . ."

But she'd already disconnected the call. Nate sat there holding the cell phone for a while. Then he gathered himself and drove off, the police station in his rearview.

31

It was nearly dark, the air swarming with mosquitoes. And in the wash of his truck's headlights, Samuel stood in the middle of the one-lane, turning a three-sixty, taking in the overgrown bushes on both sides of the road. On the left there was also a weather-beaten gray fence, buckling under the weight of a hungry vine, the impenetrable forest beyond. Other than him and the new guy there wasn't a soul for miles. No farmsteads, no houses. Just a desolate stretch of unlit road.

"You're sure this is right?" Ronald asked him.

Samuel, stunned mute, simply nodded.

"I don't understand this, sir. Why would your brother be out here?"

"Wouldn't," Samuel managed, and he walked on watery legs back to his truck, leaned against it for support and to think. Even though he hadn't met Chipper until he himself was nine and Chipper six, they'd had an immediate connection that was supernatural, otherworldly. It disturbed him that he couldn't pick up the hum of his brother's vibrations now.

"What are you thinking, sir?"

He didn't answer and the new guy got the hint, moving off to walk along the edge of the road, kicking at rocks or clumps of broken branches or nothing at all.

Samuel returned to his thoughts. His brother wasn't exactly

easygoing, but Chipper was far less difficult than Samuel. Not as mer-
curial, kept an open mind when it came to the occasional good cheer.
Fine with his women being slutty and "healthy," running toward fat in
the same way the niggers preferred. Samuel guessed that most people
would've considered Chipper to be a reasonable guy. So, who would
want to hurt him? Who would have the balls to try? Chipper didn't
attract the vitriol and animosity that Samuel dealt with on a daily
basis, but when it came, he wouldn't shrink from it. He'd be a damn
tough-out. Tough as fanning the big half-nigger on the Yankees.

And yet he was gone, his hum silenced. Dead. Buried out here in
some shallow grave that animals would disturb eventually. Samuel
was certain of this. It was that supernatural connection that'd been
there since his father had come home with a strange boy, sheepishly
telling Samuel, "Suppose this is your brother."

"What's his name?" Samuel had asked once his shock wore off.

"I started calling him Chipper and it took."

"Why Chipper?"

"'Cause I caught him smiling a few times."

Somehow it made sense.

Now, Samuel fumbled his cell phone from his right pants pocket
and punched in Chanel's number.

"Anything?" she asked in his ear, practically breathless.

"Cold trail."

She took that news in silence.

"Chipper express any concerns about anybody lately?" Samuel
asked her.

"Meaning?"

"Anybody he was worried about? Someone he was griping with.
Anyone who would mean him harm?"

"Nobody ever stepped to Chipper. You know this, Samuel."

He nodded despite her not being able to see it.

"A man did call the house earlier, though," she said. "I'd run a bath and popped a bottle of red, hoping that would help me calm my nerves. Of course, it didn't do—"

"What man, Chanel?"

"Investigator. Said he wanted to talk to Chipper about the past and what'd happened with Chipper's family."

"What does any of that mean?"

"Your guess is as good as mine."

"Do whatever you have to do to get this man out to your house," Samuel said, and he disconnected the call.

He'd never believed a fairy would put a dollar under his pillow for a bicuspid. Never for a second believed some jolly old fat man was sliding down his chimney with a G.I. Joe. There weren't any rabbits coming around with chocolate eggs neither.

And no such fucking thing as coincidence.

This man, whoever he might be, was in for a world of hurt if he didn't have answers to a few very fine questions.

32

Dorothy Adams lounged on the couch in the living room, snoring, with a sea of pillows surrounding her, one of the pillows clutched to her chest as if she were a heart patient in a hospital. Joshua leaned down and kissed his mother's forehead, then headed to the kitchen.

He tried to be quiet, but his mother must've heard him chopping onions and tomatoes on the cutting board or pulling the skillet from the mess of pots and pans in the cabinet under the stovetop.

"Shoe?" she called.

Joshua wiped his hands on a dish towel and moved into the living room. "Didn't mean to wake you, Ma. Breakfast will be ready in about ten minutes."

"I meant to catch you," she said.

"Catch me for what?"

"I've been talking to a nice lady from the Department of Human Services."

"What? Why, Ma?"

"Don't get upset. She told me about a program called JACC, even helped me fill out an application right on the phone. I got approved."

"I've heard about that program, Ma. I don't want any money for looking after you."

"I knew you'd say that."

"Good."

"So, I didn't bother adding you to my plan of care. I got someone coming in to give you a break, though."

"Who?" Joshua frowned. "I don't need a break."

"You're so busy with your PAC," she said, getting it right this time. "And you're the one who made a big deal about my fall."

"I can look after you," Joshua insisted.

Caring for his mother was about the only thing he got right.

"Has to be a better use of your time, Shoe."

"Pssh—" He waved that off and returned to the kitchen. He'd just cracked six eggs in a bowl when the doorbell chimed.

"Shoe?"

"I heard it," he said, wiping his hands on the dish towel again. He threw it on the counter and moved to answer the door.

The woman on the other side made his mouth go dry.

She had a rich chocolate complexion, close-cropped hair, dyed a shimmery blonde, too-bright purple lipstick. Wearing jeans with rips at the knees, and a clingy top. Up close, the added weight most definitely agreed with her.

"Shit," Joshua said, and he left her standing there, smiling on the other side of the door.

"Don't act like this, Shoe," his mother called.

He rushed past her and through the door in the kitchen to his lair in the basement. He was still dealing with the echoes of his mother's pleading voice as he banged down on the cot, sprawled on his back with his eyes closed.

It wasn't long before he heard the squeal of the door opening above him, and then the stairs groaning. He turned over on his side.

"I told Miss Dot this was going to upset you."

He didn't respond.

"I've missed you, Joshua. Seriously. I don't understand why you're acting like this. You can't even look at me?"

"Alani . . ." But he couldn't say any more. Those three syllables were difficult enough.

She came and sat next to him on the cot. She smelled the same. A light citrus fragrance. *Versace Yellow Diamond.* Alani ordered it off Amazon for a ridiculously low price. Nate was more apt to take notice of a woman's perfume, but Joshua's heart leaped now as its memory returned. He squeezed his eyes shut even tighter.

"I still love you, Joshua." Alani placed a hand on his shoulder. "I need you to know that."

No, no, no. She had no idea what she was talking about. What was there to love?

"Joshua . . ."

Shaking him and stirring up all kinds of buried feelings.

Buried shallowly, it seemed, like Chipper's grave.

"Okay," she said, tears in her voice. "Let me get upstairs. Thanks for getting Miss Dot's breakfast started."

She was at the stairs when Joshua rolled over and opened his eyes. "Thanks," he called. Alani stopped as if she'd been shot in the back. "For putting flowers on Darius's grave. That was nice of you."

"I loved your brother, too," she called from the stairs.

"Darius would be ashamed of me."

Alani turned to him. "Why would you think that?"

"Nate was more of a brother to him than I ever was."

"Your hurt is talking."

"I don't know what's wrong with me, Alani."

She dropped away from the steps and moved to sit next to him on the cot again. "You're being really hard on yourself, Joshua."

"Not hard enough."

"What have you done?"

"You really don't wanna know."

"I took you at your word that time you apologized after your slipup with Aisha Jennings," she said. "You promised it was a mistake and would never happen again. And I believed you. I didn't cut up your jeans. Didn't start checking your phone. Told Will Brock to go somewhere when he tried to holla at me."

"That was high school times, Alani."

"Right," she said. "And I was immature as hell, but I didn't start tripping after your little confession. I accept you, Joshua. Warts and all, as they say. Ain't nothing you can't tell me."

"I been sleeping with a married woman," he said.

Alani swallowed, nodded. "You . . . you care about her?"

"I'm not even sure I like her. She's . . ."

"She's what?" Alani snapped.

"Not you."

"Way you been actin', I would think that's a plus."

He'd taken part in covering up a man's murder and yet he felt making Alani feel diminished was probably the worst thing he'd done in recent memory.

"I didn't push you away because I don't love you," he told her.

"Love? You really have the nerve to be talkin' love."

"I love you so much it—"

"No," Alani said, rising to her feet. "I'm not letting you play with my emotions."

"I pushed you away for your own good."

"Wow. That is some bullshit, Joshua."

"I'm not good," he insisted.

"You looking for me to disagree? Wrap my arms around you and lay my head on your chest and swear on my mama and Miss Dot I ain't ever come across a better man than you. That what you need? 'Cause I'm so heartsick without you, I'll fuckin' make a fool of myself and do it."

"I don't need that. I just need . . . I just need you."

"I'm standing right in front of you now, Joshua. Been standing in front of you, but you haven't even looked my way."

"I've done some shit I'm not proud of," Joshua said.

"Should've had this crisis of conscience before you stuck your dick in that married woman."

"She's the least of it."

"Oh, yeah?" Alani placed her hands on her hips. "Tell me then."

And so, he did.

Told her everything.

"Look at this crap," Elizabeth said.

Mason followed her gaze. "What?"

"That's a Confederate flag bumper sticker on that truck."

"I see."

"Well, I'm glad you see it. That's wonderful, Mason."

Rather than continuing with the back-and-forth, he just handed Elizabeth her laptop bag. She was no longer barefoot, but just as displeased as she'd been since they'd met up at Birmingham-Shuttlesworth International. They'd booked seats next to each other on the plane but hadn't managed more than a few sentences the entire flight here to New Jersey. Elizabeth had written furiously in a leather-bound journal while Mason absentmindedly thumbed through a copy of *Rolling Stone* he'd picked up from Hudson News at the airport. Pretty singer named Halsey on the cover but he'd gotten lost in an article about the NYPD's Homicide squad. Lost not because he found the article so interesting, but instead because he'd found himself re-reading entire paragraphs. His mind was a ball in one of those arcade games, bouncing off everything.

"I'll handle most of the talking," he said now, standing with her in front of Duane Kelly's house.

Elizabeth glanced his way. "And I'm sure it will go well, since it's a white woman."

"That was my line. You need to come up with something clever of your own to trash me."

"Challenge accepted."

"You ever going to ease up on me?"

"Probably not."

Probably not.

Baby steps.

He'd take it.

"After you, Miss Elizabeth," Mason said, lifting his hand to indicate the path ahead.

She stared at him for a moment, then turned and moved toward the house, Mason following on her heels. A very narrow road had brought them here, to a heavily wooded area with a few scattershot properties breaking up the landscape. This one was clearly cared for, the lawn cut, the shingles power washed, and yet there was still something eerie about it. Perhaps the trees that cast it in shadows. Perhaps the woods surrounding it. Perhaps its isolation, a quarter mile away from a neighbor of any sort. Perhaps the attic window just under the peak of the roof. The window was like an unblinking eye, and the house itself gave off the impression it was holding its breath. Didn't help that the woman they were meeting had sounded as though she was deep in mourning when she responded to Mason's voicemail message. Also, very suspicious as to why he'd called, the timing of it all. Once Mason shared his theory that a group of four kidnappers—including a light-skinned woman—were targeting the descendants of men who'd committed past hate crimes, she admitted that her common-law husband was missing, and she believed a woman dressed up in a disguise was involved. She'd tracked her missing husband through his Apple Watch to a desolate stretch of road bordered by woods in Salem County. That last bit of detail had prompted Mason to hop on a plane. He just knew the four kidnappers would escalate. This sounded like their handiwork.

Elizabeth raised her hand to knock, but the door opened before she could do so. A woman with a mop of wild blonde hair took up the doorway. There was trouble in her startling blue eyes and something about her demeanor said *despairing*, but she managed a smile, a nice smile. Mason thought it was an act and felt all the closer to her for the effort.

"Chanel?" he said.

She nodded, eyed their bags. "Hope you ain't planning on moving in."

"We came straight from the airport," Mason told her. "I haven't even checked into our hotel yet. We were anxious to speak with you."

"All right. Come on in."

"Thank you."

They all settled in a room at the back of the house, a den of sorts, Mason and Elizabeth side by side on a denim-blue couch, Chanel in a matching armchair. She sat with her legs splayed, which was disconcerting even with her wearing sweatpants—a feminine woman but rough around the edges.

"Still no word from Duane?" Mason asked.

"No one calls him that," she said. "He goes by Chipper."

"No word from Chipper?"

"You don't have to do that," she said. "This won't have a happy ending."

"You never know," Mason replied, not wanting to feed into her fatalism.

She sighed. "Chipper left his truck in the lot at Lace. I asked them if I could keep it there, see if he snuck back to get it. Thought I might've been the problem and he wanted to slip away to a new life."

"Lace?"

"Strip club," she explained. "Last known sighting."

Mason processed that, said, "You two were having issues?"

"Thought you said you weren't a cop anymore. These sound like cop questions."

Mason smiled. "Old habits die hard, I guess. I apologize. Just want to get a sense of the situation to see if this is connected to my . . ."

"Case?" Chanel supplied.

"It's nothing that formal."

"Who's your client?"

"He'd rather I didn't—"

"You said something about three men doing these kidnappings," she said, interrupting him. "And there was a woman with them."

"That's right."

"Tell me about the woman."

"We're almost certain she's mixed," Mason said. "Very light skinned, whatever her background. She could pass for white."

"Taylor Swift."

"Pardon?"

Chanel shook her head. "Nothing."

"Don't discount any detail, Ms. Anderson. You never know what might be important."

"You're sounding like a cop again."

"I—"

"What's your role in this?" Chanel said, turning her attention to Elizabeth.

"Mason has a theory," Elizabeth replied, sitting up and clearing her throat now. "He thinks the four kidnappers are targeting the descendants of white people who committed horrible crimes against black people in the past."

"And Chipper's family was part of that?"

Elizabeth nodded. "There was a man . . . his name was Mingo Jack. He was hanged. Eatontown, I believe."

"I've heard of Eatontown. When was this?"

"Eighteen eighty-six."

"You've got to be fucking kidding me," Chanel said, and she laughed. "Who the hell would think to blame Chipper for that?"

"Mason's aiming to find out."

"This all sounds ridiculous," Chanel said, turning back to Mason.

"I know it does," he admitted. "My guy was just taken without being contacted, but did Chipper mention anyone reaching out to him?"

"No."

"What are they saying at Lace?"

"Like I told you, Chipper left with a woman who I'm pretty sure was wearing a disguise. It could be your girl. And it would've taken three motherfuckers to get Chipper down. So, the three guys you're saying were a part of it with her would fit."

"Chipper has a tendency to be combative?"

"Not as bad as Samuel," Chanel said, "but you wouldn't confuse him for a worker with the Peace Corps."

"Who's Samuel?"

"Chipper's big brother. Same asshole father, different mothers. Chipper eventually ended up staying with his dad. Tells you how terrible his mother was. This thing has to do with his mother's side of the family?"

"Yes," Mason said. "Tell me about Samuel, though. You say he's a rough sort. What's he into?"

"He ain't connected to this," Chanel said.

"How can you be so sure?"

"'Cause he's madder than hell right now and wants to see that someone pays for what happened to Chipper."

"What do you think happened?"

"Aren't you here to find out? You got a hard-on when I told you about the Apple Watch."

"I'm sorry. I know this isn't easy for you."

"You think? Chipper is probably buried out in the woods some-where, and that's what you come up with? It isn't easy?"

Mason knew better than to feed her anger. "I'd like to talk to Samuel."

"Well, you're in luck then," Chanel said, smiling.

One of the biggest humans Mason had ever seen up close stepped into the room. He wore a motorcycle vest over a tight black T-shirt that strained against his biceps, Faith, Family, and Folk emblazoned on the shirt in white letters. Mason could see the cruelty in his eyes. "Chanel should've added that luck is relative," the man said in a coarse voice that fit his size. "One man's luck is another man's misfortune."

34

Isiah had only spoken with Rachel once since she'd stormed out, and the conversation had been strained, painfully so. And yet his spirits weren't as troubled as they could be, the days slipping by like something oiled, largely because he'd spent much of the past ninety-six hours here, parked in a clearing in an otherwise heavily treed woods. The woods served two functional purposes: one, they gave him a great vantage point of Chipper's house, and two, they provided cover, so Chanel didn't see him.

He'd seen her, though.

Twice she'd ventured outside. Once to a GameStop, and then the post office to mail whatever she'd bought. A second time to make a run to the grocery store, returning with an armful of Acme bags tied off at the top, same way Rachel did it. Isiah followed at a safe distance on both occasions. Two opportunities to flag Chanel down, or leave a note in her mailbox—or, in the case of the grocery store run—tucked under her windshield wipers.

He couldn't say what had stopped him. Maybe her resemblance to his sister, Julie, was too much of an emotional bridge to cross. Regardless, watching her kept his mind off Rachel. He felt good about that. Even though so far, he'd been too cowardly to follow through on the reasoning he'd convinced himself was the point for being here. Today would be different, though. He just needed the right moment, and then he'd let Chanel know Chipper's fate. An anonymous note in her mailbox—that seemed to him the right way to deliver the hard news to her.

Sure.

He shook his head and raised the binoculars he'd bought after his first day out here. Looking through the scope, he saw Chanel had opened the blinds. That was a new development. On the other days, not only had she kept them closed, but no lights burned inside either. And Isiah had stayed well past nine o'clock each evening. The other thing he noticed was a second vehicle parked alongside Chanel's Honda. A truck with a Confederate-flag sticker stuck to the bumper like spinach in someone's teeth.

One by one, he trained the binoculars on each window of the house, hoping to get a glimpse of Chanel's visitor. Or visitors. Unfortunately, he didn't pick up anything in the windows. A bad feeling boiled in his gut just the same. It was that Confederate-flag sticker, sure, but also an intuition something bad was brewing.

He had a feeling he should probably leave but found he couldn't. What was he worried about anyway? No one could see him from this distance. He was safely hidden. And it was important he get a close look at who'd come in the truck.

In the meantime, he desperately needed to urinate. He set down the binoculars and stepped out of his car, careful as he closed the door. He stepped just as carefully over the bed of broken twigs and fallen leaves as he moved deeper into the woods. His piss steamed as it swamped the ground at the base of an ancient oak. It wasn't lost on Isiah that everything started to fall apart with Scott York. He pictured the scene in Alabama, the noose in particular.

He shook himself off, zipped up, and was headed back to his post when he heard something. An approaching car. He quickened his step, getting to his own car and yawning open the door without caring what sound it made with its rusty hinges. He grabbed the binoculars off his seat.

The car sped around a deep curve in the road, flashing past Isiah's hiding spot in the woods without noticing him, and pulled up in front of Chipper's house. A reflective sign propped up in the rear window. Lyft. An attractive, unusually curvy white woman with jet-black hair and porcelain skin emerged from the car. She was barefoot a moment but paused to slip on sandals. Moving out after her was an older white man. He pulled bags from the car. A dark leather laptop bag, a duffel he draped over his left shoulder, a mottled blue travel tote he hung from his right. Isiah stood up straight, recognizing something in the man's bearing, how he carried himself. "Shit. A fucking cop?"

The woman had a certain demeanor as well, as if she were on a bad date. Isiah homed in on her and noticed first the painted-on jeans, then the logo and words on the T-shirt she was wearing. He gasped. His heart galloped. He knew the organization. They were based out of Birmingham, Alabama. Their website offered a comprehensive history of lynchings in America. He'd searched it several times since they'd started their work.

Isiah stumbled back to his car and snatched his cell phone from the charger plugged into the cigarette lighter. The number he needed was among his *Favorites*, and despite all the anger he felt toward this person he didn't hesitate to call it. Isiah knew he couldn't deal with this brewing situation alone.

Someone picked up after what felt like a million rings.

"Nate," Isiah said. "We have a big fucking problem."

35

Chipper's brother, Samuel, shrugged out of the motorcycle vest and held it in a fist by his waist. Two other men walked in behind him. The one to his left was heavily bearded and covered in tattoos, including two lightning bolts, side by side, high up on his neck, and the number 88 in a small font by his right eye. An absolute freak show. The man to the big guy's right wouldn't have garnered a second look in most settings. He had pale blue eyes, no facial hair, and could've used one of those fidget spinners the kids liked to play with to keep themselves calm.

The big guy carefully laid his vest across the shoulders of the armchair and told Chanel to make herself scarce. She bit her lip and trembled as she hurried from the room. Mason watched her go with a sense of dread.

Samuel took Chanel's place in the armchair. He closed his eyes, worked his neck in circles. Like he was warming up for something.

Mason had no desire to find out what.

"I'm glad you're here, Samuel," he said. "I've got some questions that'll hopefully lead to us finding out what happened to your brother, to Chipper."

Samuel kept twisting his neck.

"Do you know of anyone he was having problems with?"

Moving on from cracking his neck to cracking his knuckles, his eyes still closed.

"I appreciate anything you can tell me."

"What's your client's name?"

Mason didn't immediately register that Samuel had spoken to him, because he still hadn't opened his eyes, the words coming from somewhere unseen, like a ventriloquist's trick.

"I'm sorry, could you say that again?"

Samuel's eyes flashed open, and he trained them on Mason. "This client of yours who was kidnapped. What's his name?"

"I'm sorry," Mason said. "But I can't share that information without his permission."

"Call him then."

"I'm afraid—"

"What's your name?" Samuel said, turning to Elizabeth.

"Elizabeth."

"You've heard of the seventeenth-century Flemish painter Peter Paul Rubens?"

She shook her head and Mason could see she was afraid. Samuel saw it too.

"Just making conversation, Elizabeth," he told her. "You've nothing to worry about with me. I've no use myself for Rubenesque women. Not even to root around in the mud with."

"Wh-what?" she said, lifting a hand to her breast.

"Your client's name," Samuel said to Mason, back on him.

"Why don't we focus on—"

For a big guy, Mason was stunned by how quickly Samuel moved. He was up out of the armchair and snatching Mason up from the couch by his collar in a blink. Biting down on Mason's right ear just a beat after that.

"Ah . . . Jesus . . . shit . . ." Mason yelled, trying to wriggle free, but Samuel's clamp on his ear only intensified.

It was on fire and might pull apart at any moment.

In the close distance Elizabeth screamed, her voice like a psychedelic nightmare.

Somebody else was calling Samuel's name, probably the nondescript guy, because it sounded as though he wanted the big guy to stop.

And, shockingly, he did.

He dropped Mason to the ground like a sack of laundry, stood to his full height, wiping his mouth with the back of his hand.

Mason's eyes were blurred by tears, but he still made that out as well as blood on his fingers as he touched his shredded right ear. He scooted backward on his ass until his back touched the couch. Elizabeth laid a shaky hand on his shoulder.

"Jesus Christ!" he said, looking up at Samuel. "What the hell was that?" Elizabeth's hand squeezed. "You fucking bit me."

Samuel didn't respond, distracted as another man entered the room. This one also bearded and tattooed. "What do you want, Logan?"

"We've spotted a man watching the house," he announced.

"Watching the house?"

"That's right," Logan said. "With binoculars."

"One of us?" Samuel asked.

"Nope. Some Watermelon American."

"Don't let them leave," Samuel said to the initial two men, indicating Mason and Elizabeth with a nod, and then he followed Logan, the messenger, from the room.

36

"How did you get here?"

"Walked."

"You're bullshitting me?"

"Not from my house," Nate said. "I parked back by the main road, in the lot of a bar and grill called Woody's, very apt, I guess. Then I walked from there through the woods."

"Why?"

"Aftermarket cherry bombs don't exactly make for a quiet entrance."

"Too bad you're an insecure asshole and felt the need to make all those modifications to your Explorer."

"We're still doing this, I.T.?"

"Doing what, Nate?"

"You unlocked?" he asked, nodding at I.T.'s car. "I need to sit."

"You mean to tell me big bad Nate's feet are hurting?"

"I.T. . . ."

"It's unlocked, it's unlocked."

Nate shoved past and opened the passenger door of the car, sitting down hard inside with the door left ajar. I.T. joined him a moment later. They were both quiet, looking in the direction of Chipper's house. I.T. picked up his binoculars after some time and peered through the scope. Nate sat up straighter. "And?" he asked.

"Not seeing anyone."

"Let me have a look."

"You think you're going to see something I don't, Nate?"

"It's very possible."

"Fuck you. Must I remind you about the Apple Watch?"

"All four of us missed that, I.T."

"Only one of us is a superior asshole who doesn't make mistakes."

"You've broken one of our commandments," Nate said, "but I'm the superior asshole?"

I.T. frowned. "What commandment?"

"We could hack their phones, their online accounts, whatever. But none of us would ever go anywhere near where they lived."

"We?" Isiah laughed at the notion. "I'd love to see you try to hack an account."

"You shouldn't be here. What were you hoping to accomplish?"

"None of your fucking business."

"I'm curious why you called me," Nate replied.

"Because you got us in this shit. When I saw the woman's T-shirt, I knew we had a problem. We used some of her organization's research. It's too much of a coincidence. And then the man."

"You said he looked like a cop?" Nate said, moving on.

"One hundred percent. Clean and neat, rigid, military haircut."

"For all Chipper's girlfriend knows, he's missing," Nate said. "This could just be a detective getting a statement from her."

"Out of state, carrying overnight bags, and traveling with that woman?"

"You're right," Nate admitted. "That's too much of a coincidence."

"So, what do we do?"

"I'll keep eyes on the house for a bit. Then I'll head back to the bar. I expect they'll get picked up by another Lyft. I'll follow it."

"What if it comes before you make it back to the bar? It must be close to a mile hike, much of it uphill."

"They'll be here a while," Nate said. "No worries."

"How can you be so sure?"

"Intuition," Nate replied. "You got the plates from the car that brought them here?"

"Yes."

"Go work some of that I.T. magic. See if you can trace it to the owner. Once you do, we'll have Rachel talk to him, see what she can learn. Maybe they said something during the ride."

"You think the Lyft driver is going to talk freely with some random woman?"

Nate smiled. "This is Rachel we're talking about. She'll get him to spill. Your girl's got skills."

I.T. glared.

"What's the look?" Nate asked him.

"You fuck her?"

"Fuck *who*?"

"Rachel."

"What are you talking about, I.T.?"

"Don't play dumb, Nate."

"I'm not playing anything."

"Rachel," I.T. said. "Did you fuck her?"

"Are you serious? She's your fiancée."

"So?"

"As difficult as you can be, in the end, you're my friend," Nate added. "*Both* of you are."

"Rachel maybe, I'm not sure about me."

"What's the matter with you? Did you two have a fight?"

"I don't trust you, Nate."

"That's fine. You trust Rachel, though?"

I.T. didn't respond.

"Really? You think that poorly of your girl?"

"There's something with you two," I.T. insisted.

Tell him? Nate wasn't sure that was a good idea, but his friend was clearly tormented. Whatever Nate might say and do, he cared about the fool. "There's nothing between me and Rachel," he whispered. "I helped her deal with a situation, is all."

I.T. frowned. "What situation?"

"I'll let Rachel tell it."

"Why hasn't she already?"

Nate shrugged. "Talk to her."

I.T. looked off in the distance.

"Binoculars," Nate said, holding out his hand.

I.T. handed them over without even glancing in his direction.

"Find that Lyft driver," Nate told him. "All the rest of this shit can be settled later."

"What situation did you help her with, Nate?"

"Find the Lyft driver," he repeated. "I'll catch up with you later and we'll plan next steps. We'll have to bring Joshua and Rachel up to speed."

"Why wouldn't Rachel come to me if she had trouble?" I.T. said.

Nate sighed, said, "She didn't think you could handle it. I'm sorry, man."

Nate stepped out of the car then, closed the passenger door. After a moment, I.T. started the engine and slowly rolled out of the woods, turning left toward the main road.

Nate shook his head, strolled to the edge of the clearing, and lifted the binoculars to his eyes. He didn't appreciate much about the outdoors, particularly its bugs. There were several different spiders that could be scary large—especially the females—and often they garlanded tree limbs with filaments of silk that hid in sunlight. Cobwebs as wide as a few feet, sturdy, too. Nothing he wanted to walk through unawares. Add in the time in Alabama's swamps and he'd drifted even further from appreciating nature and all its oddities and curiosities. It didn't help that today brought another wave of heat, sweat dripping from his hairline and stinging his eyes. A circus of odors in these woods that clotted in his nose and throat.

"Fuck this."

Nothing was happening at the house anyway. Might as well move back uphill to his Explorer and wait in comfort with music and air-conditioning.

But he decided on five more minutes, and that turned out to be a good decision. Maybe. There was movement along the side of the house. Nate quickly lifted the binoculars.

Two men making their way toward the front lawn. One stood about five-nine, was built like a bulldog. He was tattooed, bearded, dirty looking. The other was the height of a standard doorway and just as wide, familiar in some way. Nate trained his binoculars on the heavyweight.

"Damn," he said, realizing at once.

The guy favored Chipper.

A larger model, unbelievably.

And he and the bulldog were walking in this direction.

Nate quickly turned on his heels and started trampling through the brush, up a steep slope toward the main road. The terrain was uneven as well, so he stepped carefully, not wanting to turn an ankle. He wished there was a switch to dim the daylight. He felt naked out here.

He risked a glance over his shoulder. Didn't see them, but he could hear them. One of the men was loudly whistling the melody of "Ten Little Indians." Or maybe the minstrel-era version where they'd replaced the Indians with ten little niggers.

Nate pushed that thought aside and picked up his pace. When he came upon a cleared trail, he paused a moment to catch his breath and risk another glance over his shoulder. Nobody in sight, but the loud whistling continued. They were closing in. He wiped sweat from his eyes and took in a large gulp of air.

Turned to continue but pulled up short.

A man stood blocking his path. The man's smile revealed teeth stained by tobacco. His eyes were missing light. Nate didn't know guns but instinctively figured the one trained on him could do some damage. "Easy, partner," he said, raising his hands.

"Partner? I look like I'd want to throw in with you for anything, nigger?"

"Good point," Nate said. "Step aside and I'll be on my way."

"Samuel would like a word with you first."

Nate frowned. "Samuel?"

"Chipper's brother."

"Never heard of any Samuel or Chipper," Nate lied.

"Drop those binoculars on the ground and empty your pockets."

"Why?"

"'Cause I'll blow your damn head off, you don't do what I tell you, boy," the man said, the gun wagging with his every syllable.

Nate dropped the binoculars.

"Pockets," the man said.

"There's no money in my wallet, and my cell phone is one step above a flip."

"Do it."

The whistling was getting ever closer.

Heart hammering in his chest, Nate pulled out his wallet. He hesitated, and then tossed it near the man's feet. As he'd hoped, the gunman glanced down. Nate charged him, heard the air whoosh out of the man as they collided. The gun skittered from the man's hand and they both went to the ground, but Nate was on top. He bruised his knuckles on the gunman's face. Punch after punch after punch. Once he knew the threat was eliminated, he searched the ground for his wallet. He was reaching for it when he heard a crack, then another.

Both cracks sounded like a felled tree.

Someone had jabbed at his left shoulder.

And at his lower back, right side just beneath his ribs.

A sensation as if he'd been burned with a cattle brand.

Shot, he realized. He'd been shot.

He staggered to his feet and there was another crack and the ground spit up earth by where he stood.

He stumbled forward, grabbing hold of tree limbs to use like kernmantle climbing rope, yanking himself up the rise. His left shoulder and right lower back screamed in pain.

Voices behind him. But no more of the fucking whistling. Thank God for that.

He moved on with awkward baby deer steps, his long legs eating up chunk strides of ground.

Sleepy.

He just wanted to close his eyes for a moment's rest.

But he didn't. He pressed on through sheer will and determination. Thinking about that made him giggle. It sounded like a recruitment commercial for the armed forces. *Sheer will and determination. Be all that you can be. Ask not what your country can do for you. The few, the proud.*

Very fucking funny.

He felt delirious in laughter.

So much so, he didn't even notice one more step forward would take him over the edge of a bluff of some kind.

He took the step.

Part III

37

"**You and Isiah** aren't speaking?"

"We talked once," Rachel said.

"You seem tired."

"I fell in love with Isiah because he was steady, dependable, free of drama."

"So very different than your previous relationships."

"Yes," Rachel said. "I made a lot of bad choices in the past. If the guy was tall, dark, and handsome I didn't consider whether he was faithful, intelligent, and . . ."

"And?"

"Slow to anger," Rachel said.

"Mmm."

Dr. Legg's office was appointed in the style of a trendy family den. Grass cloth–wall coverings, which gave it a sense of warmth. White shelves stacked with books, a variety of figurines, and, for some odd reason, not one but three globes of the Earth. Flowers, lots of flowers. A dartboard. The only emblems suggesting that you were in a psychiatrist's office were the two locked file cabinets tucked away in one corner.

Rachel shifted her position on the couch. It was too comfy in her opinion, built to mold to your shape, easy to lull you into whispering your darkest secrets. Meanwhile, Dr. Legg sat less than ten feet from her, in a chair with an overhead lamp behind it. Could've been a nice little reading nook. A cup of tea and the latest Kennedy Ryan. Or, in the doctor's case, probably Nora Roberts.

"You're right, I am tired," Rachel heard herself say. "I haven't been sleeping."

"I see." Dr. Legg nodded thoughtfully. "Is there anything else on your mind? Or just the spat with Isiah?"

"It was a bit more than a spat. We haven't gone this long apart in all the time we've been together."

"Five years?"

"Six come September."

"That's a real commitment."

"I used to think so."

"You no longer do?"

"I don't know what I think anymore," Rachel told her, and she hid her hands from view, pinching the webbing between the thumb and index finger of her left. A painful impulse to steer her toward caution in what she confessed.

"You blame Isiah for what's happening with your relationship," Dr. Legg said.

"Is that a question?"

"I'm not sure," Dr. Legg replied. "Is it, Rachel?"

Tea lights. Dr. Legg's office had lots of tea lights as well. Scented. Her favorites appeared to be lavender and garden mint. She always asked at the start of their sessions for permission to light a few of the candles. The lavender was overpowering for Rachel—it lodged in her throat like kernels of popcorn, and she struggled to keep coughing fits at bay. Still, she never objected.

"Do you blame Isiah for what's happening with your relationship?"

"Yes," Rachel said. "I suppose I do."

"For accusing you of being unfaithful?"

"He didn't word it that nicely," Rachel said, her hands back on her lap. Dr. Legg seemed to notice, and that angered Rachel. She bit the inside of her jaw. "He accused me of *fucking* Nate."

Dr. Legg's cheeks blossomed a fiery red, and though she wore no pearls to clutch, her delicate fingers still reached, briefly, for the collar of her blouse. "How would you have responded, if he'd worded it more . . . nicely?"

The quick recovery further angered Rachel. "You know I don't do well with hypotheticals, Doctor."

"Could you try in this instance?"

"No."

"Respect is important to you?"

"Just me?" Rachel said. "You'd be fine with your husband accusing you of fucking some other man? Or woman?"

"I've had arguments with my husband that left me feeling disconnected from him. Is that what you're experiencing, Rachel?"

She smiled at the doctor's agility. Such a slippery bitch. A manner that could lull you in like the soft contours of the couch.

"Rachel?"

"As I've told you, I'm not sure what I'm feeling, Doctor. But I am tired of talking about me and Isiah. Can we move on?"

"Let's discuss Nate then."

Rachel shifted in her seat again. "Absolutely not."

"Why is that?"

"This whole thing with Isiah is because . . ."

"I'd love for you to finish your thought, Rachel."

"I'm done talking about all of this."

"You first came to me after your assault," Dr. Legg said. "Do you remember the emotions you were dealing with then? Mostly that you felt so alone. I encouraged you to open up to Isiah."

"I couldn't involve him in that," Rachel said, waving her hand.

"But you were comfortable telling Nate?"

Because all she'd wanted was revenge, for her attacker to hurt, to suffer. Isiah's gentleness was one of his best qualities. But she needed rage. Fire as searing as her own. Nate offered that.

"Rachel . . ."

"Why are we rehashing this?" she barked at Dr. Legg.

"I believe it's relevant to what is happening with you and Isiah now."

"I don't know how it could be."

"I've never asked what Nate did after you told him about your assault. I could guess the particulars, but I'd rather not. What I do know is that whatever it was, it helped you tremendously. And I imagine Nate's support must call up some emotions. Those emotions are tricky for you. You've never really wanted to talk about it."

"Including now."

Dr. Legg pressed on anyway. "Try to remember what you felt after Nate's help."

Rachel glanced away, said, practically in a whisper, "Appreciative."

"And what about Isiah? What did you feel toward him during that time?"

"Nothing," Rachel answered. "He wasn't involved."

"So, you felt nothing for Isiah."

"I didn't mean it like that," Rachel said, turning back to face the doctor. "You're twisting my words."

"What would Isiah have done if you'd told him about the assault?"

"How would I know?"

"I'm sure you've given it some thought."

"I really have no idea, Doctor."

"Okay."

"Don't do that," Rachel said.

"Why are you getting upset?"

"Isiah would've helped me through it . . . in his own way."

"You're confident of that?"

"Yes."

Dr. Legg smiled at her. "I'm wondering then, Rachel, why you didn't tell him what happened to you. Why you didn't give him a chance to support you through it. Why you confided in Nate instead."

It was a good question, a wonderful question. Rachel sat there a long time, working through an answer.

"He didn't notice anything was different with me," she said finally. "After I'd been assaulted."

"Isiah?"

Rachel nodded.

"And . . ." Dr. Legg prodded.

"Nate did."

"I see."

"That's the thing with me and Nate," Rachel told her. "We're too much alike. He can . . . he can see inside me."

"Sounds like a relationship with some depth."

"I need to go now, Dr. Legg," Rachel said, rising suddenly, as if from a slumber.

"We have twelve more minutes."

But Rachel was out the door.

38

Topsy-turvy. **The phrase** floated in Mason's head. The anchor of an old song by the Manhattan Transfer. It meant upside down, a state of utter confusion—exactly how he felt in the moment. His pulse wasn't racing, but it wasn't exactly hushed, either. His shredded ear throbbed like a stubbed toe and burned as if the big guy, Samuel, had taken a blowtorch to it. The room was a Tilt-A-Whirl. And Elizabeth appeared to be in shock. She'd stopped gripping his shoulder and fell back against the couch cushions, gone still as a breezeless day. Despite everything else, she was Mason's greatest concern. He couldn't say for sure what this was, but he knew it wasn't good. It gutted him that he'd brought Elizabeth into it.

"Why are you holding us?" he asked.

The question was directed to the clean-shaven guy with the pale-blue eyes. But of course, the freak show, with two lightning bolt tattoos high up on his neck, the number 88 inked by his right eye, a beard like a cheap Christmas wreath, of course he was the one to reply. "You heard Samuel. We're to keep an eye on you until he returns."

"You haven't answered my question. Why are we being held against our will?"

"Try not to look at it like that. Try to see it as a few committed,

righteous patriots working together for some sort of understanding.
We need to find out what happened to Chipper."

Mason frowned. "Patriots?"

"Yes, sir."

"Who are you people?"

"Committed, righteous patriots," the freak show answered.
"Thought we'd just established that."

Mason looked at the other guy, the normal-looking one. He
turned away and moved to the edge of the room, focused on the ceiling, the walls, everything but Mason and Elizabeth. Uncomfortable
with what was happening here. Mason tucked that knowledge away
for later. It might prove useful.

"You all some sort of group?" he asked.

"Brothers," the freak show replied.

"No sisters in your group?"

"You ask too many questions."

"Samuel's your leader, I presume."

"Far too many questions."

"What do you call yourselves?"

"Just sit there and be quiet a minute," the freak show yelled.
"You're giving me a damn headache with all the questions."

Mason decided not to push his luck. He quieted. And thought.
He didn't know much about these alt-right groups that were in the
media, but Samuel's gang of misfits appeared to fit the bill. Except for
the normal-looking guy. He could've been an altar boy at Our Lady of
Saints, a first-year history teacher at some high school, a rookie officer
back home with the BPD. It was unnerving that someone so ordinary
would be involved with these sickos. Mason touched his ear, his fingers coming back dry. The blood had clotted, but that didn't change
the fact that the big guy, Samuel, had nearly bitten the ear off. Sickos.

"I need to use the bathroom," Mason announced. He turned to
Elizabeth. "How about you?"

She didn't process he'd even spoken to her, so he asked again. This time she shook her head.

"Where is it?" he said to the two sentries, casual and confident, leaving them no room to question whether he should get the opportunity.

"I'm not watching over another man taking a piss," the Freak Show said.

"You'd rather a fellow patriot soiled his pants?"

Freak Show's eyebrows knitted. "What now?"

"I'll show him the way," the other guy said.

Mason smiled. "Appreciate it . . ."

"Ronald," he offered.

Mason rose to his feet, knees cracking with the effort. He gave Elizabeth a reassuring smile that bounced right off her. There was a strong possibility she was in shock. Her lack of affect was concerning. Mason had to do something to lift her out of her malaise, and fast. Would she even be able to move if he put them in position to make a run for it? He leaned down and took hold of her chin, raised her head. Once she met his eyes, he said, "I need to go see a man about a horse. I won't be long. Yell if anything . . . if he starts doing anything to you."

An almost imperceptible nod. She barely blinked.

"I ain't no rapist," the freak show called out. "If that's what you're insinuating."

Mason gave him a smile, partly in surprise at the freak's vocabulary, partly to exude a sense of calm he didn't feel. "Not insinuating that at all . . ."

"That trick isn't gonna work on me," he said.

"Okay then." Mason nodded at Ronald. "You lead and I'll follow."

To Mason's surprise, Ronald stepped out ahead of him and into the hall. Heart starting to hammer, Mason trailed him. He balled his right hand into a fist. There's a big bundle of nerves behind the ear, a very sensitive area. Hit it right and lights out. The back of the head or neck was another option. Good old rabbit punch. Near to the brain stem, could be dangerous and potentially lethal if struck.

Mason lengthened his stride to get closer to Ronald.

Started lifting his arm.

Ronald pulled up short, though, and Mason crashed into him. It knocked the wind from his lungs. Dazed him. Still, he made out the booming voice just beyond them at the other end of the hall.

"What the fuck are you doing, Ronald Owen Atkins?"

"He . . . he needs to use the bathroom."

"Are you really this dumb?"

"Sir?"

Samuel bulled his way forward, pushing aside Ronald, rag doll–tossing Mason against one of the walls. The pain was immediate and excruciating. Bile rose from Mason's stomach and for the second time today his eyes watered. He risked a glimpse at his left shoulder and saw the grotesque bump where his arm bone had popped out of the shoulder socket. He fell to his knees, clutching at his left side with his right hand, and bit down on a scream.

Samuel took hold of Mason's damaged shoulder.

"No, please, don't—"

And wrenched it back into place.

Mason vomited, some of it spotting the front of his shirt. It didn't get on Samuel, but the big guy appeared to take offense just the same. He shoved Mason aside and kicked him in the back.

Facedown on the ground, Mason closed his eyes and prayed for this nightmare to end.

"Bring him back in the room," he heard Samuel say. "I've got more I'd like to ask him."

Elizabeth had finally stirred. Her eyes welled with tears immediately upon seeing Mason as he was ushered back into the room. He dropped down on the carpet, several feet from her, humiliated to be covered in his own puke.

Samuel took the armchair again. "Nate Evers," he said.

No one else spoke.

"Name doesn't mean anything to you?" he asked Mason.

"No," Mason replied.

"I need you to check with your client then to see if it means any-thing to him."

"I'm not involving him in this," Mason said, defiant.

"No?"

"No."

Samuel tossed something. Mason couldn't lift his good arm quickly enough, so it bounced off his chest and landed on the carpet next to him. A scuffed, brown leather wallet.

"For you to understand how serious I am," Samuel said.

Right hand shaking, Mason flipped open the wallet, the unsmil-ing face of a black man staring at him from the driver's license tucked behind the clear insert inside. Nate Evers. An address in a place called Irvington. "What did you do?" Mason stuttered.

"Our country a favor," Samuel replied.

"I don't think anyone is going to thank you for your service."

"Maybe not," Samuel said. "Nonetheless, the nigger was watching this house. My brother's house—my brother who has just recently gone missing. Two plus two, as they say. I would've liked to have asked this Nate Evers why he was so interested but you don't always get what you want."

"Why didn't you ask him?" Mason said, fearing the answer.

"Afraid that after we shot him," Samuel said, smiling, "the nigger nosedived over a cliff."

Could this really be happening?

A hitch in his voice, the man named Ronald said, "Sir? You killed him?"

Samuel turned to him. "We'd be within our rights. You should've seen the nigger wailing on Polk. Luckily, Logan got off a few good shots, at least two of 'em true, before this Nate Evers went over. There's a slim chance he's alive down there, I guess."

"You're not going to check?"

"What for, Ronald Owen Atkins?"

"Like you said, he could be alive. We might be able to save him."

"What you're suggesting sounds downright humane."

"We—"

"The niggers are born from monkeys, Ronald Owen Atkins. They've got the advantage when it comes to physical endeavors of any sort. If anyone could drag themselves up out of that gulch, it would be a nigger."

Elizabeth openly sobbed.

"Sir, I don't think it's a good idea to leave him down there without—"

"Jesus Christ, you're a soppy bastard; gullible and humorless to boot. You think I'm an idiot? Of course we're checking. Logan and Polk are making their way down to where he fell as we speak. And let me tell you, the nigger would be better off dead, because if Polk gets his hands on him . . ."

Ronald relaxed his shoulders.

Samuel turned back to Mason. "I need you to call your client and ask him if the name Nate Evers means anything to him."

And again, Mason told him, "I'm not involving him in this."

"You really want to die on that sword?"

"I may reconsider if you let Elizabeth go."

She looked into Mason's eyes then, and even knowing there was a possibility he wouldn't make it out of this alive, Mason felt content. Bella had been the love of his life, and though that had diminished, though it had broken his heart into shards, Elizabeth had ignited a new flame of hope. The thought of that made it to his face.

Elizabeth smiled back at him.

That was everything.

Her bravery in this awful situation was everything.

"Be a shame to separate you two," Samuel said, ruining their moment. "It's obvious to me you're a matching pair. So, no, I think we'll
hold on to your dear Elizabeth. And you can hold on to your client's
anonymity. There are other ways for me to get the answers I want."
He turned to Ronald. "My memory fails me the older I get. You're on
Facebook, correct?"

"Sir?"

"Facebook? Do you have an account?"

Ronald nodded. "I do, sir."

Samuel queried the others in the room, everyone except for
Elizabeth and Mason. All affirmatives. They had either Facebook accounts or some other form of social media. Gab. MeWe. Parler.

"There's my point," Samuel said. "Even degenerates like you all are
on social media, and I'm betting this Nate Evers is as well. How 'bout
we get on the interweb and see? We should pay special attention to
his friends once we find him." He moved over to Elizabeth, bent down
in front of her like a baseball catcher. "I couldn't help but notice your
laptop bag. I imagine you brought along your actual laptop, too. Mind
if we use it? Or is it just for your chubby little fingers?"

She lifted a hand to slap him, but he grabbed her by the wrist.
Mason attempted to rise, and the freak show stepped in front of him,
shook his head.

"Save us the trouble now if there's a password," Samuel said to
Elizabeth, tightening his grip on her wrist.

"Lawrence thirty-three," she said, grimacing. "Capital L."

Samuel let her wrist go. He turned to his men. "Who's good on
the interweb?"

Ronald raised his hand, said, "I'm decent."

"Jesus fucking Christ," Samuel barked. "We aren't in grade school."

"Sir?"

"You don't have to raise your fucking hand to get called on."

"Sorry." Ronald lowered his hand.

Weak link, Mason thought, not for the first time.

"See if you can find this Nate Evers online," Samuel told Ronald. "We have his driver's license to compare with any profile pics you might find."

Ronald moved over to Elizabeth's laptop bag. "You mind, ma'am?"

"Just take the damn thing," Samuel barked.

Ronald hesitated, and then took it. He sat on the couch and placed the bag on his lap, unzipped it and pulled out the laptop. After a while, he said, "What's the Wi-Fi password here?"

"Chrissakes," Samuel said. "Take that out and get the password from Chanel. Don't come back until you've found something."

Ronald sulked from the room.

"Gas station robber," Samuel said, shaking his head. "Hard to fuckin' believe."

"You're not going to get away with this," Mason told him.

"We probably wouldn't," Samuel said. "If there were any witnesses."

They both fell silent after that.

Not a word spoken until the man named Ronald came rushing back into the room. "I have something," he said, practically breathless.

"Go ahead," Samuel told him.

"Mostly political stuff from Evers," he said. "Articles he shares, stuff like that. He doesn't really write anything himself."

"Okay."

"Usually," Ronald added. "I did find a post from a few years back announcing the formation of something called a PAC. It got a bunch of likes and comments, including from a guy who's also involved in it with him."

Samuel cocked his head. "You have my attention."

"This guy's the opposite of Nate. Basically, has put his whole life online. Turns out the woman he's marrying—Rachel's her name—is also part of this PAC with them."

"Are there any pictures of her on his account?" Samuel asked.

"Lots. He's clearly smitten with her."

"Light-skin black woman, could pass for white?"

"Definitely."

"Okay, go ahead."

"The oversharer is named Isiah Thomas."

"You're shitting me. Like the basketball player?"

"More like Linsanity."

"What's that mean?"

"He's a gook."

"Mmm."

"In one of his posts, he linked to an article about some guy who was busted for growing marijuana. The article gives a street and block, plus a picture of the weed grower's house. Isiah commented, 'my neighbor.'"

Samuel smiled. "So, we know where this Isiah Thomas lives?"

"That's right."

Samuel nodded at the freak show. "You and Frog go check him out."

Mason watched with a growing sense of doom as Samuel then turned to Ronald.

"Never thought I'd ever hear myself say this," he told him, "but . . . I must tell you, Ronald Owen Atkins, I'm absolutely chuffed."

39

Isiah drove in a crawl down the residential block of three-bedroom co-
lonials. The sidewalks were littered with leftover white bracts from
the flowering dogwood trees that flourished in late spring. The street
overflowed with vehicles, making parking impossible, so he continued
another two blocks and pulled into United Fellowship's lot. A few
others had cleverly thought to leave their cars there as well, heathens,
as Joshua's mother would call them, because there was no evening
Bible study or revival services, the inside of the church dark as a funeral suit. Isiah turned off the engine and sat there a moment, willing
his hands to steady. They resisted his effort. Fuck it, he said to himself,
pocketing his keys and climbing out.

A few minutes later, he pulled up short in front of a humble
house with a whisper of a lawn baked brown despite the protruding
head of a sprinkler system. A walking path led from the street to
a jerry-rigged wheelchair ramp constructed with a two-hundred-
dollar budget of lumber, non-slip paint, and prefab handrails from
Home Depot. Isiah had spent the better part of two weekends
helping to build the ramp. He eyed it as he plucked his cell phone
from his pocket and punched one of the Favorites icons from the
call menu.

"Hey," he said. "I'm out front. We need to talk."

The front door opened, jolting him even though he'd been expecting it.

"This isn't really a good time, Isiah."

"I'll be as quick as I can," he replied. "Need to bring you up to speed on a few things."

"You should've called ahead. I would've told you I couldn't do this now."

"Trust me," Isiah said. "You need to hear this. It's about . . . our work."

Joshua's nostrils flared, but he yawned the door open wide. Isiah stepped inside.

"Where's Miss Dot?" he asked, seeing her normal spot on the couch wasn't occupied.

"Caregiver's helping her wash up."

"When did you get a caregiver?"

Joshua shut the door with a soft click, locked it, and shuffled off toward the kitchen. Isiah frowned but followed his friend down into the basement.

"So, talk," Joshua said, dropping down at the head of the cot where he slept.

"You okay, bro?"

"Didn't you say you'd make this quick?"

"Yes, I did."

"You should probably get started then."

"Why are you so uptight?"

"Isiah . . ."

"All right, all right." He moved over to the area of wall beneath the basement's one window, leaned against it. Nate's spot whenever they congregated down here. "I've been watching the guy's house," he began.

"What guy?"

"You know who I'm talking about."

"Wait a minute," Joshua said. "Why would you do that?"

"Couldn't stop thinking about his girlfriend and what she must be going through," Isiah said, shaking his head.

He wasn't ready to admit he'd been back there, to the spot where they'd buried Chipper, and he'd been tinkering around on that abandoned property, that he'd placed motion-sensor cameras there that would capture anyone who came near the grave and send a video to his email. That he'd been torn as to whether he should let Chanel know Chipper was dead.

"I hope you're not about to tell me she spotted you," Joshua said, pulling him back in.

"No. I was discreet."

"What then?"

Isiah glanced at his watch, a Peugeot he'd picked up at Kohl's for under a hundred dollars. Though it lost a minute or two off the actual time with each passing week, he couldn't bring himself to replace it. Change, he was coming to understand, wasn't easy for him. He'd thought a lot about that over the past few days. "Little while ago, someone showed up at the house."

Joshua frowned at him. "Are you going to dole this out like cough syrup?"

"A man and a woman," Isiah went on, "clearly out-of-staters. Man carried himself like a cop. The woman was wearing a T-shirt . . . for December's Promise."

Joshua stopped frowning and sat up straight. "Shit. What the fuck, Isiah?"

"They were dropped off by a Lyft," he continued. "I called Nate about it, and he came right away. He sent me off to track down the Lyft. He believes Rachel could talk to the driver and find out if the cop and woman said anything during the ride. Might be something there that'd tell us what they're up to. Their showing up must be connected to us."

"Shit," Joshua said again.

"Nate stayed back to watch the house a bit longer. We figured they'll need another Lyft. He'll follow them, hopefully to the airport. If they're staying here . . ."

"We're fucked," Joshua said.

"Maybe."

"How are you going to find the Lyft driver?"

"Got his plate," Isiah told him.

"You know someone at the DMV? I can't imagine you can hack into their system."

"Dark web isn't just for selling fentanyl without a prescription," Isiah replied, "or hiring someone to kill your spouse or significant other."

Joshua blew out a breath.

Isiah heard the door to the basement open, the stairs creak. He came up off the wall.

A familiar voice called out, "Joshua? Is everything okay down here?"

"I'm just talking to Isiah."

"Miss Dot's all cleaned up. I started dinner."

She came into view at the foot of the stairs. Looked first from Joshua and then to Isiah, a frown forming once she saw him.

"Hey, Alani," he said, waving and smiling. "Long time no see."

She turned on her heels and rushed back upstairs.

Joshua groaned like the steps.

"Caregiver, huh," Isiah said, smiling.

"Shit."

"How long has this been going on?"

Joshua looked at Isiah, as though seeing him for the first time. "What are you talking about?"

"Thought you two were kaput."

"Kaput? How old are you, man?"

"Broken up," Isiah said. "Consciously uncoupled. Better?"

"Not really."

"So how long have you—"

"She knows what we've been doing," Joshua blurted. "And what happened."

"You mean—"

"Yeah."

"Everything?"

"Everything," Joshua said, nodding.

Isiah took a moment to process that. "How did she find out?"

"I told her."

"Fuck, man. Why?"

"You've been hanging out watching the man's house. You have to ask?"

"Confessing something to your estranged girlfriend that could get you and your friends sent to prison," Isiah said, "was something you had to do?"

"Pretty much. And we weren't estranged. I just needed some time to myself. There was a lot for me to process."

"That's the point, Joshua. She's been processing, too. No telling how many dudes Alani's processed with since the two of you were last together. You don't even know what she's about now. Woman that pretty isn't just sitting around waiting on—"

"You've said enough, Isiah."

"Don't get upset. I like Alani. Always have. She still friends with loudmouth Crystal, though? You know Alani tells that girl everything. I can't say I'd trust either of them with something this . . . weighty."

"It doesn't fucking matter what you'd trust her with. I trust her."

"Damn, man." Isiah ran a palm over his scalp. "Nate's going to lose his shit when he finds out."

"You should worry a little less about Nate, and spend more time . . ."

Isiah's head rose and he eyed Joshua. "More time what?"

"Nothing," Joshua said. "Why don't you get to work on finding that Lyft driver?"

"More time what?"

"Let it go."

"Can't, you were about to say something. More time what?"

Joshua stood up. "I need to go have a word with Alani. You and I can talk later."

"I'm here now, bro."

"I'm not doing this, Isiah."

"More time what?"

"How many times are you going to say that?" Joshua asked. "You're acting like a child."

"Good you recognize that," Isiah replied, "'cause I'm about to start throwing shit. More time what?"

"You're the dumbest smart person I've ever known," Joshua told him.

"Is that right?"

"You know, from the start we weren't sure about you. Nate asked Rachel directly whether we could expect you to stand tall. And she didn't answer right away, just so you know. Despite that, we put our faith in you and now you're looking to fuck everything up."

"How long has Alani been back? A week? A few days?"

"What does it matter?"

"You're right, it doesn't matter," Isiah said. "Whatever the timetable, it hasn't been long. And you confessed everything to her? Sounds like Nate should've been wondering whether you could stand tall. Alani didn't need to know what we did."

"I don't lie to her," Joshua said.

"That's relationship goals." Isiah chuckled, shook his head.

"You need to ease up."

"Fuck you," Isiah yelled. "You motherfuckers have been underestimating and talking shit about me the entire time we've supposedly been friends."

"Supposedly? You're letting your emotions speak for you now."

"Isiah the milquetoast Asian."

"Never heard that from me," Joshua said. "Must be how you feel about yourself."

"Me?" Isiah shook his head, deepened his voice. "I've got knowledge of self, bro. My people are kings, queens, rulers of the universe. The original people."

"You're mocking us for being black and proud?"

"Nah, bro. Do you."

"You should go, Isiah."

"You know Alani is a Hawaiian name? Means 'precious' or 'orange tree.' Black people accuse others of appropriating your culture, but you all are well acquainted with that yourselves."

"You have issues, Isiah. And I can't help you resolve them."

"Rachel told me she had to choose," Isiah said. "And although you can't get her to eat spaghetti or cevapi, even though she's totally committed to her blackness at the expense of everything else, it's black people who've given her some of the hardest time."

"You're rambling."

"Darius might still be here if it weren't for this ignorant shit."

"We're not bringing my brother into this," Joshua said. "Absolutely not."

"You've got issues, too, bro. You weren't feeling him dating that Italian girl."

"Isiah . . ."

"If Sofia had been in your hood," Isiah said, "she might not have been safe after dark either."

"Time for you to go," Joshua told him, moving over and taking him by the elbow.

Isiah shrugged the hand aside. "You tell Orange Tree that Darius was in that neighborhood because you made it clear to him he shouldn't bring that white girl around here?"

"You stupid motherfucker."

"Imagine if Rachel didn't have to choose, if I never got called a Chink . . . if you'd been more supportive of Darius's choices."

At that, Joshua was on him, bunching up the collar of Isiah's shirt, hot breath in his face. "You need to leave, before I hurt you."

"Take your hands off me, asshole."

Joshua released him.

They stood there, watching each other, both of their chests heaving.

"Get the fuck out of here," Joshua said after a while.

Isiah nodded and took to the stairs. Something good was in the oven, the kitchen warm with spices.

Alani was in the living room with Miss Dot, looked as though she was doing something with the older woman's hair.

Joshua's mother's face lit up. "Isiah? My goodness, look at you. I didn't know you were here. How you doin', sweetie?"

"Just a quick pit stop, Miss Dot. I'll catch you later."

"Alani made—"

He shut the front door behind him as he moved outside. Timing was everything, he realized, seeing a spot now along the curb out front wide enough to accommodate two vehicles. He walked down the wheelchair ramp and headed for his car, parked back at the church.

Fuck Joshua.

Fuck Nate.

Rachel . . . he wasn't sure how he felt about her. Disappointed? Angry? One thing was for sure—he needed to start thinking about himself. If the shit hit the fan, the three of them would likely shift into survival mode, self-preservation. He could be all kumbaya if he wanted, but that was a party of one. They'd been the ones to break the covenant. He never felt more alone than he did in that moment.

Probably the same emotion Chipper's girlfriend was dealing with, the cop and the woman notwithstanding. It would be cruel to leave her forever wondering about her boyfriend's fate. A show of cowardice if you got right down to it. Isiah was finished with being afraid to step out and forge his own path. If Joshua could confess all their sins to Alani, and Rachel and Nate could be united in some dark secret, then Isiah could give a grieving woman her closure.

He made it back to the church and slid inside his car. He rooted through his glove box, pulled out the vehicle owner's manual, flipped pages until he came to one that was blank. He carefully tore it out. He used the ballpoint pen he always kept on him to compose notes, big block letters, using his left hand. He creased the page and folded it in half.

He'd head back to Chipper's place now, to his hidey-hole in the woods, and when the sun slipped from the sky he'd trot over and trap the note under Chipper's girlfriend's windshield wipers. Or even drop it in her mailbox.

Either way, she'd know.

And that would be one less thing on Isiah's conscience.

He drove with the radio on low.

Approaching the turnoff, he glanced to his left at Woody's Bar and Grill.

Nate's Explorer was still parked in the lot. The shock of seeing it made Isiah miss the turn. He circled back and slammed to a stop alongside the SUV, primed for another fight. He leaped from his

vehicle, tromped over to the Explorer, but it was empty inside. The
hood cool to the touch.

What the hell? Nate hadn't returned yet.

Isiah's anger dissipated and a chill fell over him.

It didn't seem right Nate wouldn't be back by now.

Something was wrong.

40

"Samuel?"

Chanel was as surprised as Samuel was to find herself in the doorway, calling out to him, interrupting him in the middle of what he was doing. Since he'd banished her earlier, she'd watched television and tried to block out what was happening in the house she'd shared with Chipper. When that hadn't worked, she'd taken a long, hot shower, then dressed in a plain white T, mud-colored jeans, a choker around her neck, coral rings on both middle fingers. A look she'd tried to recapture from a rom-com she'd watched with Chipper. He'd loved the woman in it.

Samuel took her in, frowning. "You need something?"

"Talk to you a minute?"

"I'm kind of busy," he said, motioning at Mason and the others.

"Just be a minute."

"Keep an eye on our guests," Samuel told Ronald, and then he followed Chanel from the room. She beat him outside. Heart ricocheting in her chest, she fumbled in her pocket for the old joint she'd found in her panties drawer earlier. She also grabbed the gas-station booklet of matches, tore one off, struck it, and relit the joint. She drew the smoke into her mouth, held it there and moved the joint away from her lips, then inhaled the smoke deep into her lungs along with an intoxicating bouquet of oxygen.

"Could you be any more pitiful," Samuel said, nodding at her, wearing an expression of distaste, "out here smoking marijuana like some nigger?"

"Little weed never hurt anyone," Chanel replied. "Clears your head."

"You sure your head can withstand any more clearing?"

"What's that supposed to mean?"

"You called me aside," Samuel said. "I thought you had something important to say."

"More like ask."

"Get to it."

"What are you after with these people?" she said.

"I don't understand the question, Chanel."

"Mason. Elizabeth."

"They know something about what happened to Chipper."

"I'm not sure that's true."

"Really? Well, if my clear-thinking, weed-smoking sister-in-law doesn't believe they know something, then I should march right in there and bid them adieu."

"I heard Frog and the new guy talking." Chanel paused to take another puff. "Some black guy was watching the house?"

"We've dealt with that. Now, if that's all, I need to get back to—"

"You shot him?"

"Me personally," Samuel said, "no."

"I don't think this is still about Chipper for you."

Samuel frowned. "No?"

"You want to hurt somebody. That's clear. Doesn't matter who, either. It's just a bonus if they happen to be involved with what happened to Chipper."

"You should stop smoking, Chanel. It's well documented that stuff kills brain cells."

"Chipper wouldn't have wanted any of this," she insisted.

Samuel laughed. "Chipper would want me to go scorched earth

on these motherfuckers. Guess you were too busy shaking your ass and showing off your pudenda to any man with a dollar to really get to know my brother."

"Pudenda?" Chanel wondered.

"My brother was better than me," Samuel continued, shaking his head. "I'd never think to domesticate one of my whores."

"You've never liked me."

"I won't deny it."

"Because I made Chipper stop running with you and your merry band of fools?"

"Fair trade," Samuel said. "I gave him my blessing to move on from me and the brothers once you agreed to stop selling yourself for the price of a Happy Meal. You have no idea how much it humiliated my brother to have a damn stripper as his girl. You can't help who you fall for, though."

"You're a cruel man. Chipper *was* better than you."

"Why did the stripper wear panties?"

"What are you talking about?"

"To keep her ankles warm," Samuel said, smiling. "How is a stripper like peanut butter?"

"This is stupid. Why don't you—"

"They both spread for the bread. Chipper had a bunch of them, Chanel. Joking about you himself kept others from doing it first."

"He loved me," Chanel whispered. "I'm not gonna let you poison that."

"Sure enough. And it appears his final act of love for you was going off with a Taylor Swift look-alike that brought him a whole heap of trouble."

"Fuck you, Samuel."

"Are we done here?"

And when Chanel didn't respond, he headed back toward the house. A bounce in his step.

41

The sound of movement.

Nate listened, suddenly alert.

He blinked his eyes into focus, and then pushed upright onto his elbows. He needed to stand, to stretch some distance between himself and the men making their way down the slope. But his body was racked with so much pain, especially in his right leg, his mind blanked for a moment. It was much cooler down here, the soil like potter's clay along the banks of the narrow, slow-moving creek. A fringe of skunk cabbage and arrow arum beside the whispering water, the ground in this part of the woods littered with glass bottles, crushed aluminum cans, bald rubber tires, even a refrigerator streaked with tears of rust. Nate just the latest junk illegally dumped here.

No.

He gritted his teeth, stood to his full height, a white-hot flare sparking in his leg as he sloshed through the creek, water seeping into his shoes. On the other side, he collapsed behind the cover of a bush that was two heads taller than him, its branches sprouting from the crown of a thick, white, fleshy taproot. The bush had purplish stems and was covered in pixels of near-black berries. If it was poisonous, he'd get a rash, or worse.

"Christ, what the fuck . . ."

Nate snapped alert again, peeked and saw that two men had made it down the crest of the hill and were looking for him on the other side of the creek. The bulldog and the man who'd cut Nate off on the path and pulled a gun on him. The man Nate had pummeled and left for dead. There was a scowl on his face now as he turned a circuit, revenge no doubt ticking through his blood. "He couldn't have made it far after that fall."

The fall.

Nate registered for the first time that he'd tumbled at least twenty feet. And he'd been shot as well. Twice. Both grazes but it was still a damn miracle he was breathing, intact if not hurting. He nearly cried out in a peal of grateful laughter.

The bulldog slapped at his arm. "Getting eaten alive."

The insects were bad along here. Wood ticks, yellow jackets, mosquitoes. The mosquitoes were insidious, freckling not only Nate's arms but also his neck and face. Another miracle: that he was able, for the most part, to ignore them.

Not so much for the bulldog.

"Fuck this," he said, retreating toward the slope.

"You're giving up?" the other man said.

"Damn skippy, Polk."

"I'll keep looking."

"Suit yourself," the bulldog said, and he slapped at his arm again, stomped up the crest of the hill.

The other man, the revenant, Polk, let out a breath and scanned the panorama. Nate leaned back and closed his eyes as Polk's gaze fell in his direction. Had it been like this for Darius? Cornered and wondering whether this was his last breathing moment.

Heart crashing against his ribs, Nate reopened his eyes, saw Polk had his back turned, looking elsewhere. It didn't appear as though he wanted to move. Or was capable. Afraid. Nate smirked.

Classical violins and electric guitars wiped the smirk off his face.

Shit.

He struggled to dig his cell phone from his pocket, silence it.

The ringtone he'd programmed into his phone to indicate a call from I.T. *"Turbulence"* by the South Korean boy band ATEEZ.

When Nate quieted the smartphone, Polk was four yards from him. "Come out, come out, wherever you are," he taunted.

Nate searched the ground for a swollen limb, a hunk of rock, a Budweiser bottle, something. Nothing in sight or reach.

"Guess I'll come to you then," Polk said.

Nate scrambled to his feet, conscious of the noise he was making and the pain in his right leg, both unavoidable. Outrunning Polk was impossible, leaving Nate with just one option. Two actually. Stand his ground. Or attack.

He was strongly considering the latter.

Medical experts would say the two gunshots Nate had taken—one on the right near his rib cage, the other in his left shoulder—were tangential, superficial, but that distinction didn't minimize the hurt they left behind. He needed the wounds cleaned up, bandaged, possibly even stitched. He needed rest, not a fistfight.

"I'm gonna kill your black ass," Polk growled.

Experience is the best teacher, but Polk hadn't learned a thing with Nate's earlier wallet diversion. Off in the distance, a female blue jay sung like a child's rattle. Closer still, a titmouse whistled *peter-peter-peter*. Distractions that made Polk glance up in the trees. The split second Nate needed. He came out of hiding and hit Polk square in the jaw, rattling the man's teeth but also swelling his own hand. Dumb move. Should've hit him in the throat, a softer target.

Polk recovered quickly, let out an animal roar, and went on the attack himself, wrapping Nate up and piledriving him to the ground. With his full weight on top, Polk was able to use the leverage to pound Nate's head on a hard tree root beneath them. Nate knew the science behind head injuries. With each blow, his brain cells were stretching and twisting, his blood vessels leaking chemicals his brain used to communicate. Electrical activity dampening.

He had to get Polk off him.

He managed to reach up and gouge the man's eyes.

But Polk closed them tight, bobbed and weaved and continued banging Nate's head on the tree root. Nate's scalp felt like it was about to split apart.

He forced his body to go slack. Became dead weight.

Polk paused a moment.

And Nate head-butted him. Twice.

Polk fell away, dazed, on his hands and knees, a baby discovering he could crawl.

Nate shook his head to clear the cobwebs and stalked up behind Polk, scarfing his right arm around the man's neck. Forearm pressed tight to one side of Polk's throat. Bicep pressed tight to the other. Polk squirmed but Nate had all the leverage now. He leaned back and brought Polk with him, easing his left arm behind Polk's head. He pushed forward.

Same chokehold Daniel Pantaleo had used on Eric Garner.

Same chokehold the police had used on countless other black men that hadn't been caught on camera.

Low on the neck.

Pressing into the man's carotid, stopping blood flow to his brain.

Five Mississippi and Polk was still struggling, squirming, and wiggling, attempting to break free. Ten Mississippi and he began to quiet.

Fifteen. His arms dropped to his sides.

Twenty. His shoulders deflated and he sagged into Nate.

Twenty-three. His legs fell straight, the toes of his feet pointed in opposite directions.

Out cold.

Nate let him go, let Polk's body drop.

Breathing heavy, he reached into his pocket and lifted his cell phone to his ear. He'd connected the call, left the line open so I.T. could hear. "Please tell me you're close by."

"What's going on, Nate? Did that man—"

"You close, I.T.?"

"In the lot of Woody's Bar and Grill."

"I'm making my way back toward the road. Pick me up."

"Nate, you—"

He ended the call, pocketed the phone. With the limp, it took him longer than he would've liked to travel back to the main road, took up all the reserves of energy he had as well. He was drenched in sweat by the time he broke from the trees. Luckily, I.T. was waiting, engine running, his passenger door opened. Nate plopped down inside, lay back with his eyes closed.

"Jesus Christ. You're bleeding."

Nate's head swirled.

"It's all over your shirt."

"They shot me," Nate managed, his throat dry, raw.

"Wait. *Shot* shot?"

Nate opened his eyes to blurry vision, double images, the adrenaline wearing off. "I need you to get me somewhere."

"A hospital."

"No," Nate said. "Heather."

"Who the hell is Heather?"

"She'll . . . she'll know what to do."

"Is she a doctor or something?"

"Something," Nate said, and he gave I.T. the address. He was already drifting as his friend punched in the house number and street on his phone, so out of it he never heard the woman from Google Maps direct even one turn.

"Nate?"

A hand on his shoulder, shaking him.

He opened his eyes.

Vision even more blurry, a kaleidoscope of I.T.s.

"We're here," I.T. said.

"Ring her bell first. Give her a heads-up."

"Heather, right?"

"Yeah," he said, and he reached over, took ahold of I.T.'s arm. "Thanks, man. You really came through for me."

I.T. nodded.

Nate watched as I.T. rushed up the path toward the house. Watched as I.T. banged his fist on the front door. Watched as it opened and a woman came into view. She'd recently showered, a garnet flush to her porcelain skin, reddish-blonde hair slick and the color of squash when wet. Confusion and then concern in her green eyes.

I.T. must have asked her who she was.

Nate stopped watching and closed his eyes, right after she mouthed, "Nate's wife."

42

Years ago, at a strip club of all places, one of the dancers had asked Mason why he'd become a cop. He'd been off duty, working extra hours as a bouncer at the club. So used to standing wide-legged with his arms crossed, he couldn't find a comfortable position on the velvet couch in the lounge. A glass of ginger ale was on the table in front of him.

"Well?" the stripper, Bethany, had prodded.

Mason thought a moment and then started to speak. "First year on the job, I encountered addicts of every stripe, plus gangbangers, thieves, men who beat their girlfriends and wives, an idiot who got behind the wheel after drinking the heart out of his Saturday night and plowed down a bunch of folks leaving early Mass at Church of the Ascension."

"Any wayward strippers?"

Mason smiled. "More than a few."

A gleam in her eyes, Bethany said, "Guess you're gonna tell me you joined the cops to change the world."

"By myself?" Mason replied, snickering. "Can't say I had much motivation in that regard."

"What then?"

"Thought it'd be cool to bust heads." He'd paused to take his first sip of the ginger ale, a crinkle in his expression. "It sounds terrible, I know, but I had a lot of bottled-up aggression and taking down all of those . . . I was just energized by it, that's all."

Moving from the memory, he glanced over at Elizabeth now, and when she met his eyes, he smiled and gave her a nod. After everything that had happened, he wasn't surprised when she didn't reciprocate. She hugged herself and continued shivering. Mason blamed himself. He needed to turn the tide while he had the chance, while Samuel was off speaking with Chanel.

"What did you do before this?" he called out.

Ronald was just as dazed as Elizabeth. It took him a moment to realize Mason was talking to him. "What?"

"Before this," Mason said. "What did you do?'

"I don't know what you're talking about."

"You guys are a baby KKK, aren't you?"

"What? No. We're patriots."

"Cut the shit, Ronald."

"You don't know me, man."

"I know you better than you know yourself," Mason replied. "You want no part of this. I can see it in your eyes."

Ronald looked back at him, unblinking.

"You have options," Mason said.

"Do I now?"

"Sure. Convince the big guy to let us go." Mason smiled. "Or help us get out of here."

"Don't think I'll take either of those doors."

"You're not like the rest of them," Mason said. "I've been watching you closely. You're disturbed by all of this. You've gotten yourself into something and you're looking for a way out."

"That right?"

"You have family, Ronald?"

"Most do," he said.

"Wife or girlfriend? Kids?"

Ronald shifted in his seat. "Little girl."

"What's her name?"

"None of your business."

"I have a daughter. Her name's Nicole."

"I know what you're trying to do," Ronald said, "It's not gonna work."

"We're just talking, Ronald. That's all. And I'm trying to show you it doesn't have to be this way."

"You're wrong on that."

"I think you're scared, Ronald. Afraid to back out now that the ball's rolling."

"Scared?" Ronald scowled. "I did time, brother. Didn't flinch through any of it. You don't know shit about me."

"Doing time doesn't mean you're built for what's going on here, Ronald. I could name twenty men who did time and jump at their shadows now. You don't belong with Samuel and his brothers."

"I *am* one of his brothers."

Mason laughed.

"What's so funny?" Ronald said, frowning.

"You," Mason told him. "So funny you're sad. I'm trying to help you, *brother.*"

Ronald nodded, pursed his lips. "Knew an old man named Max," he shared. "Ran a little convenience store where I grew up. Cheapest motherfucker you ever seen. Candy on the shelves was all dusty, like it was in some black ghetto."

A different tone. Mason realized immediately that he'd pushed too hard, and it was backfiring.

"Listen, Ronald, why don't you—"

"Come to find out Max wasn't his real name. Hebrew name was Mordechai."

Mason swallowed. He didn't like where this was going. The

expression on Ronald's face alarmed him. He'd misjudged. Maybe Ronald wasn't the weakest link.

And as if intuiting Mason's thoughts, Ronald settled exactly who and what he was. A wicked grin spread across his face. It could've belonged to Samuel or any of the others. "Know what me and a friend of mine did to that old Jew when we caught up with him at the dumpster behind his place one night?"

Mason shook his head. "I don't need to hear this."

Ronald told him anyway. "Beat the kike right out of him."

43

Idling in her car in front of Isiah's house, Rachel looked in her rearview mirror for what felt like the millionth time. The street was as quiet as a testing room. A short while ago, two white guys in a pickup truck had slowly rolled past, but so far that was it. There were still a few hours of daylight remaining, the sky a mix of fire and sea. No telling how long Rachel would have to wait for Isiah to show. And her bladder felt as though it might burst any minute.

Desperate times called for desperate measures. Seeing Isiah's neighbor backing out of his front door, Rachel climbed from her car and rushed toward him. He turned, eyes colored in a bubblegum tinge.

"Hey, Derby," Rachel said, giving a small wave. "Sorry to bother you. Can I use your bathroom?"

He stole a glance next door, no car in Isiah's driveway.

"No idea where he is," Rachel explained. "I'm having quite a day. My cell is dead. And I misplaced my key."

Her cell had plenty of charge, and she'd dropped the house key in Isiah's mailbox after she stormed out the other day. A vindictive move now that she thought about it. Anyone could've come across the key and robbed Isiah's place. This wasn't exactly a prosperous neighborhood. Isiah, though, he hadn't even reacted the one time they'd spoken after the argument, just saying "Yeah" when Rachel asked whether he'd recovered the key. Surely his attitude toward her would've thawed by now. She had much she needed to tell him.

"I was heading out," Derby said, breaking her thoughts.

"I'll be quick, I promise."

He pursed his lips, then turned and led her down a long entry hall. A door lay open to one of the rooms off the hallway. Rachel peered inside. It was windowless, dank. A crowd of plants were arranged on folding tables beneath a mess of fans and lights. Derby, she knew, sold top-shelf sinsemilla—unfertilized female cannabis plants—and all manner of exotic weed. Even after several arrests, he hadn't given up his business. She couldn't say she blamed him, there was art in what he was doing.

He had a stunning setup.

Derby backtracked, brushing her aside. He eased the door shut, pressed his back against it. "Bathroom's just around the corner, first door on the left."

"Oh, sorry. Thank you."

In the bathroom, Rachel went over again in her head what she would say to Isiah. She'd read once that the ancient Egyptians had fifty words for sand, the Eskimos one hundred words for snow, and she was prepared to bombard Isiah with every word for love that came to mind. For once, she'd allow herself to be vulnerable enough to grovel for *his* acceptance. It would be humbling, but necessary.

A knock sounded at the door. "You fall in? I need to get going."

"Wiping now," she called, smiling as she heard Derby's hurried retreat down the hall.

She would tell Isiah about the time Derby had offered her a smoke and more. Also, that she'd turned it all down without hesitating. Hopefully in that experience alone, Isiah would recognize her commitment to their relationship. If not, she'd confess that every boyfriend she'd had before Isiah had been terrible for her and to her. Cheaters, emotional abusers, and Solomon, who'd put his hands on her that one time and thought croc tears could make it right.

Isiah was better than the sum of them all.

She flushed the toilet, washed her hands, dried them on the towel hanging from a ring above the sink.

Derby was waiting by his front door, walking back and forth across the rug placed there. He glanced at his watch and sighed when Rachel came into view.

"Have I made you late?" she said.

"It's fine. But I need to leave now."

Outside again, she abandoned her car and watched from Isiah's porch as Derby pulled away from the curb in front of his house, gunning the engine of his Corvette as he took off down the street.

"Asshole," she whispered.

This made her think even more about Isiah. She was truly lucky to have him in her life. He was one of the good ones. Thoughtful, considerate, prepared to spend—

"Shit," she said out loud, jarred by that last thought.

Prepared.

Isiah was not only prepared to spend the rest of his life with her, but he was also prepared in general. Sparked by a sudden recollection, Rachel leaped to her feet and trotted down the side of his house to the backyard. She found a fake rock back along the fence line, tucked underneath a bush Isiah never bothered trimming. It wasn't a particularly believable rock when it came down to it, but a spare key was inside. That's all that mattered.

Rachel's stomach churned as she slid the key in the back door lock. Stepping inside, she felt tired down to her marrow. A shower would do wonders, she decided. It was important that she be sharp when she spoke with Isiah.

She stripped out of her clothes and dropped them in the hamper in his bedroom. She grabbed two towels from the hall closet, committing on the spot to washing her hair as well. She laid the towels on the edge of the sink in the bathroom. She used her cell phone to pull up the R&B playlist Isiah had arranged for her and set the phone beside the towels.

Jagged Edge's "*I Gotta Be*" filled the bathroom like steam.

Rachel turned on the shower, tested the water with her fingers, regulated the temperature until it was just right. She stepped under the showerhead and let the jet spray work its fingers into her weary back muscles. With the release of tension came an old memory. Two months in with Isiah, and him standing by the doorway of his kitchen, frowning, a black, rectangular bar in his hands.

"What's this, Rache?"

"Soap," she'd said, looking up from loading his dishwasher.

"Where's my shower gel?"

She'd stood to her full height, nodded at the soap bar. "That's infused with shea butter, plantain, and palm oil."

"You tossed my shower gel, didn't you?"

"Your skin will thank me."

She grabbed a bar now, wet it under the spray, and rubbed circles over her body, calling up a rich lather. She rinsed and repeated the routine, her eyes closed as the hot water prickled her skin. She felt dirty enough for ten washings.

After lathering her hair with shampoo and conditioner, she let it sit for a moment, and then rinsed it out, noticing that the hot water was running its course. The shower gurgled and belched as she turned it off. Old plumbing. She and Isiah would eventually have to upgrade to a place that was more modern, and bigger, too, she thought, touching her damp stomach. They'd agreed that starting a family would be a priority. As if to augment the point, "*Can't Take My Eyes Off of You*" by Lauryn Hill came on. Rachel was smiling as she stepped from the shower.

But the smile faltered within seconds.

It took that long for her to process what she was seeing.

Or, more accurately, what she wasn't.

Her stomach tangled up like the strands of her wet hair.

The two towels she'd carefully laid on the edge of the sink were no longer there.

44

Samuel watched the clock on the wall, thinking about his brother. After a while, he smiled and, speaking to no one in particular, said, "She walks in beauty, like the night / Of cloudless climes and starry skies; / And all that's best of dark and bright / Meet in her aspect and her eyes."

"What?" Mason, the only one in the room who appeared to have heard him.

"My father was an enigma," Samuel said, emphasizing the "was" with the widening of his smile, a hateful smile. "Big and rough as tree bark, but he was always reading. Always making us memorize some quote or line of poetry. I think he believed having those words in our heads would somehow wash away the stench of who we really were."

"Sounds like he made an effort to raise you right," Mason said.

"Chipper never took to it, the reading, the memorizing. He'd rather be out working on something, using his hands."

"You do understand we had nothing to do with whatever happened to your brother, don't you?"

Samuel didn't respond.

"How long has your father been gone?" Mason tried.

"Those lines are from Lord Byron," Samuel said, ignoring the question.

"Poet?"

"That's right."

"Learn something new every day."

"The knowledge sharing has been pretty one-sided."

Mason looked into his eyes. "What are you doing here? Elizabeth and I have nothing to do with your brother. You should let us go."

"And let me guess," Samuel replied. "You won't tell a soul about me, about all that's happened?"

"Will you let us go?"

"Almost eight years," Samuel said.

"What?"

"That's how long the old man's been gone."

"I'm sorry to hear that. I lost my—"

"Car accident," Samuel cut in. "Insurance company suspected the brakes had been tampered with. They did an investigation but couldn't come up with anything conclusive. My brother and I were the only beneficiaries."

Mason gave him a knowing look, and Samuel nodded, another smile playing at the corners of his lips. A record day for him, despite everything. Chipper was the smiler. The chirp of Samuel's cell phone interrupted the moment. Mason let out a breath as Samuel answered the call. "Yeah?" A beat of silence to listen, then, "Okay."

He pocketed the cell and turned to Ronald, who'd been sitting by quietly this entire time. "Go with Logan and Polk back to the compound. Take Elizabeth with you. Mason will stick with me."

"You're staying here, sir?"

"No," Samuel said. "Kaleb and Frog are closing in on Rachel. I'd like a word with her."

And then he turned to Mason, a dazed-looking Mason. "Up," he said, directing him with a raised arm.

It pleased him that Mason stood without complaint.

45

Heather casually slid a Marlboro pack from her pocket and tapped out a cigarette, which she lit with a black Zippo lighter that had a cherry-red rose carved into the metal. She blew out soft whorls of smoke, squinting as she took Isiah's measure. "I need to know what you guys are into," she said. "And don't bullshit me."

"You're Nate's *wife*," Isiah replied, shaking his head.

"Are you going to keep saying that?"

"I'm shocked, sorry."

"Expecting Michelle Obama?"

"Wasn't prepared for a wife of any kind," he said. "But, yeah, wouldn't have pegged you for Nate's type."

"Nate's full of surprises," she said.

"We can agree on that."

They were in her den, a space with lemon-yellow walls and white crown molding, a fireplace with its large hearth painted coal black, a red sofa and two red gingham-checked chairs. There was a painting of a nude woman mounted to the wall above the sofa, her lacy white bra lifted to expose breasts swollen with milk and the curve of a belly, her legs splayed open to a nest of mahogany-brown pubic hair. Heather had described it as her own forgery of the first painting she'd ever sold, not long after she'd dropped out of nursing school. A validation of the decision. She sat beneath the painting now, Isiah across from her in one of the chairs. She'd cleaned up Nate's wounds and left him in a deep Tylenol sleep in her bedroom. She leaned forward to crush the light of her cigarette out in a handcrafted ceramic ashtray on her coffee table. It was also one of her creations.

"How long have you two been married?" Isiah asked her.

"More questions? Nate told me you were annoying."

"He's one of my closest friends, and an hour ago I didn't know you even existed. I hope you understand that I . . . yes, I have questions."

Heather sighed. "He stayed here with me for about three weeks before we realized it probably wasn't going to work out."

"This was when?"

"How about you answer *my* question now, I.T.?"

He blinked. No one other than Nate ever called him that, and so Heather clearly shared an intimate relationship with his friend. Rachel and Joshua would be blown away by that. Isiah wondered how Nate could've had this secret life without any of them knowing about it. Or was that an assumption?

"One more question. Does Joshua know about you and Nate?"

Heather shook her head. "None of my friends or family either."

"Can I ask why?"

"You're pushing your luck."

"I apologize for that."

Once again, Heather sighed. "As soon as June hits, I turn lobster red, even if I slather on SPF fifty. Knowing him as you do, you understand it's a serious dent to Dashiki Boy's reputation to have me on his arm."

"Dashiki Boy," Isiah said, letting it play across his tongue and mind, and then smiling. Best description he'd ever heard given to Nate. He could appreciate now what his friend must've seen in Heather. She had spunk.

"What are you guys into?" she said again.

"I think Nate should be the one to tell you."

Nate had suggested something similar earlier, regarding Rachel. Isiah hadn't liked it. But now he understood.

"That's a bullshit response," Heather told him.

"Maybe. But it's only right he tells you himself."

"You need to leave then."

"I'd like to stick around to make sure Nate's okay."

"I'll handle Nate, don't you worry."

"That's what I'm most concerned about," Isiah said, smiling to let her know he was kidding. Sort of.

Heather stood. "I'll walk you out."

"I'm sorry if we've gotten off on the wrong—"

She moved from the room, leaving him to his unfinished thought. Isiah waited a moment and then rose to follow her. She was by the front door, holding it open.

"Look, I—"

"Whatever mess you and Nate have gotten into, fix it. I don't want any more problems showing up on my doorstep. You understand, I.T.?"

He nodded and left.

For home.

46

Chanel glanced around in surprise. She'd grabbed her wallet, cell phone, and ring of keys, and clomped away from the house with no clear destination in mind. The only imperative was that she put some distance between herself and Samuel, so that had been her only focus. Or so she'd convinced herself. But clearly her subconscious had been at work because here she was now at the secret spot Chipper had shared with her shortly after they began dating. A rickety bridge, blocked off from traffic with concrete dividers. An unnerving vantage of the Raritan Valley train line below. Chipper liked to climb up on the guardrails, dangling his feet over the side. Chanel didn't have the stomach for that. The trains blurring by wobbled her footing as it was; it took every ounce of her courage to get close enough to peek down at the tracks. Heights had always been a problem for her.

Today, however, without giving it any thought, she hopped up on the guardrail. Surprisingly, although she'd never dared to ride a roller coaster and saw no romance in rooftop bars, her stomach didn't drop. She eyed the train tracks and looked off in the distance in anticipation of the next rumble. Nothing moved from miles away, and so she let her mind shift, focused instead on the next few moments and what needed to be done. She bit her lip, Chipper's voice in her head.

You're just gonna give up? Thought you were tougher than that.

She looked down again and swallowed. Easily a thirty-foot drop. No one could survive the fall. At least she didn't believe so.

She licked her lips and took a deep breath.

It wasn't exactly giving up, just rejiggering a life that didn't hold a lot of meaning for her anymore. Sometimes you simply needed to throw up your arms and admit you didn't have the strength, resiliency, the fortitude, and fight to keep going. And as cowardly as that might seem, Chanel didn't care. Samuel's words had wounded her, broken her, but he'd also done her a favor. Through his hate, he'd given her permission to accept this new course. And it was freeing to realize all the plans she'd made for the future ended right here, right now.

Easily a thirty-foot drop.

As Chanel was taking in another lungful of oxygen, a dark-blue sedan with tinted windows edged up close to the concrete dividers blocking access to the bridge. Its horn tooted. Chanel sighed and swung her legs back over the guardrail, stood and headed for the car.

Tonique's sister stepped out and waited as Chanel approached. She was taller than Chanel expected, close to six feet, probably not more than twenty-five, a cascade of jet-black and burgundy box braids hanging down past her shoulders, a long contrail scar against the smooth dark sky of cheek beneath her left eye. She was wearing a snug teal-blue T-shirt and a black skirt she could only wiggle into while lying on her back. Her hands were veiny and sturdy, her eyes hard.

"What are you frowning about, Renessa?"

"You looked like you were ready to jump."

"I wouldn't," Chanel said. "Appreciate you coming out to give me a ride. Tonique said you wouldn't mind."

"Look, I've been there myself. It's okay to—"

"You ready to go?" Chanel said, cutting her off. In no mood for amateur psychoanalysis.

"Okay, I'll butt out," Renessa said, raising her hands. "The truck is at . . . your old workplace?"

"Lace."

Renessa frowned again. Clearly, she didn't like the strip club. Didn't like her sister working there. Chanel found it all so very hypo-critical, that kind of high-minded morality, especially considering Renessa's role in what lay ahead.

"It's an honest living, Renessa."

"What is?"

"Dancing."

"Sure."

"What's your problem with it?"

"Don't want my sister to be another Briar," Renessa said, speak-ing softly.

Chanel had no response to that. The Summer of Briar, as she thought of it, had affected everyone at the club, her more than most because of their friendship. Women were always vulnerable to men with bad intentions, but that summer had been particularly heavy with distressing news. There was Holly Abramson, a blonde with eyes the vivid blue of dishwashing liquid and long, pianist fingers. What Chanel considered an endearing pouch of baby fat around the young wom-an's waist that was especially pronounced whenever she sat on a piano bench. Holly had been on summer break after a surprisingly sanguine freshman year at Berklee College of Music in Boston. Clark Burroughs strangled her with an extension cord he kept in the back of his work van. The cord left a mark around Holly's throat that looked like the inking of a snake tattoo. In the crime-scene photographs that were leaked online it was easy to make out the tiny pinpoint spots sprinkled like pepper across her eyelids and cheeks. Petechial hemorrhages, Chanel learned they were called.

Magdalena Montgomery was another. Some kids had been kick-ing around a soccer ball in a field of knee-high grass when they came upon her. Her panties had been ripped off her and tied in a make-shift blindfold to cover her eyes. Her mouth was stuffed full of dead grass and dirt. All but two of her fingernails were broken, likely in her struggle to get free. At the time of her murder, she had been a practicing ob-gyn for a little more than six years. A month before the end of her life, Eric Connelly had delivered a carton of benzalkonium chloride towelettes to Magdalena's practice and was immediately besotted by the raven-haired doctor. Magdalena apparently hadn't noticed Connelly sitting in her parking lot every day after that initial interaction, wearing shades in December.

And then there'd been Briar.

A little too close for comfort.

The other women were nothing more than stories Chanel had come across in the news.

Meanwhile, she and Briar had shared a set to Nine Inch Nails' "Closer" the last night anyone had seen Briar alive.

"You really know someone who'll give me ten for the truck?" Chanel asked, coming out of those memories. "Even though I don't have papers on it?"

Renessa was momentarily thrown off by the quick change in subject. "If it's in the condition you told my sister it is."

"Chipper took good care of it."

"Tonique said he run off on you. That true?"

"Called me from the road," she lied. "Told me to sell it and start a new life for myself. So that's what I'm going to do."

"Ten thousand is a lot of money," Renessa said. "But hardly enough to start some new life."

"More money than I've ever had at once," Chanel told her. "I'll put it to good use."

They hardly spoke during the drive. Other than Briar and Tonique, Chanel had never really had any close female friends. She found women annoying. And even with Tonique, they'd seldom hung out away from the club.

Chipper's absence made her ache even more.

"I'm going to drop you here," Renessa announced.

Chanel looked up in surprise.

The road in front of Lace.

"You don't want to see the truck for yourself, Renessa?"

"No. I'll give you a call later about getting it to my guy."

"I really appreciate this," Chanel told her. "I'll have to thank Tonique again for connecting us."

"She said you helped her sell a bike once?"

Chanel smiled. "Yeah, I sure did. Your sister and I have had a few adventures."

"I bet. She's at the zoo with Amerie. Playing mommy for a change."

"Tonique's a good mother. She loves her daughter."

"Mmm. I'll call you later about the truck."

The car was already moving as Chanel eased the door closed. She stood there and watched until it disappeared in the distance. Chipper might've had a book's worth of stripper jokes, and Renessa clearly wasn't happy with her sister working at Lace, but Chanel felt no shame for her time at the club. Every one of the women working there had her own story of hard luck and trouble, but, ultimately, they'd all done something that should be celebrated—they'd refused to roll over, instead took their gifts and monetized those gifts to provide for themselves and their families.

No shame at all in that.

47

"Isiah?"

Rachel wasn't surprised when he didn't answer. There was a hostile crackle in the air that Isiah wouldn't have wrought. But even with the certainty there was someone else in the house with her, she'd never felt more alone. Or, at the same time, more exposed. The door to the bathroom was cracked open and she stared at it—at its busted lock. If it weren't for that, she would have barricaded herself in here and called 911. She could still try, of course, but whoever had moved the towels would be on her before she punched in the first of the ones.

Mouth gone dry, she tried to call up some spit and couldn't. Not knowing what else to do, she just stood there, her heart banging against the cage of her ribs, water dripping off her and pooling on the tile like dog piss. Goose bumps prickled her skin and the glucose in her blood spiked. Spiked enough for her to summon the courage and energy to take a soggy step forward. Just one step and she stopped again and listened for sounds. Nothing but Lauryn Hill issuing from her phone.

She took another step, waited a beat, and then took another. Just a few more feet and she'd be close enough to snatch the towel off the hang bar ahead of her on the wall. It was a bit scummy from Isiah constantly drying his hands on it and never throwing it in the wash, but she didn't care. She needed to be wrapped in something.

She took another step and reached for the towel. To her dismay, it snagged on the hang bar as she grabbed at it. The bar humming like a tuning fork, Rachel grimaced and paused to listen for approaching footfalls. Still only the soft R & B, so she braved another step forward and was able to get a better grip of the towel. She swaddled herself in it.

She swallowed and took the last few steps to reach the door. Despite the steaming-hot shower she'd taken, the handle remained cool to the touch. She pulled the door inward and immediately lurched back. Two men stood there in the hallway. One had eyes that bulged from their sockets. The second man's face was wreathed by a rowdy beard. He was littered with tattoos, holding a towel in each fist.

His smile stole Rachel's breath.

"You really lose yourself in a shower," he said. "Didn't even hear me walk in before."

Rachel thought of several responses but couldn't get her mouth to form the words.

"Samuel can't wait to meet you," the man added. "Better get some clothes on. And for fuck's sake, turn off that coon music."

48

Samuel kept pace with long strides as up ahead of him Mason trampled through the brush, working his way, as directed, toward the lowering sun. He was breathing wildly through his nose, silent tears painting streaks down his face. Crying over the woman, Elizabeth.

"Halt."

And like a whooped puppy, Mason came to an immediate stop, bent over with his right hand on his knee, his damaged arm snugged up against his stomach as if he was trying to hold together his innards.

"Adrenaline not helping with the pain?" Samuel nodded at Mason's left side.

"What are you doing with Elizabeth?"

"That's your biggest concern right now?"

"She has nothing to do with any of this."

"Makes you angry, doesn't it," Samuel said, "that I had my men take her? Furious, even. Furious enough to strike me."

Mason didn't respond, but it was clear in the set of his jaw, and how his eyes blazed, he was considering just that. Striking Samuel.

Smiling at the notion, Samuel said, "Ever heard of Tyrtaeus?"

"I've had my fill of history lessons."

"A Greek elegiac poet," Samuel explained, undeterred. "During the time of the Second Messenian War. He was what they called a state poet, charged with riling the Spartans to fight to the death for their city."

"I said I didn't want to hear any—"

"You wouldn't think a life-or-death battle would require any motivating, but I can tell you from experience it certainly doesn't hurt."

"I don't care."

"That's good. Makes for an interesting dynamic between us. You have nothing to lose, and as a rule I don't lose."

"You're not going to get away with any of this."

Samuel trudged closer, said, "You're going to hit me until you can't lift your arm."

"What?"

"Preferably in the face. But careful with your hand. I have a hard skull."

"You're nuts."

Samuel slipped out of his vest, peeled off his shirt, tossed it at Mason. It landed by his feet. "Wrap your hand. Need to protect those knuckles."

"I won't," Mason told him.

"How difficult do you imagine it will be for me to *rile* my men to have a little fun with Elizabeth?"

Mason's nostrils flared.

He reached down and picked up the shirt, awkwardly wound it around his right hand, used his teeth to knot it in place.

"Throw short, compact punches," Samuel told him. "You'll generate more power."

Mason growled and unfurled a haymaker that snapped back Samuel's head. A second punch had the same effect. Samuel grinned, his teeth painted red, and he spat blood. Started chanting, *"Not where the missiles won't reach, if he is armed with a shield."*

Tyrtaeus.

Another punch rocked him back on his heels. He rubbed at his jaw, both surprised and pleased by Mason's strength. *"But getting in close where fighting is hand to hand, inflicting a wound . . ."*

49

The walls in the narrow corridor were hung with prints from Picasso's Blue Period—*The Death of Casagemas, Evocation, Two Sisters*. Somber, difficult art. Beggars, street urchins, the old and infirm, all depicted with an intensity that bled out through the canvases. Although each portrait was magnificent, Nate ignored them all and walked on, his footfalls little more than a whisper. Finally, after what seemed like endless miles of carpet, he came upon a door. It was painted a rich bloodred and marked with a private sign. His hand fell to the doorknob and twisted it open. He was surprised to find Heather inside, sitting cross-legged on the floor. She looked up, smiled, and said, "Hold that pose."

Nate froze.

"Still getting used to the charcoal," she told him, raising a General pencil for him to see. "It's amazing. I get a darker value with two layers of charcoal than I could with even five of the graphite."

She blew charcoal dust from the drawing pad, lifted what looked like putty—a kneaded eraser—and used it to clean up portions of the sketch, in the process creating distinctive highlights. Reductive drawing. The changes brought a smile to her face.

"So, you're a murderer?" she said, casual. When she looked up the smile had vanished. Tears of blood leaked from her eyes.

Nate came awake with a start. Lights burned overhead and from a standing lamp in the corner of the room. A ripple of cold moved through him. A headache throbbed on the right side of his head. He had the sort of cotton mouth a gallon of water couldn't slake. And glancing down at his right side, he saw squares of white bandage wrappings. Touching them softly made him wince. A matching bandage pad was on his left shoulder. His knuckles felt raw. His leg ached.

Battered and bruised.

Though he was steady enough while lying across Heather's bed, he instinctively knew once he stood, the room would begin to tilt and whirl.

He struggled to his feet anyway.

And sure enough, the room became the eye of a tornado. Using the furniture for purchase, he limped his way out into the hallway.

Where he heard voices.

He made his way toward them.

". . . couldn't just turn him away."

"You could have. You just chose not to."

"That's not fair."

"You've exposed yourself to all kinds of legal entanglements. You said someone shot him? I mean . . . Jesus, Heather, that's insane. Whatever he's into, you're into it now as well."

Nate cleared his throat as he reached the doorway of the living room. Heather turned, her brow furrowed, distorting the features of what was normally a very lovely face. But she wasn't Nate's concern at the moment. He focused his attention instead on the man standing less than a foot from her. The *him* Nate had referred to when he'd called Heather after his run-in with that police detective. He wasn't as tall as Nate, but that was just a quibble, for only an inch or two separated them. Nate thought of the man's strange granola complexion as dirty, practically mange. And in startling contrast to his vivid blue eyes, his hair was black as the ace of spades. It had to be dyed. Were blue eyes and hair that black even genetically possible?

"Speak of the devil," the man said.

"Good to see you, too, Keith," Nate replied.

50

Three vehicles splattered with dried mud were parked in the clearing beyond the trees. Mason noticed the bumper stickers that would've made any reasonable drivers switch lanes. Guilt by association. One of the vehicles was a hulking black SUV. Another was a tricked-out Honda Accord. Lastly, a pickup truck with more dents than wheels. Samuel moved toward the SUV, creaked open the driver's-side door, reached across, and started it. Key must have already been in the ignition.

Samuel joined him a few feet from the SUV. There was bruising on his face and just looking at it made Mason's right hand ache. "How many of you are there?" he asked Samuel.

"Enough."

"So, you were expecting trouble?"

"What do you mean?"

"Why else would you hide these vehicles here? Bring an army?"

Samuel smiled, said, *"Der liebe Gott sleckt im detail."*

"I'm sorry?"

"God is in the detail."

"What does—"

"Old German proverb," Samuel explained. "It's changed over time. From detail to *details*. From God to devil."

"You're a smart man, Samuel. Don't you think this has gone too far?"

"Get in."

"Why do I need to be involved in this?"

The big guy moved back to the SUV, turned, and gave Mason a look that made him wither and open the passenger door, ease inside.

"I'm doing you a favor," Samuel said, once he'd slid behind the wheel, "leaving your hands free."

"I won't be a problem."

They rode in silence. Perfect condition for all of Mason's fears, anxieties, and regrets to rise to the surface like earthworms after a torrent. He found himself thinking about both Elizabeth *and* Bella. And Nicole and his grandson. It stunned him that losing his job would not be the worst thing to happen to him this month.

"Settle in," Samuel said, breaking his thoughts. "We have a bit of a drive ahead of us."

Like they were partners.

"Where are we going?"

Samuel didn't answer.

Mason closed his eyes, not for sleep but to block out the dark thoughts intruding upon his mind. It didn't help. In fact, closing his eyes had only made the dark thoughts more vivid. Now he had images.

He kept his eyes closed.

He deserved this pain.

Eventually, they came to a stop.

Mason sat up, blinked open his eyes, yawned. He'd fallen asleep. How callous did you have to be to allow yourself rest in a situation like this? He was a horrible person and deserved whatever was to come.

Still, his eyes watered when he fully grasped their surroundings. A lonely one-lane, both sides of the road choked with bushes, nothing else as far as his eyes could see. No farmsteads, no houses. "Hey, Samuel, listen . . ."

"Get out," Samuel told him.

"I won't say a word to anyone about you."

"Out!"

Mason fumbled at the door handle, dropped down to the ground a moment later. He shut his door carefully, while Samuel slammed his, a sound like a gunshot that made Mason flinch.

Samuel lumbered around the back of the SUV, came up on Mason, looming over him. Mason nearly shut his eyes again. But Samuel turned away, stared off in the direction they'd come from.

"I thought you were going to talk with the woman."

Samuel didn't respond.

After a while, Mason heard something moving toward them from a distance. Then he saw it. A truck. Samuel cracked his knuckles and grunted.

The truck pulled in behind the SUV.

The freak show and a man with bug eyes—presumably Frog—stepped out. A woman stepped out as well.

Samuel moved toward them.

And Mason did, too, for some reason.

Freak Show said, "She's cranky. Made her listen to Daughtry the entire drive. Think she would've preferred Whitney Houston. Maybe that Ruben Studdard. Whatever happened to him anyway?"

Samuel stopped so he was standing a foot in front of the woman, just looked at her. To her credit, she held his gaze. Mason was impressed by the tall, eggnog-colored woman, with slick, wavy brown hair, mint-leaf eyes, and the demeanor of an animal with claws. The big guy may have met his match.

"Say something, motherfucker," the woman demanded.

"Where did you bury my brother?" Samuel asked, obliging her.

"Don't know what you're talking about. But if he's as ugly as you, he should be buried. More than six feet, preferably on his stomach."

Samuel chuckled and Mason's stomach dropped. The big guy wasn't easily amused. His laughter had nothing to do with joy.

"We've combed through your fiancé's social media," Samuel told the woman. "There's you, Nate, and Isiah, of course. Your fourth is a cipher."

Her face slipped and all her bravado with it.

"Obviously, we'll get Isiah. We already have you. We shot Nate."

"Wait. What?" she stammered. "You shot Nate?"

Samuel smiled.

"Is Nate dead?"

"Who's your fourth?"

"Fuck you."

"Possibly later." Samuel faced the freak show. "You have her phone?"

"The rhythm and blues jukebox? Sure thing."

Samuel wagged his fingers.

Once he had the phone in hand, he started pawing at the screen. It was like a child playing with a toy, his meaty hands, fingers like sausages, working through the phone. "Ah . . ."

He tapped twice.

Speakerphone.

Ringing.

Then a man's pinched voice. "Rache? Where are you? I've been sitting outside your place. It's bad. Nate's been—"

"Isiah?" Samuel said, cutting him off.

A long pause. Mason could only guess at what Isiah must be feeling, hearing Samuel's cruel voice on the line instead of Rachel's.

"Who the hell is this?" he said after a moment.

"My name's Samuel Wayne Pringle. I'm just here with your fiancée, trying to jog her memory as to where you all buried my brother, Chipper. Rachel's having quite a bit of difficulty remembering. We thought you might be able to help."

51

Joshua's cell phone rang out.

He frowned at the screen.

"Who is it?" Alani asked.

"Isiah."

"You're not gonna answer?"

"After all that shit he was talking . . ."

"Might not be smart to alienate him," Alani said.

"He'd have to implicate himself, if you're suggesting he might turn on us."

The phone rang again.

Joshua glanced at the screen, shook his head. "Persistent motherfucker."

"I was mean-mugging him earlier," Alani said. "But in all honesty, I like Isiah."

"Can't say the same. I wouldn't piss on him if he were on fire."

"Oh, Lord, Joshua. You don't mean that."

"He said a lot of shit about Darius and me."

"You were both emotional from what I heard."

"Fuck him."

This time the phone didn't ring. An alert sounded that Joshua had received a text message. "See what I mean?" he said. "Persistent as fuck."

He tapped the screen and went completely still.

Alani noticed the change in him. "What is it?"

"Rachel," Joshua said, standing. "Isiah says she's been kidnapped."

52

Chanel returned home to find the place was empty. Samuel and his cretins were gone. That should've thrilled her, made her feel a million times better, but all it did was leave her with the burdens of silence. She thought about calling Tonique, but then remembered she was out for a day with her daughter. There was no one else for Chanel to even consider calling, so she went into her bedroom, plopped down on the bed without pulling back the covers. Staring at the ceiling was like watching a movie screen. Images of the day and circumstances in which Chipper had thrust himself into her life.

It'd been Chanel's third time up and down the block, and only then did she notice the rusty Norton parked on the curb by the main road. Someone had sheared a motorcycle cover in half and hung the remains over the flank of the ancient bike, painted the word *Reclamations* on it. There was an arrow painted on it as well, directing customers down a narrow alley next to a retired strip mall anchored by a shuttered laundromat. At one time there'd been a Chinese restaurant in the strip as well, the sign still intact even though the inside of the space was bare.

She'd turned down the alley and had to immediately veer to the right as a hog roared past, a woman with flame-red hair riding pillion. She held up her middle finger to Chanel like a hitchhiker's thumb.

The shop had two bay doors and they were both raised. Chanel parked in front of them. Even from her car she could hear a whirring sound coming from inside. Probably a drill. She eased out of her car and moved toward the bay doors.

The shop was crowded with rows of bikes. Three bright red hydraulic lifts loomed beyond them. Gas tanks of every shape and color hung from the ceiling like butterfly chrysalises. A black-and-white sign attached to a support pole in the center of the shop floor stated the going rate for mechanic work at eighty-five dollars an hour.

Chanel tracked the source of the sound she'd heard outside. A drill, just as she'd suspected. Its operator placed the tool on the oil-stained concrete floor and retrieved a red shop rag and an unlabeled bottle of spray from a table off to the side. He wore a wool cap, despite the heat, and had tattoo sleeves on both arms, his earlobes stretched grotesquely by moon and sun piercing plugs. He didn't glance Chanel's way, but she could tell he'd registered her presence.

Another man was disguised by a black welder's helmet and long sleeves and bulky nitrile gloves. He was working a blow torch.

There was only one other worker in the shop. He was crouched down and working on another bike with a Tekton torque wrench. The wrench clicked and he rose to his feet and ran a rough hand down the length of the bike. Chanel's mouth gaped. He was well over six feet tall, and bulky with muscle like some comic book creation. But he was touching that bike in a way that made her skin tingle. She let out a breath and the man turned and spotted her. He looked embarrassed for a split second, then recovered with a toothpaste commercial smile and walked over. "No one's supposed to be in the shop but the laborers," he said, holding the smile while his gaze traveled over her.

Normally when she wasn't working at the club, Chanel would be wearing baggy sweatpants and a threadbare T-shirt that'd been through too many washes. But for what she was here to do she'd slipped on a pair of heels, pleated shorts, and a thin, flowery blouse. She hadn't dressed up fishing for compliments, though. She'd dressed up to be taken seriously. Her friend Tonique was counting on her.

"All sales are final," the man said.

Chanel frowned. "Excuse me?"

"Your mister read in some magazine that off-road dirt bikes are enjoying a renaissance and he bought one without clearing it with you first. You're worried he's gonna kill himself on it, even though he just straddles the thing and posts pictures on Instagram. He thinks it gives him the appearance of an *edge*. Edgy plays well, even in the suburbs."

Chanel fell in love with the big man in that moment. It stunned her that anyone could think that was her life. The suburbs. Jesus.

"He probably refused to come see if I would buy it back," he continued. "But you figured you might be able to persuade me."

"There's no mister," Chanel told him. "But I do have a scrambler I'm looking to sell."

"A scrambler you're looking to . . ." His words faded as he worked through the calculus of what she'd said.

"It's got low pipes that give it a nice rumble." Chanel nodded at the worker still fussing around with the blow torch. "An amazing bike, really. But I'm not sure now that I want to sell it to you. Not sure you can give it the proper love and care it deserves. It shouldn't take your guy over there more than a minute or two to budge that rotor bolt."

The man regarded her with curiosity. "I think I've misjudged you," he said. "You know a thing or two."

"Slutty aunt," Chanel explained. "Lots of biker boyfriends. I pay attention to everything."

"What's your name?"

"Chanel."

"Of course it is."

"What does that mean?"

"The name suits you, is all," he said.

"What's your name?"

"Duane. But everyone calls me Chipper."

"Why?"

"I'm loads of fun. Guaranteed to keep you smiling and feeling good about the world."

"Is that right?" she said, eyeing his grease-stained fingers, his ratty work clothes.

"I clean up rather nicely," he said.

"Who do I talk to about my bike?"

"That'd be me," he said. "Owner and operator."

"It's not actually mine," Chanel admitted. "A friend's old man gave it to her so she wouldn't take him back to court for an increase in child support. I told her I could help unload it. Get her at least a month's rent. She knows nothing about bikes."

"A month's rent," Chipper said, smiling. "Hope she's in a one-bedroom."

"That's not nice," Chanel chided.

"Where's this bike?"

"Parked in the lot where we work."

"We?"

"My friend and I," Chanel said. "Tonique."

"Exotic name."

"She's from the Bahamas."

"Mmm."

"So, are you interested?"

"Most definitely."

"Are you talking about the bike?"

Chipper had simply smiled at that.

They'd had their issues—his practically moving into Lace once he discovered she worked there, and then criticizing her at every turn for earning her living on a pole; her bitching about the racist assholes he drank beers with at his brother's sad little commune—but eventually they'd bartered exits for themselves, and apart from Chipper's wandering eye and an oftentimes hostile, bigoted outlook, life had mostly been good ever since.

God, she missed him.

She'd do just about anything to lay eyes on him one last time.

53

All the Righteous Boys knew about the forested region in northern Idaho, about forty miles south of the Canadian border, which erupted in gunfire on August 21, back in 1992. They knew all about the Weaver family, particularly Vicki, who was shot to death by an FBI sniper while standing in her cabin with her ten-month-old daughter, Elisheba, in her arms. They knew all about the eleven-day standoff and gave a nod to what happened those years ago with a sign at the entrance of their own compound—a sheet of plywood that could've been a makeshift basketball backboard that they spray-painted with two large interlacing Rs, one burgundy and the other bright yellow.

"People conflate Ruby Ridge with what took place several months later in Waco, Texas," Samuel said, continuing his narration of days gone by as they sped past the sign. "The Branch Davidian compound. The comparison irks me, though, to be honest. Those folks were a fringe religious group . . . of all races."

Rachel didn't respond, and neither did the man seated next to her in the rear of the SUV, Mason. He was a curious one. Didn't strike her as either a foe or ally. And they hadn't secured his wrists, as they'd done hers, and yet he was being held against his will, too. He kept sniffling like his nose was running.

"Seventeen acres," Samuel added, waving his arms to indicate the expanse around them, "every inch of it completely mongrel-free."

Rachel looked out her window. A cloud of dust kicked up as they traveled down a long, impossibly straight dirt road, blurring past a slanted rock-climbing wall, a plowed field with soccer goals at each end, the dregs of old campfires. In the grass, every so often she spotted charred pieces of wood, which made no sense, that is until she recognized the bottom half of a cross tamped in the ground like a rosebush trellis.

She couldn't believe it. These fools burned crosses for sport.

Jesus.

Rachel had no idea what was coming, but she knew this was the end of something, and would've given anything for the chance to tell Isiah how much she truly loved him, how sorry she was they'd wasted the past few days, time they could have spent together, making new memories.

She blinked.

No way would she allow these people to see her cry.

"Are you ready to tell me who your fourth is, Rachel?" Samuel asked her.

"Never," she replied.

"I'm very sorry to hear that."

They turned down a paved road that branched off to the right and came to a stop in front of a tiny log building. It looked to Rachel like a storage shed of some kind. Samuel climbed out of the SUV, shut his door gently, and then creaked open Rachel's door. The bearded, tattooed guy who'd been driving stepped out next. And Mason, too. They all stood around, peering into the SUV. Rachel let out a breath and hopped down from her perch.

"We're doing a reading from *The Death of the West* after dinner," Samuel told her, looking into her eyes. "You're welcome to join us."

Rachel ignored him, glanced around at the landscape instead. Dismissive.

The only power she still held.

Samuel grabbed her arm at the elbow, a tight hold she couldn't break free from, and guided her toward the log building. The bearded, tattooed guy ran ahead, disengaged the lock, and opened the door. Samuel shoved Rachel inside.

She wheeled around as he handed Mason a stainless-steel buck knife, with the wood handle facing out. "You're on sentry," he told him. "She makes a move . . . fillet her."

"I . . . Don't put this on me."

"Either do it," Samuel barked, "or you'll pay her debt."

Mason sagged. "Elizabeth?"

"Safe." Samuel smiled, clapping Mason on the shoulder. "For now." And at that, he stepped outside and closed the door behind him.

Mason went still a moment, then recovered and jiggled the handle. Locked.

He turned and looked at Rachel, pursed his lips.

Her stomach turned to water as she saw the change in his eyes. As she saw the way he tapped the knife against his palm. Like someone more than capable of using it.

54

"What do you want?"

Chanel's voice was rougher than Isiah had envisioned it would be, gravelly and full of smoke, a mournful note in it. He was already off balance, and hearing her now, sounding so damaged, only added to his feeling of vertigo. Which wasn't a good mix with the ferment already settled in his blood. Though he'd been compelled to do something, anything, he wondered now whether dialing her number was a mistake. If so, it would be one of many he'd made. Why not another?

"Who the hell is this?"

"I think you know," Isiah said.

After a lengthy pause, Chanel spoke again, a new steadiness in her voice. "You're one of the four?"

"That's right."

"Which?"

"Isiah."

"You've got some nerve calling me, Isiah."

"I want to know how to get in touch with Samuel."

"Trust me, that's the last thing you want."

"I don't have time for this, Chanel."

"Oh, you know my name."

"Are you hearing me?"

"You might've gotten the drop on Chipper," she said, "and Lord knows how. But you've gone and screwed yourself now. Samuel's as wicked as they come. He doesn't give two shits about fucking people up. He *likes* it."

"Duly noted. Where can I find him?"

"What did you do to Chipper?"

It didn't surprise him that she'd ask, but he was still caught a bit off guard. "Samuel has someone," he stammered. "Someone extremely important to me. Will he hurt her?"

Chanel's laughter said it all.

"I'm right up the road from you," Isiah told her. "Inside Woody's Bar and Grill. We should talk in person. Come alone."

"Who are you to dictate anything to me?"

"I need your help."

"I'm not the helping kind."

"I've read up on Briar Stewart. What was available in the beginning when she was newsworthy. That didn't last long though, did it? I mean, who gives a shit about a missing stripper." When she didn't respond, Isiah went on. "You do. She has to be missing for five continuous years in Jersey before being officially declared dead, and so you haven't given up hope, have you, Chanel?"

She didn't respond.

Isiah said, "Saw you buy something from GameStop the other day. Gift for Briar's daughter?"

"You'll tell me what you did to Chipper?" she replied, speaking softly. "Come alone."

Isiah disconnected the call. Stood on watery legs and stumbled toward the restroom. His heart was beating in his throat by the time he reached it. He shouldered his way inside, checked that it was empty, and, relieved to find it was, set up station in the last stall, the only one backed by a window he might be able to prize open and climb out of.

It took a couple of tries for him to work his zipper, and then several moments more until his bladder released. His piss sounded angry as it broke the toilet water.

He shook off and washed his hands at the sink, warm water, no soap. Couldn't look up at his reflection in the mirror.

Chanel was stepping inside the restaurant as he weaved his way back toward his table. He didn't bother trying to catch her eye, didn't wave at her, and yet she was standing over him as he settled back into the booth. "You can sit," he told her.

Again, everything about how he'd envisioned her was wrong. He'd pictured her sitting across from him, clutching a pocketbook tight to her chest, mascara running down her face. But Chanel's eyes were dry. She tossed what looked like a man's wallet and a tangle of keys on the table and took a seat.

"Thanks for coming," Isiah said.

"How did you know about Briar?"

"Watched the interview you did with News 12 on YouTube. None of the other dancers were willing to speak on camera. It was clear to me you're a woman of principle."

"Everyone's forgotten her," Chanel said. "But I won't. Ever."

"I was right about you buying gifts for her daughter?"

Chanel actually smiled. "I still talk to Briar's mother. She told me Lily really wanted Super Mario Maker 2."

"Samuel has my fiancée," Isiah said, getting back on track. "Where would he take her?"

"The compound, I would imagine," Chanel told him.

Isiah sat up. "How do I get there?"

"You?" She shook her head. "Most likely rolled up in carpet."

Isiah reached across the table and laid his hand on her wrist. She pulled away. They stared into each other's eyes for the longest time. Shockingly, it was Chanel who broke first. "You're crazy to even think about going there."

"Nothing to lose," Isiah said.

"That's not true at all. Samuel will make sure you lose plenty. And that you feel each loss in your soul."

"I don't care. I have to get Rachel away from him."

"You'll tell me where to find Chipper, if I help you?"

"Do you one better," Isiah told her. "I'll take you to him."

"I know Briar's dead. And I know Chipper is as well. That you had a hand in his death." She let out a long sigh. "Knowing and *knowing* are two different things, though. Isn't that what you were counting on? That after everything with Briar, I'd need to know for sure with Chipper."

Isiah opened his mouth, but no words came.

Chanel picked up her wallet, her keys, and stood. "I'm simple to figure out, I guess," she said, looking down at him, hurt in her eyes. "Come on. I'm driving."

55

Sean Patrick Adams. One of the first disturbance calls Mason took his rookie year on the force. Eight-year-old boy. Birth father high as a kite, decided to stalk his ex, a literature professor, and ended up snatching their son instead. In a cocaine fog, cut his son's throat. Their graves are green, they may be seen—the words etched on the boy's granite headstone in a cursive he'd yet to learn, would never learn. William Wordsworth, Mason discovered. From a poem titled "We Are Seven." A ballad of four-line stanzas that had made him blink, the first time he read it, as if sand had blown into his eyes.

He opened his fingers now, let the knife from Samuel clank off the wood floor.

"What's your deal?" the woman, Rachel, called to him.

"A masterpiece of loneliness," he replied, forcing a smile.

"What does that mean?"

"It's from a song," he explained. "John Waite."

"You have a head full of random song lyrics?"

Mason nodded. "Can't sing a lick, so it's the next best thing."

"A wannabe crooner who doesn't like knives."

"Seems you have me pegged, Rachel."

"What's your involvement with these people?"

"What's yours?"

"This won't work if you respond to my questions with your own."

"I see you can't handle not being in control."

"Forget I said anything."

"Scott York," Mason replied. "Name ring a bell?"

"I don't think so."

"You're lying."

"Okay."

"You and three men kidnapped him, took him into the swamp, hung a noose around his neck."

"Sounds like a movie to me."

"No conscience," Mason said. "I knew you all would be cold but . . . man."

"I'm done talking to you."

"We're just getting started, Rachel. What have you done to Samuel's brother? Chipper?"

"Done. Talking. To. You."

"Bad things have happened in the past," Mason acknowledged. "I will give you that. But what gives you the right to eke out your own sick brand of justice? Torturing Scott York because of something his grandfather did . . . it's insane."

"You don't know what you're talking about."

"Enlighten me."

"No," she said, shaking her head. "You've had plenty of time to do that work yourself."

56

Nate glanced at his watch again. It hadn't moved but a few clicks in the last hour, as far as he could tell. Sighing, he rubbed the tension from the back of his neck, then lumbered toward the kitchen, barefoot and shirtless, the belt at his waist looped tight to keep his pants from falling off. He pulled an ice-cold Budweiser from the refrigerator, popped the tab on the can, raised it to his lips for a healthy swallow. It was meant to be sipped while fishing, practically tasteless. He glugged the rest of the can, pulled out another. Popped the tab and let muscle memory take over.

"You should go easy on those."

He turned to his lawfully wedded wife, standing in the doorway beneath the *My Kitchen Prayer* sign. "You worried about Keith? I think he can spare a few beer-flavored waters," he told her, and took another swallow, grimacing through the taste. Despite what was happening between him and Heather, he couldn't deny his lingering feelings. Simply looking at her made him ache all over. And that had nothing to do with being shot and beaten.

"Keith would actually be pretty excited to see you mixing Tylenol and alcohol."

As always, Heather knew exactly what to say to get a reaction from Nate. He set the can on the counter, abandoned more than half-full. "Didn't mean to chase you two out of here."

"Keith felt he and I could speak more freely at the park."

"Nice romantic stroll?"

"You really want me to answer that?"

"No," Nate said, surprising himself with the candor.

They stood there in silence for a long stretch, just staring at each other. Nate's mind flipping through images of better times. It troubled him that Heather might not be willing to even acknowledge a better time. Worse, might not even remember one. It hadn't lasted long between them.

"I was a little hazy when I.T. dropped me off," he said, shaking aside those thoughts. "Not sure if I let you know how much I appreciate you taking me in, cleaning me up."

Heather nodded. "Are you ready now to tell me what's going on? This have something to do with the police questioning you?"

"No."

"That's hard to believe, Nate."

"I have my flaws," he admitted. "Lying to you isn't one of them."

She placed her hands on her hips. "What's this all about then?"

"I've been kidnapping people," Nate said straightaway, before he lost heart. "Forcing them to pay reparations."

Heather laughed, and then, her face folding into a frown, stopped laughing just as abruptly. "Wait. You're serious?"

"After Darius, I started looking into old hate crimes. I'm talking 1950s and earlier. Lynchings, primarily. The stuff of nightmares, but somehow reading up on it all . . . helped."

"Lynchings . . ."

"I know it sounds crazy." Nate shook his head. "Most of the guilty are long since dead. I got to thinking about history, though. Those who forget the past are doomed to repeat it, that whole thing. So,

I asked I.T. to investigate some of the descendants. Descendants of those who'd committed the hate crimes. For some reason, I needed to know what they were up to."

Heather continued to stare at him, not exactly gawping, but close to it.

"And a funny thing happened," Nate continued. "I.T. discovered that history was indeed repeating itself. One of the descendants was running an insurance scam on people in senior living facilities throughout Mississippi. Another was—"

"White," Heather said, interrupting him.

"Pardon?"

"The people you've been kidnapping. White?"

"That doesn't matter. I'm not talking about decent people, Heather. These are the sort of men you'd—"

"White?" she asked again.

Nate took in air, then another sip of his beer, then forced himself to look into her eyes. "Not always," he said.

"But mostly?" Heather shot back.

Nate sighed. "You remember showing me that wood engraving of the colonists killing the Pequots? You're very aware of the violent history of this country. And who usually caused the bloodshed."

"Kidnapping a bunch of white people changes that?"

"Never said it was a bunch. Only nine so far."

Heather sat down at her glass-topped table, buried her face in her hands.

"It sounds insane," Nate told her scalp. "But with what happened to Darius, we—"

"Obviously I.T. is involved," she said, looking up. "Who else?"

"Joshua and Rachel."

"Your little friend group," she said bitterly. "The people who matter most to you."

"You upset I didn't ask you to join us?"

Heather ignored that, asked, "How did it go from kidnapping to you being shot?"

Nate wasn't ready to tell her about Chipper. "We messed up. Targeted the wrong person."

"Are you in further danger?"

Nate shrugged.

"Whose idea, Nate?"

"What are you asking?" he said, frowning.

"You came up with this?"

Nate moved over and sat across from her, placed his hands on top of Heather's.

"I am so fucking stupid," she said, and bit her lip, her eyes watering.

"We weren't doing this just to be doing it, Heather."

Something flashed across her face. "This was happening while we were together?"

"We went on pause when you and I went to Hawaii."

"On pause."

"Our honeymoon," Nate said. "It was only right."

Heather laughed, shook her head, let out a breath.

"I get it," Nate said. "This is a lot to digest."

"The beer's all yours."

"What?"

"I ended it with Keith."

Nate wasn't sure how to respond.

In the void, Heather said, "You're hung up on color. How could we possibly expect it to work between us?"

"It's different with you."

"Except when it's not. We're out at a restaurant or a movie or, fuck, I don't know, the Verizon store, and some *beautiful Nubian sista* gives you a nasty look."

"I don't believe that's ever happened."

"No," Heather said, "but you were always looking for it. I had to fight for your attention whenever we went out. Your eyes were constantly roaming. Like you were looking to see how people were reacting to you. To us."

"I like to people watch, Heather."

"I'm so fucking stupid," she said again.

"You're not."

"You've started some kind of race war," Heather said, "and I'm on the other side. The white devil."

"I don't hate white folks."

"No?"

"Just the ones who've done wrong to my people."

"How can there ever be any meaningful change if it's *your* people and *my* people? If we keep pitting ourselves against each other?"

Nate shrugged. "Race is a complex issue."

"Lee Boyd," Heather whispered.

Nate frowned. "Who?"

"Lee Boyd Malvo, John Allen Muhammad," Heather said. "The DC snipers. I was about eleven when that happened. Lee Boyd looked just like one of my classmates. Benjamin Moseley. The kids at school started treating Benjamin like a disease. No one would play with him at recess, eat with him at lunch. And then one day . . . I just went over and sat down at his table. Neither of us even said anything while we ate. Benjamin cried on his food, didn't bother wiping away the tears. I will never forget that. The humanity in it."

Nate swallowed.

Heather said, "Basquiat did a lot of good, but I've heard rumors he was emotionally abusive in relationships. Maybe even physical."

Nate licked his lips.

"Jovan Belcher," Heather said. "My college boyfriend was a huge Chiefs fan. Droned on and on about them. Belcher had thirty-three tackles during the 2012 season. Chiefs started the year one and ten.

You know what was most significant about that season, though?
Belcher shooting his girlfriend nine times with their three-month-
old baby in the other room."

"I don't see how this—"

"Everyone I mentioned is black," Heather said. "And I could keep
going, come up with all kinds of examples of black people behaving
badly. Committing their own crimes of hate. But to what purpose?
Will that bring us closer together? Bridge this huge divide we have
between us?"

"There's no huge divide, Heather. I love you."

"You keep saying."

"Sounds like you don't believe it."

"Oh, I believe it," she said. "And that's what makes what you've
done even more hurtful. I can't have you looking at me and seeing . . .
what do you even see when you look at me?"

"The beautiful woman I married."

"*White* woman," Heather corrected.

"Color of your skin means nothing."

"Right."

She stood then, bumping past Nate, making her way to one of
the lower cupboards. She opened it and pulled out several items
from the bottom shelf. Placed them down gently on the countertop. Pulled something from the freezer, too. Despite his best efforts,
Nate couldn't see what the items were because she stood in a way that
blocked his view.

"Heather?"

"Dinner should be ready in less than an hour," she said
matter-of-factly.

Clearly not interested in engaging him in further discussion.
Nate nodded even though she wasn't looking in his direction. Heather
moved to the sink, turned on the tap, tested the water with her fingers.
Only then did Nate spot the package of frozen New York strip steak

on the counter. Heather was a vegetarian. Keith as well. It was one of the initial reasons she'd fallen into that rebound relationship, Nate knew. Partnerships worked best when the two people had things in common.

"Heather..."

She picked up the package of meat, held it under the water flow, her back to Nate as she stared out at the backyard through the window over the sink.

Nate left her there, with her quiet sadness, the music of the running faucet water. His hands had a slight tremor in them as he settled back in bed. The adrenaline of being around Heather again had masked his bodily injuries, but he couldn't as easily dismiss the turmoil of his thoughts.

Better that he focused on something other than the conversation they'd just had.

Joshua needed to be brought up to speed with everything that had happened. Rachel, too. He had to check in with I.T. to see whether there was any progress on tracking down that Lyft driver.

Nate bit his lip and squeezed his eyes shut tight. Took several deep breaths to silence the noise in his head. It worked on the noise. But the tremor in his hands only deepened.

Still, he managed to reach for his phone and dial I.T.'s number.

Straight to voicemail.

He'd try again later. After he finished eating his steak. After he figured out how to tell Heather she was right. Right about everything.

57

Dizzy from the heat, Mason sank to the wood floor beneath one of the two windows in the log building, gently set the knife down beside him, and took several long, deep cleansing breaths. As his heartbeat slowed from a gallop, he lifted the tail of his shirt and dabbed at his forehead, wiped sweat from his eyes. The vomit on the shirt had dried to a crust that scratched his face like a beard.

"What did you do to your shoulder?"

He ignored Rachel and groaned his way back to his feet. It took oxygen to speak, and energy, too, and he would need reserves of both to finish the job. Using his right hand, he jabbed the point of the blade in a gorge of the putty helping to hold the window in place, and then hammered the butt of the knife with the side of his fist. After a couple of strikes, the putty flaked up and crumbled.

"You think you know me, what I've done, but you don't."

He really wished she would stop talking. Despite how much he loathed this woman, every word out of her mouth made him long for Elizabeth. They had similar honey-inflected tones, it was like listening to a song.

"Yes, we were involved with your client. But Scott York isn't some innocent snowflake. He's a horrible man. Chipper, too. And they aren't the only ones. I could tell you some stories."

Mason gritted his teeth and hammered the knife butt again. More flakes of putty. Soon he'd be able to use the knife blade as a pry bar, carefully removing the vertical strips along the sides of the window, the wood strip stretched across the upper stash.

"Stop! Someone's coming!"

It took him several seconds to realize Rachel was saying something of real import this time. Still, he managed to snick the blade back into the handle using the wall as a second hand, and stumbled over to a corner, away from the window.

Samuel stepped inside.

He left the door gaped open behind him, the fading sun at his back, and fixed his gaze on Mason, asking, "Is she behaving?"

Mason nodded. "So far so good."

"What about you?"

"I'd say the same," Mason replied, chuckling, keeping his voice light. "So far so good."

"Is that right?" Samuel moved from the doorway, clopped his way over to the window, tracked his fingertips along the sill, picking up crumbs of the putty in the process. Frowning, he crushed the crumbs into an even finer dust.

58

The long day was winding down, the sky gone the gray of an old blind woman's eyes, and Chanel looked as weary as Isiah felt. While he'd expected plenty of tears and a boatload of hate from her, instead he got cigarette smoke and a warm breeze that lay on his skin like the exhaust from a muffler. She drove with purpose, silent and squinting, with both windows cranked down, a stick from a box of Parliament 100s bobbing between her teeth.

"Say something," Isiah implored her, sickened by the silence.

She paused from tapping her fingers on the steering wheel, evidently thinking. "Tell me about your gang."

"We're not a gang."

"Kidnapping, murder . . . you could've fooled me."

"Who says we—"

"Cut the shit, *Isiah.*"

Here was some of the anger he'd expected.

"I know you're upset," he said. "Once I'm satisfied Rachel's safe, I'll take you to Chipper, just as I promised. You have my word. Okay?"

"What's your word mean to me?"

"Nothing," Isiah admitted. "But I'm asking you to trust me anyway."

"If you won't tell me about your gang, then tell me about Rachel."

"I don't see what—"

"Rachel," Chanel said, raising her voice.

Isiah sighed. "What do you want to know?"

"Whatever you want to tell me," Chanel said.

Isiah's turn to think.

"Potcakes," he whispered after a moment.

Chanel frowned. "I didn't hear you."

"Potcakes," he said again, and cleared his throat. "We've been researching . . . we're getting married. We've been researching a lot of stuff around the wedding, the honeymoon. At one point we were considering Turks and Caicos, but a photographer living there that Rachel follows on Instagram posted a picture of a dog just lying in the middle of the road. Clearly malnourished. They call 'em potcake dogs in Turks and Caicos because the locals feed them the caked remains of the cooking pot. Rachel cried when she saw the post and Turks and Caicos came off the honeymoon list."

"Bitch cares about dogs, but not people, huh?"

"I know you probably think . . . look, we never—"

"No one owns these potcakes?" Chanel asked.

Isiah sighed. "I don't think so. You see them all over the island."

"Maybe they're just displaced," Chanel said. "Maybe someone's somewhere worrying themselves sick about them."

"That's—"

"This is us," she said, making a hard turn off a desolate road.

Isiah reached to brace himself with the dashboard and was still slammed into his door. He looked out in time to see a sign of some sort at the entrance of the compound but couldn't make out what was written on it. A cloud of dust kicked up as they traveled down a long, impossibly straight dirt road, blurring past a slanted rock-climbing wall, a plowed field with soccer goals at each end, the dregs of old campfires. He couldn't help but imagine the landscape through Rachel's eyes, what she must've been thinking, feeling, as she took all this in.

Assuming she was here.

If she was, he would get her out. No matter the cost.

"Stop a moment."

Chanel jammed the brakes. The front end of her car did a snake weave. She punched the gearshift into park. The tears Isiah had originally anticipated were there now, they'd just been delayed. Chanel tossed the cigarette she'd been smoking out the window, wiped her eyes with the back of her hand. "Fucking things taste like shit," she muttered. "Chipper was always getting on me about lung cancer."

Isiah felt for her, but now wasn't the time for sentiment. "How will this go, Chanel?"

"What do you mean?" she said, snuffling her nose.

"If Rachel's here, where will Samuel have her?"

"My guess would be either up at the main house or in the log building."

"And when—"

"Actually, I don't think she'll be in the main house," Chanel cut in. "Samuel is especially cruel. He'll most likely have her in the log building. Now that night's fallen, she'll be in the dark. There's no electricity."

"And where is this building?"

"Main house is at the end of this road. There's a road just before it that branches off to the right. Only paved road in here, you can't miss it. The log building is down there."

"Okay."

"We can't just ride down there, though. You can see the turnoff from the main house. And there's always someone watching."

"What do you suggest?"

"I don't even know what you're planning."

"Makes two of us."

"You're crazy," she said.

"I'll think of something."

"I could let you out here. Samuel stays in the main house, but the brothers live in trailers. The trailers are down that road ahead of us, off to the left. If you follow it through, it loops around behind the main house and comes up on the log building from behind. That'd be your best bet."

"Won't the brothers spot me?"

Chanel glanced at her watch. "They'll all be up at the main house now. There are evening exercises. They last well into the morning."

"You know a lot about this place."

"Chipper used to be . . . he was involved at one time."

"Oh yeah?"

"Don't give me that look," Chanel said. "People can change. Besides, he had every right. Samuel bought this place with money they got from their dead daddy's life insurance."

"I'm going to go ahead and get out here then," Isiah said, "and have a look around. Need you to unlock your cell phone."

"Why?"

"You're just going to head off with no way of getting in touch with me? I want to put in my number."

Chanel hesitated a moment, then unlocked the phone and passed it over to him. Isiah tapped the screen and punched at it for a moment. Then handed it back to her like something marked fragile. "I'm *Gene Kan* in your contacts. Text me if anything jumps off that I need to know about. I'll do the same. Or if I have questions. Or any requests. Be discreet. Don't let anyone see you texting."

"I'm working for you now?"

"No," Isiah said, "you're working for Chipper."

It was a cheesy line, insensitive really, but he couldn't take it back now. Luckily Chanel didn't react to it in any discernible way he could tell. She seemed numbed by everything that was happening. And

Isiah certainly related to that. He couldn't believe he was doing this even as he made a move to hop out of her car. Chanel grabbed his arm. He released the door handle and turned back, facing her.

"Yeah?"

"Be careful," she told him.

"Thanks."

"'Cause if Samuel kills you before I get a chance to see for myself what you fucking done with my Chipper, I'm gonna be royally pissed."

59

"Nepenthe," Samuel said softly, wiping the dust from the windowsill off his fingertips and onto his shirt. Edgar Allen Poe had used the word to significant effect in his poem "The Raven," rhyming it with "lent thee" from the previous line. It carried the Greek prefix ne, meaning "not," plus penthos, meaning "grief" or "sorrow," and once referred to a potion used by the ancients to make one forget pain and suffering. A mythical concept. If only such a thing truly existed. "I'll take that knife from you now, Mason," he added.

"You caught me," Mason admitted, his voice quavering. "But I want you to know, if we'd have gotten out, we wouldn't have mentioned a word about you or anything that's happened here to anyone."

"Knife, please."

"Are you hearing me?"

Samuel's long stride brought him face-to-face with Mason, and the man sighed and slipped the knife in Samuel's hand like an exchange of money, albeit a transaction under duress. "Thank you, Mason. Now, let's you and I go see about Elizabeth." He turned to Rachel, cowering off to the side. "You can cool your heels for now."

The room in the main house where they had Elizabeth was adorned with faux wood walls and a carpet that had never met a vacuum. Elizabeth was slumped in a rigid plastic chair that had to be cutting into her generous backside, a rag knotted behind her head and gagging her mouth. Her ankles were scrunched together with loops of duct tape, but Samuel had ordered her hands left free. Leaving her hands free would allow her a sense of control, of freedom, that would be dashed as soon as she realized—even though she wasn't bound at the wrists—there was no getting out of here. Until Samuel was ready to release her, that is.

Which wouldn't be anytime soon.

He was pleased that she didn't register a presence as he and Mason stepped into the room.

Perfect. That meant she was broken or nearly so.

He loosened the rag from her mouth, dropped it to the dirty floor, and then took ahold of her chin, gently lifting her head so their eyes met. "Guess who's here to see you?"

It was as though she were looking right through him; he pressed on, nonetheless.

"Mason, announce yourself," he called over his shoulder.

An indecipherable sound, like a hum.

"Gag." Samuel smiled, shrugged his shoulders. "Anyway, Mason says hello. If you'll look over to your left, you can see him in the corner. Feel free to give a wave."

She glanced that way, two of the brothers had Mason pinned down.

"Let's play a little game," Samuel said. "What do the following have in common? The Roman Praetorium who guarded Julius Caesar, the three hundred Spartans who spilled blood during the Battle of Thermopylae, and the Wild Geese Irish soldiers who fought for a century against France."

Elizabeth shook her head.

"Unbowed loyalty," Samuel said. "I demand it from the brothers. It's more important than their belief in our mission. Your boyfriend betrayed my trust."

Elizabeth was listening to him, though she did not respond. At least not with words. A single tear ran a course down her right cheek. Her chin trembled in Samuel's hand.

"I'd love your input on how I should deal with Mason's sedition."

Now more than one tear trailed down Elizabeth's face.

Samuel let her head drop to her chest, dug in his pants pocket, and came out with a knife. The one he'd taken back from Mason.

He flipped it open.

Crouched down.

Mason hummed into his gag again. Elizabeth produced a breath that sounded like someone's last.

And, in one slash, Samuel turned the duct tape around her ankles to strips.

"Stand up," he told her.

She did.

"Turn around."

Ruffling and rumbling behind him. Mason fighting the brothers. A losing fight. Samuel didn't even bother looking. Elizabeth turned as Samuel had directed.

He ignored her tremors as he bunched her T-shirt and heaved it up to her shoulders, as he undid the clasp at the back of her bra, as he guided her around so they were facing again. "Remove your brassiere," he commanded.

"Please . . ."

"Remove it."

Barking the order would've made her flinch. Saying it so calmly, as he'd just done, made her tears flow more freely, made her sob. Despite that, she worked the bra off, pulled it from her sleeve like a magic trick. Samuel held out his hand and she passed it to him.

Mason screamed into his gag.

"Most men are fascinated by breasts," Samuel said, impassive. "I don't understand why."

Elizabeth's throat rippled as she swallowed.

"They're just glandular and fatty tissues. Mostly fat. Which we abhor otherwise, but when it comes to breasts . . ." He shook his head.

"What do you want?" Elizabeth asked, her first real words in some time.

"I've seen the way Mason looks at you," Samuel told her, smiling. "I think that punishing you would actually cause him the most suffering."

"Jesus, help me," she whispered.

"Would you prefer a bite or burn, Elizabeth?"

"No . . . please."

"I'm hungry, just so you know."

Again, the sounds of a struggle behind him. Mason was nothing if not persistent.

"Well?" Samuel said.

"Burn," Elizabeth managed, teetering.

Samuel steadied her by the shoulders. "Whoa there. I'm not trying to throw out my back picking you up."

"Why are you doing this?" she stammered.

Samuel didn't respond. He removed a Zippo lighter from his pants pocket, flicked the ignition wheel, and let the flame lick at the knife blade. Once the stainless steel was heated, he nodded at Elizabeth. She understood and raised the front of her shirt without complaint, closing her eyes and biting her lip, turning her head, balling her hands into fists.

More screams from Mason into his gag.

More rustling and fighting.

"Do you know the word nescience, Elizabeth?"

She opened her eyes, turned back, facing Samuel. "No."

"Ignorance," he explained. "A lack of knowledge. I'm at a disadvantage because I don't have all the pieces to the puzzle. No way for me to put this together without all the pieces."

"We've told you everything we know."

"Not everything."

Elizabeth frowned.

"The name of Mason's client, please."

Elizabeth looked over at Mason, then said, "Scott York."

"Mmm." Samuel nodded. He turned to the two brothers. "Take these apostates back to the log building. I'm sure the half-breed is lonely."

60

There was a mound of compost beside the first trailer Isiah came upon. The pile was about four feet tall and constructed like a layer cake. Built upon a foundation of leaves and twigs, which were themselves coated with a sheet of dark soil. A third layer of grass clippings, vegetable refuse, and green plants, and then an icing with more of the dark soil. Putrid was the word that came to mind. The pile smelled like rotting eggs. Isiah couldn't believe anyone would willingly live with that enduring odor at their doorstep. But someone was squatting here.

Lights burned inside the trailer.

He held still and listened.

Quiet, a piercing silence that was its own sound.

Maybe Chanel knew what she was talking about. It didn't seem as though the trailer was occupied now.

Crouching, Isiah shuffled past it. On the other side, he discovered a large cistern collecting rainwater that fed into an outdoor shower. And beyond that, a vehicle. A beat-up old Chevy Silverado pickup truck with all its windows lowered. It was shocking to see keys dangling from the ignition. Isiah stole a glance at the trailer, then eased the keys out, pocketing them.

The sun had plunged from view, the sky the color of duct tape, leaving him the cover of darkness to move about freely. He took in a full breath and continued. The next trailer also had lights burning inside. And was currently unoccupied. No compost pile, but a Camry parked alongside the trailer.

Isiah shook his head and pocketed this second set of keys.

Further up the road, his heart kicking at his ribs, he paused to lean against a tree. Thoughts crowded his head as he worked to settle his breathing. This was crazy, a suicide mission. And what good would that do Rachel if he was killed before getting her out of here. He should just call the police and explain everything. Give them the address of the compound.

Of course, that would put him, Rachel, and the guys in serious legal jeopardy. And he couldn't allow that to happen. What they'd all done was born of good intentions. Yes, they'd veered off course and pushed it too far. But didn't Darius deserve that effort? Some action, however drastic? He did, Isiah believed, and so, no matter how frustrated Nate made him, he couldn't help but swell with adoration for his friend. Nate had felt the anger they'd all been contending with, and he'd refused to sit by idly as it poisoned and killed his spirit. He'd elected to do *something*. A crazy, insane, off-the-wall something, sure, but that's what Darius's senseless death required.

Isiah took another breath and stood up straight.

It was on him from here on out.

He pushed away from the tree and surveyed the area. It took him a moment to recognize the remnants of a burned cross stamped in the ground less than thirty feet from him. That was startling to see. To his right, he noticed the side of the trailer he'd just passed was draped with an oversize Confederate flag. And there was some sort of marking on the tree, he also realized. It was difficult to make out, so he plucked his cell phone from his pocket and used the flashlight feature, steadying it on the bark.

"You've got to be kidding."

A swastika.

It was absurd, these three symbols of hate so prominently displayed within yards of one another. If Isiah weren't seeing them with his own eyes, he wouldn't have believed it.

He felt suddenly emboldened. These people were so cartoonish in their hate their advantage in numbers was slipping his way. Their foolish symbols and foolish ideology couldn't possibly match deliberate action and careful thought.

When Isiah came to the next trailer, discovering it empty like the others, and found yet another pickup parked beside it with keys hanging there for the taking, and found a filled red gas can in the truck bed, well, he had the spark of an idea.

No pun intended.

61

Samuel didn't have very much use for God. Prayer, though, prayer captivated him. And he saw nothing contradictory or faulty in his thinking because there was something pure and beautiful in giving thanks and in finding hope through supplication. He and the brothers were an ekklēsia—a Greek word that meant "an assembly," a "called-out people"—and therefore it was incumbent on all of them to not only recognize but welcome the power of prayer. Samuel, as their leader, foremost of all. He looked around the log building at the brothers he'd pulled from the reading at the main house. Kaleb, Polk, and Ronald Owen Atkins stood at attention in a loose circle, surrounding their guests, and would assist him with that old Scottish rite of offering up a cross to a crackling fire of rebirth once they all stepped outside. And though the guests—Mason, Elizabeth, and their newest congregant, Rachel—might not fully appreciate the cross-burning ceremony for all its potency, it would be unlike anything they'd ever experienced before.

Samuel would make certain of that.

He swept the beam of his Maglite to shine in Mason's face and asked him, "Have you heard about the plague of grasshoppers in Minnesota? Back during the 1800s?"

Mason squinted but didn't respond.

"They called them grasshoppers at the time," Samuel continued, focusing the beam on Elizabeth, "but we later learned they were actually Rocky Mountain locusts."

She didn't react, either. Mason held her close, rubbing at her back, cooing to her as if she were a chubby little toddler.

Samuel walked the light to Rachel.

She stared into its brilliance, barely blinked.

Samuel smiled at that, passed the flashlight to Ronald Owen Atkins, then pulled out his knife, flipped it open, ran his rough fingers along the edge. The newest brother was wise enough to spotlight Samuel without being told, enabling the guests to see the seriousness etched into Samuel's face, and the knife held in his fist.

"Over about a five-year period, 1873 to '77, these grasshoppers, these locusts, descended on Minnesota crops and, well, you can imagine the destruction. As the growing season of '77 approached, entomologists looking into the situation found billions of grasshopper eggs waiting to hatch. Eighty thousand square miles in the state and fifty thousand of 'em impacted." Samuel shook his head. "The entomologists warned that the previous four years would look like child's play once those new fuckers hatched."

"Kill us, if you will," Mason shouted. "But enough of your pointless and boring stories."

Samuel wasn't surprised by Mason's hubris, false as it may have been. Headless chickens could run around for seconds after being decapitated. That last gasp, he found it rather enduring. He moved closer to the three, towering above them. "Minnesota had only gotten its statehood twenty years prior. Most of the farmers were living in log cabins, plank houses, still figuring how to eke out a living. There weren't any pesticides, any insecticides. No answer for those irritant grasshoppers that could strip an entire field bare overnight. So, feeling understandably desperate, the people petitioned the governor, John S. Pillsbury—yeah, just the Pillsbury you're thinking of, from the baking flour family—and asked him to declare a statewide day of prayer. And he did. April 26, 1877. A day of fasting, humble submission, and prayer."

Mason's nostrils flared.

"It was an unseasonably warm day," Samuel went on, "their dedicated prayer day. Perfect conditions for those eggs to hatch, for those murderous grasshoppers to wiggle to life. And they did. Gives new meaning to a *wing* and a prayer, doesn't it?"

Samuel's little attempt at humor fell flat. Tough crowd. But he couldn't stop now. He had to give them the rest. This last bit was the best part. "But something else unusual happened that night. Chilly rain, which changed to sleet, and then to snow. Freezing temperatures and snow for two full days, and then, on the third day, a Sunday no less, a full-bore blizzard. All those little grasshopper fucks froze to death. Isn't that something?"

None of them responded, of course.

Samuel didn't care.

"Chipper and I didn't always see eye to eye," he announced. "But I loved him best I could. Same could be said for him with me. And you motherfuckers know exactly what happened to him. So, either you're going to tell me what that is . . . or you're going to need something even more miraculous than that day of prayer to save your souls. I'll butcher you and not lose a wink of sleep."

"You won't get away with this," Mason replied, his voice a pitiful rasp. He didn't believe his own words.

"Rachel," Samuel said. "I'm growing weary of all this. I need to have all the pieces. Who is your fourth?"

"Fourth what?"

He sighed and tapped the knife against his leg. "People talk about filleting something, and I'm not sure they know what it means. You see, you can only fillet something that has a tenderloin."

He moved toward Rachel, and she took a step back.

"The tenderloin runs along both sides of the spine," he went on, "and is usually butchered as two long snake-shaped cuts of meat."

He held up the knife.

Five paces from her.

He took another step forward.

A knock at the door paused him in his tracks.

He turned, frowning, barked, "What?"

The door creaked open.

Chanel stepped through and looked at everyone, pursed her lips.

Samuel's frown only deepened. "What are you doing—"

Frog stepped in behind her.

He should've been up at the main house, participating in the reading, educating himself on the war being waged between the old culture and the new in these Divided States of America.

"Chanel, Frog, I'm busy here. You two need—"

Frog said something Samuel didn't make out.

"What's that?" he asked.

"Fire," Frog said. "In three of the trailers."

And Samuel was moving without thought of anything else, all the brothers except Frog on his heels.

62

After Samuel rambled through that soliloquy about prayer, Rachel had decided to try it on for herself, and like manna from heaven, or water turned to cabernet sauvignon, it was looking as though she'd been blessed with a miracle. The guy with the bug eyes lingered in the doorway of the log building, alternating between squinting in the direction Samuel and his men had run off to and keeping a guarded eye on the prisoners the giant had carelessly left behind.

The woman Rachel knew as Chanel, Chipper's girl, said, "Don't worry, Frog. I'll watch 'em. I imagine the brothers need all the hands they can get to deal with those fires."

"I'm not sure—"

"Just go, Frog!"

He flinched as if he'd been shot, gave a mean eye to Mason, less of one to Elizabeth, none to Rachel, and then he turned to Chanel and nodded and took off.

Her shoulders sagged and she huffed out a breath. Then she stilled herself and faced Rachel and the others. "Isiah has a vehicle waiting for you all. You've gotta move fast, though."

Isiah?

Rachel wasn't sure she'd heard correctly. "My Isiah?" she asked, frowning.

"Who else, Taylor Swift? Now come on."

Chanel stepped outside, holding the door open for them. Mason practically had to carry Elizabeth; she leaned her weight on him. Meanwhile, Rachel's legs were like wet noodles, but she managed to keep pace.

"Isiah's waiting for you," Chanel said, pointing off to their right. "Should be just around that bend. There's a back road in."

Mason tumbled down the path in that direction, still propping Elizabeth up and dragging her along.

Rachel paused by Chanel. "I don't know why you're doing this but thank you."

She could've but didn't raise her hand to block Chanel's slap.

Face stinging, Rachel took off in a trot to catch up with the others. And sure enough, just around the bend, Isiah was assisting Mason with easing Elizabeth into the rear of a Toyota Camry. They laid her down like a pregnant woman going into labor.

Isiah forced something in Mason's hand after they shut the rear door. Mason frowned at whatever it was, and then lifted the tail of his shirt, fumbling near his waist. Rachel was just reaching them and only heard the last of what Isiah was saying: ". . . her off safely and then get on a plane and never look back. Forget you ever heard of us."

Mason nodded. He jumped behind the wheel and fired up the engine.

Isiah looked up and smiled at Rachel.

She fell into his embrace.

"Getting you out of here," he whispered, rubbing circles on her back. "They didn't hurt you, did they?"

Rachel didn't have words. Tears flowing, she simply shook her head.

"Nate's been shot, but he's okay."

Rachel nodded.

"Chanel filled me in," Isiah went on. "She believes this Mason is a good guy."

Rachel came up off his chest. "What did you just give him?"

"Car keys," Isiah said, avoiding her gaze.

"Isiah?"

"You need to get out of here," he said, looking at her again. "Mason will protect you."

"Protect me? Wait, you aren't coming?"

"I'll be right behind you all."

"I'll ride with you," Rachel said.

"You need to get moving now," Isiah insisted. "Those fires won't keep them occupied much longer."

"What are you doing?"

"I have to let Chanel know . . . something."

"You're still on that?"

"It's the right thing to do," Isiah said.

"Who's to say she won't go to the police?"

"I trust her."

"Samuel and his men know where you live," Rachel said. "My place, too, I would guess."

"I gave Mason the address to Nate's wife's place."

"Did you say Nate's *wife?*"

"I know," Isiah said, and laughed. "No time to explain. You need to go, Rache."

"You'll be right behind us?" she said again, taking his hand, giving it a firm squeeze. He squeezed hers in kind.

"Yes."

"I can't believe Nate's marr—"

"I know. Now go."

She was almost at the car when Isiah called for her. She turned back.

"You know I'd never let anything bad ever happen to you, right?" he said. "That you could always count on me?"

"Without question."

"I can't tell you how happy it makes me to hear that, Rache."

"And I never slept with Nate. I wouldn't do that to you. He wouldn't either."

"I know it."

"Hurry up," she told him. "Don't keep me waiting long."

"I won't. Now go," he said.

"Right behind us?"

"Yes. Go. I love you."

She slid inside the Camry, barely had the door shut when Mason took off. He wheeled around the bend and hit the main stretch into the compound, that long, impossibly straight ribbon of dirt road. A cloud of dust kicked up as they roared past one of the side roads where the three trailers broiled thanks to Isiah's fires. There was a flurry of activity down there.

Rachel couldn't help but smile.

And then she looked up at the rearview mirror and the smile faded.

Nothing else but that billow of dirt road behind them.

63

Samuel slowed in disbelief as he came upon the trio of burning trailers. Logan retrieved the rusted toolbox he stored beneath the steps of his, hefted it, then rammed one of the front windows, spiderwebbing the glass after three tries, shattering it altogether after a fourth. The moron let out a cry like a wounded animal as he was lifted off his feet. It took a moment for him to roll over and sit up on his elbows, for him to realize it wasn't a gas explosion but rather a person who'd knocked him on his ass.

"Samuel? What the fuck, man?"

"Fires need oxygen to stay burning," Samuel told him. "You just fed it."

"Sorry, man. I didn't realize."

"Fuck out of my way, Logan."

"Hey, man. No reason for you to—"

Samuel grabbed ahold of Logan, forced him to his feet, and tossed him aside. That taken care of, he covered his mouth and nose with the collar of his shirt and stepped inside the trailer, where he was greeted by a wall of smoke that was spreading like spilled milk. Knowing the importance of every second, he tracked his way to the kitchen area, the most likely source of the fire. There were wadded-up heaps of paper towels on the stovetop, everything spattered with grease, a flame practically licking the ceiling.

Smart.

He and the brothers were dealing with a clever gang of arsonists.

Samuel couldn't help but to be impressed.

He turned at the sound of hacking coughs.

Logan had dusted himself off and was limping through the trailer now. Ronald Owen Atkins had finally decided to join the party as well. Not surprisingly, neither of them thought to cover their face. Breathing in smoke, cyanide, and carbon monoxide; probably already at toxic levels. And the density of the smoke meant the most flammable objects in the trailer wouldn't have to come in direct contact with the source blaze to ignite. Soon those objects would spontaneously burst into flames, everything in here would. The dining table, the chairs, the tattered paperback of Michael Bray's *A Time to Kill* splayed open on the countertop. Eventually all the oxygen in the trailer would be sucked out, the rest of the windows would shatter, and the temperature might climb as high as fourteen hundred degrees Fahrenheit.

Samuel looked around for something to snuff out the flames. Extinguisher, pot lid, baking soda.

The door of the trailer clapped open again. Frog.

His eyes were bugged out more than usual when he reached Samuel at the edge of the kitchen. "What's the prognosis?" he asked.

"Who's watching over our guests?" Samuel said, talking through a fistful of his shirt.

"Guests?"

"Mason, the heifer, and the half-breed."

"Oh," Frog replied. "Chanel's looking after 'em."

Samuel nearly laughed. The arsonists were smart all right. A diversion and a jail break. Chanel wouldn't be that difficult for them to overwhelm.

It's how he would've done it.

Frog appeared to realize it in that moment, too. "Shit. You don't think—"

Samuel moved toward him, fists at the ready. But he heard a sound that stopped him cold.

Running water.

He wheeled around.

Logan stood by the sink, nozzle outstretched and pointed at the lumps of glowing paper towels on the stovetop.

Samuel scrambled in that direction. "No!"

Water would make a grease fire spread faster. You needed to smother it instead.

Logan released a spray.

Leaping flames engulfed his clothes and did the same with Samuel's as he wrestled the nozzle from Logan's hand. The other man screamed, danced around, a fireball that quickly.

Samuel could feel the flames eating through his own clothes, searing his skin, a heat like the fires of hell. He was also a fireball. Melting skin sluicing off him like a snake.

Damn clever gang of arsonists.

64

Isiah had a broad, towering tree in his backyard growing up, a scarlet oak. In the fall, it shed reddish-brown leaves, and spit egg-shaped acorns with bitter kernels. He used to pop off the hut top of those acorns and suck on the seeds, which said something about him, he supposed. It was as if he expected them to turn sweet at some point, even though that wasn't within their nature. Still, he was enthralled by that tree and its versatility, how it could thrive in a wide range of soils except alkaline, and while it preferred moisture, certainly, it did have some drought tolerance.

His father encouraged his interest and took to using arboriculture metaphors to explain to Isiah some of life's greatest mysteries. "You're mature enough to start understanding some things," he remembered his father telling him, a few days after Isiah's ninth birthday. "There are layers to everything in this world. If you want to succeed, you'll have to look beyond the bark, past the cambium, try to see your way to the heartwood."

It was a remarkably nuanced conversation for his dad. Not to suggest Isiah's father was a stupid man, but no one would have confused him for an academic either. His worldview was simple. A man paid his debts and didn't complain even if it meant he worked his hands raw, all while sacrificing himself for the good of those he loved and was responsible for. Isiah had found it interesting that his parents fit together like a tongue and groove even though his mother liked to quote Charlotte Brontë and could tell you the counterpart of an aria was the recitative, and his dad was, well, not cultured in that same way.

Isiah wiped his clammy hands on his pants now and tucked those old memories into the back of his mind. He squared himself and started walking around the bend in the road.

Chanel was pacing in front of the log building, her face illuminated by the flashlight feature of her cell phone. She frowned and nearly jumped out of her skin as Isiah scuffled closer. "You came back."

"You doubted I would?"

"They made it out safely?"

Isiah nodded. "Watched them roar past the trailers and out of the compound."

Chanel hugged herself, as if there was a chill in the air. "You'll . . ."

"Yes," Isiah finished for her. "I'll take you to Chipper now. Where's your car?"

65

Mason left the compound and turned onto a secluded road, giving the Camry gas, the wind blowing hot against his face through his open window. He drove on into the night, past fields of wild grass, old farmhouse buildings slumping like stacks of damp cardboard boxes, useless tractor equipment rusted the color of dirty bricks. A forgotten and desolate wasteland. No wonder the Righteous Boys had chosen to call the area home.

Beside him, Rachel shifted, moving her gaze from her sideview mirror to look his way. "Isiah gave you an address to drop me?"

He wished she would be quiet. It was difficult enough contending with the other voices already bouncing around in his head. Elizabeth was rather lucky right now, fast asleep in the back. In shock, but still. Better than dealing with everything of the moment. The decisions to be made.

"Mason?"

"Yes," he said. "Isiah programmed the address into Google Maps with a phone he took from one of the burning trailers."

"Why aren't you using it?"

"Considering," he told her.

"Considering what?"

Getting Elizabeth to safety was Mason's priority, but that didn't

diminish his other obligation. Through all his failings, his shortcom-
ings, he was a lawman. And a damn good one, he liked to believe.
Rachel and the three men she ran with should be held to account for
what they'd done.

"There isn't enough evil and division in this country?" he said.
"You all felt the need to take it upon yourselves to blame white people
for . . . for . . . you tell me."

"I'm not having this conversation. Please just take me to Isiah."

Mason brought the Camry to a complete stop, literally in the
middle of a crossroads. A dark and isolated route stretched both ways
in either direction parallel to them.

"What are you doing?" Rachel said. "Keep driving."

"Why did you do it?"

"Do what?"

"Kill Samuel's brother."

"Who said we—"

"No more bullshit," Mason shouted. "I'm not putting my safety
and Elizabeth's on the line for you if you don't answer my questions."

"To hell with this," Rachel said, reaching for her door.

"Don't even think about it." Mason quirked the locks. "Isiah gave
me more than just the cell phone, Rachel."

She turned back to face him, her eyes aflame. "What are you
blathering about?"

Mason lifted the tail of his shirt and the flame in Rachel's eyes
flickered. The barrel and sight on the .38 were chopped off close to the
cylinder. The grips were neatly wrapped with black electrician's tape.
No telling how many bodies were on the gun. Mason didn't want to
be responsible for adding another.

"You wouldn't," Rachel said.

"Why did you kill Samuel's brother?"

Rachel let out a breath and took him back to the beginning.

Darius.

The anger that had welled up in her and her three friends after his senseless death. How impotent they'd felt. The pervasive hopelessness.

Then their plan.

And how it had gone so terribly off the rails.

"Bound to," Mason said. "Targeting people just because someone from their family did wrong umpteen years before."

"The people we kidnapped were deserving."

"How do you figure?"

"You're working for Scott York, right?"

Mason didn't reply.

"You don't know about him and the Creek Indians?" Rachel said.

"No idea what you're talking about."

She told him.

Mason swallowed. "Any of those . . . Creek Indians get hurt? Physically, I mean?"

Rachel nodded.

Mason said, "He told me you targeted him strictly because of what his grandfather did."

"And you took him at his word?"

"No reason not to."

"That's why we did what we did," Rachel said. "Everyone should get that benefit of the doubt."

Mason wasn't sure how to respond to that. He moved in his seat, and was about to try when Rachel's eyes widened.

Following her gaze, Mason turned to his left.

Headlights barreling toward them.

Plenty of time for the driver to change course.

But they didn't.

In fact, the pickup truck accelerated. The nose adjusting for a teeth-rattling collision.

All Mason could do was brace for the impact.

66

Chanel and Isiah paused at the end of the path down from the log building, listening for trouble, the main house off to their right, a hundred yards or so. Felt like three times as much. But they had to take that walk. Chanel had parked her car in the dark shadows alongside the house.

"You can drive," she said, her voice a fossil of itself, shrunken and fading to bone gray. She dislodged a ring of keys from her pocket and tried to press them into Isiah's hand.

He frowned and moved his hand away. "What's wrong? You're not looking well."

"We shouldn't waste time talking. Take the keys."

"Are you really up for this?"

"I have to see him," she whispered.

"Not if it's going to make you—"

"Oh, for fuck's sake." And she was off and jogging toward the main house, sipping the air, tasting the smoke.

Isiah's footfalls slapping the ground behind her.

She reached the driver's side of her car before him, and even though he moved immediately to the other side, the passenger side, he said, "If you really need me to drive, I can."

Chanel didn't answer.

Chirp-chirped her locks and groaned open the door. Dropped down behind the wheel and let out a long breath. Isiah settled beside her and gently closed his door. "I know this is . . ."

But she didn't hear the rest. Instead, she glanced up at the rear-view mirror, and that's when she noticed him. His smile turned her stomach to broth, but she didn't react in any noticeable way. No gasp, no hand to the mouth, not even silent tears.

The sight of him. Wet, weepy, brownish-pink skin swelling with blisters. Hair singed.

Samuel, looking every bit of someone raised from the dead.

"Going somewhere?"

Isiah jumped at the sound of Samuel's voice, fumbled at his door handle but couldn't get it to open. He looked over at Chanel, and she wanted to give him a hug, tell him to run and not look back. The surge of emotion surprised her. He was a killer. Chipper's killer.

Samuel said, "Neither of you have anything to say?"

"You're . . . injured," Chanel managed.

"Quite observant, sis."

"You need medical attention."

"Scarring will probably suit me," Samuel said, shrugging. "Sometimes you eat the bear, sometimes the bear eats you. Where were you two headed?"

"Chipper," Chanel said, speaking softly.

"Ahh." Samuel looked at Isiah. "And you are?"

"I-Isiah," he stammered.

"Your mother didn't teach you to not play with matches?"

"She—"

"The diversion of a fire was an impressive play," Samuel said. "But all for naught, I'm afraid."

Isiah frowned.

"I'm admittedly paranoid," Samuel explained.

Isiah's frown only deepened.

Then Chanel let out a sound, covered her mouth with her hand. "Oh my God, I forgot. Trackers. He doesn't really trust the brothers. He puts trackers on all their vehicles."

67

Ringing in her ears. Nausea. Blurry vision. Several seconds lost to confusion. Rachel managed to crank her door open to stick her head out for some fresh air. She wasn't confident she could stand.

Screaming.

Tapping.

The haziness was slowly lifting, so it took a moment for her to make sense of what was happening. Elizabeth sitting up in the backseat, screaming like a banshee. Mason behind the wheel, a shower of glass in his lap, tapping Rachel on the arm. Saying something to her as well.

Despite her best efforts, Rachel couldn't process what he'd said. "Come again?"

Mason shoved her from the mangled Camry. Popped the trunk and leaped out behind her. "Over there," he said, taking her by the arm, pointing at the woods.

Rachel stumbled toward the tree line. Stepped wrong and lost her footing. Who'd thought to make the ground wander and gyrate like a level in some video game?

She scooted on her ass to an oak, turned and rested her back against it.

Mason opened the back door of the Camry and pulled Elizabeth out, shoved her toward Rachel. The trunk of the car was raised like the arms at a railroad crossing.

Mason yanked something from his belt and staggered through the Camry's headlight beams to the pickup truck that had run into them. He opened the driver's-side door and excised a dazed man with an untrimmed beard, a billboard of tattoos on his skin, and what was most likely a new limp.

One of Samuel's men. Rachel remembered him from the compound. She was thinking more coherently now.

"Move," she heard Mason say, and the guy did as he was told, settling at the back of the Camry.

"You don't think I'm getting in a fucking trunk," he said.

"Would you prefer lead poisoning?" Mason said, flashing something.

The old .38, Rachel realized.

Samuel's man climbed into the trunk, but not before saying, "Samuel knows exactly where you are, asshole. You can't escape his reach. He's omnipotent."

Mason slammed the trunk on the guy's head. Then he turned to Rachel and Elizabeth. "Let's go."

The two women rose at the same time, using each other for strength.

"Truck took the least of it," Mason said. "It'll still drive."

"What did he mean by that?" Rachel said. "Samuel knows exactly where we are."

"I'm thinking a tracker," Mason said. "You two get inside the pickup. I'll make sure it's clean."

It wasn't. Rachel looked out as Mason stomped on a little black box he'd found on the underside of the pickup.

"I'll take you to where Isiah asked," he said as he eased inside the truck. "And then Elizabeth and I are getting the hell out of this state."

Rachel nodded, went quiet.

Not another word spoken until Mason parked in front of Nate's wife's place.

"Thank you," Rachel said.

"Right." Mason, terse.

Elizabeth at least offered a tiny smile.

Rachel stepped from the pickup, gently closed the door, watched a moment as the truck edged away from the curb and disappeared down the block. She sighed and strode down the sidewalk toward the yellow colonial. The porch decorated with two vintage rocking chairs and several colorful arrangements of potted plants. Nate's wife had some style.

Rachel pressed a finger to the bell.

It took a series of rings for an answer. The door swung open so sudden that Rachel lost her balance from surprise. And that wasn't the only surprise. A woman stared out at her from behind the screen. A woman with an egg-white complexion and green eyes not much different from Rachel's.

"My God," the woman said. "Your face."

"Argument with a dashboard," Rachel said, smiling through the pain. Her thoughts were much clearer now at least, her head less murky. Though she did have a splitting headache.

"You're probably concussed."

"Probably. You're Nate's wife?"

"Heather," the woman said. "Come on. The boys are in back."

Rachel followed Heather to the rear of the house. Yellow must've been her favorite color because she'd painted the walls in the den a bright lemon. Nate beamed from a red sofa, with a thick wool blanket laid across his lap. Joshua's shoulders relaxed and he let out a breath as he took in Rachel from his perch on a red gingham chair.

Rachel stepped fully into the light of the room and both men frowned.

"Oh, shit," Nate said. "What happened to your face?"

But that wasn't Rachel's concern now. "Where's Isiah? Bathroom?"

"Weren't you just together?" Nate said.

"He's not here?"

"Not yet," Nate replied. "Samuel and his men took you?"

Rachel nodded. "That's right. To a compound. Isiah found it with help from Chipper's girl and got us out of there."

"Us?"

"Mason and Elizabeth. They're from—"

"That's the last you saw of I.T.?" Nate said, cutting her off.

"Yes."

He looked over at Joshua. "What did I.T. say to you?"

"That Rachel had been kidnapped but he was handling it. That I should come where you were convalescing. We'd all meet up. His last text to me was the address here."

Nate picked up his cell phone, punched in a number, held the phone to his ear. Rachel was able to make out Isiah's recorded voice. Nate disconnected and dropped the phone beside him on the couch. There was a storm in his eyes. "Straight to voicemail."

"What do we do now?" Rachel asked.

"Probably not the smartest thing . . . but do you think you could direct us back to the compound?"

Rachel thought a moment before responding. "I believe so."

Nate looked at Heather, something unspoken communicated between them, and then he was pushing aside the blanket and grimacing as he made it to his feet.

68

"**I'll take you** to your brother," Isiah announced. "And this all ends. You don't retaliate."

"Just let you and your people go?" Samuel said.

"You shot Nate. Kidnapped Rachel. And now you have me. Enough is enough."

Samuel looked at Chanel. "What do you think, sis?"

"I . . . I just want to find Chipper."

"You trust this man?"

"Yes," she said, with no hesitation.

Samuel rubbed his chapped hands together. "Let's gather the brothers and get moving then."

It took some time for them to assemble. Chanel was stunned by their number. The group had grown since she'd made the deal with Chipper for him to leave them behind. This wasn't some fringe group of Twitter terrorists. There were more than twenty of them, hard-eyed, hyperfocused, loyal to a man with a heart as dark as the bottom of a well. Samuel's sway over them was terrifying. They moved about quietly, like drones. It took seven vehicles to handle them all. Kellogg, his skin blued by tattoos, shoved Isiah into the back of a hulking SUV. Back when Chipper was still hanging around, Kellogg wouldn't even curse in Chanel's presence, but now he made no attempt to conceal the semiautomatic he held like a drinking glass. He slid in beside Isiah and pressed the gun to his ribs.

Samuel placed a raw, blistering hand on Chanel's shoulder. "Why don't you sit in back with your boyfriend, sis?"

"He's not my boyfriend."

"Is that right?"

"What are you going to do to him?"

Samuel smiled, shrugged.

"Chipper wouldn't have wanted any of this, Samuel."

He turned from her then, faced the new guy, Ronald, who to Chanel looked like an accountant decent enough at hiding a heroin problem. In the moment, though, he was jittery, kept clicking his jaw and grinding his teeth. Samuel flipped the keys to the SUV at him. Ronald bent and picked them up off the ground. "I'm driving, sir?"

Sir?

"Stick to the speed limit, Ronald Owen Atkins. We don't want to call attention to ourselves."

"Right," Chanel said. "Don't call attention to yourselves. With a convoy of SUVs plastered with Confederate bumper stickers." She couldn't have explained where the outburst came from, but when Samuel looked at her, she swallowed and held his gaze. Fear couldn't live inside her if she was going to take this ride.

Samuel said, "Let's get to Chipper. He's waited for us long enough."

It was a surprisingly tender sentiment, especially coming from Samuel, so when Ronald opened the rear door of the SUV for Chanel, she climbed in without protest. Isiah turned and looked at her as she eased in beside him. Ronald closed the door and took his spot behind the wheel.

Samuel drum-tapped the dashboard. "And we're off."

Isiah directed them to one of the state's many back roads, and Chanel focused out the window at the passing landscape, breathing through her nose to steady her heartbeat. Was she truly up for this? Hard to say. She wanted to see Chipper one last time, needed to see him, at least that's what she craved in her mind, but it wouldn't be pleasant, she knew that, too. What she was going to see was just a shell. The Chipper she'd loved and shared a life with was gone. For good. She felt Isiah's leg touching her own and shifted away. He was a killer. Chipper's killer. She had to keep reminding herself of that, as false as it rang in her mind.

There wasn't any talk from anyone until, hours into the drive, Isiah said, "Slow, slow."

The accountant hit the brakes, skidded.

Chanel's heart thudded and she blinked.

"Turn in right ahead there," Isiah said, pointing. "Just past that clump of bushes. There's no path carved out, but your vehicles can manage it."

"This?" Samuel said a beat later, after the convoy had driven through the opened gate, an abandoned Cape Cod ahead of them lit up by the riot of headlights.

"Yes," Isiah said.

There was a cacophony of slamming doors as they exited their vehicles. A vigil of cell phone flashlights. Ronald opened Chanel's door and she sat there, willing herself to move. Beside her, Isiah said, "It's okay," and he gave her hand a squeeze, something in his voice giving her strength.

Kellogg grabbed Isiah's arm and pulled him from the SUV. Isiah landed awkwardly, turning his ankle.

Chanel hopped out by herself.

"Show us," Samuel said to Isiah.

Limping, he led them through the overgrown yard, walking

slowly, counting off steps. He looked up toward the Cape Cod, then stopped and tamped at the ground with the toe of his shoe. "Here."

A slight hump, but the dirt packed tight, nothing anyone would really notice. Easy enough to walk back and forth across without re-alizing what you were trampling on. Chanel's eyes started to water.

No one moved to comfort her.

She would've shoved them aside had any of the brothers done so.

"Start digging," Samuel called out, and the next sounds were shov-els scraping at the displaced earth, his men grunting from the exer-tion of reopening the hole.

Chanel slipped away.

Settled by a tree, farther back in the yard, desperate to be alone. But of course, Samuel wandered over.

"I don't feel like talking," she told him.

"Me either."

Second time today he'd surprised her with a hint of tenderness. They stood there, shoulder to shoulder, watching the brothers dig. Isiah paced, despite his twisted ankle, playing with his hands, looked as though his lips were moving. Chanel wondered how he and the three with him had done it, how they'd killed Chipper, and though she knew Isiah had played a part, she decided it couldn't have been a prominent one. There was something inherently gentle about him. Noble, even. She couldn't picture him holding a gun or knife. Couldn't imagine him capable of pulling a trigger on someone or sink-ing a blade hilt-deep into warm flesh.

Beside her, Samuel winced. His wounds from the blaze must've been oozing pus because the taint of an infected odor stung her nos-trils. If he wasn't already, she suspected he'd be feverish in no time.

The only thing keeping him going now was likely his hateful resolve.

"You're not letting this end here," Chanel said.

It wasn't a question, but Samuel answered, "No."

The accountant yelled that they'd found something and stumbled back from the hole, wiping at his mouth. He folded over and vomited in the grass. Samuel took Chanel's elbow and forced her toward the grave. Later, she'd question why she let him. Probably numbed by the horror of it all.

Isiah headed them off as they neared the grave. He looked into Chanel's eyes. For her, it was like staring at her own reflection; his eyes were haunted, sad. He told her he was sorry.

"On your knees," Samuel said.

Isiah turned to face the grave and dropped down, crossed his arms over his chest. Samuel loomed over him. "I never had any intention of letting you go, Isiah Thomas."

"Never thought for a second that you would, Samuel."

"I'll hunt down your friends as well."

"No," Isiah said. "I don't think you'll be doing that."

"You're a fool."

"Yes," Isiah said, and he half turned, looked up at Chanel. "Yes, I am."

"Take my brother out so we can make the switch," Samuel directed his men. Then he called for Kellogg, asked for his 9mm Hellcat. Once he had the compact pistol, he stepped to Chanel, tried to force it into her hand.

This time she resisted.

"You should get the honor," Samuel told her.

"I don't want it."

"You realize what this man did to Chipper?"

"I know," Chanel said. "But I won't kill him for it."

"Hmm." Samuel turned the gun on her, let it kiss her temple. "My brother would be disappointed in you, sis."

"You didn't know him as well as you think, Samuel."

"I could fill this hole with the both of you," he snarled. "You and Isiah Thomas."

Chanel nodded, the gun biting into her skin. "You could."

"Look down in the hole."

She did.

It was Chipper. But it wasn't the Chipper she'd grown to hate and love. That Chipper had a crooked smile, a devilish streak, was prone to foolishness but also could be tender and bursting with love. That Chipper came from people who'd been passed over by the world, hard, dusty people, and coming from them had shaped him, sure, but hadn't defined him. That Chipper took her to secret places, both physical and in his heart, and in doing so made her aspire for more than was promised by her own passed-over, dusty history.

"Rack the slide," she told Samuel. "Slam a round into the chamber."

Her slutty aunt's boyfriends loved their guns as much as their bikes. She'd learned it was best to hold the semiauto close to your chest, get a good hold on the grip with your strong hand, that you should keep your finger off the trigger and grip the slide with your palm and four fingers. A push-pull motion. The strong hand pushes, slide hand pulls. And you should let the slide move forward on its own. Otherwise, you might fuck up the ammo feed or pinch your skin.

"Bitch," Samuel muttered, and he lowered his hand. He turned his attention back to Isiah. Chanel stepped away from the grave. She contemplated going back to the SUV, but a strange thought hit her. She didn't want to leave Isiah with these motherfuckers in his final moments. Not that he needed her. She noticed him looking up toward the heavens, smiling.

Chipper didn't have an ounce of religion or faith, but she hoped he prayed at the end.

Isiah's smile held as Samuel touched the gun to his chin, tilting

Isiah's head up. He continued staring at the heavens, calm, composed, at peace it seemed.

"I'll not sleep until all of you have met your maker," Samuel said. Isiah's smile widened.

Chanel noticed it then, a security camera, positioned up in the eaves of the Cape Cod with the lens facing down at the grave. Isiah wasn't glancing at the heavens. She looked at him, that smile still full on his face, and understood. Where was this video feed going? The police? Samuel had no idea he was being recorded about to commit a murder. Maybe later Chanel would feel shame for not warning him about the camera, for siding with a man who'd taken everything she loved from her, but in this moment she kept quiet.

Even as Samuel raised the pistol and blew the smile right off Isiah's face.

69

Heather's windshield was paintballed with bird shit just out of reach of her stripped wipers. Though not a starving artist, she lived frugally where she could in respect for that possibility. A car was just a car, for instance, and she didn't put much effort into keeping hers clean or on a maintenance schedule. Tires pushing the edge of bald, a tick in the engine that sounded like a steel pot catching rainwater, a blender when she braked. Never had any of that bothered her, but she felt badly now because it only added to the distress Nate and his friends were experiencing. She shouldn't have insisted on coming along with them, that she do the driving.

"Anything?" she asked her rearview, eyes trained on Rachel in the backseat.

"Nothing looks familiar," Rachel said, shaking her head, a quiver in her voice.

"It'll come."

By now, Heather had a rough sketch of what was going on. The four of them had been playing with matches and gotten burned. They'd done real harm to a man named Chipper, and his brother, a cross-burner with psychosis, was aching for revenge. Had a band of brothers from other mothers that would kill in backing him up.

And I.T. was in their jaws.

"I'll never forgive myself if anything happens to him," Rachel cried.

"Don't even think like that, honey." Heather glanced at Nate, sitting solemnly quiet beside her in the passenger seat. "From what I've heard, there's nobody smarter than I.T. He'll have worked out a plan. You'll all be laughing about this tomorrow."

"Stop there," Nate said, pointing at a gas station up ahead. "Someone inside might know something."

"Good idea," Joshua managed from the back, first he'd spoken the entire drive.

Heather nodded and blurred past the fuel islands and screeched to a canted stop in front of the convenience store addition—*On the Run* lit up in bright neon lettering across the facade above the entrance.

"I'll go in and ask around," Joshua said.

Nate shook his head. "I've got it."

"You shouldn't even be out here, Nate. Y'all shouldn't carry all the weight on this. 'Bout time I made myself useful."

"Both of you sit this out," Heather said, opening her door. "I'll go in."

Of course, Nate, stubborn as they came, hobbled from the vehicle, cutting her off by the entrance of the store. "We'll do this together."

Something inside Heather flared at the tenderness in his voice. She bit her lip, nodded. They headed straight to the cashier. White girl with a face of angry red acne, sleepy eyes, dyed blue hair showing its original roots.

"Ever heard of the Righteous Boys?" Nate asked her.

"Rap group?"

"No."

She shrugged.

There was an older white man by the cooler area, tugging an armload of snacks. He hadn't gotten the memo about the summer heat. Heather took in the man's steel-toed boots, stiff Dockers, flannel shirt under a Carhartt jacket and approached. Flashed her friendliest smile. "Righteous Boys?"

"I'm sorry?"

"Looking for these guys," she told him. "They stay around here somewhere. Call themselves the Righteous Boys."

"Don't sound like anyone I'd know about."

"Thanks anyway."

"You got it."

She found Nate down one of the aisles, leaning on a stand of Coca-Cola two-liters. He stood up straight once he caught her watching. "You're hurting," she said as she approached.

"I'm fine. Just want to find Min-su."

"Min—"

"His Korean name."

Heather nodded. "Well, no one here knows anything. You ready to get going?"

"Need to hit the head," he replied, handing her his phone. "Hold this for me."

Later, it would be this moment that Heather would remember with the most clarity. This moment that justified her insistence on coming. No sooner had Nate disappeared inside the bathroom than his cell phone pinged. Heather punched in his four-digit code, worry and hope powering her fingers. Not a text, rather the notification of an email.

From I.T.

The email's subject line: Motion Sensor Recording.

"Oh . . ."

Nothing written in the email, just an attached video.

With a growing sense of dread, Heather tapped the screen, activating the recording playback. Weeds and tall grass, the yard of an apparently abandoned property, the shadowy outline of several men, men with shovels.

"Shit."

A growing mound of dirt, and then one of the men stumbled away from what had to be a gaping hole in the earth. Looked like he vomited in the grass. And then there was I.T., standing next to a woman and a man about Nate's height but bloated with muscle.

Heather blinked, her eyes starting to water.

She leaned a hand against the soda display as the video reached the awful part. She tapped it off and fumbled the phone into her pocket. Took in several deep breaths. Pushed back her shoulders.

Glad now that she'd insisted on coming.

Nate didn't need to watch this video.

A beat later, he emerged from the bathroom. He looked weary and in tremendous pain. Heather didn't know how exactly, but she would get him through this. And then they'd see.

"Sorry," he said, joining her. "My stomach's a mess."

She bit her lip, couldn't keep the tears from falling.

Nate frowned. "What is it?"

No words would come.

"Heather . . ."

"Min-su," she said, her voice phlegmy with emotion.

Nate shook his head, staggered backward a step.

"An email," Heather told him. "A motion sensor video. I.T. and several men. Men with shovels. A backyard with overgrown weeds."

"Nah," Nate said, shaking his head. "Nah."

"I'm so sorry."

"Nah . . ."

She'd never witnessed Nate crying before and seeing the eyedropper tears spilling down his face, his beautiful brown face, that triggered a strength she didn't realize she possessed. She moved to him, wrapped him in her arms, held him tight even as he trembled.

The tight hug may have been bad for his injuries, but she didn't think so.

"We have to go talk with Rachel and Joshua," she whispered.

Nate made a noise in his throat, nearly toppled over.

Heather took his hand.

And they shuffled together out of the store.

Rachel was sitting on the hood of Heather's car. She came off it, smiling. "There was a grain silo. I remember now. And then a little farther along was the turnoff. We gave up too soon."

Heather nodded, said, "Honey . . ."

70

If not for the Toyota Prius parked in the small lot, he might've thought he had the wrong place. There weren't all the empty spaces anymore, several other vehicles here now. Much had changed over the last year. Elizabeth's work was of greater significance with everyone chanting Black Lives Matter. Mason wasn't there yet, but when he spent time with his grandson, he did it with a certain pride. Zion was smart as a whip. He used words in everyday conversation that had Mason fumbling for a dictionary. Nicole had said Elijah read to Zion every night and Mason saw clearly it was making a difference. He'd told Elijah so, complimented him for the efforts he took with his son, Mason's grandson.

Grandson. There were still days when it was hard to believe. Not the biracial thing, the fact that he was old enough now to be somebody's grandfather.

Mason shook aside those thoughts and glanced at the brand-new sign on the front lawn. It was still bordered with boxwoods, azaleas, and hydrangeas, and listed the sole occupant of this ranch house as *December's Promise*.

He shut off his engine and sat there a moment, working up his nerve. After a while, he said, aloud, the necessary step of pep talks whenever he was gearing up to visit with Elizabeth, "Mask up, Mason, and get to it."

He reached for his glove box, pulled out the black cloth mask, worked the loops over his ears, and fit the material so it was fully covering his mouth and nose. He didn't ever want to be one of these fools he saw wearing their masks like chinstraps. This coronavirus thing was raging and required people to make the right choices, choices of self-sacrifice and caring for their fellow man. In fact, Mason imagined that's how all the issues plaguing the country would have to be dealt with.

He sighed and slid out of his car.

Walking across the lot, he played over exactly what he would say to Elizabeth.

"I'm definitely keeping my social distance from you," a voice called out, interrupting his prep. "Are you talking to yourself?"

Mason chuckled. How had he missed her, sitting in a lawn chair on the side of the building, sipping at what looked to be sweet tea?

"Miss Elizabeth," he said, taking her in. Barefoot, as usual. Her mask matched her eyes.

"What do you have there, Mason?"

"Toasted coconut cream pie," he told her, holding up the white Styrofoam container. "The place over in Irondale is trying to make a go of curbside pickup."

"All we've been through and you're still with the bribery?"

All they'd been through. It was amazing that she could be so hopeful, still, after the experience with Samuel and the Righteous Boys. Mason found her hopefulness to be one of her better qualities, and she had several great qualities.

"Don't look at it as bribery," he said. "Consider it an offering of . . ."

Love, he wanted to say, but, for some reason, the word stuck in his throat.

"Gimme," Elizabeth said, waggling her fingers, mercifully saving him.

Mason did as she asked. And sat in the lawn chair she'd set up for him, six feet apart from her own. "You ever going to stop playing dirty, Mason Farmer?" she asked, removing her mask and cutting into the pie with a plastic fork, shoveling a piece in her mouth. After a few seconds, she closed her eyes and moaned.

Mason took in a breath.

"You've really brightened my mood, Mason," Elizabeth announced. "I hadn't realized how much I needed it brightened. Thank you."

Mason's gut roiled at that. It was good to see her smiling, happy. How long would that last, though? Particularly considering what he wanted to say to her. What he needed to say to her.

"You mind if I take this thing off a bit?" he asked, indicating his mask.

"Can you keep your distance?"

"All right, I'll just leave it on then."

Elizabeth laughed. "Go ahead, Mason. I set us up out here so we could see each other's faces for a change."

He slipped the mask off, placed it in his pocket.

"Not fair," Elizabeth pouted.

"What's that?"

"You've got your Gillette razor and electric clippers, which is apparently all you need . . . and I've got my roots growing in and a desperate need for a trim."

"You look just fine to me, Miss Elizabeth."

"Your nose is growing."

"I mean it."

She studied him a moment, then said, "Okay. Spit it out, Mason Farmer."

He looked into her eyes, frowning. "What do you mean?"

"You think I don't know your expressions by now? This hangdog look is 'I have something on my mind but I'm afraid I'll come off as an asshole if I say it.'"

"That's scary," he said. "I think I'll put the mask back on."

"Don't you dare. Tell me what's on your mind."

Elizabeth smiled as she waited. A stunning smile, Mason believed. It reached all the way to her violet eyes. That hurt because if he was truthful with her now, if he told her what was truly on his mind, the smile would likely vanish. She'd been through a lot. They both had. And he truly hated to think of himself as adding to her burdens.

"Mason . . ."

He cleared his throat, sat up straighter in his chair, working to gather his thoughts. Finally, he said, "This protest is when again?"

"May twenty-sixth," Elizabeth said coolly.

"I'm hearing it could get ugly."

"Uglier than the police barging into a woman's apartment and shooting her dead while she's sleeping?"

"They had a no-knock warrant," Mason argued.

"Don't get me started. There are all kinds of issues with those. But how do you serve the warrant when Glover, the actual target, was no longer living in the apartment? How did they not know that?"

"They made some mistakes."

"I'll say. And we're going to make sure Mayor Fischer holds those three cops accountable. They should be arrested and charged with murder."

Mason grunted.

"You feel differently?" Elizabeth asked him.

"I'm not sure what I feel," Mason said. "Sadness, I guess. I wish none of this had to be."

"I suppose sadness is a start. As long as it's for Breonna and not the cops who took her life."

"What do you think protesting will do?"

"I told you. We want the cops arrested and charged with murder."

"And you think . . . you think some people holding up Magic Marker signs and chanting outside the mayor's office will make that happen?"

"Come to Louisville with me, and you'll find out firsthand."

"Nicole says white folks are getting involved in these protests now to ease their consciences. As if we're the saviors and can just jump in and make everything better. And if things truly do change, we'll take credit for solving a problem we created in the first place."

"I can't argue with any of that."

"I don't think that's why you're doing it, though, Miss Elizabeth."

"I'd like to think not, but . . ."

"But?"

"My conscience does need some easing, Mason. Doesn't yours?"

He thought about the four kidnappers back in New Jersey. Nails still called from time to time, asking whether Mason had made any progress on tracking them down. He was still paying the reparations even though they hadn't contacted him since the day in the swamp. Mason told Nails he was doing his best, but the kidnappers were a tricky bunch. It surprised Mason to be taking their side, thinking of them more as vigilantes than murderers. But none of the four were at all the monsters Mason would've believed them to be before he discovered more about them. Were they angry? Absolutely. So much so they'd been willing to risk everything, just to be heard in some way. Maybe someday he would have the courage to return to New Jersey, look them up, and make sure they knew he at least had heard them. Probably it wouldn't matter, but you never knew.

He looked over at Elizabeth and something hard inside him softened. He was glad in that moment to not be wearing the mask. And though he might think very differently later, for now he'd come to a decision—one that surprised him and thrilled him at the same time. Thrills had been rare since the day he'd come home to a noiseless house and a note from Bella. *For me to be free, I must set you free.* The divorce left him heartsick but was also a relief. Last he'd heard, his ex-wife was in therapy and working to get back her life. He couldn't imagine letting anyone rummage around in his head, fancy degree or not. So far, he'd resisted the idea of talking to anyone.

Except Elizabeth. She was able to help him untangle his emotions.

"Heard a lot about this chocolate and walnut pie they've got over there in Kentucky," he announced, a smile tugging at the corners of his mouth. "Think it's called Derby-Pie, Miss Elizabeth."

"What are you saying?" she asked, matching his smile.

"Some things I need to experience for myself before I can pass judgment."

"Are you talking about the pie?"

"Absolutely," he said, smiling even wider. "You know me so well, Miss Elizabeth."

71

For the past several months, Alani had picked up the habit of watching the women around her, particularly those with thin, tight bodies. This one had eyes the color of cayenne pepper and freckles sprinkled across her brown face like the stars on a child's wallpaper. She wore a long, flowing skirt and sandals and a close-fitting halter top, her breasts small but perky, one of the spaghetti straps falling off a shoulder to reveal the tattoo of a pair of dice. Her hair was natural, a close black Afro cut, and standing across from her, Alani was fascinated with the interlocked hearts dangling from the woman's earlobes, plus her other earrings as well, and the studs in her lip and nose.

It was just the two of them in the restaurant now, some mix-up with both of their orders, and therefore it didn't require much on the woman's part to catch Alani staring at her.

"Figures they'd mess up the two black girls' food," she said, lowering her mask to speak.

"Did those hurt?" Alani asked, to head off any kind of awkwardness.

"I'm sorry?"

"I like your piercings."

"Oh, thank you," the woman said, a splotch of fiery cheeks joining the penetrating eyes and lurid freckles.

"Did they hurt?"

"Like a bitch."

She went on to explain the piercing near the top of her ear was called a rook. The one that looked like a crumb was an inner conch. Her slender fingers rose to the small flap of cartilage directly in front of her ear canal.

"Tragus," Alani said.

"Okay, look at you. You know about piercings?"

"A lil' somethin' somethin,'" Alani told her. "I'd been telling my boyfriend I wanted to get my belly button done, but . . ."

"Not too late," the woman said, eyeing Alani's rounded stomach. "Congratulations, by the way. How far along are you?"

"Seven months."

"Your first?"

"Probably last, too," Alani said, smiling through her mask. "I don't like not being able to see my toes. Not to mention what this'll do to my body."

"You have a doula?"

Alani frowned. "What's that?"

"Guess not," the woman said, laughing. "Girlfriend of mine had one. She raved about the experience. Woman gave her all kinds of emotional and physical support throughout the pregnancy and childbirth."

"My boyfriend has got that covered," Alani said. "He's gonna be a great father."

"That's good. Too many of our sistas out here going at it alone."

"That wasn't about to be me," Alani told her. "I would've stalked Joshua's ass to the end of the world if he tried to play me. And Miss Dot—his mama—would've backed me up."

"You got Mama on your side? I heard that."

"Picking up this dinner for her," Alani said, looking toward the counter area. So far two people had come in and grabbed their take-out orders from the designated table the restaurant had set off in a corner. With the virus raging, the dining area was closed.

"Do you know the sex?"

Alani looked back at the woman. "Huh?"

"Your baby's sex? Did you find out, or—"

"Boy."

"Nice. You have a name in mind?"

"Isiah," Alani said, and her voice cracked.

"I like that name."

"It has meaning for us," Alani said.

"I hear that. I'm Jamila, by the way."

"Alani."

"Wishing you and Joshua nothing but blessings with your baby," Jamila said. Finally, her order was ready.

"Real nice talking to you, Jamila."

"Take my number," she said, and winked. "I can hip you to a place in Newark to get that belly-button piercing. Or you could take a train to the city, check out a spot near Times Square."

Alani's order came out as she was programming Jamila's number into her phone, so she sent Joshua a quick text as well, letting him know her mission was complete—she had Miss Dot's chicken parmigiana—and she would be heading home now.

As was the case whenever she left the house, Joshua had his cell phone close by and responded right away. Told her to be careful, aware, to keep her head on a swivel. Sounded like military talk to her and she didn't like it. Couldn't imagine bringing little Isiah into some covert operation of a life. She responded to Joshua's text with the eye-roll-and-tongue-out emoji.

He hit her back with a smile.

She set the bag with Miss Dot's dinner on the passenger seat in her car, configured her seat belt so it wasn't pressing into her stomach, checked her rearview, and started driving. Five minutes in, she heard a knocking noise. Sounded like it was coming from the engine, an issue of late. Joshua had been talking about checking YouTube for troubleshooting videos, but he hadn't gotten around to it yet. Tomorrow, Alani would just take it in to her mechanic.

She turned onto a lonely stretch of highway less than five miles from home, and was about to flip through the radio stations when another loud knock startled her. The car slowed without her pressing the brakes and tendrils of smoke rose from the hood.

"Shit."

She pulled over to the shoulder, managed to reach down and engage the hood latch, and stepped out. She didn't know a thing about cars, so this was all pretense. Gave her a sense of importance. Since she'd gotten pregnant, everything was about the baby. That's the way it should be—she wasn't complaining—but it did leave her with a feeling she was being erased, bit by bit each day.

It took some work to get the hood lifted. And some more to figure out how to make it stay up. She used the flashlight feature on her cell phone to see what she was doing. Not that it mattered. Taking in all the parts under the hood made her head spin.

"Now," she said. "How do you lower this thing?"

She was fiddling with it when headlights approached from behind her. The vehicle, a truck, reduced its speed some but kept moving past her.

"Asshole," she muttered.

Not that she wanted the driver to stop. Joshua would've lost his shit. It just would have been nice to see that people still cared. This virus and all the political shit were making it clear that people were terrible. Maybe even wicked deep down in their souls. She felt some guilt for bringing little Isiah into this dark, cruel world.

Headlights again.

Coming from the opposite direction this time.

She glanced up and was dumbfounded to see it was the same

truck that had just passed. And in her bewilderment, she didn't move fast enough when it decelerated and made a casual U-turn, coming to a stop in the road with its headlights strong in her face.

No one with an ounce of decency would do that.

Alani squinted and shielded the glare with a hand.

The driver's-side door of the truck opened, and she was able to make out the outline of the man who emerged.

A big, big man.

Had to be close to seven feet tall, she thought, even though she wasn't good at that sort of thing—guessing heights, weights, people's ages.

"I see you're having some car trouble," he said, coming closer into view, his skin mottled, scarred, as if baptized by fire.

And Alani knew. The realization made her knees go weak. But she stood there, resolute, firm, strong. Joshua would've been so proud of her. And he wouldn't have been the only one.

Eyes beginning to tear, Alani touched a hand to her belly.

ACKNOWLEDGMENTS

I'm fond of saying "It takes a village . . . " to describe the importance of community in achieving any deed. Writing a book is no different, though it might seem to be a solitary endeavor. I'm blessed to have had some wonderful people in my corner throughout this process and want to take a moment to acknowledge them.

Jackson Keeler, my agent, for believing in me from the start and helping me through countless drafts to shape *Smoke Kings* into a novel we are both immensely proud of. Scorpio energy!

Carl Bromley, my editor, thank you for molding the book even more once it touched your desk. Cheers!

All the wonderful, hardworking, and passionate people at Melville House: Dennis Johnson, Valerie Merians, Carl Bromley, Mike Lindgren, Sofia Demopolos, Michelle Capone, Beste Miray Doğan, Ariel Palmer-Collins, Janet Joy Wilson, and Sammi Sontag. I appreciate each of you for everything you've done and continue to do to cultivate reading and literacy. Publishing quality books is a heroic mission that is not often enough recognized. You all are top-notch!

To all the independent bookstores, authors I've interacted with on social media, readers, reviewers, etc.—appreciate you!

Don Winslow . . . thanks for the early blurb that helped us build momentum for the novel!

My family, friends, and loved ones. I can't call you all by name, but you know the impact you have on my life.

I especially want to acknowledge my mother and brother, plus my wife, T, and children, A&M (sounds like an HBCU). James Baldwin famously said, "Not everything that is faced can be changed but nothing can be changed until it is faced." Thank you all for giving me the strength and support to face the many challenges of life.

Lastly, I have a mantra and it has guided all my steps thus far and will continue to do so with the steps that remain: "Blessed is the man that trusteth in the LORD, and whose hope the LORD is." Amen to that!

ABOUT THE AUTHOR

Jahmal Mayfield was born in Virginia but currently resides in New Jersey. In addition to writing crime fiction, he serves as the director of a nonprofit program that provides employment support to people with disabilities. *Smoke Kings* was inspired by Kimberly Jones's passionate viral video, *How Can We Win?*